Proof of Innocence

The Innocence Trilogy

Proof of Innocence

Price of Innocence

Premise of Innocence

Other romantic suspense and mystery by Patricia McLinn

Romantic suspense

Ride the River: Rodeo Knights

Bardville, Wyoming Series

Mystery

Caught Dead in Wyoming series

Sign Off

Left Hanging

Shoot First

Last Ditch

Look Live

Back Story

Cold Open

Hot Roll

Reaction Shot

Body Brace

Secret Sleuth series

Death on the Diversion

Death on Torrid Avenue

Death on Beguiling Way

Death on Covert Circle

Death on Shady Bridge

Death on Carrion Lane

PROOF OF INNOCENCE

Book 1, The Innocence Trilogy

Patricia McLinn

PROLOGUE

Four and a half years ago
Bedhurst, Virginia
Thursday, 2:47 p.m.

NOVEMBER WIND SKIED down the county courthouse's steeple, plunged three brick-covered levels, and blasted any mere human braving the backside of Courthouse Hill.

Prosecutor Maggie Frye's sole concession to its assault was dipping her head as she marched, coatless, up the steep grade toward the courthouse's back door. A damned hurricane wouldn't keep her from Courtroom One.

The jury had a verdict in *Commonwealth of Virginia v. J.D. Carson.*

For the murder of another woman denied the fullness of her life, denied the chance to grow old among those who loved her.

No.

She would not open that door.

She could only gain justice for *this* victim. For Pandora Addington Wade.

This trial. *This* verdict. *This* defendant.

J.D. Carson, a boy from the wrong side of the tracks who'd turned his life around in the Army, but then killed the one person who'd always believed in him. All because she'd refused to run off with him.

A success story gone very, very wrong. Tragically wrong for Pan Wade.

But Maggie could at least get J.D. Carson convicted. She could do that much this time.

Sure, she was on edge.

Because of the need to get a conviction.

Because this was her first murder trial as lead prosecutor.

Because the jury was out only two hours, meaning her post-trial re-acclimatization was barely started. That odd period when she bobbed up, disoriented, like a deep-sea diver without good equipment. Blinking into the light, forced to recognize the world beyond the witness chair, bench, and jury box had gone on while she was immersed in the trial.

That all explained this strange unsettledness. Nothing to do with the past.

She overlapped the edges of her suit jacket. The wind meant business here in the Blue Ridge Mountains. She was accustomed to a tamer version in Northern Virginia. Possibly hot air coming across the Potomac River from D.C. tempered it in Fairlington County.

"We should go around to the front entrance," said Nancy Quinn, assigned to her from Fairlington as paralegal, assistant, and—Maggie suspected—babysitter.

"This is faster." She didn't alter her route.

Ed Smith, her second chair, hurried to hold the metal backdoor that accessed a utilitarian stairwell to Courtroom One.

Like her, he was an outsider in Bedhurst County, but with far less experience, since this was the first murder trial he'd worked on.

His charcoal suit was wrinkled, his pants scuffed the floor. Had he dressed like this all along?

Possibly.

Probably.

She hadn't noticed.

Up the stairs, he stepped ahead again to open the courtroom door. "Full house."

Word spread fast around here. Or no one had left since the jury went out.

"She's the one came from the city to prosecute," someone in the back row muttered with a disapproving sniff.

As if she'd had a choice.

Her boss, the Commonwealth's Attorney of Fairlington County, assigned her the case, so here she was.

In Bedhurst County, the Commonwealth's Attorney office consisted of exactly one part-time lawyer. He'd claimed a conflict of interest in this case, requiring prosecutors from other counties be brought in. Not that unusual for rural one-CA counties.

But this specimen had waited to the last second to back out, left her inadequate files and a stubborn, chauvinist sheriff, then departed on a sudden and extended vacation as she'd arrived. No doubt a cover-his-ass move to ensure he couldn't be blamed, no matter the outcome.

All around, a great case.

None of that mattered.

Pandora Addington Wade was what mattered.

She looked toward the front of the courtroom and saw, inside the railing dividing spectators from the working area, defense counsel—one Dallas Herbert Monroe—talking with the victim's family, who sat in the first row. The victim's mother smiled at Monroe, her father shook his hand.

Sucking up to the family of the woman his client murdered. That was low, even for a defense attorney.

Though Pan's parents *had* favored the defense, indicating they didn't believe Carson was guilty—or wouldn't believe it.

On the other hand, Rick Wade, the estranged husband, now a widower, stared straight ahead without acknowledging Monroe.

Ed stopped to greet two young women—one with her crossed legs extending into the aisle where they couldn't be missed. A middle-aged man across the aisle appeared mesmerized. A chemical redhead beside him was decidedly less entranced.

"Judge Blankenship's two daughters. Been here every day," Nancy murmured as if to fill in gaps for Maggie.

Pan Wade's parents and husband had testified, so Maggie knew everything about them she could cram into her head. The rest of the spectators? She'd swear she'd never seen them before.

But Nancy couldn't possibly know that.

Nancy tipped her head to the middle-aged man and redhead. "Also regular attendees, Eugene Tagner and the third Mrs. Tagner."

Then, not returning Maggie's look, Nancy glided into a seat behind the prosecution's side.

In the next row sat Teddie Barrett, who'd also testified. He bobbed his head and smiled broadly. Maggie forced herself to smile back.

It wasn't his fault, it was hers for getting caught flat-footed.

Monroe's cross-examination shredded Teddie's testimony. He hadn't recognized it, as happy at the end as at the start. Everyone else in the courtroom had. Including the jury.

But she'd given them enough to counteract that. She was sure she had.

Inside the railing's gate, she placed her briefcase on the prosecution table, and gave Monroe a cool, level gaze.

He was in her territory. Not by chance.

With a smile and a tip of his head that artfully tumbled a hunk of silver hair, Monroe shuffled back to the defense table.

She sat, then raised the briefcase lid.

Pan Wade's wedding portrait stared up from atop legal pads, files, and notes. Pan faced away, except her head, looking over her shoulder at the camera. You barely noticed the dress, the veil, the earrings. You saw the wide smile, the soft eyes, the slight, questioning head tilt.

A nice woman.

A thoroughly nice young woman.

As always, Maggie touched the briefcase lid's suede pocket, feeling for the edge of the plastic sleeve inside it, leaving the sleeve where it was.

Ed Smith slid into place beside her, as the court reporter, a wiry man about thirty, unbuttoned the cuff of his white shirt's left sleeve and folded it back.

A side door opened.

A bailiff escorted the straight-backed defendant with a solicitous touch. A law enforcement officer of fifty being solicitous toward a man twenty years younger, half a foot taller, and packing considerably more muscle could have been amusing.

She found nothing amusing about J.D. Carson.

Not when she first read the file and especially not after she encountered his powerful composure in person. This was not a man who would lose control and explode in anger. When J.D. Carson killed, he meant to kill.

"All rise!"

All rose. All sat. The court reporter spread his well-kept hands like a pianist. The door next to the jury box opened.

Maggie had never seen proof of the folklore that a verdict could be read from jurors' body language or expressions. Besides, in minutes she'd know the verdict rather than trying to divine it.

And yet, she watched the jury enter. Every time.

Ever since—

No.

She blinked. Refocused.

This jury.

She studied their faces, peering into the shadowed hallway beyond the door to see the next. Each face appeared unchanged, with the exception of a deeper solemnity.

Yet there was something … *off.*

It prickled at the hair at the base of Maggie's skull. It twitched the ends of her fingers.

Without looking away from the jury, she widened her focus. The judge, clerk, court reporter, bailiffs, all watched the jury enter. Beside her, Ed watched, too. At the defense table, Monroe did the same. His bulk blocked her view of the defendant's face, but most defendants couldn't take their eyes off the people about to tell them their fate.

All as expected.

What the hell was the matter with her? She did not indulge in this sort of crap. *Something off.* For God's sake, she sounded like—

Like someone she wasn't. She pulled her chair in tight and square to the table.

Then she did something she never did.

She faced away from the entering jury.

And met the direct, hard gaze of the defendant, now visible around Monroe.

He wasn't looking at the jury.

He was looking at her.

The boy from the wrong side of town, who had been championed by Pan Wade from childhood, who had been trained as a warrior, who had come home on leave last summer, and who had murdered Pan Wade because he couldn't have her.

If anyone deserved the ultimate punishment it was this guy.

What if he's innocent?

Words spoken in Maggie's head by a voice she'd sworn to forget. A voice she'd swear she *had* forgotten.

Now it flooded her.

She no longer heard the scrapes and slides as jurors took seats in the box. She no longer smelled the blend of dust, despair, and legalities. She no longer felt the disorientation of returning from the depths of a trial.

That voice.

Smooth, gentle even. She'd hated it. From the first question, she'd hated it. Felt it leading her away from where she'd needed to be, what she needed to do … Yet she hadn't known how to stop it. Or how to stop herself.

Until that final question.

Are you sure? Are you absolutely certain?

A touch on her arm.

She jolted, swung around. And met only the innocuous concern of Ed Smith.

"Maggie—?"

She silenced him by turning away, again facing the—*this* defendant.

Carson's right brow ticked upward.

"Have you reached a verdict?" the judge's distant voice asked.

"We have, Your Honor."

"Are you—?" Ed started.

"Fine. I'm fine." Quick words, from the side of her mouth.

She focused on the clerk carrying the written decision to the judge, waiting for it to be read, then returning it to the jury foreman. The defendant and his attorney rising.

"We, the jury…"

This was the moment.

She touched the pocket in the briefcase lid.

Had she succeeded in making the jury see the truth? Would they put this murderer away? Prevent this happening to another woman?

What if he's innocent?

She stopped.

Stopped breathing, stopped thinking, stopped waiting.

"…find the defendant…"

She turned her head again.

To most observers it would appear the defendant was looking at the jury. She knew better. He looked at her.

"…J.D. Carson…"

His eyes were dark, unreadable. She didn't look away. Not this time. Not as she had from that other defendant so long ago.

"…not guilty."

CHAPTER ONE

Present Day
Saturday, 5:20 p.m.

LAUREL BLANKENSHIP TAGNER slammed the door of her blue Lexus SUV, a gift from the judge, birthday before last, and leaned against it, arms crossed under her breasts.

She'd learned at thirteen to show off what she had. She had considerably more to show off, not to mention considerably more ways to show it off. That didn't mean you shouldn't make the most of the basics. Because it was too damn easy for people to take you for granted, to treat you like you were just anybody.

Well, not anymore.

She'd shaken things up plenty with Eugene and nobody would take her for granted now.

She smiled.

She'd shaken up Charlotte big-time, too. Her sister getting all cross-eyed over the possibility of her being single again hadn't entered Laurel's mind while she'd made her plans. It was pure, sweet bonus.

Charlotte had been beside herself with Laurel living back at Rambler Farm these past weeks. Even before Laurel had a little fun with Charlotte's husband.

Ed Smith. God, even his name was boring, which matched his moves in bed—and with Ed, it was *always* in bed.

Sure, she'd let him screw her some before he'd settled for Charlotte, but Ed hadn't been enough for her four years ago and he sure as hell wasn't enough for her now on.

She had bigger fish to fry. And dammit, she wanted to get on with it instead of standing here freezing her ass off.

If he wasn't here when the sun dropped behind the ridge, she wasn't waiting around.

He hadn't even bothered to call directly. Besides, why the hell had his message said to meet out here in the damned woods anyway? He knew she wasn't an outdoors kind of woman.

That was one thing she'd liked. He did know—and appreciate— what kind of woman she was.

But she should have told him to forget it when he'd suggested this.

Although there'd been one second when she'd told him how things were going to be from now on…

Laurel rubbed her arms under the light sweater she wore. Too light for this early in spring, but his message had said to wear it for old-time's sake. What the hell, might as well give the guy a bone. Besides the silk weave showed off her figure, and after this, she was going to Shenny's. It was Saturday night, and she deserved to celebrate.

Damn him, where was he? It was cold. The noises from the woods were creepier by the second. Not just birds making a racket, but rustlings. Animals or something.

Hadn't the judge talked about mountain lions at breakfast? She hadn't paid much attention, not like Charlotte, hanging on his every word. Her older sister liked to pretend he was discussing issues with her, when he was really making sure she filled the library decanters before he took his cronies aside tomorrow.

More got done at the judge's Sunday afternoons at Rambler Farm than the rest of the week put together. Charlotte was forever saying that. As if she'd started the whole thing, instead of filling in where Mama left off.

A new sound caught Laurel's attention. It wasn't the hum of a motor she'd been expecting, but it had damn well better be him. From habit, she adjusted her posture, dropping her arms to the best position under her breasts and cocking one hip to draw attention to the length of leg below her skirt.

The figure came from an unexpected direction and was hard to make out.

Hell, she didn't care what direction he came from. Her wait was finished. Now, to get this over with.

CHAPTER TWO

Sunday, 9:14 p.m.

"YOU HEARD?" **SHERIFF** Roger Gardner demanded.

No pleasantries, no easing into it. Just a city-bred cut to the chase.

Dallas Herbert Monroe rocked back as much as he could in his easy chair, wishing it were the chair behind his desk, which allowed more latitude, and studied the younger man from beneath lowered lids.

He'd adopted this pose early in his career. It masked when the pilot light on his mind fired up. No sense warning other folks when you were about to strike. Lost half the advantage of having a devious mind if folks knew you were fixing to be devious.

Not that he needed to do the lowered lids much these days. His mind still fired up with enough regularity to keep his skull from freezing—no, that hadn't changed, thank God.

What had changed was the face that stared back at him from the mirror while he shaved each morning. Under eyebrows trailing the rest of his hair toward silver, skin pouched and folded until it resembled another eyelid.

Come to think of it, a second layer of defense might be handy now that he was supposed to be on the same team with the sheriff.

This new sheriff was sharp. This would take some handling.

"I heard," Dallas said with a slow nod. "A tragedy. One so young, one so beautiful. Judge Blankenship will be devastated."

Something crossed the other man's face. "He is."

"Ah." Gardner had gone to Rambler Farm first. Courtesy or politics? Or could the sheriff suspect someone there?

"Had a devil of a time keeping him from heading right to the scene," Gardner added. "Had a devil of a time keeping half the county from tramping all over the scene."

Dallas nodded. "That's why I stayed put. You got lights out there? I can go with you now."

Dallas braced himself against the chair's worn upholstery. Ruth would have had it re-covered years ago. But she'd been gone more than a decade and he hadn't had the heart to change it.

The sheriff didn't budge from the couch across from him. "Not sure this is going to work, Dallas."

"I'm the duly elected Commonwealth's Attorney for Bedhurst County. It's my duty—"

"You're also the defense attorney from a murder that took place at the same spot, with the victim another attractive young woman."

Yes, Roger Gardner was sharp. And he'd done his homework. The murder of Pan Wade and J.D.'s trial predated Gardner's election as sheriff by four years.

"He was acquitted." Dallas's voice was harsher than he would have liked.

"He's in the county. And even more connected to you now."

"I told you when you called, J.D. was here with me yesterday evening, well into the night. You can't be saying he's—"

"I'm not saying anything except that in a county with seven homicides in a decade, only two have not been domestics or bar fights—and both those were killings of attractive young women at the same hidden-away spot in the woods practically on your boy Carson's doorstep."

He couldn't let Gardner shut him out of this investigation.

Too much rested on it.

He'd been sitting here thinking about that, trying to work it all out ever since word came about Laurel Blankenship Tagner.

"As the duly elected Commonwealth's Attorney for Bedhurst County, I'm going out there with you. As will my associate."

"Dammit, Monroe—"

Evelyn appeared at the arched opening. "Can I get you gentlemen anything? Coffee? Something else to drink?"

"No thank you, Mrs. DuPree," Gardner said, a flicker crossing his face.

The same flicker that had crossed his African American features the first time he'd come into Monroe House and met the solid black woman who served as Dallas' housekeeper.

She'd told the sheriff half a dozen times to call her Evelyn. He hadn't listened. And yet, Dallas thought, the younger man probably believed he was being respectful.

Dallas also declined her offer of coffee with thanks.

When she left, he took up the conversational reins Gardner had dropped, as had surely been Evelyn's intent by timing her arrival then. Dallas knew she was still listening from the hallway, and she'd have an opinion to share later.

"Sheriff Gardner, let's be honest here. You need me. You don't know this county. I do." A modest understatement. No one knew this county the way Dallas Herbert Monroe did. And no one knew that better than Dallas Herbert Monroe. But modesty never went amiss.

"I know having you anywhere near the case until we know for sure if it's connected or not to the one four and a half years ago is—"

"Who better to tell you if the two cases are connected than the defense attorney from the first trial?"

"Oh, I can think of a couple people just as good," Gardner said with cutting dryness. "Starting with the murderer."

Dallas settled deeper into his chair. So, now the real haggling began.

CHAPTER THREE

Monday, 8:12 a.m.

"**HOPE YOU HAD** a nice weekend, Ms. Frye—you deserved it after that verdict Friday."

Maggie smiled at the front desk guard as she went through the security screening. "Thanks, Robert."

"Got to love when they come back fast and right," he said.

"Absolutely."

Most mornings Maggie Frye walked the four flights to her office in the glass and concrete Fairlington County Justice Center, counting it as both aerobics and weight-training, considering the heft of her briefcase, which never lightened no matter how some crowed about paperless offices.

But today she headed to the elevator.

She was treating herself.

The Millerand jury had returned a guilty verdict late Friday, putting away a rapist after an hour of deliberation.

That should prevent other women going through what Dustin Millerand's two victims had. At least until he got out.

Winning the case gave her more ammunition to get Vic Upton to name her deputy when the current deputy retired in the fall.

Plus, the quick verdict had left an unburdened weekend to run errands, do laundry, buy groceries, and wake to the fact that winter had retreated from Fairlington County, Virginia.

Daffodils bloomed beside her townhouse's front steps. She hadn't planted them since moving in twenty months ago, but if they were a carryover from the previous owner, she should have noticed them last spring.

Oh, wait.

The Dorset case. The stalker tracked through his mother's DMV records. No, she wouldn't have noticed daffodils then.

The doors slid open on the fourth floor and she turned right.

"Maggie." A familiar male voice came from behind her.

Her mood dipped. She kept walking.

"I could need to talk to you about a case, you know."

She stopped, faced him. Dark blond hair, sparkling blue eyes, upper-crust looks—and even more appealing in his police uniform because of it. Must have ceremonial duties today. "Is this about a case?"

"No, but—"

She pivoted to continue in her original direction.

"You are so damned unforgiving." He followed.

"According to you there was nothing to forgive."

"There wasn't. It didn't mean anything."

"Not to you, obviously. And now it doesn't mean anything to me."

"I meant with her, not with you, Maggie."

"I meant both."

She tugged the outer office door handle. He spread his palm across the glass surface. Balanced between his push and her pull the door remained static.

"The prosecutor takes one piece of evidence, becomes judge, jury, and executioner?"

"Not original, Roy. And I doubt Officer Hundley would appreciate you calling her a piece—even of evidence."

"I don't want to play word games, Maggie."

Because he never won? asked the voice in the back of her head previously silenced by his gorgeousness.

"I stayed away while you were trying that rape case," he added. "Now it's over and I want you to listen to my side."

"No, you want me to agree you've done nothing wrong and we can go on the way we were. I told you before, we can't." She looked fully into his blue eyes. "I don't want to."

"You're going to kick me out of your life? Give up on what we had? Forget how it was? And—"

"Yes. Yes. And yes. Good-bye, Roy."

She tugged hard on the handle, wedged the door open with her briefcase and slipped inside.

"Good morning, Nancy. Isn't it a beautiful spring day?"

Nancy's gaze slid past Maggie, then back. "It's been a beautiful spring day for two weeks. And you can stop talking like a dropout from finishing school. He's gone."

Maggie looked around. Nothing but hallway beyond the glass door.

"Roy Isaacson isn't used to hearing no," her assistant observed.

Nancy liked to say she'd held every job in the courthouse except judge and Commonwealth's Attorney—in other words, all the important jobs. She knew everyone and their secrets.

"He'll get used to it."

"With him glowering like a thundercloud, word will get around. Belichek and Landis will be pissed if they don't hear it from you."

She hadn't told her assistant she'd broken up with Roy. But Nancy knew everything about everyone in the building, plus half the metro area.

"I'll call them."

"Vic will be up later. Sheila couldn't say when. The Post story must have him on the prowl." Nancy frequently warned that, with Maggie's success nipping at Vic's heels, Maggie should beware of him kicking her in the teeth. "Also, your cousin called. Jamie. Not Ally. She wants you to call her back as soon as possible."

Maggie grunted. She'd have felt obligated to call Ally back immediately, with what she had going on in her life. Jamie could wait.

✦   ✦   ✦   ✦

"HEY, MAGGIE," DETECTIVE Tanner Landis' telephonic voice topped background noise announcing he was in the car. "Good going on the Millerand case."

Landis always checked caller ID before answering his phone. It was one of the smaller reasons she most often called his partner, who never bothered to check caller ID, because he answered every call with a barked "Belichek."

But for this call Tanner was the better option.

"Thanks. I, uh, wanted you and Bel to hear this from me."

"Oh, Christ. You're going to a big-bucks corporate firm."

"No. Why would you think that?"

"It's my recurring nightmare."

She grinned. "Aw, Landis, I didn't know you cared."

"Care? I am deeply, passionately—" His next word was blurred by the call-waiting click. "You got to get that, Mags?"

She checked caller ID. The Sunshine Foundation. "No."

"Family, huh?"

Another reason she generally preferred Belichek. Not that he wouldn't draw the same conclusion, but he'd keep it to himself. Usually.

"Shut up, Landis." She nearly said her personal life was none of his business, but relented, considering what she'd called to tell him. "Do you want to hear what I have to say or not?"

"Yes, ma'am, Ms. Assistant Commonwealth's Attorney, ma'am. Please."

"Roy and I broke up."

There was a slight pause, then Landis spoke away from the phone's mouthpiece. "Mags dumped Isaacson."

"I didn't say that. I said—What did Bel say?"

"He said *Thank God*. A sentiment I second. And I know you didn't say you dumped him, but if he'd dumped you, you would have gone into clam mode and never said a word, ergo my superior detecting skills tell me you dumped him."

"Why *Thank God?*"

"She wants to know why you said *Thank God*, Bel."

"He's an asshole" came through clearly.

Landis spoke in her ear, "In another sentiment I second, Bel says—"

"I heard. Why didn't you say anything?"

"And risk the wrath of Frye? Sometimes you gotta wait for a case to develop, instead of forcing it. That's my reason. As for Bel, he was being his usual tactful self."

Belichek being tactful. That would be something to see.

"Yeah? Well—" Nancy appeared in the open doorway. "I gotta go, Landis. We'll continue this later."

"How about lunch? We'll be there. Got court this afternoon."

"Sure. Sounds good."

"And I promise not to tell you more than twice you're better off and you deserve a hell of a lot better. No promises about Bel—you know how he goes on and on."

Nancy, standing in the doorway, nodded at the phone after Maggie hung up. "How'd they take it?"

"They'll survive."

"I imagine you made their week. Jamie's on line two."

Nancy's subtle way of saying she was done fending off Maggie's cousin.

Maggie picked up the receiver.

CHAPTER FOUR

VIC UPTON, COMMONWEALTH'S Attorney for Fairlington County, slapped a fold of newsprint on Maggie's desk. He could have sent it digitally, but Vic liked the sensory impact.

She didn't look up. She continued writing, fast and strong, bringing order to the week ahead.

This newsprint thwap wasn't bass enough to be the entire *Washington Post*, which would mean Vic had dumped a Page One problem on her desk.

Once—just once—she'd screamed when Vic dropped a complete Sunday *Post* on her desk. It had been barely six a.m., she'd spent the night in the office, and she'd been asleep with her head on the desk that Sunday morning. The four-pound thud had reverberated in her head all day. The professional headache had endured considerably longer. But it had been worth it in the end. She'd won that case, too.

This thud sounded like the local section alone.

The story about the Millerand trial had been in the Saturday Metro section, but Maggie didn't waste more than a millisecond considering whether Vic was here to congratulate her.

Her cousin's congratulations on the verdict had been subdued, though she supposed sincere.

Jamison Chancellor didn't get enthusiastic about justice. She reserved her enthusiasm for her starry-eyed venture aimed at making the world a place where everyone walked hand-in-hand in perfect peace.

Even worse, she kept trying to drag Maggie in.

Jamie had started today's installment by extolling the beauty of the spring day and mentioning she'd driven past Maggie's place and seen daffodils blooming there.

"Don't give me any credit. The previous owner must have done it," Maggie said.

There was a slight pause. "Ally and I planted them last fall."

Shit. "Right. Of course, I remember."

Jamie laughed. Another reason Maggie tried to avoid these calls. Jamie's laughs were frequent. Too genuine, too affectionate, too ... familiar.

"No, you don't. But it's okay. We planted them on Vivian's birthday and she would love them blooming for you now. And—"

"Jamie, I have to go. I got behind during the trial and have a pile of work on my desk." Not true. Everyone expected the trial to take longer. Her calendar was blocked out.

"I won't keep you. I wanted to tell you the Foundation's annual fundraiser is coming up and—"

"I'd have to check my schedule."

"Nancy says it's clear."

Damn both of them—cousin and assistant. "Jamie, I really have to go."

"Okay. Just—promise me you'll think about it. It would mean a lot to ... to have you there this year. Ally is coming. Please. Just say you'll think about it."

Some people failed to see the rock-hard tenaciousness beneath Jamie's sweet expression and starry-eyed ideas. Maggie had known better since they were kids.

She also knew the only way to get off the phone was to make a promise she had no intention of keeping.

"I'll think about it."

After disconnecting, she set to work on a list of tasks sure to keep her mind off that promise. She'd still been at it when Vic strode in, unannounced.

Maggie finished writing the current item on her list, then capped her pen.

Vic snorted. A single sound standing in for past diatribes on her using pens "anybody can buy at Staples, for God's sake, when you have a Waterman set honoring your family's foundation."

Maggie gazed at the newspaper Vic had deposited on her desk.

Not the *Washington Post*. The *Bedhurst Bulletin*.

The headline word *Murdered* caught her first.

Not in Fairlington, so not in their jurisdiction. Could be Vic was crowing over a colleague's misstep.

Then she saw the complete headline

Bedhurst Woman Murdered in seventy-two-point type. Beneath it, in only slightly smaller type: *Similarities to Unsolved Wade Murder Cited.*

"Shit."

"That about covers it." Vic occupied a chair in a space-gobbling spread of arms and legs. "Judge's daughter, too. The same judge, right?"

So, Vic *was* crowing over a colleague's misstep. Hers.

Though misstep was too mild. Try utter failure.

Picking up the newspaper to bring the text into focus, she pushed aside everything else.

Use your brain, Frye.

Her practiced scan locked on the name—Laurel Blankenship Tagner, daughter of Judge Kemble Blankenship—and said briefly, "Same judge."

She went back to the start of the article.

Laurel had failed to show up for a gathering at her father's home at noon Sunday. Friends and family realized no one had seen her since Saturday afternoon. Authorities were called. Someone thought to check the service road entrance to Bedhurst Falls—*the same location. God, the same location*—and Laurel Blankenship Tagner's body was found just before sunset Sunday.

The authorities acknowledged there were similarities to the murder nearly five years ago of Pandora Addington Wade. No one had been convicted of that murder.

The location of the body was one similarity, authorities indicated there were more, but had not released details.

Maggie breathed out, slow and deliberate. Similar didn't have to mean the same murderer. Similar could mean someone who'd followed the Carson case, in other words, anyone in Bedhurst County.

Or the sonuvabitch she'd failed to get convicted could have killed again.

"Is it the same guy?" Vic demanded.

"Hard to tell from this." She sounded calm. Good. "Could be. Could be a copycat. Could be unrelated."

Vic stretched one leg kept passably lean by a daily sacrosanct hour in the gym. "In that backwoods county? With who the victim is—another woman from one of the county's top families, like your victim—and where the body was found? And those other similarities the newspaper doesn't have?—I got word the body was found in the same position. Face down, arms and legs spread out. No sexual assault. The area around the body brushed, like last time, no footprints, or any other marks."

Almost certainly related.

She grunted, started reading at the top again. "Where was Carson?"

"There, in Bedhurst. With his defense attorney. Alibied to the hilt."

Maggie's stomach tightened.

Under the headlines, a three-column studio photo of a young woman with dramatic makeup emphasizing come-hither eyes and mouth. Maggie squinted at the photo. Pulled up a memory. The judge's daughters sitting in the courtroom, awaiting the verdict. This one with the sex-kitten mannerisms. Unlike her companion, a square-faced woman who dressed as if Talbots were racy.

"I'm going up there," she said abruptly.

Vic straightened from his initial slouch, then slid down again. To the untrained eye it might appear to be the same sprawl.

"The hell you are."

"Monroe is Commonwealth's Attorney now and the sheriff was elected last fall and he's an outsider, from Richmond. Monroe—"

"How do you know?"

She flipped her hand, dismissing his question. "Monroe will run rings around him."

"Even if it is Carson, Monroe can't defend him. Not in Bedhurst

County, not since he was elected Commonwealth's Attorney."

"He won't have to defend. He can make sure there's no case. As CA, he can refuse to prosecute Carson."

"Jesus, Maggie, I know you don't have much use for defense attorneys from that thing when you were a kid, but you make it sound like Monroe would throw a murder investigation to protect a former client. The citizens of Bedhurst must think better of him than you do or they wouldn't have elected him. Besides, it's not our case. I just thought you'd be interested."

Like hell.

He'd thought he would bring her down a peg after Friday's verdict. It was how he kept his staff from nipping too hard on those ambitious heels of his.

"It's still my case." She took a breath, kept the words reasoned, but firm. "The rape trial wrapped up faster than we expected. My desk will never be clearer than it is now. And God knows I've got vacation time coming."

"Listen, Maggie, we all have a case or two like this. The ones that go bad, the blots on our record that haunt us. But trying to make it right can make it worse. Let it go."

He thought she wanted to make it right so it didn't dim her record's sparkle? Of course, he did.

In the face of her silence, Vic heaved a breath. "Actually, the sheriff has requested you up there."

"To prosecute." It would be one hell of a trick to get named special visiting prosecutor on the case, but for a second chance to put Carson away she'd call in every favor.

"Not to prosecute. He wants you and Monroe to fill him in on the earlier murder."

CHAPTER FIVE

1:38 p.m.

MAGGIE BRAKED AS she entered Bedhurst County.

Not from any desire to contemplate bright green rolls of country rising beyond picturesque fences. She'd abruptly remembered being ticketed twice in speed traps four and a half years ago.

The town itself was announced by the usual outriders of chain stores and fast food places. Quickly, streets narrowed and trees crowded close to the curbs. After a spate of brick ramblers and cape cods, the houses grew larger and the lawns deeper. Finally, a band of one-time grand houses converted to business-use opened to the town square.

None of it jogged any memories until she reached the courthouse. *That* she recognized.

All red brick, white trim, and restrained columns, the hundred-plus-year-old Bedhurst County Courthouse was venerable and well-proportioned, in stark contrast to the graceless municipal buildings huddling down the hill behind it. That's where she'd had a window-less closet passing for office space as special visiting prosecutor.

She found a parking spot across from the courthouse steps, where the likeness of General Joseph Bedhurst still rode his bronze horse on a landing halfway up to the front entry.

A blustery breeze snatched at the car door as she opened it. She reached back for her lined raincoat. Bedhurst hadn't gotten the memo about spring.

The entry to the sheriff's department was at the back of the courthouse, in a basement revealed by falling-away ground. She should check in with the sheriff.

But straight ahead, two doors down Main Street from where she stood, the wind swung an old-fashioned wooden sign on a metal arm: Dallas Herbert Monroe & Associate, Attorneys-at-Law.

The man who had won J.D. Carson's freedom. The man who provided him an alibi now. The man who, after forty years as a defense attorney, had run for—and won—the part-time job of Commonwealth's Attorney for Bedhurst County.

The sheriff could wait.

Maggie opened the black door beneath the sign and crossed a worn threshold, her entrance announced by a small bell. A sliver of space to her left held the barest essentials of a waiting room—three chairs and a magazine rack. Straight ahead a wide hall clogged with teeming barrister cases disappeared into dimness. A yard down on the right she saw an open doorway. Farther back, a gap in the barrister cases on the left indicated another door.

A creak came from deep down the hallway. She squinted but saw only shadow. Must have been an old-building settling noise. God knows the building was old, and it looked as if it might settle right into the ground.

"Have a seat!" came Monroe's muffled voice. "I'll be right with you."

Maggie tracked the voice to the office on the right. Piles of folders, books, and notepads listed from nearly every surface. The top of a silver-haired head showed beyond a three-foot pile on the corner of a desk that could have doubled as a battleship if it wouldn't have sunk under the load.

"Monroe."

He came out of his chair. "My dear, my dear!" A broad smile rearranged folds and wrinkles. To reach her, he weaved around an island of books with practiced ease. "It is a delight to have you back among us. It's been entirely too long. Four years and—"

"It could have been another forty years for my taste." She met his handshake with her abridged, professional edition.

"Oh, my dear, I am crushed you would have preferred to stay away. We take such pride in our fair corner of Virginia—and do call me Dallas."

She raised her brows. "I was referring to another murder."

His face fell instantly. Holding her captive right hand in both of his, he drew her to a settee on the wall opposite the front windows. "Horrible. Horrible."

She withdrew her hand, but sat. To her knowledge she had never encountered a horsehair sofa before, but this had to be the real thing. No one would make modern upholstery jab this way.

"All of Bedhurst County is most grateful you have come to assist us in this horrible time. With the murderer of Pan Wade never found—"

"Never convicted."

Sharp eyes under heavy lids flashed, but he didn't rise to the bait. "We must find this person, and Sheriff Gardner wisely recognizes he needs assistance."

"I understand you say you were with Carson?"

"Indeed. J.D. and I were together all of Saturday afternoon and through the evenin', well past midnight."

Alibis were meant to be broken. That's what an old prosecutor had told her.

"Can an independent party verify that?"

He patted her hand, ignoring her question and its implications.

"What we need to concern ourselves with is whether the murder of Pan Wade fits in with this—" The sound of the outer door opening, the bell, and the door closing reached them. Monroe never paused. "—horrible murder of the judge's daughter, and if so, how. I was mappin' a strategy when you arrived."

Monroe's attention shifted past her right shoulder.

"Ah, here you are, and bearin' our catered luncheon." The smell of burgers and fries brought Maggie's head around, even before Monroe added, "You remember J.D., don't you, my dear?"

"Welcome back to Bedhurst, Ms. Frye."

CHAPTER SIX

J.D. CARSON STOOD at the office's open doorway, holding a cutaway cardboard box with bags stamped Cheforie's Burgers. His dark eyes watched her.

Refusing to show shock, she studied him right back. He had those eyelids some people called sleepy. A scar slashed a diagonal across his chin, starting half an inch from the corner of his mouth and disappearing under his jaw. A single deep dent of concentration marked the spot between his brows. He stood military erect.

Unlike court, where he'd worn a suit and tie, he had on a well-worn polo shirt tucked into jeans. But there was more different about him. What was it?

"Better weather for you this time," he said.

The voice hadn't changed. Unhurried. Calm. Steel beneath each word.

"Quit discussin' the weather and get that food in here, J.D. We took the liberty of orderin' for you, Maggie," Monroe said as Carson put the box on an open patch of the conference table.

Both of them, acting as if this were a social call.

She'd known he was still in the county, known Monroe provided his alibi, but what the hell was this? Had Carson left the Army to become a gofer?

"Come sit and have your lunch," Monroe continued. "We can start workin' as soon as we've reacquainted body and soul. J.D. put together a preliminary report on this tragic murder and—"

"Carson did?" she interrupted.

Apparently unfazed by her lack of greeting or anything else, the man in question sat at the conference table with his back to her and bit into a burger.

Monroe paused in peeling the final corner of shiny paper from his burger. "Of course. J.D. is my new associate, so—"

"*Associate?*"

"Yes, indeed, passed the bar last fall. First try. Then—"

"*He* went to law school?" Maybe a law school couldn't legally keep out a man found not guilty, but even if it hadn't come up on any of her periodic database checks of Carson's name, she surely would have heard about a former murder defendant applying to law school. And would have done her damnedest to stop him.

"J.D. followed our fine Virginia custom and read for law. Other states have abandoned their heritage, but Virginia maintains the tradition. So, like Mr. Jefferson and Mr. Madison and Mr. Monroe— Did I tell you I'm a descendant of that esteemed gentleman's cousin? Although—"

"You let him read law with you." Maggie didn't bother making it a question.

Among the government and criminal databases she checked regularly, she'd never considered members of the bar association.

"No, no. He needed wider experience than I could give, having remained in Bedhurst County nearly my entire career. Why, I'm not at all sure the Virginia Board of Bar Examiners would have approved me. Rules and regulations measure each step of a lawyer overseeing the reader's legal education."

"I read with Chester Bondelle of Roanoke." Carson didn't turn. "His number's 434-555-4305."

And she'd damn well check out Chester Bondelle the first chance she had.

Had Carson commuted to Roanoke? Because according to the official record, he'd maintained residence in the shack near Bedhurst Falls he'd inherited.

Damn, damn, damn. She should have dug deeper.

"Since he's my associate," Monroe was saying, "of course J.D.'s workin' with us in assistin' Sheriff Gardner with his investigation."

She stared at the back of Carson's head. That's what was different—his hair. It had grown out from the military cut. Because he'd never gone back to the Army. Because he'd stayed here to study law and pass the bar.

Why?

Carson stood. "I'll finish my lunch at my desk, leave you two to talk."

Without looking at her, he walked out.

"You mustn't—" Monroe started.

At a distance a male voice rose. Irritation, though not the words, clear.

Monroe's gaze slid to the back wall of his office, as if he could see what was happening in the depths of the building.

Monroe focused on her again, the break in his manner smoothly mended as he murmured solicitously. "You mustn't let this bother you, and you should eat before it gets cold."

"Not let it bother me? The man I tried, the man charged with a similar murder—"

"Found not guilty."

"—the only man ever charged, because nobody else has been charged with Pan Wade's murder, not in four and a half years." He muttered something. She overrode it. "The only man charged and brought to trial for one murder involved in the investigation of a similar murder? And I'm not supposed to let it *bother* me?"

He swept a hand through the air. "When you've grown accustomed to the changes, you'll—"

"You can't do this, Monroe."

"It's done."

"Even with you giving him an alibi for now, he's a suspect."

He didn't allow himself to be drawn. "This is the way it is, so—Where are you going?"

"To talk to the sheriff."

"The sheriff knows."

"He doesn't know what I'm going to say about it."

Commonwealth v. J.D. Carson

Witness J.D. Carson (defendant)
Cross-Examination by Assistant Commonwealth's Attorney Margaret Frye

Q. Isn't it true that you and Pandora Addington Wade were together at the restaurant and bar called Shenny's on four consecutive nights before she was murdered?

A. Yes.

Q. You've heard witnesses testify that you sat close together—no space between them at all was the testimony—is that your testimony?

A. Yes, we sat close.

Q. You also hugged her on at least one occasion?

A. Yes.

Q. Did you talk about your relationship on those occasions?

A. Yes.

Q. Did you also talk about her marriage to Richard Wade at that time?

A. Pan did.

Q. Pan did? You were silent on the subject?

A. Yes.

Q. On the last occasion you were there together—the evening before Mrs. Wade's murder—you wrote the name and address of a housing complex near the base where you were stationed and gave the paper to

Mrs. Wade, isn't that true?

A. Yes, I wrote down the information for a housing complex near where I am stationed.

Q. Had you talked about her moving there?

A. Yes.

Q. Did you argue about it that evening?

A. No.

Q. You were heard to argue—

Mr. Monroe: Objection, Your Honor. Assumes facts not in evidence.

Ms. Frye: Your Honor, Theodore Barrett testified that he heard the defendant and Mrs. Wade—

Mr. Monroe: And admitted on cross-examination that he couldn't hear anything clearly from where he was, Judge.

Ms. Frye: Only after defense badgered and—

THE COURT: Enough. Objection is overruled. Witness will answer the question.

A. No, we didn't argue.

Q. You argued because she wouldn't run away with you and—

A. No.

Q. And you shot her—

A. No. I did not.

CHAPTER SEVEN

PHONES RANG IN syncopation as Maggie entered the sheriff's department.

"The line at the high school should be operating, transfer the Tagner case calls to Abner. You keep things running here and—Yes?" The speaker, a tall, thin man with skin a richer version of his brown sheriff's department uniform, had caught sight of Maggie.

A gray-haired woman wearing a headset grunted and lowered herself into a battered leather chair. She punched a button, said, "Sheriff's Department," and one ring dropped out of the race.

"I'm Maggie Frye, from the Fairlington County Commonwealth's Attorney's office. Are you Sheriff Gardner?"

The man nodded and they shook hands. "Come on back to my office."

He sorted old-fashioned message slips on the way down the short hall and dumped half in the trash can in his office. The rest he slid into a folder. She took the chair he indicated. He sat on the edge of the desk.

"I appreciate your agreeing to help us, Ms. Frye." He blinked, dark lids covering blood-shot eyes for an extra beat. She recognized the signs. The man hadn't slept the past two nights.

"Call me Maggie, but I haven't agreed. How can the man prosecuted for the first murder be involved in the investigation?"

"Prosecuted and found not guilty," he said.

"Carson has to be a suspect for this murder. The prime suspect."

"No evidence against him, but I haven't eliminated anybody." He narrowed his eyes. "And let me be very clear. I'm leading this investigation."

"But—"

"That's not what I need you for. Listen, Dallas has me by the short-hairs and knows it. They recruited me from Richmond to run here. Took office four months ago. I've got to know if this murder is connected to the other one, and fast, but what do I have to work with?

"My predecessor has dementia and judging by his reports he wasn't right for years. The deputy who assisted him on that investigation died of cancer. The judge from that trial is grieving his daughter's murder. That leaves crap reports and a transcript I don't have time to read. You'll help some, but, no offense, you don't know this county any better than I know Los Angeles.

"Dallas says he'll help, but only if Carson's included. What am I going to say? A lot of folks here think Carson never should have been charged—not all, but a lot. And he was acquitted. Now he's a lawyer in good standing. So, I take the package deal, and ask for you to balance things out.

"Another thing, Ms. Frye—you said Carson was prosecuted for the first murder. That's jumping to a conclusion that this one's a sequel. We don't know that. Yet." He stood, tucking the folder under his arm, and she also rose. "Look at it this way, if Carson is guilty, he's where I've got two upstanding citizens watching him, including a hot-shot prosecutor from the big city."

"Monroe? He's on the other side. Makes it two against one."

"I'd take those odds with you being the one. Or are you going to quit on me, leave it two against none?"

"I haven't decided."

"Decide fast. If you're staying, we're meeting at the high school at three-thirty to try to keep this coordinated, not leave gaps, not run over each other."

"One more thing, Sheriff. I intend to prosecute this case."

"We have to catch the sonuvabitch before anybody can prosecute. If there's a conflict between my investigation and you possibly prosecuting later, you do what's right for the investigation or I'll throw

you out of my county. There're plenty who can prosecute a case—
assuming we get the sonuvabitch—but you're the only one who can
give me the prosecution's view on the Wade murder."

He was right.

But another factor might push her toward the decision Gardner
wanted her to make.

She'd told herself for more than four years that the jury had spoken in the Carson case and that was all there was to it.

That wasn't all there was to it.

Either she'd prosecuted the right man and got the wrong verdict or
she'd prosecuted the wrong man and got the right verdict.

Either way, a murderer went free and she was responsible.

Again.

FROM THE SHADOWY back corner of Courtroom One, J.D. Carson
squinted through hazy afternoon sunlight polishing the wooden
benches and floor.

The first time he'd been in this courtroom he hadn't been old
enough to go to school. He'd come to see if it was true his mama was
going to jail.

Many times after he'd sat back here, silently watching.

Being on trial for murder he'd been in the same spot Nola Carson
had routinely held.

After he'd passed the bar, he'd sat in each seat in the jury box to
know what they would see when he stood before them as an attorney.
He'd even sat behind the bench, the best seat in the house.

After that, J.D. thought he truly knew this courtroom. But he'd
never seen it from where Margaret Ellen Frye stood now, dragging her
knuckles across the aged wood of the prosecution table. Right where
she'd stood four and a half years ago.

One spot he'd missed.

That was a mistake, and he couldn't afford mistakes.

CHAPTER EIGHT

2:27 p.m.

"Papa?"

Charlotte Blankenship Smith hadn't called her father that since she was thirteen. Mama had been sick for a full year by then and relying on Charlotte for organizing, phone calls, checking on workmen—all that allowed the household to run and the entertaining to continue as befitted the judge's position.

Laurel, almost four years younger than her, had declared Papa was for babies. She'd called him Judge, and he'd liked it. Soon Charlotte had dropped Papa for Judge.

He gave no sign of hearing Charlotte now, sitting in the darkened library, his head tipped, staring at the mahogany piecrust table beside his wing chair. The table needed dusting before allowing visitors in. The whole room did.

He insisted she turn everyone away today. But Rambler Farm would soon be filled with people again, as it should be.

"Judge?"

He lifted his head slowly. "Charlotte. You're here."

She had sat across from him for eight minutes.

"Judge, we need to talk about the arrangements. The sheriff's office says it will let us know as soon as the body can be released." Dorrie at the sheriff's office had also said that woman prosecutor who'd tried J.D. was back in town. A factor Charlotte would think about later. "If we make decisions now, everything can be ready."

He squeezed his eyes closed. "You do it, Charlotte. I ... I can't ..." Tears slid from between his eyelids.

"I'll take care of it." She patted his hand, feeling the raised veins and the nubs of the knuckles. "I'll take care of everything."

She closed the door behind her, gathered her tablet and phone from her desk near the kitchen before heading to the sunroom. It was more efficient to keep her work tools here than at Second House where she and Ed lived, across the circular drive.

She added a notation. While waiting for her father's attention, she'd noticed the paneling on the library's fireplace wall—original to the 1804 core of the house—needed lemon oil.

Clouds' shadows deepened the green of the velvet lawn. Crocuses bloomed around the base of the birdbath. Still wrapped tight, buds of daffodils and tulips stood tall. The azaleas would show well this year. By fall, mums planted last year should have caught hold for a good display, too.

Summer was hardest. She'd have two plantings of annuals again to keep the beds fresh. Not wilted like they had been on that July day going on five years ago when Pan came by.

To cry about her marriage to Rick Wade falling apart.

Pan had married the hometown hero, the high school and college football star who had come home to his family's businesses when he didn't make it in the pros. Had come home to Bedhurst's favorite daughter, the one everyone loved as soon as they set eyes on her. Sweet Pandora Addington.

But when Pan's ideal life was falling apart, she'd come to Charlotte.

"It was so much simpler when we were all in school. You and me and Rick and Scott and J.D. and all the others. I miss those times," Pan had said.

Charlotte didn't miss them. Not one bit.

"Charlotte?"

She jolted at Ed's voice. She wasn't used to him being here during a weekday.

"Sorry, honey." He sat beside her. "I didn't mean to startle you. What are you doing? Can I do anything to help? Do you need anything in town?"

"No, you can't help." Did he know the Frye woman was back? Was that why he wanted to go to town? "I'm planning the funeral."

Planning Laurel's funeral, thinking about Pan.

"Oh, Charlotte. Don't worry, honey. They'll catch him. They'll catch whoever did this."

She focused on him. His eyes were red, his hair uncombed.

He'd gone out with the search parties, of course. But now everyone knew where Laurel was. No more wondering if she would be late. Or what she was doing or might do in the future. No more upset. It was all settled.

J.D. HAD CLOSED to within ten feet of the prosecution table when Maggie Frye pivoted. Controlled, but fast enough to make her collarlength hair swing. The flaps of her long raincoat opened, showing black slacks and dark green blouse.

"Ms. Frye, Dallas sent me to make sure you have a place to stay tonight."

"Someone from my office is making arrangements."

"She tried. She called where you stayed before. But Paula had a knee replacement and she's not open. Your assistant tried to reach you, but reception can be spotty. The sheriff's office had her call our office for a suggestion." *Our office.* He said that easily now.

"Any chain will do. Or I passed a place coming in. Something Manor."

"Closest chain's in Lexington. And Dallas said to tell you you can't stay at the Piedmont Manor."

Her shoulder moved, more a twitch than a shrug. "I'll be fine."

"If you don't believe Dallas, go back and ask the sheriff. You can't stay there."

She was fast. His words indicated he'd seen her leave the sheriff's office. That left a gap—the gap when she'd stood by the prosecution table, thinking fierce thoughts. She was wondering what he'd been doing during that time.

She was also clear to read. It was one of her strengths as a prosecutor. Juries believed her, because they saw she believed in the defendant's guilt.

"Dallas has a guesthouse," he said. "Private drive. Easy walk to the office and here. He said for you to try it tonight. You can leave your things and be to the high school for the meeting."

"Fine." She wanted this trivial matter settled. "How do I get there?"

"I'll lead you."

"Just tell me."

Oh, yeah, she was easy to read. "There are quirks, and Dallas doesn't let anyone have the key until they've been warned."

She cut a look toward him without connecting, grabbed her purse, and passed him.

He matched her pace across the marble lobby floor. Held the heavy wooden door for her. He waited until they'd started down the outside steps to say, "It's going to be hard working together if you can't look me in the eye."

She stopped. Her cold glare belied his accusation. "We are not working together."

"You're leaving?"

The glare's temperature shot up but everything else about her cooled, especially her voice, as she continued down the steps. "Why are you determined to be involved in this investigation?"

"I'd think that was obvious."

"You're going to say it's to clear your name."

"And you're thinking it's so I can interfere with the investigation."

"A logical conclusion."

"A logical premise. For a conclusion you need—" He let an extra beat emphasize the final word. "—evidence."

"I had evidence. I never prosecute someone if I have any doubt about their guilt."

This woman threw her cards on a table like a B-52 delivering bombs. He wasn't surprised, not after watching her in court.

"A jury didn't agree with you. And you've missed another explanation for why I want in on this—I don't want any more dead women in my county."

Her phone rang. As they crossed the street to the red Honda with the Fairlington County sticker, she fished it out of her bag one-handed and answered with the ease of practice, never breaking stride.

"Frye. ... Yes, I heard." She looked directly at him. He leaned against her car, holding up his end of the stare. "Yes, that, too. ... He's here. ... That's right, J.D. Carson. ... He's offered to lead me there now to check it out. ... Yes. I'll call you immediately. ... I will be."

She disconnected the call, maintaining eye contact.

He nodded, pushing off the car. "Smart, letting your office know who you're with and where you're going."

"I'm a smart person."

"No need to prove it to me." He'd seen how smart she was first-hand. It could have put a needle in his arm. "I'll lead the way."

He wasn't entirely sure until he pulled his truck out of the alley beside the office and her red Honda followed.

A left, right, left and into the dead-end dirt lane to the rear of the generous grounds around historic Monroe House. He parked the truck with the nose stopping shy of the weathered wood fence that marked the end of the lane.

She pulled in beside him, in the spot closer to the guesthouse's door. She had too much speed and had to hit the brakes hard. The Honda's front end dove low, but the bumper still connected with the fence, not with enough force to do any damage to fence or bumper, but enough to set the old wood shuddering.

She was already out of the car when he came around to her driver's side. He blocked her path, pointed at the fence.

"You pushed your luck. There's a drop-off to the creek bed forty, fifty feet down. If you count on that fence holding you, you're going to find yourself smashed up."

The red in her cheeks deepened in a way no makeup could reproduce. Whether she'd been distracted by the wild grounds threatening to swallow the little guesthouse or she'd been questioning herself for coming to such an isolated spot with him, she hadn't been paying attention to her driving. And she was pissed. At him. At herself.

"I'll remember that."

He led her to the single broad step flanked by rhododendron bushes behind budding azaleas. Clouds had rolled in, working toward smothering the sun, and the thick rhododendrons added to the gloom.

He showed her how the front door's handle had to be lifted up and jiggled for the key to fit. Only when she'd done it successfully did they go inside.

"You've got a nice view from the porch." He gestured toward the screened porch that ran six feet deep along the back and was partially cantilevered over the drop-off to the creek.

Bushes had blocked the view until he pruned them four years ago.

She made a sound, like she approved of the flickering sunlight on the opposite bank shifting across soft greens of new leaves and stark blacks of rain-soaked trunks. What she said was, "Anything else?"

"Heat." He pointed to a handle with a hot pad tied to it. If she didn't know to use the hot pad to turn it off there was no use telling her anything. "Never put the heat on when you have this lamp plugged in. It's a fire hazard, combining those two."

He waited. She said nothing. He saw the *It's almost May, I'll never need to know this* look folks from other places got. If she didn't figure out that the weather in these mountains didn't operate by the calendar there was no use telling her that, either.

He led the way to the kitchen. "This faucet has to be dripping to get the shower to run. If the refrigerator starts sounding like a motor boat, unplug it, let it sit five minutes—full five minutes—then plug it back in. Any garbage, take to the main house. The raccoons don't take no for an answer. Don't leave the door open or you'll have them for roommates."

He kept up his monologue, as if he didn't notice she always stayed closer to the door than to him.

Narrow steps led to the bedroom and bath. She went to the seat under three wide windows that reached to the ceiling and looked over a steep porch roof, then across the gully to the woods. He never got between her and the exit.

"There's a closet." He pointed to a door next to the bath, then to a door on the far side of the bed, next to the windows. "That's storage. Kept locked."

She didn't say a word.

"Any questions?" he asked when they were on the front step again.

"You could have gone back to the Army, why stay here? Why law?"

He'd meant about the guesthouse. But he should have been ready—surprise and directness gave her cross-examination muscle.

"I went into law for the big bucks. Didn't you?"

He held up the key. When she put a palm out, he dropped it in. She made no move to go inside, to turn her back on him.

Most people had no fear because they had no distrust of him. Some let good manners push them into pretending they had no fear. A few showed fear.

None of the above for Maggie Frye.

He got in his truck, made a proficient three-point turn and pulled away.

Before the magnolia blocked his view, he checked the rear-view mirror. She was still standing there, watching his truck. Making sure he left.

Commonwealth v. J.D. Carson

Witness Terence Pratt, Colonel, U.S. Army (prosecution)
Direct Examination by ACA Frye

Q. Thank you for that summary of the defendant's military career, Colonel Pratt. What it comes down to is that the defendant has been trained to kill, isn't that so, Colonel?

A. He is trained to fight. In some instances that might call for employing potentially lethal force.

Q. Certainly being in combat, as the defendant has been, would call for—as you say—employing potentially lethal force, would it not?

A. In some circumstances. Even in combat there are fewer instances for an individual to face the decision of whether to employ potentially lethal force than many civilians believe.

Q. Do those instances exist in combat?

A. As I said—

Q. Please answer the question.

Defense. Objection, Your Honor. The prosecution is badgering her own witness.

THE COURT: Overruled. I will allow it, though, Ms. Frye, I don't recommend pushing the bounds with your own witness. Colonel, if you will please answer the question.

A. Yes, they exist.

Q. Thank you, Colonel Pratt. Now, the training the defendant received that you listed for us, that would include knowing how to fire a weapon?

A. Yes.

Q. Including knowing how to fire a Smith & Wesson M&P 9-millimeter, the same model the victim, Mrs.—?

Mr. Monroe: Objection. This witness has no way of knowing the model of Mrs. Wade's weapon.

THE COURT: Sustained.

Q. Did the defendant's training include how to fire a Smith & Wesson M&P 9-millimeter?

A. Yes.

Q. Did the defendant earn awards for marksmanship?

A. Yes.

Q. Was excellent marksmanship a prerequisite for the special training you mentioned earlier?

A. Yes.

Q. Was knowing the inner workings of a gun a prerequisite for the special training you mentioned earlier?

A. Yes.

Q. Knowing the inner workings of a gun would include being familiar with how to load a gun?

A. Yes.

Q. In fact, his training included being able to load a gun blindfolded, relying only on his sense of touch, did it not?

A. Yes.

Q. In the special training the defendant received, did he learn how to disable someone without leaving a mark?

A. Yes.

Q. Did he receive instruction in how to move into and out of an area without leaving any trace, including by obscuring sign of his movements?

A. Yes.

Q. Thank you, Colonel Pratt. One last thing. If you would refer again to the recommendation you wrote for the defendant, will you please read the highlighted sentence just above your signature?

A. It says—the one sentence?

Q. Yes, please. If you will read the one highlighted sentence.

A. In summary, Carson is an exemplary graduate of this program with a grasp of all the skills required for special operations—in fact, one of the best I have ever seen.

CHAPTER NINE

3:33 p.m.

MAGGIE WATCHED SHERIFF Roger Gardner cross a border of bare floor to reach the rectangle of industrial carpet protecting the high school's basketball court.

Cafeteria tables rimmed the rectangle with gaps for passage to the middle, where three tables formed an H. Rivers of cords flowed across the floor to computers, phones, lamps. Attached to portable whiteboards were a county map and several photographs.

"Sheriff got this set up fast," she said to Dallas Monroe.

He had been standing with J.D. Carson when she came in. Carson stayed put when Monroe advanced to greet her, expressing delight at her staying in his guesthouse.

"He's had us all runnin' drills to set up for disasters, but this isn't the kind of disaster we were preparin' for." His blue eyes, faded almost to the color of skim milk, were sorrowful.

Gardner stopped, facing the pockets of conversation. Everyone quieted.

He met Maggie's eyes. She nodded once. She was staying.

"Crime scene folks are processing, won't join us." Racing the weather, everyone knew. It had rained yesterday before Laurel's body was found and looked ready to start again. "Those of you not here this morning, this is how it breaks down…"

The sheriff and a state trooper headed the investigation. They would coordinate with those processing the scene, witness the autopsy.

Four officers from neighboring counties, each paired with an auxiliary deputy, would canvass the community. A local deputy and a state investigator would organize preliminary witness interviews and create a timeline. Another local deputy would be reachable here at all times to coordinate.

Scanning the men and women gathered, Maggie identified jurisdictions by uniform. One man was harder to place. Mid-thirties. Smooth brown hair cut with precision. A white shirt that almost seemed familiar, though how any one white shirt could be familiar, she didn't know.

"Everything comes to me," Gardner said, "with copies to Abner and keep a copy yourself. Abner will keep a log. If you think I've missed something, speak up. But nobody acts on his or her own."

Monroe shifted his weight.

"Nobody, and I mean nobody—" The sheriff looked at Monroe. "—is a freelancer. Nobody talks to the media except me. Anybody does, you're out and I'll look real close at obstruction of justice."

The rest wasn't any more than the newspaper and Vic had told her—with one notable addition.

Laurel Blankenship Tagner had been garroted.

Pan Wade had been shot with her own gun, which had been left at the scene—wiped clean.

Whatever had been used on Laurel had not been left at the scene, although from the injuries, the experts said a stick or rod had been used to tighten whatever had been around her throat. Nothing of Laurel's was missing. Working theory was the murderer brought the materials and took them away.

But did the different methods matter? The Army trained J.D. Carson to expertise in those and other methods.

Both women's bodies had been left face down, neatly posed, no clothing missing or disturbed.

"Once the garrote was around her neck, anybody could strangle her by twisting the stick or whatever the hell it was." Gardner's gaze swept the gathering. "We're going to the crime scene when we finish here. If you think you have a reason to see it, check with me. You go with me now or not at all."

"What about them?" The demand came from a tall man. People between them kept Maggie from seeing more than the tan t-shirt of the auxiliary deputies. She thought he looked toward Carson.

The rest of the gathering looked at her.

"Dallas Monroe, Maggie Frye, and J.D. Carson are going to help out. Sort of an adjunct to the main investigation. Some of you might not know Maggie. She's an Assistant Commonwealth's Attorney from Fairlington County. She was up here as special prosecutor on Pan Wade's murder. That's all."

"Do you have instructions for our special unit?" asked Monroe in the split second before the listeners broke ranks.

She had to admire the old lawyer. With one question, he'd announced they were "special"—a different matter entirely from Gardner's "sort of an adjunct"—and they reported directly to Gardner.

The sheriff's expression said he might like to disband the "special unit" on the spot. "I'll be back to you in a minute."

The well-dressed man she'd noticed started after the sheriff.

"Scott, stay here, boy," Monroe said.

"They need my expertise." The younger man followed the sheriff's back with his eyes. "To keep the record of the investigation. Interviews and—"

"They got deputies for that. We'll need your help."

"I'm working only for you? Not the investigation?" It was an accusation.

"We're part of the investigation," Monroe said mildly.

"That's a waste of my skill. The sheriff—"

"Has made his decision."

The younger man opened his mouth, closed it, and walked away.

Beside her Monroe sighed. "You have family, Ms. Frye?" He didn't wait for an answer. "Young Scott Tomlinson's my cousin's boy."

She didn't talk family with anybody, much less Monroe. Besides, young Scott had to be her age, no boy at all.

"Padding the payroll with your relatives at the government's expense?"

"You are a viper, woman," he said approvingly. "Scott'll earn his keep, don't you worry. Besides, he's providin' transcripts from J.D.'s trial."

Ah. That's why Scott Tomlinson and his shirt looked familiar. The always-a-white-shirt, turning-his-cuffs-back-precisely court reporter.

"That boy was a godsend to his mother when his father was gone," Monroe said, apparently continuing a conversational thread she would have cut off at the start if she'd caught it. "Had a fallin' out. Thank heavens they healed the breach not long before she died, the little insurance she had helped him get by. It hit him hard." Monroe sighed again. "Family."

With a murmur about the map, Maggie escaped to the whiteboard.

Carson was there, studying I.D. photos of the victims and general shots of the crime scene.

She spotted on the map where Laurel Tagner's body had been found yesterday and Pan Wade's nearly five years ago. She also located Judge Blankenship's Rambler Farm, where Laurel had been living since leaving her husband three months earlier, according to Carson's preliminary report she'd read before the briefing.

The cabin where Carson had been staying at the time of Pan Wade's murder was impossible to pinpoint within the irregular green-shaded area surrounding Bedhurst Falls. He'd inherited it, not from family—reports on his background said the best his relatives did was hand-to-mouth—but from an elderly woman.

If Maggie hadn't been keeping Carson in her peripheral vision she would have missed his assessing look at the photo of Laurel, then the one of Pan. As he started that go-round a fourth time, she'd had enough.

"What?"

One dark eyebrow flickered. He didn't pretend not to understand. "There's a resemblance."

She studied the photos. Differences jumped out first. It required mentally stripping Laurel's flashiness, but then, yes, there was a resemblance. Long, light brown hair with red glints, distinct eyebrows against fair skin, full mouth. The eyes were different. Pan's had a softness. Not Laurel's.

"You're saying they're a type? You're saying this could be a serial killer, and this is his type? Nearly five years between murders could be long for a serial killer. Unless he was off somewhere. Perhaps, spending most of his time in another city, training. But now he's back full-time, a possible trigger."

He gave no sign her parallels to his circumstances got under his skin.

"Are you testing if I know that up-to-date research says many serial killers don't stick to the rigid timelines and MOs popular media portrays? I do. What I'm saying is, in a general way, they look like each other—and you."

"*Me?*"

"You'd have to grow your hair, but there's a similarity. Of course, you're older."

She snorted her skepticism and disdain.

"And there's the fact you're all from complicated families."

"I beg your pardon? What do you think you know about my—?"

"Google's a wonderful thing." He walked away.

J.D. Carson had researched her on the Internet. And not just her, her family. *What the hell?*

"Ah," came Monroe's drawl from beside her. "J.D.'s right. There is a resemblance amongst the three of you."

She sent him a look, but he was studying the photos. Or pretending to.

"Eavesdropping, Monroe?"

"An eminently useful means of acquirin' information," he confirmed. He stood with his hands behind his back, pushing out his paunch. He'd used that pose in the courtroom. It contributed to a kindly uncle persona.

She moved to the other end of the whiteboard.

A new voice came at her.

"You're a fool." It was the *What about them?* guy. "You'll get sucked in by Carson like all the rest."

Before she responded, he strode away as Monroe called her name.

The sheriff, Carson, and Scott Tomlinson were with him.

Carson was saying to the sheriff, "Looks like you got it all covered. What can we give you?"

"History."

"You mean the first murder," Scott said.

Gardner's gaze flicked to Maggie, "First murder or unrelated murder? That's what I need from you folks—context, background to start toward answers. I've read a report that could pass as a text and a few incomplete newspaper clippings. That's all I know about the Wade murder. That's not enough—not nearly enough—to say if these murders are connected. I want you to organize the details on that case so I can determine if there are parallels."

"We'll need free rein to interview people from the first case," Monroe said. "Witnesses—"

"Law enforcement—besides the former sheriff," Maggie said.

"Wasn't anybody beyond him and his deputy who died. Unless you mean Rick Wade." Gardner jerked his head toward the man who'd asked *What about them?* and accused her of being a fool.

The memory clicked. "Pan Wade's husband."

"Yeah. He's an auxiliary deputy. Was then, too, though he didn't work on her case. At least they did that right. Look, it's up to you how you start. If you give me what I need I'll leave you be. If not, I'll step in."

Maggie followed Gardner.

"Sheriff." He slowed, didn't stop. "The defendant and the husband of a murder victim? How can you—?"

"Because I have to. This whole county's Wades and Addingtons and Tagners and Blankenships. Unless they're Monroes. I'm doing damn well not to have any of Laurel's immediate family involved. If I eliminate anyone related to Pan, too, it'll be me and one state guy left. Besides—" He shot her a look. "—if Wade wasn't involved we might not have found Laurel when we did. He suggested the spot be checked and was the first there."

She cursed.

His wan smile acknowledged her sentiment. "Says he wasn't there more than two minutes alone. No sign he went into the scene. But I agree. It sucks. You coming to the scene? Dallas and J.D. are, along with some added techs."

"Yes, I'm coming. Sheriff, I know you're up against it. But I want to add someone to this cozy little group you want me in." To even the numbers, if not the odds. "Ed Smith. He was my second chair. He's in Lynchburg. That's close enough—"

He was shaking his head. "Smith married Judge Blankenship's older girl, Charlotte. This victim was his sister-in-law. I told you, they're all related."

He started off, then added, "You know, with Rick Wade around you'll only be the second-most certain Carson's a murderer."

CHAPTER TEN

4:19 p.m.

NANCY ANSWERED ON the first ring. "Where are you?"

"Driving to the scene," Maggie said. At the speed of a funeral cortege, stuck behind official vehicles.

"You're staying?"

"Is that approval I hear?"

"I don't express opinions about legal matters."

Maggie suppressed a snort.

Nancy Quinn had been a single mother with two kids and three years on the police force when a suspect shot her, shattering her right femur.

She'd told Maggie she would have returned to the street if it hadn't been for her kids. A desk job in the police department would have rubbed salt into the wound, but she hadn't strayed far, first trying court reporting, then becoming indispensable in the Commonwealth's Attorney's office.

When Vic assigned Nancy to assist on the Carson case four and a half years ago, Maggie had been half terrified, half grateful. She'd had the same mix of emotions when Nancy opted to become her assistant on their return to Fairlington. That hadn't changed.

"I'll request your complete file out of storage and a fresh transcript," Nancy said.

"No need on the fresh transcript. The trial court reporter's providing copies."

"For free?"

"I don't know. But, apparently, it's not totally out of the goodness of his heart. Monroe's hired him. Plus, he seems interested."

"One of those."

Nancy didn't think much of legal system employees who viewed investigations and trials as fascinating pastimes. *Court reporter needs to concentrate on getting each word down accurately, not try to put pieces together and reach a conclusion.* And that, Maggie suspected, was why Nancy left court reporting. She hated sitting back and letting other people run the show.

"Nancy, what do you know about becoming a lawyer in Virginia by reading the law?"

No hesitation. "Reading the law was how lawyers studied for hundreds of years, serving an apprenticeship with an established lawyer. For example, Thomas Jefferson read the law with George Wythe in Williamsburg. The Virginia Bar Association spells out regulations and requirements now."

"I never heard of this," Maggie grumbled.

Nancy reeled off names. Maggie recognized a respected judge in the Tidewater area, a real estate law specialist around Richmond, and the author of several journal articles she'd admired. "All read for law," Nancy concluded. "Have to be able to work alone and be a self-motivator, but for those who can't afford tuition or can't go to law school for some reason it's a great alternative."

"Some reason like having been tried for murder. Carson, the guy we prosecuted up here, is now a lawyer, thanks to this throwback system."

There was something in the quality of Nancy's silence.

"You knew?" Maggie demanded.

"I heard."

"Why didn't you—? How?"

"Roger Gardner's brother's married to my cousin. I saw Roger over the holidays, after he was elected."

Maggie rubbed her forehead. She'd thought Nancy's web of connections covered the D.C. metro area. She'd been thinking too small.

"Roger mentioned Carson becoming a lawyer," Nancy said. "Flew through the bar exam."

"I don't care if he got the best scores ever. Just because a jury was blinded by sentiment doesn't make the evidence go away and it doesn't make this guy innocent."

"Innocent isn't up to a jury—only guilty or not guilty."

Maggie drew in air to keep her lungs too occupied to talk. "I want all the background on Chester Bondelle from Roanoke."

MAGGIE FINGER-COMBED HER hair straight back to stop it from dripping in her face.

Rain had started as the convoy parked along the edge of a paved county road. The new arrivals trudged past police barricades and up a rough path beside a dirt road that ran perpendicular to the county road. The forest's underbrush crowded them on the right, Across the dirt road to their left, the ground rose sharply toward a tree-studded ridgeline.

After a distance Maggie equated to three blocks, the dirt road ended in a clearing. As it had four and a half years ago, yellow crime-scene tape encircled most of this clearing. At one o'clock of the rough circle, the path slid into the forest and out of view.

Inside the yellow tape and under tarps, crime scene specialists worked with methodical efficiency.

With the rain, some people left for other duties. But Carson stayed, so she did. Not that she expected him to pocket evidence with an audience. But he'd stayed for some reason.

"How much will they lose because of the weather?" she asked Sheriff Gardner.

"Not much." He didn't take his eyes off a squat man taking soil samples. "They started last night and have been working steady. The bad news is, they're telling me there isn't a lot to get. No tire tracks except hers. No footprints."

Just like Pan Wade's murder.

The only recent tire tracks had been Pan's car. No footprints, not even hers, because of spiraling brush marks someone had taken the time to create with a bushy evergreen branch.

"Dirt was brushed out all around the body, out to the gravel," Gardner finished, his description of this crime scene echoing Maggie's memories. "Somebody knows how to cover his tracks."

Carson was trained to slip in unnoticed, to kill, to leave no trail.

"What about the body? You know about the note the ME at the district office in Roanoke found in Pan Wade's mouth at autopsy?"

That piece of information wasn't in Sheriff Hague's records, probably the only reason it hadn't been public knowledge before the trial. She'd saved that detail until the expert's testimony.

"This victim went to Roanoke, too. No note," Gardner said.

Her phone rang. It was Belichek. As usual he wasted no time on niceties like hello.

"You're running around on some old case with a murderer?" he demanded. "Is your head up your ass? Is everybody's heads up their asses there?"

"Yes to the first. No to the second. Possibly to the third."

"Maggie—"

"How did you know about this?"

A tech called to the sheriff, who squished across to the tarp-roofed area.

"Nancy. When we came to pick you up for lunch."

"Lunch. I totally forgot."

"No shit."

"I'm sorry. I didn't—"

"No problem." Bel hated apologies. "Do you need help? I could—"

Maggie saw Dallas Monroe and Scott Tomlinson standing tucked under a line of trees, sheltered by the umbrella Scott held. Monroe appeared lost in miserable contemplation of the mud at his feet. Tomlinson was looking at the far side of the clearing.

Maggie followed the direction of his gaze.

"Not now. Thanks, Bel."

He grumbled something, then, "I hope to hell you know what you're doing. And why you're doing it up there."

Carson stood alone, outside the yellow tape, his back to the clearing, facing the evergreen-encrusted ridge rising in front of him. The camouflage slicker he'd put on when the rain started blurred into the vegetation. He took a step, and she realized he was at the opening to a path she hadn't seen before.

A few more steps and he would be invisible to those in the clearing.

"Bel, I gotta go."

Commonwealth v. J.D. Carson

Witness Terence Pratt, Colonel, U.S. Army (prosecution)
Cross-Examination by Dallas Herbert Monroe

Q. Colonel Pratt, you said Captain Carson here is trained in these skills Ms. Frye had you reciting, is that so?

A. Yes.

Q. And that training, does that include more than how to do the thing?

A. Absolutely. It entails being in control of the abilities taught to you. That control, that discipline is taught right along with each skill. Control and discipline are instilled under rigorous circumstances. That is essential to the training.

Q. Thank you, Colonel. Thank you. Now, Colonel, with all that training and discipline, though, it's possible—just possible, mind you—that some fellows you've got in there don't take all the training the best way, and you need to keep tabs on them, maybe wash them out of the program, is that right, sir?

A. Yes. There are periodic reports on candidates during training, assessing their abilities and especially the matters you've mentioned—control and discipline.

Q. So, in those reports on Captain Carson was the assessment of his control and discipline ever anything less than the top grade?

A. No, sir.

Q. Might say he was one of the best you'd ever—

Ms. Frye: Objection. The defense is trying to testify again, Your Honor.

THE COURT: Sustained. Mr. Monroe, questions, not speeches.

Mr. Monroe: I do apologize.

Q. Let's open it up all the way then, Colonel. In his entire career in the Army, from the time he entered as an eighteen-year-old, was there ever any official or unofficial reprimand or notation or concern or a taking him aside in an informal manner—was there anything at all—that might indicate Captain Carson had any difficulty with discipline or control?

A. No sir. On the contrary, he was commended in the highest terms possible for his performance and was specifically cited for his cool and disciplined approach.

CHAPTER ELEVEN

MAGGIE SCOOTED AROUND the clearing, skirting the yellow tape, fighting for footing on rain-slicked grass. Carson was out of sight.

She almost missed the path. She'd gone two strides past before a rustling made her backtrack. Examining the area between two dripping bushes, she saw a rough path open up.

Literally up. It zigzagged narrowly on the incline toward the ridge-line. Something—someone—moved above her. She put her head down and started climbing.

The webbing of trees overhead cut some of the rain, but the branches dripped splotches onto the path. Odors of wet earth and last fall's rotting vegetation were nearly as tangible as the moisture.

The path sucked her flats deep, letting muck ooze up the low-cut sides and brush clammily against her insteps. She grabbed stout branches or saplings' trunks to help pull herself up. She fought the flaps of her raincoat every step. Trying to be quiet was hopeless.

The heavily ridged soles of Carson's running shoes left distinctive marks in the soft ground, but the few times she glanced ahead she saw no other sign of him.

She had to be more than halfway to the ridge. She was getting winded, but no way could she rest with him getting farther away every second.

Her right foot slid. She grabbed for a bush, her hold skidded off the wet trunk, and her right hand came down hard on coarse twigs, leaves, and other detritus of the forest floor. Her left arm windmilled for balance, but she was going over backwards, and it would be a rough trip down.

An iron grip encircled her left wrist.

"Hold on," he ordered.

She clasped her hand around Carson's wrist, strengthening the bond.

With one hand, he held her up until she had both feet under her and on relatively solid ground.

"I'm okay." He released her immediately. "Thanks."

Without responding, he continued up the path. How far ahead had he been? She hadn't seen him, yet he'd reached her in almost no time.

She started after him.

"You shouldn't come up here." He didn't look back.

"I'm not afraid of a little mud."

"Going into these woods alone with a man might not be the smartest thing to do. Two women who look like you—" She snorted. It didn't ruffle his flow. "—have ended up dead. Granted, I have more reason to be afraid of you, since you're bent on a do-over to get me convicted. And maybe you think to right other old wrongs?"

She bypassed the irrelevant question. "This murderer doesn't operate when he's exposed. The sheriff knows I'm with you." Maybe. But surely Scott did. He must have seen her follow.

"Two isn't much of a pattern to bank on. And logic isn't much of a weapon against murder. You're willing to gamble your life on that?"

"I don't see it as a gamble. Besides, you wanted me to follow you. What *are* these things?" In annoyance, she shoved away a stiff cluster of big, streaming leaves slapping her face.

"Rhododendron." Still moving, he looked back. "You think you know I wanted you to follow, because...?"

"Don't tell me you didn't rustle those bushes on purpose when I'd passed the opening." She hated she was puffing while he didn't seem the least bit pressed. "You had Special Ops training—and excelled. So, you did it on purpose."

"Better to know where your enemy is," he muttered.

Her sentiments exactly.

She didn't say that. She probably didn't need to. Whatever else he was, J.D. Carson wasn't stupid.

Climbing behind him, her eyes leveled with where the hem of his slicker caught on the top edge of his jeans pockets. It highlighted the hard shape under those pockets. The muscles working in perfect, powerful rhythm to get him where he wanted to go.

She kept her focus on the ground in front of her.

Her puffing eased by the time she followed him into a clearing that was a smaller, rougher version of the crime scene, including a track of narrow ruts roughly parallel to the dirt road below.

Without moving, Carson examined the ground.

"What are you looking for?" She finger-combed her hair again, the rain sluicing from the ends under her collar and down her backbone. She squelched a shiver.

"Don't know until I see it."

He gazed along the rutted track, frowning, then slowly walked the outside of the hard-packed area, examining the pale, sprouting grass around it.

The rain came harder in the clearing. It slid off the ends of his hair and dripped in his face. He made no move to wipe it away, barely blinked when a drop hit his lashes.

Having completed his circuit of the clearing, Carson walked past her toward an opening opposite from where they'd climbed up.

She was on his heels when he edged into the path, his head barely moving, but his eyes taking in everything.

His hand slashed the air, gesturing for her to move to the side. "If you have to come, get behind me. In my footprints. Not in the middle."

"Nothing this narrow has a middle. And I'm coming, all right." She plastered herself against the prickly wall of vegetation. "What are you looking for now?"

"Nothing." They'd gone maybe twenty yards when he stopped. "Nothing," he repeated, but it sounded different. "Let's go."

He gestured for her to lead back the way they'd come. She hesitated. It was pure instinct not to turn her back on him.

His expression didn't change.

He stepped around her, leaving one additional footprint in the path, before retracing their steps.

A branch slapped sticky wet leaves against her cheek, like cloth soaked in sugar water. She pushed it away impatiently.

"Why aren't there better paths?"

"Deer aren't as picky as you city types." He gestured to indentations in the mud.

They resembled elongated teardrops. Now she saw the tracks were everywhere, crossing and re-crossing each other.

"This is a deer trail? Why in hell are we on a deer trail?"

"I'm on it because I wanted to see if any humans used it lately. You can supply your own motivation."

"What difference are you saying it would make if humans used it lately?"

"Maybe none. Doesn't matter. Only deer've been there."

"What about the one from the main clearing toward the waterfall—aren't you interested if anyone's used that path lately?"

It was also the path that eventually led to his shack in the woods.

The path he'd testified he took after leaving Pan Wade—alive—in the clearing.

The one Teddie Barrett initially said he was on when he heard Carson and Pan arguing.

It had been broader, better used four and a half years ago. Now it had mostly gone back to the wild.

"I know that's been used. My tracks were there from last week, though not as far as the clearing. After Laurel was found Sunday, there were a lot of other tracks added."

"Your footprints must have been as far as the clearing. You're still living in that cabin and that's the only way to get to it. You must be parking there—"

His head shake sent off a spray. "Built a private road four years ago. This is park land. Okay to use it now and then. Not permanent. My road comes in further along the county road."

He crossed the clearing to the edge of the dense vegetation on the slope they'd come up, and squatted, balancing on his toes.

Her calves and thighs ached from the climb. Her feet were stridently complaining that her flats had long ago forfeited their sensible status. And the only level spot to mimic his position and see what he was seeing would put her hip to hip with him.

There was a log on his far side. She stepped over it and sat. Under an overarching fir tree and between bare branches, a view of the crime scene below opened like a curtain had been raised.

The clearing in the middle, the entrance to the path to his old shack on the left, the first few yards of the road to the right. If someone had been here at the time of the murder—either murder—there'd be one hell of a witness.

Carson said dryly, "Good thing we're not hoping to find evidence there."

"Evidence?" She looked at the log. "Of what?"

"Nothing this time."

"What does that mean?"

He didn't answer. He squinted at the area spotlighted by yellow ribbon, where figures in slickers toiled.

Now she got it. This pantomime was meant to lead her to ask a certain question. Then he'd give her a piece of information he was dying to dump on her while making it seem she'd wormed it out of him.

He didn't know she'd trained under the master of that technique, Vic Upton. And she'd learned the solution was to not ask the question.

The figures below were fading. Despite the rain and the woven roof of the forest some light had filtered to them, but soon wouldn't be as generous.

Carson stood. "I'm going. If you don't want to let me loose in the woods alone, you better come, too."

She rose without comment. He squinted toward the crime scene, murmured something. That was part of the technique, too. She didn't ask what he'd said. Besides, she had a pretty good idea it was a repeat.

"Nothing. This time."

CHAPTER TWELVE

10:24 p.m.

MAGGIE PILED PILLOWS against the headboard of the guesthouse's double bed, adjusted the lamp, placed her open briefcase on the far side of the bed, and slid in between the covers.

She hesitated, her hand at the opening of the lid pocket. She limited herself to running her finger across the outside surface, feeling the edge of the plastic sleeve that always stayed there.

At least some things were where they belonged.

Just now, when she'd reached for the green tube of facial cleanser it hadn't been where it belonged.

The toothpaste, floss, and glass with her toothbrush huddled together where she'd put them when she unpacked this afternoon. A few inches apart sat moisturizing lotion. In between, where the facial cleanser should reside, was an empty swath of vanity.

She'd widened her view, and there was the cleanser. On the right side, between her makeup and hairdryer.

She put things in the same place. Always. It helped her put her hands on necessities even in the depths of a trial.

But there was the cleanser on the wrong side.

Listen, Maggie, we all have a case or two like this. The ones that go bad. … Let it go.

The hell with that. The hell with Vic Upton's ambitious pragmatism.

You're bent on a do-over to get me convicted. And maybe you think to right old wrongs?

What exactly did J.D. Carson think he knew?

She adjusted her position and took out the copy of the original investigative file into the murder of Pan Wade.

It didn't matter what Carson thought he knew. All that mattered was catching him.

Or, she mentally added in strict fairness, whoever the murderer was.

She began to read.

The file was even worse than Sheriff Gardner said and she remembered.

Next up was her case summary of *Commonwealth of Virginia v. J.D. Carson.*

Maybe Scott Tomlinson would have the complete and certified trial transcript tomorrow. When Nancy sent the material from her files she'd also go over the dailies where she'd made notes during the trial.

Finally, she re-read the preliminary information Carson had written on Laurel's murder. It was concise, organized, and devoid of commentary or local color.

When she'd finished, she made a call.

"Belichek."

"Got some time, Bel?"

"Yeah. Shoot."

She outlined the case she'd made four and a half years ago in her opening statement, then built up layer by layer through testimony.

J.D. Carson, home on leave from the Army, had been seen with the victim numerous times in the days before the murder. Witness after witness provided observations of a man falling deeper and deeper for this woman.

The day before the murder, he called about off-base housing where he was stationed. Why would he do that if he wasn't anticipating Pan returning with him?

But her estranged husband, his family, and her family all were urging Pan to give the marriage another try.

She had told her hairdresser she was meeting Carson that afternoon, and expected, the hairdresser had testified, "a turning point."

It added up to a woman returning to her husband, cutting off Carson, a man who was no stranger to violence. He knew how to take the life of a man—or woman—in a cold heartbeat.

Maggie had told the jury they didn't need to know what was said between Pan and Carson, because they had the evidence of what happened.

They were sighted in her car, turning off the paved county road that provided back access to Bedhurst Falls Park and surrounding woods that had been Carson's second home since childhood. The next morning, Pan's body was found in an isolated clearing.

Dirt around her body had been carefully brushed out. But on the path leading into the woods toward the shack Carson had recently inherited, had been two clear prints. His.

Two of his dark hairs had been found on her clothes. A strand of her hair was found wrapped around his shirt cuff button.

Pan had a broken fingernail, but no useful DNA was found under any of her nails. He'd had no marks on him, but the shirt could have protected him.

They'd found a note in his handwriting about off-base living with Pan's body.

"Practically the only piece of evidence that didn't get spread all over the county before the trial, because it wasn't found until the autopsy at the regional ME's office," she told Bel. "They kept it to themselves except for the official reports, unlike the locals. They found the paper in her mouth, like it had been shoved in there. Which logic says was the action of someone angry and taking something very personally."

"What did your guy say?" Bel asked.

She suppressed the urge to say he wasn't her guy, instead delivering the facts. Carson acknowledged giving Pan the note, but said it had been the previous day and their conversations had shifted to her trying to make her marriage work.

He'd said he left Pan in the clearing, taking the path through the woods to his home. He'd stayed there, alone, until a phone call the next morning from Pan's worried mother. He said he'd immediately searched the clearing and found Pan dead.

"What's Carson's connection to this second victim?" Bel asked.

She smiled without humor. "The sheriff will tell you that figuring out if Laurel is the *second* victim is the job of this bizarre task force I've been maneuvered onto."

"You don't get maneuvered, Mags. And I still wanna know if he's connected to the latest dead body."

"Of course he is. Everyone in this damned county lives in everybody else's pocket. He seems to have been a frequent visitor to her father's place—Rambler Farm. Don't let *farm* fool you—it's an estate. Plus, the older Blankenship sister went to school with Carson, Pan Wade, and Wade's estranged husband."

"What about that estranged husband? Was he looked at for the first murder?"

"He had an alibi. I don't remember the details of it." She scribbled a note to herself. "I should remember the details."

"That case landed on you like a pile of bird shit at the last minute. You were too busy trying to get bird shit out of your hair to look around at the rest of the flock."

Despite herself, she chuckled. "Thanks, Bel. I wonder about the current victim's estranged husband's alibi, too."

"Another estranged, huh?"

"Yeah. This guy also has three exes before Laurel. I wanted to go there tonight to interview him—there and to Rambler Farm to talk to the judge and the sister. Laurel had been staying with her family since the problems with her husband. But Monroe said it was too soon to intrude on their grief. God, like you should give people a week to come up with their story."

"Surprised you didn't go on your own."

"I would've. But the sheriff said no because he was conducting a round of interviews with them tonight about Laurel. I wanted to go along, but Gardner didn't want me since I'm only supposed to be looking at the earlier murder."

Bel made a noise that might have been sympathy. But she suspected it was for Sheriff Gardner, not her.

"Instead, Monroe insisted I have dinner at his place with him and Carson."

"Learn anything?"

"Only that Carson wasn't murdering anybody tonight between seven and nine-fifty-five. And Dallas Monroe can talk non-stop for nearly three hours."

"He's a lawyer, isn't he?"

She gave an obligatory *huh* of amusement. "Gardner says he wants the details of the Wade case organized, but he's swamped. What he really needs is comparing and contrasting of the circumstances and victimology of Pan Wade's and Laurel Tagner's murders."

"He'll love you telling him what he really needs."

She ignored that. "And if I catch Carson in inconsistencies, place him where he says he wasn't, get a line on a real connection between him and Laurel, I can nail the bastard this time. Get enough to convict—"

"Whoa. You're not just putting the cart before the horse, you've got the cart miles down the road. Quit trying to go from nothing to a mountain of evidence. The mountain—"

"I know, I know. The mountain starts with a pebble," she mimicked his frequent lecture.

"That's right," he said evenly. "It's pretty simple, Mags. You've either got one murderer or two, with this recent one using what worked for the first murderer. Concentrate on which it is, and keep an open mind about the rest. Who and ifs and all. You don't start with a vision of the mountain. You let the pebbles piling up say what the mountain's going to look like."

CHAPTER THIRTEEN

Tuesday, 7:12 a.m.

THE OLD-FASHIONED BLACK telephone rang as Maggie's hand touched the guesthouse doorknob.

She picked it up before the second ring.

"Maggie! Come on up to the house. Evelyn's made us breakfast." Dallas Monroe's voice boomed. "Just follow the path from the back door."

He hung up before she could reply.

She wouldn't have declined anyway. She had things to get straight with Monroe. Besides, she was hungry.

The path started as a narrow passageway between thickets of what Carson had identified as rhododendron bushes. Branches met overhead, creating a dim, moist tube. Just short of the main house, one side opened to a large oval of lawn bordered by beds with green shoots poking through the soil and climbing over the dried husks of last year's plants.

"Come in, come in," Monroe called. He held a door open in a one-story frame addition to the three-story brick house.

The warm scent of eggs and bacon wrapped around Maggie. She sucked it in with an unconscious inhalation.

"Wonderful, isn't it?" He smiled widely as his hand at her back urged her into a long, narrow kitchen spattered with sunlight. "If you thought dinner was good, wait until you taste Evelyn's breakfast."

Maggie had briefly met Evelyn DuPree, a black woman with gray working its way from her hairline to the crown of her head, the night before. Now, she smiled, said hello, and gave Maggie the once-over in two seconds flat, before returning her attention to a pan of scrambled eggs. "Sit down. Dallas, get the girl juice and coffee."

He waved Maggie to a seat at a table by the windows and quickly complied. He settled into his chair and Evelyn delivered plates with portions of eggs already on them, one in each hand and the third balanced against her forearm.

"Evelyn, my love, will you marry me?" Monroe breathed in, his eyes almost closed.

"No."

"You wound me to the heart."

"Remember you only eat like this every two weeks or you won't have any heart at all."

He faced Maggie with an air of pointedly ignoring Evelyn's comment. "How do you like my little guesthouse, my dear?"

"It's fine." Evelyn's forehead wrinkled at the curt word. Maggie added, "It's lovely. Thank you for letting me stay there."

"Not at all, not at all. Delighted."

"There is one thing, Mo—Dallas. I'd like to have all the keys in my possession while I'm here."

Her host emitted a gust of laughter. "My dear, you might as well ask me to give Sisyphus a hand with rollin' that rock up the hill in hell—it's as useless a task."

Evelyn smiled. "He hands keys out like candy on Halloween. About all anybody has to do is show up and say Trick or Treat."

"How many keys?"

Monroe lifted his hands. "I have no idea. I don't recall askin' for any of them back."

Evelyn considered. "Scott, of course, and Rick Wade, and Eugene Tagner for a couple nights, and the sheriff. Before that, we had Ed Smith and Abner—one of the deputies—and of course J.D. You'd think Dallas was running Bedhurst's version of Boys Town."

"You know they're all here for your cookin' when it comes down to it, Evelyn, and you love havin' guests."

"At least this time it's a woman," Evelyn grumbled, but with a hint of a smile. "She's bound to be better about bringing the garbage up to the bins, keeping the raccoons from rampaging."

Maggie brought the conversation back on topic. "Carson stayed here?"

"After the trial," Evelyn supplied, as Monroe ate. "Until he got his place in the woods squared away. Worked on it hard, but what with studying law and all, it took nearly two years."

So, Carson had a key to the guesthouse, among a cast of thousands.

That misplaced tube of cleanser. *Had* she been forgetful? Or was there another explanation?

"You mind drivin' this mornin', Maggie? My car's in for a tune-up."

She jerked her attention back to Dallas. "Driving where?"

"Here and there. Talkin' to folks who knew our victim well. That's what J.D. and I are tacklin' first thing. Figured you'd surely want to come along."

"All those interviews were already done, besides the trial files will be delivered today."

"Ah, Pan Wade's case, yes. But people are out there." He swept his arm in a gesture she remembered from the courtroom. "Files stay put, never changin', but people don't. Longer we wait, the more time for them to forget somethin' about Laurel or remember somethin' that never was."

"About Laurel?" So his mind was also on comparing and contrasting the two murders, though, clearly he'd be searching for differences to put Carson in the clear. That was okay. She could make this work to her advantage. Still, no reason to make it too easy. No reason at all. "We're supposed to get the sheriff up to date on Pan Wade's murder. He doesn't need his investigation duplicated."

"How're we to tell him if the cases are connected if we don't know a thing about *this* murder? We gotta gather facts."

She was being pushed. Any doubt was erased by the bright, curious way he watched her.

She didn't like being pushed. Even when it was in the direction she wanted to go. Besides, it set a bad precedent to fall over at the first push.

"When will Scott have copies of the official transcript? If those are ready, we should—"

"Won't be a while yet. Give the boy a chance."

The first batch of material from Nancy wouldn't arrive via messenger until later in the day. Besides, she wasn't about to let Carson and Monroe go off on their own.

She paused, as if her mind weren't made up. "All right. On the condition we start with the witness from Carson's trial who heard Carson and Pan arguing—Teddie Barrett."

"Hah! I showed on cross-examination he heard nothing of the kind."

"You took advantage of him, confused him, and—"

"Stop!" Evelyn commanded. "Leave that behavior in the courtroom, it's not fit for the breakfast table. Now, Dallas, you tell this girl straight out that poor boy died four years ago." To Maggie she said, "He was riding his bike out Falls Road like he liked to, and somebody must've hit him, knocked him and his bike right off the bridge and down I don't know how far, poor soul."

"Hit and run? He was killed in a hit and run?"

"That's right. Hit and run accident. Though how they can call it an accident I don't know when somebody's so evil he doesn't stop to help, especially a soul as harmless as Teddie Barrett."

CHAPTER FOURTEEN

To J.D.'s THINKING, the uninspired modernity of Eugene Tagner's house should have been cited for littering concrete boxes on Dry Creek Ridge.

He'd said as much to Pan. She'd said spending money wasn't the same as exercising good taste.

Louelle, who'd previously worked for Eugene's parents, answered the doorbell and ushered them through a yawning hallway with a chandelier that resembled pickup sticks, and into a study where black leather, chrome, and glass fought for domination.

Earlier, J.D. had stepped into Monroe House in time to hear Maggie's clear voice stating their first stop would be to see Teddie. He'd waited out of sight until Evelyn explained.

When he entered, Dallas was saying they'd start with Eugene Tagner.

Maggie immediately said, "We should talk to Teddie Barrett's family."

Dallas tsked. "Four years after the fact? Talking to next of kin right after a murder is good sense. Four years after an accident—tragic as it might be—is not. Eugene first."

J.D. had seen Maggie want to argue, recognizing she was being manipulated. Then he'd seen her wonder why she was being manipulated. He'd seen the moment she'd decided watching Dallas question Eugene might answer that.

She'd been even more eager than Dallas to get here, judging by her driving, which had Dallas clutching the dashboard dramatically. She'd paid no attention.

J.D. had felt no concern. She drove fast, but she drove well. She was a most competent woman.

He'd recognized that when she tried to convict him of murder.

He'd confirmed it in more detached circumstances on three occasions when he'd watched her prosecute other defendants.

He'd stayed tucked into the back of those courtrooms, but he needn't have bothered. Completely focused, she'd gotten three guilty verdicts.

Yes, Maggie Frye was most certainly competent.

Eugene arrived. A combination of a swayed back and an officious walk sent his rounded belly before him like a herald.

"Dallas, how kind of you to support me during this tragedy. Tragedy." His loud, high voice bounced off the walls and surrounded them.

Dallas introduced "my colleague from Northern Virginia, Maggie Frye." Tagner said hello, his gaze cataloguing her charms.

But J.D. suspected intelligent eyes, eloquent mouth, and stubborn chin weren't charms that would appeal to Eugene, even when they were accompanied by that body.

Subtle charms didn't suit Eugene.

He liked blonde and buxom of the sort nature never created. Plus, he liked twenty-two. He'd married his first twenty-two-year-old when he was twenty-four, his second at twenty-nine, his third at forty-three and his fourth at forty-six, three years ago.

Eugene nodded dolefully as they each expressed their condolences.

"I don't know what to do with myself," he said. "My heart's ripped right out, right out. This is such a tragedy. We were happy as two peas in a pod, peas in a pod."

"Mr. Tagner, your wife had left you, you couldn't have been too happy," Maggie said.

Eugene's mouth flopped open. Dallas glared at her.

"Now, Eugene," Dallas soothed, "why don't you just tell us what you know."

"Know? Nothing! That new sheriff won't tell me a thing. All I know is my darling wife's been most cruelly taken from me. I know what some are saying," he added. "But no one from outside can know what passes between a man and his wife, between a man and his wife."

"So true," Dallas murmured. "But tell us, you and Laurel had a bit of trouble, isn't that right?"

"No more than any couple."

"Enough trouble for her to move back to her father's house," Maggie said.

Eugene breathed out noisily through his nose. "The judge missed her." He turned to Dallas again. "You know how crazy he's always been for Laurel. But we were going to break it to him Sunday that her visit to Rambler Farm was over and she was coming home to me."

Two peas back in the pod.

"In fact, I was the first to get worried when she wasn't there at Rambler Farm. I knew how excited she was to let everyone know she was coming home. I was the one to raise the alarm, to say something was wrong."

Dallas nodded. "Now, Saturday—?"

"I was here. All day, and all night. Had friends here for poker. You know the kind of thing. You can ask Louelle."

"You didn't have plans to see Laurel, spend time together Saturday night?"

"No need, what with her coming home soon. Besides, that way it would be a surprise for everyone Sunday. A happy surprise."

He shielded his eyes, as if to hide tears.

"The sheriff will need the names of your poker guests, Mr. Tagner," Maggie said.

"Gave him the list yesterday." He dropped his hand. His eyes were dry.

J.D. recalled a line he'd heard. Eugene was shaken, not stirred by his wife's murder.

"It must be a pure consolation to you, Eugene, to know sweet Laurel was comin' home. And don't you be chewin' on the fact that if you'd raised her allowance early on instead of tellin' her she was gettin' all she'd get, you could have had more time with her." Dallas gave a convincing a-thought-just-occurred-to-me start. "Perhaps she wouldn't have been killed at all. But don't you be thinkin' about that. No, you console yourself knowin' you saw the light at the end."

"That's right, that's right." Eugene licked his lips. "I did see it her way. And that's what I told her. Came right out like a man should, and said I'd been wrong. A woman—a young, beautiful woman like Laurel—wants pretty things. I wouldn't have loved her as much as I did if she hadn't been the kind to love beautiful things, now would I?"

Dallas nodded. "Makes sense. There's one thing kind of confusin' to me. I was down to a bar association meetin' in Lynchburg while back. Picked up Henry Zales at his office, saw his last client headin' out as I pulled in. I'd take my oath it was Laurel in that blue vehicle of hers."

J.D., walking to the wide window on the side wall, glanced at Maggie. Not even knowing the significance yet, he could see her mind working to figure out how fast she could have someone check out Zales.

Taking too long formulating his answer, Eugene said, "What if she did talk to Zales? Doesn't mean anything. Just checking what was what, background. I knew. She told me."

"Background on what? Because Henry practices divorce law."

Eugene swallowed "What if he does? We were working out our differences and she was coming home, like I said. If that's all—"

"You've been seeing Renee." J.D. didn't turn around.

"That's not—"

God, the idiot was going to lie about something two dozen people could testify to?

"You've been seeing Renee," he repeated.

"I, uh... A man doesn't stop having feelings for a woman he's been married to, even if the marriage didn't work out."

"Those differences cited in your divorce from Renee weren't irreconcilable after all?" Dallas asked, dangerously mild.

"Marriage connects you to another person in a way that doesn't go away. Doesn't go away."

In the reflection of the room J.D. caught movement. Dallas. His wife had been gone a long time, but it hadn't seemed to change his feelings. Was that why he and Evelyn didn't act on the relationship most of the county knew about?

"Was anything bothering Laurel the past few weeks, Eugene?" J.D. asked, watching his reflection. "Besides the two of you being apart."

Eugene squinted toward him. "You mean those phone calls? I couldn't say they bothered her exactly. Just irksome. The phone ringing and no one there. All hours. Why she was halfway to thinking I was making those calls, accused me of checking up on her, but then one came on her number she'd hardly give anybody. Liked to keep it free for emergencies, she always said. And I was sitting right there in front of her. So, she knew it wasn't me."

"What did caller ID say?" J.D. asked.

"She said the number didn't show. I told her she should block numbers not identifying themselves, but she said you never knew when there was a call you wanted to take from one of those numbers."

Another reflected movement.

J.D. shifted for a better angle.

Maggie Frye was a million miles away, thinking something none too pleasant. Something that made her mad at herself, the way she'd been when she tapped the guesthouse fence.

Eugene looked from J.D. to Maggie and back, then to Maggie again. The repeated motion appeared to snap her out of her reverie.

For an instant she met J.D.'s gaze.

She immediately shifted her focus. "Mr. Tagner, who were Laurel's friends?"

"Friends?"

"Who did she do things with? Social things."

"Most often we went out for my business. Dinners, dances, and such. And Rambler Farm, whenever the judge had something, of course."

"I mean her close friends, personal friends, girlfriends. Someone she'd confide in. Someone she'd go to lunch with, go shopping with."

Eugene shook his head. "Laurel never went shopping with anybody. Said she didn't want the clerk's attention divided."

"She must have had friends."

"We neither of us needed anybody else."

"You met her at J.D.'s trial, didn't you?" Dallas asked.

"Well, I'd known her a long time—barbecues and lunches and such at Rambler Farm. I didn't know she had an eye for me, too, though. Wasn't until we talked there at the trial—" He tipped his head toward J.D., as if acknowledging a service. "—that we first saw what we had, knew we were meant to be together."

"Did Laurel talk about Pan Wade's murder?" Maggie asked.

Eugene blinked. "Why would she?"

"She must have had thoughts about it, about the case." When Eugene didn't respond quickly, she added impatiently. "She was at the trial every day."

"She thought it was a terrible tragedy, like all of us." His toneless delivery removed meaning from the words. "And Pan was unlucky enough to be in the wrong place at the wrong time when some drifter passed through. Damned shame. Damned shame."

Maggie stared at the man. "Surely, Mr. Tagner, you haven't missed the similarities between Pan Wade's murder and that of your wife."

"But..." Eugene's jaw sagged. "There can't be. I mean. That would mean ... that would mean they'll never know who killed Laurel? Just like they never found who killed Pan."

J.D. read Maggie's expression easily—she believed she knew exactly who had killed Pan and Laurel.

CHAPTER FIFTEEN

"WERE YOU EVER going to get around to asking about Pan Wade's murder?" Maggie demanded of Dallas once back in her car.

"My dear, my dear, this is not Washington, D.C., or its environs. Here in Bedhurst, rushin' to a point will just get you stuck. There's a certain rhythm, an accepted way of doin' things."

Her *huh* scoffed. "You showed no sign of looking for a connection between the two cases as Sheriff Gardner asked. As if you were strictly investigating the current case."

"How else could we hope to give the sheriff our expert opinion on whether the two cases are related? By definition, we must gather information on this case in order to hold it up against what we know of the past case."

Information. Like Teddie Barrett dying four years ago in a hit and run? Why hadn't she known?

Because other than tracking Carson's steps through official records, she'd cut her ties to the Pan Wade case. She hadn't interviewed the jury, talked with the family, or kept in touch with Ed Smith. She'd gotten the hell out of Bedhurst, like a frightened child pretending it never happened.

And now another woman was dead.

She forced her thoughts to the present and got out the words expected of her. "Questions should be on specifics that directly correspond with Pan Wade's murder."

"Not at all. That would limit our enquiry to a disastrous degree. We don't know what we don't know until we know it."

A muffled sound from the back seat brought Maggie's gaze to the rearview mirror. Carson's expression was unreadable. Beside the scar near his mouth a dent dug in.

He'd gotten information out of Tagner, particularly that Laurel had been receiving strange calls. Or calls she'd said were strange.

I told her she should block any numbers not identifying themselves, but she said you never knew when there was a call you wanted to take.

A memory had strobed through Maggie's head. Sitting across from Roy at the Thai restaurant, the tang of peanut dressing on a salad she ate only to have the dressing. The discreet burr of his phone. He checked the screen, hit a button, disconnecting it.

"Need to call back?" Being on-call all hours came with the job, his and hers.

"Blocked. Probably a wrong number."

Suspicion flared. She snuffed it. Instead, she said to Roy almost exactly what Tagner said to Laurel. Roy gave nearly the same response.

A month later, feelings had nothing to do with it. Evidence proved Roy was seeing—and screwing—Officer Hundley.

Had Laurel's calls been a signaling system with a lover? A lover as yet unknown?

Maggie looked in the rearview mirror again, trying to view Carson as other women might.

His longer hair made him less austere without softening the angles of features a sculptor could have roughed in. If the sculptor had gone back to refine and smooth, Carson could have been handsome. As it was, his rawness might appeal to some women, while scaring others.

Laurel had not seemed the type to be scared.

If Laurel truly didn't confide in anyone, no one could confirm—or deny—a possible relationship with Carson.

No one could confirm or deny Tagner's version of the calls, either. Or of their relationship.

"How'd you know about the calls, Carson?" she asked abruptly.

"I didn't. Not until he told us. Just fishing."

She grunted. "What were you trying to discover with the comments about him seeing his first wife?"

"Second wife, not first. Wondered what he and Renee were talking about."

"Maybe he was asking advice about Laurel."

Dallas chortled. "Maggie, Maggie. You've been workin' far too hard if that's all you know about men and women."

Carson added, "Renee might have been telling Eugene any number of things. How to patch up his marriage with Laurel sure as hell wasn't among them."

"You don't believe everything was fine in the marriage?"

"No."

She asked Dallas, "You?"

"No," he agreed with uncharacteristic brevity.

"Stupid to lie about it," Carson murmured.

"He can't help it," Dallas said. "Money's made things comfortable for him. He doesn't know how to cope with anything not comfortable, so he pretends it doesn't exist."

"Three former wives, he must have had some unpleasantness," Maggie said dryly.

"Ah, that's what lawyers are for, to handle such unpleasantness."

"You represented Tagner in his divorces?"

"I did not," Monroe said with such affront that Maggie's lips twitched.

"How'd you know the divorce from Renee was irreconcilable differences, then?"

"Everyone in Bedhurst knows."

Carson said, "It would be interesting to talk to the lawyer who's handled Eugene's divorces. Especially about a pre-nup or other agreement with Laurel."

He was right. That was a smart place to look, especially if you wanted to steer the investigation away from another path.

"Where does Teddie Barrett's family live?"

Dallas trumped her plan. "Not now. They're expectin' us at Rambler Farm. Make a right-hand turn at the highway."

―――――――――

Commonwealth v. J.D. Carson

Witness Theodore Barrett (prosecution)
Direct Examination by ACA Frye.

Q. Mr. Barrett, where were you at approximately 6 p.m. on August 12th?

A. (Inaudible.)

Q. Mr. Barrett?

A. (Inaudible)

THE COURT: Teddie, quit laughing now, and answer Ms. Frye's questions.

A. She called me Mr. Barrett.

THE COURT: That's how we do things here. No more laughing now.

A. Yes, sir.

Q. Where were you at approximately 6 p.m. on August 12th.

A. That's the day Pan was killed, huh? Well, then I was at the park.

Q. That's Bedhurst Falls Park?

A. Uh-huh.

THE COURT: You need to say yes or no, Teddie.

A. Okay.

THE COURT: Ms. Frye?

Q. Teddie, were you at Bedhurst Falls Park on August 12?

A. Yes.

Q. Now, what did you hear there that day?

A. I heard birds and lots of squirrels and the waterfall, and the breeze in the trees and—

Q. Did a time come when you heard voices? People's voices?

A. Oh, yeah, that. I heard voices.

Q. How were the voices, Mr.—Were they happy? Soft? Sad? Loud?

A. His was loud, real loud.

Q. What were they saying?

A. Couldn't hear the words precisely, just the shouting.

Q. What did you do after hearing these loud voices shouting?

A. I got on my bike and rode home. Didn't want to hear no more shouting.

Q. I don't blame you for wanting to get away from such a scene. One more question: Could you tell whose voices these were?

A. Pan's and J.D.'s.

Q. That's Mrs. Wade—Pandora Addington Wade—and Mr. J.D. Carson, the defendant?

A. (laugh) Sure.

Q. Thank you. The Commonwealth has no further questions for this witness at this time. Your Honor, a break for lunch now…

THE COURT: Too early, Ms. Frye, too early. We'd best get on with it while we can. Mr. Monroe?

Mr. Monroe: The defense is ready, Your Honor.

THE COURT: Very well, then.

CHAPTER SIXTEEN

EVERYTHING ABOUT RAMBLER Farm was welcoming—the graceful tree-lined drive, the crisp white paint, the wide porch with pots of bright yellow pansies flanking forest green steps.

Everything was welcoming except the woman who opened the gleaming black front door.

Charlotte Blankenship.

Charlotte Blankenship Smith, Maggie corrected herself, remembering the sheriff's news that Ed Smith had married the judge's older daughter.

Charlotte stared at the trio on the threshold with the blank expression of someone whose mind was a million miles away and wanted to keep it that way.

Expected at Rambler Farm, her ass. Dallas Monroe would lie about what color the sky was.

Charlotte's green boiled wool jacket matched the porch steps but added an unpleasant cast to her complexion. The cropped jacket focused attention on where a black watch plaid skirt bunched around a thick waist. Maggie was no clotheshorse, but she suspected a super-model would look dumpy in that outfit.

"Oh, Charlotte, my dear..." Dallas took the woman's stiff shoulders between his hands, and kissed her cheek, while her arms remained at her sides, a tablet in one hand. At the same time Dallas pivoted her, gaining entry to the house. "Words cannot express how deeply we feel for you in this tragedy."

To the accompaniment of continued murmurs of condolence,

Dallas maneuvered himself and Charlotte deeper into the hallway.

Smooth, Maggie thought.

Carson gave a nod, signaling her to go ahead of him. The motion cast a shadow on his lower face that might have been mistaken for a smile.

"Charlotte, my dear, you remember Maggie, don't you? Maggie Frye, she appeared before the judge a while back. And you know J.D., of course."

"I'm sorry for your loss," she said simply.

"Real sorry about Laurel, Charlotte," Carson said.

Charlotte's gaze flicked to him, then Maggie. "I remember you."

The tone was impossible to read. Maggie got to the point, "We're here to talk to Judge Blankenship."

Charlotte's gaze went to a door down the hall. "The judge can't see anyone."

"We need to—"

Dallas spoke over Maggie. "We understand, Charlotte. Perhaps later this afternoon he'll be ready to receive us."

"Yes, that should give me time."

That comment made no sense.

Not happy, Maggie said, "In the meantime, we have questions for you, Charlotte."

"I spoke with the sheriff already, and I have a great deal to do."

"I'm sure you do," Dallas said. "You are the judge's rock."

"Yes. I am."

Maggie clamped down on the desire to tell him to shut up, and focused on Charlotte. "Surely you have time for questions concerning your sister's murder."

Without another word, Charlotte pivoted and strode deeper into the house.

Maggie followed, not caring if her passengers did or not. They couldn't leave. She had the car keys.

A door on the right opened as Maggie passed.

Judge Blankenship emerged from gloom—she got an impression of dark bookshelves, dark leather, dark wood.

"Charlotte?" he blinked as he stepped into the hallway.

"I'll take care of it, Judge. No need to trouble yourself."

"I thought I heard…"

"Judge." Dallas stepped forward, gripping the taller man's arm. "We can't begin to tell you how our hearts are breakin' for you."

Another blink, then a gradual straightening, like a deflated balloon granted a puff of air. "Oh. Yes."

"Judge—" his daughter started.

"I'll see them." It held a trace of the authority Maggie remembered from Courtroom One. "Nice of you to come, Dallas, J.D."

Carson stepped forward, murmuring something Maggie didn't hear. The judge shook Carson's offered hand and placed his other hand on Carson's shoulder.

Carson showed every sign of respecting the man who had presided over his trial for murder, that feeling appeared mutual, and no one but her seemed surprised.

"Very well." Charlotte maneuvered around her father and closed the door behind him. "Come this way."

She led them to a sitting room looking over the side lawn. Dallas, Charlotte, and the judge sat on the sofa, Maggie and Carson took chairs at opposite ends of the coffee table.

"And perhaps you remember Ms. Frye, Maggie Frye," Dallas said to Blankenship, his tone gentle. "She appeared before you several years ago."

"Ms. Frye, yes. Pan Wade."

"I'm sorry for your family's loss. In fact, we hoped to ask you—"

"I saw Laurel just Thursday at the Café," Dallas cut in. "As bright and beautiful as ever. Did she show any change Friday or Saturday? If anything happened, or you saw a change…?"

"Not at all. She was, as you say, her bright and beautiful self. That morning, before she went out for the day, she hugged me and said how much she loved me."

Parallel tracks formed between Charlotte's eyebrows.

They didn't disappear as Dallas proceeded to ask gentle questions for ten solid minutes.

Perhaps to allow a grieving friend an opportunity to talk about his daughter. But to Maggie they added up to a subtle investigation of Laurel's murder.

The judge didn't give them a single piece of new information.

Dallas pulled in a breath, and Maggie slid in.

"Judge Blankenship, were you aware of any connection between the case that brought me here before—Pan Wade's murder—and your daughter, Laurel."

He stared off into the distance. Beside him, Dallas gave her a heavy-lidded smile. Could have been genuine, but she doubted it.

Just as Maggie was about to repeat her question, the judge said softly, "No... No, I wouldn't think so. She was at the trial, of course, as everyone was."

"Did she and Carson have a relationship?"

"J.D.?" The grieving father turned to him, as if trying to get his thoughts straight. Then he said, "Knew each other, of course. Nothing more."

"Did she talk about his trial?" Maggie pursued.

"At the time, certainly there was discussion—nothing untoward, you understand. My family knows not to discuss a case. But I'm certain Laurel commented about who was in the audience and such. She is—was—a social person."

"Anything more recent about the trial or Pan Wade's murder?" He started to shake his head. Maggie broadened the question. "Anything about Pan at all?"

The head-shake continued.

"I know of no connection. Pan was Charlotte's friend, not Laurel's. Laurel's several years younger and had her own set. But Charlotte and Pan were always close."

If she hadn't been watching the judge, sitting next to Carson, Maggie would have missed the flicker across Carson's eyes. He didn't share that assessment of Pan and Charlotte's relationship.

"Charlotte?" Maggie prompted. "Do you know of any connection between Pan's death and your sister? Anything at all."

"No."

Maggie wasn't ready to be cut off with that bland negative. "But there was at least one, Charlotte. You went to Carson's trial for the murder of Pan Addington Wade." No one even blinked at the mention of Carson being tried for murder. It wasn't so much that they ignored the gorilla in the room as none of them seemed to recognize it *was* a gorilla. "Every day, wasn't it?"

"Yes."

"Why?"

"Why?"

"Why did you go every day? Because your friend had been murdered, because you wanted justice for her?"

Charlotte regarded Maggie as if she weren't very bright. "Everyone went."

"It's where Charlotte met Ed—Ed Smith—her husband," Judge Blankenship inserted.

A pleased expression replaced Charlotte's frown. "That's right, Judge."

"Yes, I heard. Congratulations, Charlotte," Maggie said. "Ed's a great guy."

The other woman's pleasure smoothed out to nothing. "He has a fine legal mind."

"Yes, of course." Maggie hadn't seen signs of legal excellence from Ed. On the other hand, that wasn't normally why people got married.

"Judge, if you don't mind, I have a question," Carson said. The older man nodded permission. "Had Laurel been receiving odd phone calls?"

"Odd?"

"Calls that might have made her uneasy or didn't make sense to her."

The judge shook his head, then stopped to look at his older daughter.

She said, "She frequently got calls she didn't want us to know about."

Charlotte clearly put Laurel on the outside of the *us* she created with a tip of her head toward her father. Maggie wondered how Ed fit with that *us?*

Charlotte rose.

"It's time you rest, Judge."

✧ ✧ ✧ ✧

MAGGIE DIDN'T FAULT Carson for asking about the calls, she decided as they followed Charlotte to the front door.

On the surface, trying to confirm Tagner's account was good sense.

But was there more? Had Carson truly made a lucky strike asking Tagner about the calls or did he know more than he was saying?

If he made the calls, it wouldn't make sense to bring attention to them. But if someone else did, focusing on the calls would be a fine diversion.

As for the judge saying there'd been nothing between Laurel and J.D., that wasn't definitive. Lovers were known to keep their relationships secret for all sorts of reasons.

They had descended the porch stairs when a voice stopped them.

"Maggie? Maggie Frye? It *is* you!" Ed Smith came across the drive with his hand outstretched and a smile lighting his plain face. "I was at Second House and I *thought* it was you. It's good to see you."

Maggie met his hand. He clasped it in both of his.

"Hi, Ed. Good to see you, too. I'm sorry it's under these circumstances."

"It is tragic, just tragic. Such a vibrant personality. The judge is devastated."

"And your wife?"

Ed responded as if it she'd made a statement, rather than asked a question. "You're right. It's the worst thing imaginable. But, Maggie, to see you again—how long are you here for?" He still had her hand.

"That's not clear."

"She's assistin' the sheriff with his inquiries, along with J.D. and me," Dallas said from the passenger side of the car.

"I see." Though it was clear Ed didn't. "We'll have to get together,

Maggie."

"I'd like that."

Carson stepped forward, his hand out to Ed. "Sorry for your loss."

Ed finally released her hand to shake Carson's. As he did, he looked beyond Carson to the house. Following his gaze, Maggie saw Charlotte standing at the door, watching.

Good-byes quickly followed. Ed went to the house as they got in her car.

Driving away from Rambler Farm, Maggie glanced back.

Charlotte and Ed stood together. Ed appeared to be talking earnestly.

OTHER THAN KEEPING an eye on Carson, the next two hours were a waste.

Dallas Monroe had to have known all they'd gather at the hardware store, grocery store, and a private home where twelve women had a bridge group were impressions, character assessments, and outright gossip.

Not a single fact. Not about Laurel Blankenship Tagner, not about Pan Addington Wade, not about a connection between their murders.

By the time Dallas directed her to park near a café for lunch, she'd had her fill of chit-chat. She finished her salad well before the men were done and took herself and her phone across the street to the small park beside the courthouse, where she could call the office in privacy.

Nancy wasn't there. Maggie left a message asking for info on Henry Zales of Lynchburg—Why did that name seem familiar?—and when she could expect the files.

She retrieved messages, noting two items concerning upcoming cases, erasing whatever Roy said, and, finally, hearing Nancy's voice.

First, Nancy said the files were on their way. Then she reminded Maggie that today was early release for the schools, which meant she'd left.

As a preliminary report on Chester Bondelle of Roanoke, Nancy listed where he'd received his degrees, said he was a member of the bar in good standing, and had a solid record as a defense attorney. She'd keep digging.

Carson exited the café, holding the door as Dallas faced back inside, continuing a conversation.

Maggie angled across the corner of the square, heading for her car parked on the other side of the café.

"Ah, Maggie," Dallas called. "You missed an interestin' conversation."

"More gossip," she muttered.

"Buildin' a portrait of the victim." Dallas had good hearing. "You know how important it is to understand the victim in order to understand the crime."

The portrait of Laurel was of a self-centered, materialistic, spoiled young woman who left her husband because he hadn't paid—as in dollar signs—enough attention to her.

How did that connect Laurel's murder to Pan Wade's murder?

From what Maggie could tell, what they had in common was each had left her husband and there was talk she was—possibly—going back to him.

The source for the about-to-return was Tagner for Laurel and Carson for Pan. Could either or both be lying to minimize his apparent motive? Oh, yes.

As Maggie unlocked the car her phone rang.

Recognizing the number, she slid the phone in her purse unanswered. Voice mail would pick up if her cousin Jamie chose to leave a message.

Dallas didn't appear to notice. Carson studied her as she got in the driver's seat.

CHAPTER SEVENTEEN

2:02 p.m.

J.D. WATCHED MAGGIE Frye try to make sense of what she was seeing.

Him, sitting in the Addingtons' comfortable family room, welcomed by Pan's parents, as he'd been by the judge. Maggie hadn't gotten that either.

She and Dallas asked the Addingtons about parallels between Pan's murder and Laurel's.

They said they knew of none, though he knew the couple wished they did—in hopes solving the current murder might also solve Pan's.

He was about to ask if they remembered Pan getting calls like Eugene said Laurel had received, when Maggie shot him a sharp look, as if to draw attention to what she would say.

"I never had the opportunity after the trial to say how sorry I was for letting you down, Mr. and Mrs. Addington, by failing to get the conviction in your daughter's murder."

Kevin Addington cleared his throat uncomfortably, but Theresa smiled. A bruised, sad smile that reminded J.D. of Pan when he'd arrived on leave.

"You didn't let us down, Ms. Frye—Maggie. We never believed J.D. killed Pan. Not for a moment. The trial only confirmed that."

"A jury's not-guilty verdict doesn't mean—"

Theresa moved her head in a slow-motion shake. "Not because of the verdict. Because of what we felt when the verdict came in and because of what we saw in J.D."

"I understand you wouldn't want to believe someone you helped could—"

"No, no, you don't understand. Yes, we felt great relief for J.D., but we also felt relief the distraction was over—the detour away from finding who really killed our girl. After the trial we hoped the investigation would truly lead somewhere. That's what J.D. said first thing. *Now we'll get him, Mrs. A. Now we'll get him.*"

He would stake his freedom that Maggie wanted to say they'd let Pan's murderer go with the not-guilty verdict. But he saw she wouldn't say it to this grieving mother.

Maggie Frye had a weakness.

Theresa Addington reached across the loveseat's arm to put her hand on his forearm. "And we will, J.D. Someday, we will. As awful as poor Laurel's death is, perhaps this will rekindle—"

"What the hell are you doing here?"

J.D. didn't need to turn to identify who'd made the demand and who'd been addressed.

Maggie's eyes widened slightly at Rick Wade's abrupt arrival, narrowed as they shifted to him and found him watching her.

Theresa's hand on J.D.'s arm tightened, as if to hold him down, but he wasn't going anywhere.

The Addingtons were too kind-hearted to shut Wade out of their lives, though J.D. knew they'd asked him not to walk in uninvited. Ignoring that was damned rude.

"I asked you what the hell you're doing here, Carson."

Wade came down one of the two steps connecting the family room with the kitchen.

Kevin stood in his one-time son-in-law's path. "Rick. We didn't know you were coming by."

Mild, yet still a reproof.

"I wanted to see how you're doing. With all this about Laurel bringing up Pan and—"

"We appreciate your caring. We're fine. It's the judge needs all our concern right now."

"Of course, but—"

"We want to talk to you, too, Rick. About—"

Wade interrupted Maggie. "Sheriff knows what he needs to know from me." He focused on the Addingtons. "There's things I'd like to talk to you about. Better things than you could hope to hear from that—"

Kevin interrupted firmly, "We've got company right now."

J.D. started to rise, Theresa clamped down on him again, and Dallas entered the fray by saying, "We were just leavin'," and positioning his hands on the arms of the overstuffed chair to hoist himself up.

"There are questions to—" Maggie started.

Dallas spoke over her. "Don't want to overstay our welcome."

"I *am* a little tired," Pan's mother said, releasing her hold on J.D.'s arm.

He stood.

With her passengers on their feet, Maggie expelled a sharp breath. "If you don't mind, Mrs. Addington, I'd like to come back…"

"Of course, my dear," Theresa said. "Any time. I'm sorry I'm not up to a longer visit now."

"You get some rest." Dallas patted her hand, then led the way out.

Amid good-byes, Maggie followed, with J.D. last. He paused beside Wade only long enough to make eye contact.

✧ ✧ ✧ ✧

"**Next, we'll call** on Renee Tagner," Dallas said.

"No."

Instead of taking offense at her, he chuckled. "You have other plans, do you, Maggie? We're captives to your whim?"

"I went along with your agenda to this point. Now I decide where we go. I've been patient enough."

She tapped at her phone for directions.

"You can never be too patient," Dallas murmured. But he settled back without further argument.

✧ ✧ ✧ ✧

GPS DIRECTED MAGGIE between two big-box stores at the edge of town, then go two blocks to where the street dead-ended in a half-weed, half-gravel parking area in front of a two-story, gray frame building that might once have been a motel.

Maggie got out of the car, leaving the other two to follow or stay where they were, while she contemplated ten rust-colored doors.

The address had simply been 743 Locust. Nothing about an apartment—or motel room—number.

She would start knocking on doors. At least she could eliminate the top five doors, since there was no staircase in sight. God, she hoped—

"Second door from the left." Carson walked past her.

Maggie caught up as he knocked. Dallas approached more slowly.

The next door to the left opened and a woman's square face appeared, anxious and confused.

"Mrs. Barrett? I'm Maggie Frye. I was the prosecutor in the case Teddie testified in four and a half years ago. I'd like to talk to you." Maggie took two steps toward her. "If we could come in for—"

"Oh! No. You stay right there. Right there."

She disappeared, the door closed. Maggie started toward it.

Carson didn't touch her, didn't look at her, but he blocked her way. "That's her bedroom. Give her privacy."

Maggie sidestepped him without moving any closer to the closed door. He not only knew the address, he knew the set-up.

Mrs. Barrett re-emerged, bustling past them on the concrete walk-way, talking fast and with a strong mountain twang.

Maggie caught the gist about of course her remembering the lady lawyer, how kind she'd been to her poor Teddie, how much he'd liked her, how excited he'd been, and at least he'd had that before he died.

The woman opened the other door and hurried in ahead of them, clearing a sagging couch and uneven coffee table by sweeping up magazines and the cardboard leftovers from fast-food meals. Through a half-open door, Maggie saw a decrepit microwave sitting on the closed toilet seat. A bucket with a few chunks of ice floating atop water stood in the bathtub and held a disintegrating carton of milk.

"I'm not rightly set for visitors. But set down, do set down, y'all."

They sat on the couch. Maggie, Dallas—sunk deep into the couch's sag—then Carson.

Mrs. Barrett removed what appeared to be a flowered sheet to reveal a chair in even worse shape. Why it warranted the protection of the sheet—?

Ah, the sheet hadn't been protection for the chair, but for a blue dress with spaghetti straps and delicate beading.

Mrs. Barrett wrapped the sheet carefully around the dress and laid both atop the aging, blocky TV.

"I do a bit of work for ladies 'round about," she said, by way of explanation, before perching her lumpy body on the edge of the chair.

Maggie started by expressing her condolences over Teddie's death, then, "If you don't mind telling me more about his ... accident?"

"If only I'd'a had one of my turns that day, I'd'a told him to stay here with his mama. But I hated to. He loved going out on that bicycle—" She pronounced it bi-SIGH-cull. "—of his. Kept it clean as could be, he was that proud of it."

Slow tears trickled down the woman's cheeks, catching in horizontal creases.

"Did he say anything before he left, Mrs. Barrett? Where he was going? If he was meeting someone?"

"No, ma'am. Nothing about meeting somebody and he near always went the same place—up to the park, to the falls. He called out *I love you, Mama* like always and went off laughin' like he did. Next thing I know, that deputy what passed on not long after was at my door, saying I should set down, he had somethin' to tell me." She stared at her slipper-clad feet. "Thought I'd never stop settin', just set there 'til I joined Teddie."

Maggie reached across and put her hand on the woman's arm. "He was a sweet boy, Mrs. Barrett."

The woman blinked, then smiled, revealing a much younger face. "He was. My Teddie was that, ma'am."

"Did the sheriff's department ever tell you anything—?"

Teddie's mother was shaking her head.

"Never heard anything beyond when that deputy said there'd been an accident, and the person what hit Teddie's bike kept going. If it hadn'ta been for someone fishin' seein' the bike come down the river, my poor boy mighta been there a long time and only his mama wonderin' where he was." She straightened her shoulders and folded her hands over her stomach. "He never hurt a soul, least of all his mama. Only thing he ever … Well, I can't say I liked his drinkin'. The drink did in my papa and more besides. But Teddie enjoyed those boys, and that's where they were most times—Shenny's. He didn't like to refuse when they offered him a drink or two—said they were right generous."

"What boys, Mrs. Barrett?"

"I don't rightly know. Teddie would talk about the other boys, this one sayin' that funny thing and that one makin' this joke, but the names came fast and it was somebody's brother or uncle or cousin. Not one in particular, but all mixed together. I didn't pay much mind."

"Can you recall any names?"

She started shaking her head and kept it up as Maggie added, "Especially around the time of Pan Wade's death? Or the trial?"

Mrs. Barrett's head stopped shaking. "Oh. Now, wait. There was something. Before that lawyer that married Miss Charlotte came and talked to him about going to the courthouse and all—he was that proud of that. Let me think. I know he was talking' about Pan Wade, but acourse it couldn'ta been her. But her husband, I think—yes, I think that was one he mentioned. And you, Mr. Dallas. Somethin' about you. And … Mr. Tagner?" Her voice lifted in question.

She was guessing at the end. Maybe she'd been right about Rick Wade. Maybe not.

"And then there was the night you brought him home, J.D. So grateful I was, because he surely shouldn'ta been in that state."

Maggie flicked a look toward him, but there was nothing to read in his expression. She focused again on Teddie's mother.

Her brow furrowed. "But that had to be after the trial, or you'da been in the jail. Oh, yes, acourse it was. Because it was early spring, but hot as scalded milk it was, and I was hemmin' up Miss Charlotte's good spring coat, sweatin' like all get out. I gave you an iced tea and—Oh. Oh."

"What is it, Mrs. Barrett?"

"Why, if I was hemmin' up Miss Charlotte's good spring coat, then it had to be right before Teddie's accident. Because I took that coat all finished up to Rambler Farm the next week, and I remember the judge being nice as could be, sayin' how sorry he was, putting' his arm 'round my shoulders. Tears in his eyes. And insisted on givin' me something extra over what Miss Charlotte paid. And now here's that poor man lost his girl, and me lost my boy."

CHAPTER EIGHTEEN

MAGGIE TWISTED IN the driver's seat toward Carson.

He continued facing the side window as he said one word, "Ask."

"You gave him alcohol?"

"No."

"His mother said—"

"She said I drove him home when he was drunk."

"How did he get drunk?"

"I don't know."

"He must have said something during the drive—"

"No."

"Surely, he—"

"No. Any more questions?"

"Not at this time."

"And I can assure you," Dallas said with full-blown sincerity, "I never sat in Shenny's bar plyin' that poor boy with alcohol. He must have confused it with talkin' to me before the trial."

———————

Commonwealth v. J.D. Carson

Witness Theodore Barrett (prosecution)
Cross-Examination by Mr. Monroe

Q. Well, now, Teddie, how're you doing today?

A. Just fine, Dallas.

Q. Good, good. You enjoying sitting up here next to Judge Blankenship?

Ms. Frye: Objection. Relevance.

Mr. Monroe: Just passing the time of day with Teddie, here, Your Honor.

THE COURT: Sustained. This isn't the Café.

Mr. Monroe: Yes, Judge.

Q. Now, Teddie, let's talk some about that day you were in the park, that day you heard voices when you were on the Waterfall Path. Was that the first day you'd been to the park that week?

A. (laugh) No. I go pretty near every day.

Q. Every day? Now that's interesting. You know, things I do every day, like getting dressed sometimes I can't remember if I put on my black shoes or my brown shoes. Does—

A. Black shoes. You got black shoes on today.

Q. Why, yes, I do, thank you, Teddie. But does that ever happen to you, that you're not sure if something happened this day or that day?

A. Sometimes.

Q. Well, I'm glad to hear I'm not the only one.

Ms. Frye: Objection. This—

THE COURT: Overruled. We're going to allow some latitude with this particular witness. Just don't get carried away, Mr. Monroe.

Mr. Monroe: Thank you, Judge.

Q. So, Teddie, what with sometimes you and me forgetting what happened one day and what happened another day, how do you keep straight something like hearing those voices at the park on that particular day.

A. They helped me remember.

Q. Who helped you remember?

A. The other people, the people who told me about it.

Q. Do you mean Ms. Frye or Mr. Smith?

A. No, not them. Way before them. When it was all happening.

Q. The same day Pan Wade was found?

A. No, I wouldn't have needed no help remembering right then.

Q. That makes sense, Teddie. So, it was some time later? Along with nodding your head, you have to say the word, Teddie.

A. Yes.

Q. It was later?

A. Yes.

Q. Do you know when it was?

A. Don't know. But not right then. And not a real long time later, like when that pretty lady there—Maggie—when she talked to me. Somewhere in between.

Q. Was it before you went to Sheriff Hague and told him you'd heard voices? That was about the middle of September—yes, here it is, September 17. Is that right?

A. I guess so. I must have remembered before I told the sheriff.

Q. Very true, Teddie. Do you remember any of the specific people who helped you remember?

A. No. It was just, you know, everybody talking. Trying to help. Because of Pan being killed and all.

Q. Okay, well, tell me this, how'd they help you remember, because maybe it's something I could use when I'm not remembering?

A. I was telling about what I heard when I was hearing the waterfall, and how I ride my bike to the park most every day, and we started working through the days like, and they told me that was the same day Pan got killed. (Unintelligible.)

Q. That's okay, Teddie. Remembering that makes all of us feel like crying. Would you like to take a little break?

THE COURT: We'll break for lunch now.

✧ ✧ ✧ ✧

MAGGIE STOPPED AT the red light off the square and felt a sudden shift in atmosphere in the car, like a plane descending. But this air pressure shift had no physical cause. She checked the rearview mirror. Carson faced the side window, his profile impassive. Nothing new there.

Dallas, too, stared out. But she remembered something from the trial: He'd stared away from Teddie Barrett that way during her direct questioning of him.

Like he didn't want to alert his prey.

She quickly looked in the direction the two men were not looking. First checking cross-traffic, then vehicles coming the opposite direction. A beat up gray sedan sat first in line. Behind it was a gleaming dark-green pickup.

She squinted against late afternoon sun. The driver of the car was a kid—good God, they let twelve-year-olds behind the wheel—but the driver of the truck…

Green light. She eased forward, trying to keep the angle right to see up into the truck's cab.

Rick Wade.

The sheriff had nailed it about the animosity between Wade and Carson.

With the Addingtons caught in the middle.

Their faith in Carson was obvious, though God knew they wouldn't be the first relatives of a victim fooled by a murderer. Charm made monsters all the more monstrous.

Wade seemed deep in thought—the kind of thought that produced a scowl—and showed no sign of recognizing her car or its occupants. Neither passenger glanced his direction.

A block down, when Maggie braked for a stop sign, Carson abruptly opened his door and said, "This is good for me. Thanks."

"Wait. Where—?"

"If you'll take me to the office, Maggie," Dallas said.

"Carson!" she shouted.

He loped in the direction they'd come from, disappearing down an alley.

The car behind them tooted.

"Office is up ahead, another block," Dallas said, as if she'd stopped because she were lost. He had his professionally benign expression aimed straight ahead.

She dropped him off with no ceremony, turned right at the first opportunity and took the street parallel to Main back to the exit of the alley Carson disappeared down. Directly across was a parking lot, if that wasn't too formal a name for an empty patch accommodating cars.

If his truck had been there, he could have gone anywhere.

Damn it. She'd accepted Gardner's arrangement largely to keep an eye on Carson, and now he was in the wind.

She could call the sheriff—

And say what? Carson jumped out of her car, she didn't like it, and she wanted an all-points bulletin?

She consciously eased the clamp on her jaw and drove on.

She found an open parking spot around the corner from Monroe's office.

She did call Gardner, but it was to recap the little they'd found out.

"You could order Monroe to stay away from anyone connected to Laurel's murder," she said.

He snorted. "As long as I talk to them first, I won't mind Dallas keeping the coals hot under folks' feet. Might help. As long as you can keep hold of his reins."

Her turn to snort.

She returned two work calls—one to a colleague, the other to a defense attorney's office about scheduling.

Jamie had called again, this message saying only to give her a call. That could wait.

The final call was from another cousin—hers and Jamie's.

Ally Northcutt, too, said to give her a call, though the phrase "as soon as you have time" added more urgency. As did Ally's circumstances.

Ally was married to a police officer who had been shot in the head three years ago as he left their home one ordinary weekday morning and had been in a coma ever since.

Maggie listened to the message again.

Surely, Ally would say if something had changed with Chad. There'd be more in her voice. Or—

"Oh, for God's sake, call her," she said aloud as she pounded speed dial.

"Hello?" The person who answered was not Ally.

"Who is this?" Maggie demanded.

"Oh, Maggie, it's you. Ally, it's your cousin."

Ally came on, as cool and unflappable as ever. "Maggie?"

"Your mother-in-law is now answering your phone? Has she planted listening devices in the house, too?"

"Yes, I know it's complicated—"

And there's the fact you're all from complicated families. … Google's a wonderful thing.

"—but it's good to hear from you," Ally finished.

In other words, Iris Northcutt was listening in. She'd never been a hands-off mother-in-law, but since Chad's shooting, she'd become an incessant presence while Ally spent all day, every day beside her husband's bed.

"Ally, you have got to tell that woman—"

"Of course, I'll be sure to tell everyone you send your best wishes. But the reason I called is Foundation business."

A door closed on the other end of the phone connection. Ally had probably gone into the bathroom.

"Can you talk openly now?" Maggie asked.

"No. But you can."

"Is everything okay?"

"No change. I called because Jamie said—"

"I told her I'd think about the damned fund-raiser. Give me a break. She doesn't harass you about going—Oh, God. I'm sorry, Ally. Of course, she doesn't. I just wish she'd let up on me."

"I know you do. As a matter of fact, she didn't even mention the fund-raiser to me, much less ask me to call you about it. I just used that in Iris' hearing."

"Oh. Good. Because I'm out of town on a case."

"Yes, I know. Jamie worries—"

Maggie's momentary chastisement fled. "*Now* what is she carrying on about?"

"She's concerned about you being in Bedhurst County again."

"That's ridiculous."

"You were upset after that case—"

"I failed to get a conviction on my first murder trial as lead. Of course I was upset."

"Was that the only reason? I did wonder if it brought up feeli—"

"No."

Silence hung between them. Silence filled with too many thoughts, too many memories. Maggie couldn't break it for fear of one escaping.

"Okay, then," Ally said slowly. In someone else, it might have sounded sarcastic. "I thought we could go to brunch Saturday. Chad's aunt is in town and will be here with him, so I'm available, and Jamie said she'd make time—"

"Sorry. I can't. You two have fun."

"You won't be back by the weekend?"

"No." The word was a decision, as well as an answer.

"I don't get opportunities like this often."

No, she didn't. Her days were a routine of sitting with her brain-dead husband and keeping their home in the condition his family thought befitted a shrine.

Maggie gentled her voice. "I know. I am sorry. But I need to be here. Sorry it didn't work out."

"Well, maybe Aunt Dawn will come back soon."

After quick good-byes, she hurried to Monroe's office.

✧　✧　✧　✧

SHE SHIVERED. SOMEWHERE behind darkening clouds, the sun must be near to dropping behind the ragged mountain line.

As her eyes adjusted to the sudden brightness of the waiting room, Carson emerged from gloom at the back of the hallway holding a coffee mug.

She hadn't been on her phone that long, yet here he was, apparently settled in. Could he have been here all along?

The front office was empty. "Where's Monroe?" she asked.

"Courthouse."

Scott appeared behind Carson, also with a mug. Was that a hint of relief she felt at having a third party here?

"Dallas asked me to clear you space at the table in his office," Scott said to her. "If you ever need anything, I'm set up in back, to take calls and such."

Carson stepped into the doorway of the room halfway along the hall, which she assumed was his office, to let Scott pass.

There was an atmosphere she couldn't pin down.

She followed Scott into Monroe's haphazard office. He restacked files, papers, and books to clear a section of the conference table. She moved a lamp to shine on the newly opened area.

After she assured Scott she had everything she needed, he went back down the hall.

She'd left her briefcase in the guesthouse, but started making electronic notes from today's interviews.

The exterior door opened and closed. The fact that the tread heading into the office was not Dallas' barely registered before a familiar voice came.

"Surprise."

She turned in her chair, not getting up. "What are you doing here, Roy?"

"Doing you a favor, babe." He placed a file box in the middle of the cleared space. "Brought these files Nancy said you wanted."

He tried to make it sound as if Nancy had asked him to make this delivery.

"A courier—" She tapped the completed label attached to the box. "—would have done fine—better, in fact."

"They don't provide TLC. I wanted to see how you're doing—" His tilted grin deepened as he looked out the window to Bedhurst's town square. "—in this metropolis."

"I've only been here overnight."

"That should be plenty of time to appreciate what you'd left behind. And to think about things."

"I'm working."

"Yeah, I heard. A cop calling in lawyers to help with an investigation. Christ." He hitched one thigh on the edge of the table, pulling his jeans even tighter. "Maybe this will be good for us. You being up here breathing in the fresh air and relaxing and—"

"I told you—"

"I know, I know, you're working. But I also know investigating a murder doesn't have to stop somebody from paying attention to the important things." He leaned closer. "You know it, too, if you think back to your kitchen last month, right after I made the Ortanovich arrest."

Important things ... In other words, him and sex.

She hadn't given a thought to him. Or to sex. Except as it might have played into the murder of Laurel.

And possibly the murder of Pan Wade.

They'd never been able to pin down evidence that Pan and Carson had been lovers. The autopsy hadn't shown any sign of sexual activity. What details would Laurel's show?

She supposed the autopsy would be done at the state medical examiner's regional office in Roanoke, as Pan's had. She needed to check—

Roy's deep chuckle snapped her attention back to him. He leaned over, slipping one hand down to her waist. "I always know what you're thinking when you get all dreamy-eyed."

She resisted his effort to draw her in, but the chair limited her maneuverability.

"Roy—"

"It's okay, babe." He slid his free hand to the side of her neck and leaned toward her. She leaned away. "You don't have to say a word."

She pushed back the chair to stand.

"Nothing has changed, Roy." She went to the doorway. "It was unnecessary, but thank you for bringing the files. Now it's time for you to leave, and no need to return."

Anger mottled his cheeks, but he kept the smile as he crowded her. She stepped back into the hall. "Depends on your definition of need, Maggie."

"Please go, Roy."

He took hold of the back of her neck with a fast move she didn't see coming. His other hand grasped her shoulder, as his mouth ground against hers. After an instant of shock, she clamped her mouth shut and jabbed the heels of both hands against his chest.

She was debating between kneeing him in the groin and stamping her heel into his foot when he released her and stepped back, trailing his hand over her cheek, still grinning—the jackass.

"See you soon, babe."

He was gone before she could express the brimstone details of where she'd like to see him.

Her arms jangled with the desire to pound something. She drew in air through her mouth, expelled it through her nose. Once, twice.

Then she became aware.

Of what, precisely, she couldn't say, but it made her turn.

J.D. Carson leaned against the frame of his office door, as if he'd been there all along.

"I've got to wonder—"

"Go ahead and wonder," she snapped, heading for the tiny bathroom beyond Carson's office that Scott had pointed out earlier.

He picked up the sentence as if she'd never spoken. "—what forensics would find of him on you and you on him after that clinch."

CHAPTER NINETEEN

3:47 p.m.

WITHOUT MISSING ANY words coming through the phone held to his ear, Belichek eyed the woman across from him.

After he hung up, Nancy Quinn immediately said, "I don't like it."

"I thought you were off this afternoon."

"I came back to talk to you. Did you hear me?"

"Uh-huh. You don't like what?" As if he didn't know.

She grimaced. "Don't play the idiot, Belichek. Landis can pull it off—barely—you don't have the looks for it. And I don't have the time. Her. Up there. Alone."

For all Maggie thought she could handle anything and everything, he didn't like this setup, either. But reveal that to Nancy Quinn, and she'd be on him non-stop.

"Bedhurst County's still part of the Commonwealth of Virginia, not some wilderness." Though you had to wonder when they let a guy go from murder defendant to an associate of the CA.

"You didn't see her there. Hell, I didn't get it, not until I knew what her normal was. Then I realized how *not* normal she'd been."

"First murder trial as first chair—"

"Yeah. And her being special prosecutor with everybody acting like she had two heads because she came from here. With a second chair who could barely tie his shoes. But it was more. It was—"

Nancy shifted her eyes, making him aware of the ears around them. All seemingly occupied with their own concerns, but rarely too occupied to miss gossip.

Especially about Maggie Frye.

The bare facts had been a source of speculation at the CA's office and police department from her first day. No way to hide a juicy piece of gossip like that.

Everything beyond the bare facts was in a lockbox inside Maggie.

He was talking to the one other person in Maggie's professional life who might have glimpsed inside that lockbox. Landis might've, too ... if he took enough time off from following his dick to think things through.

It wasn't her words. It was a look, a hesitation, an attitude, a question, then putting them together with who she was.

"The earlier case," he filled in. Using a phrase that wouldn't catch anybody's attention.

Nancy nodded. "The earlier case. And similarities."

"Similarities? The MO—"

Her slicing gesture stopped him. "Not MO. Similarities in the victim. Relationship between victim and defendant. They were ... on the same frequency."

He'd been a detective too long to scoff. Some crimes did vibrate at the same frequency, even if you didn't see similarities at first.

"That prick won't let me go up there." Nancy didn't need to say the prick was Commonwealth's Attorney Vic Upton. "Says I'm needed here. If I didn't need every dime to get my kid started at VCU this fall, I'd go unpaid. And that other prick hasn't helped."

Belichek figured Prick Two was Roy Isaacson.

"Asshole sweet-talked an idiot clerk into letting him take a box being expressed to her. Went up there, acting like God's gift to women, law enforcement, and the legal system, no doubt. Add in her cousin calling all the time. It's the annual fund-raiser. All falling down on her at once. With the biggest chunk of rock this damned case."

"What am I supposed to do?"

"God forbid you help a friend. Somebody who's damn near made your career."

"Christ, Nancy—"

She held up a hand. "You're right. Out of line. There's nothing you or I can do about the two pricks." He supposed Maggie's cousin should feel honored not to be lumped in with Upton and Isaacson. "But the sooner this case is resolved, the sooner things get back to normal."

He shifted his gaze to the corner of his desk. Its pattern of scuff marks more than once had reformed in his mind's eye to put together pieces of a case into a recognizable pattern.

No such luck this time.

"I'll make some calls." They'd be Round Two, because he'd put out initial feelers after talking with Maggie.

"That's a start. So's reading."

She dropped a file on his desk.

CHAPTER TWENTY

WHEN MAGGIE OPENED the bathroom door there was no way to avoid Scott's concerned eyes.

"Problems?" he asked from a swivel chair in front of a small desk that faced into a shallow closet.

"No."

She wrestled down the temptation to walk away. She had to work with this guy.

She went to the coffeemaker in an alcove beyond the bathroom door, and half-filled a Styrofoam cup. She held up the pot in a silent offer.

"Yes, thank you." Scott handed her a ceramic mug emblazoned "Court Reporters Get It All Down." "That was nice of your guy to bring those files. He really wanted to see you, huh?"

She grunted neutrally, handing back the filled mug.

"He sure did want it to be a surprise."

Now Maggie focused on him. "Did he?"

His smile faltered. "He came in before you got back, asked me and J.D. not to mention it. Said he wanted to surprise his girl. We said sure. Didn't want to ruin it."

At least that explained the atmosphere earlier. Scott and Carson had expectantly awaited Roy's return and the springing of his *surprise*. Though somehow she couldn't imagine Carson echoing Scott's good-natured "sure" to keeping Roy's secret.

"You and Roy were together when you were here last time?" Scott asked.

"No."

"Hard enough to keep a relationship going these days," he said with a twisted smile of commiseration. "Add in separation and it's even harder. Then, with an investigation eating your time … well, a relationship suffers."

"This one's past suffering. It's dead."

He faced her. "Oh? I'm real sorry to hear that. And you here, away from your support system. If you want to talk—"

"Thanks, Scott. I'm fine."

Carson stood in his doorway, mug in hand, making no effort to hide he'd been listening.

She walked past him and returned to work.

━━━━━━━━━━

Commonwealth v. J.D. Carson

Witness Theodore Barrett (prosecution)
Cross-Examination by Mr. Monroe

Q. Now, you said you rode your bicycle to the park that day, is that right?

A. Yeah. Every day.

Q. Do you go to the same place in the park every day?

A. No, I like to spice it up with variety.

Q. Quite right. What part did you go to that day? … You'll have to say that out loud so the court reporter can get it down.

Q. You mean Scott? Hi, Scott.

THE COURT: You need to let him do his job, Teddie, and you do your job by answering the question. Mr. Monroe, if you'll ask your question again.

Q. Certainly, Judge. Teddie, what part of the park did you go to that day we've been talking about, August 12?

A. I don't know. I mean, I don't remember.

Q. Okay, but maybe we can figure this out together. You said you heard the waterfall. Where do you like to go in the park where you can hear the waterfall?

A. That's Waterfall Path. That's my favorite.

Q. How do you get to Waterfall Path?

A. I ride all the way out Falls Road, then through the parking lot, and past the big map, and there it is.

Q. Following along on this map that's on the board, that's the main entrance to the park, is that right? You have to say it out loud, remember.

A. I guess.

Q. Now, on this official park map, it shows the path goes down to the waterfall, then loops back. Is that how you follow it?

A. Sure. If I didn't I wouldn't be on the Waterfall Path.

Q. That's a good point, Teddie. So, when you go on the Waterfall Path do you ever leave it, go behind the falls maybe or someplace else?

A. No, because then I wouldn't be on the Waterfall Path.

Q. That day, the day you remembered hearing voices arguing, did you go off the Waterfall Path? If you want to think about it—

A. I don't have to think. I know this. I never go off the Waterfall Path. When I'm on a path, I'm on the path, and I don't go off.

Q. Do you ever take the highway to get to the Waterfall Path, then sort of come in the back way by Buckley Road instead of by the main entrance?

A. No. That would be stupid, and I'm not stupid. It would be a way long way around. You'd have to ride on that road where they bring in trucks and such and then take that back path that goes to Anya's cabin—that's J.D.'s now—and it's bumpy. Real bumpy.

Q. That shows good sense, Teddie. Now, you said that day you heard the voices arguing, you could hear the waterfall, is that right?

A. Yes. And the birds and the squirrels and two snakes going through the dry grass like this.

Q. Your Honor, the defense would like to submit this videotape taken at Bedhurst Falls—

Ms. Frye: Objection. Relevance.

✧ ✧ ✧ ✧

"SCOTT!" DALLAS CALLED on his return from the courthouse.

Maggie didn't look up.

He'd settled into his chair behind his desk before the boy arrived. "I'm busy, Dallas. I'm the only one who can pull together that transcript and—"

"I know, and we do appreciate it. I just had a question that only you could answer. Louelle says for a fact Laurel was consultin' Henry Zales over to Lynchburg."

Past Scott, he saw Maggie stop typing on one of those electronic gadgets that might have shrunk in the wash and snap around to him.

"You interviewed Eugene Tagner's maid without me?" she demanded.

He switched on affable. "As it happens, I did. Though you'd best not be callin' Louelle a maid where she can come to hear about it. I was over to the courthouse and Louelle was there about her mama driving without a license again, and we got to talkin'. I could hardly stop her tellin' me. Never did care for Laurel and she wanted me to know Laurel'd been leadin' Eugene a fine dance."

Scott snorted. "Doesn't she realize that makes Eugene look even more guilty?"

"I didn't come round to mentionin' that, as it happens."

Scott chuckled.

Maggie asked, "What did she say?"

"She holds that Laurel was consultin' Henry about more than background. Scott, you've done depositions for Henry, did you cross paths with Laurel there?"

Scott shook his head. "How could I miss the significance to this investigation of Laurel seeing a divorce attorney?"

"I was sure you would have told me—us." He'd known it was a longshot. "What's been happenin' here, boy?"

He listened with half attention as Scott described each interruption and how adroitly he'd handled the issues on behalf of Monroe & Associate.

Most of his mind, was on how to approach Henry Zales. He could tell Gardner and let him… No, he'd fish that pond first.

Scott drew a breath, and Dallas plunged in. "Good, good. You did just right, Scott. Now we'd best get to the high school."

4:40 p.m.

MAGGIE'S CALL WENT through quickly. It figured the area around the high school had good reception—Gardner wouldn't have picked it otherwise.

"Belichek."

"It's Maggie." She resisted leaning against her car. Streaks of mud fanned up the side.

"How's it going?"

"Peachy. Just came from today's update of the main investigation. Unless the sheriff is holding out, it's a litany of non-evidence."

"Wouldn't blame the sheriff for holding out."

"Me, either, not considering what got around last time."

"In other words, sounds about right for this point."

She ignored that Job's comfort. "As for this *special task force*, supposedly searching for connections between the murders, I'm not sure if I'm being led around by the nose or being kept off balance."

"Hmm."

"Hmm what?"

"You're used to being in charge. Maybe some of it's working with a team."

"I work with you and Landis."

"Yeah." His tone took all agreement out of the syllable.

"You're saying I don't?"

"You mostly come into it when we've got something to show you. And you're looking at it from the court angle. Not from starting from scratch at figuring out what happened, like this. How's it going?"

"I have no idea."

"She says she has no idea," he repeated, apparently for an audience's benefit.

"Is that Landis cackling?"

"Yeah. He says now you know starting from scratch isn't as easy as you thought."

She sighed. "It's like a wadded up ball of bits of string. Somewhere inside the wad there's one long piece to take you from one end to the other of the crime. But you keep grabbing bits that don't lead anywhere except an impenetrable knot. You don't know if there's more beyond the knot or if it's the end of the string."

Without a whisper of sympathy, he said, "You keep untying knots, setting aside pieces that go nowhere and inching along the other pieces bit by bit until you find a long one and have it laid out nice and straight with no knots."

"Right."

"What knot is it you want us to untie?"

"I'm that transparent, huh?"

"A piece of glass, Mags."

"Great." Though it felt less bad than she would have expected. "The sheriff is running an official inquiry about similar murders in the state, and there's a reciprocal with West Virginia. It's the surrounding states I'd like to have checked—North Carolina, Tennessee, Kentucky, Maryland, Pennsylvania, D.C., of course. I can't make it official, but with your connections—"

"No problem."

After the call, Maggie re-checked no one was within listening distance.

Then she made another call. This one local.

CHAPTER TWENTY-ONE

6:23 p.m.

DALLAS WRAPPED AN arm around Evelyn's waist, pretending it was to distract her while he reached to dip a spoon in the simmering peanut soup.

"Sheriff's going to love this." He'd persuaded Gardner to join them for dinner, since he had to eat and they could relay what they'd learned at the same time. He doubted his efforts to get information out of Gardner would succeed, but at least the man wouldn't fall over from hunger.

"Where are they?" she asked.

"J.D.'s washing up. Maggie's at the guesthouse."

Evelyn relaxed against him. "Dallas, you be careful with that young lady."

"Mmm. I have no earthly idea what you might be referring to."

"I know you're up to something. I also know that young woman is smarter than you're crediting her for. I know one more thing—she's got her own devils, which are complications you might not see until they tow you under."

"That's two more things."

She reached back and slapped at his posterior. "Remember what I said."

"Evelyn DuPree, marry me."

"No." No hesitation, no thought. As if she had more important things on her mind.

It stung.

"Why not?"

With her dark eyes on him he realized he'd never asked that before. Asked her to marry him, yes. But never her reasons for refusing.

He repeated it, oddly urgent. "Why not? I love you, you love me."

"You're taking a lot for granted. I've never said—"

"You wouldn't sleep with me if you didn't love me, and you wouldn't sleep with me if you didn't know I love you. So, don't get swelled up like I've insulted you. I know your boys won't like it, but I won't come between you and them—if that means you going to see them without me, that's how it'll be. I won't make you change your life for me. But I could give you things, make life more comfortable for you."

Using a towel on the handle, she moved the soup to a cool burner with exquisite care. "What about you, Dallas Herbert? Will life be more comfortable for you?"

"Are you saying you think I want to marry you to have my house-keeper on hand? Is—?"

"Don't throw your lawyer voice at me."

He waited.

"You think those folks who come and pay your fees because they like saying Dallas Monroe is their lawyer will keep coming round?"

"If they don't—"

"Don't you say it. Because it's those folks with money in their pockets and willing to put it in your pockets who make it so you can be the lawyer for the other kind of folks." She cupped his cheek in her warm palm. "The folks who need you more than they know."

She looked out the window and dropped her hand. He saw Maggie approaching the back door. "There's more to be said on this matter."

"No, there's not," she contradicted. "I know you'd get by without the important folks, and I might let you do it, too. But you can't get by without the other ones—the ones who need you. And I won't let you try."

❖ ❖ ❖ ❖

MAGGIE COMPLETED HER last email and headed to the bathroom to wash her face.

Having handled necessities from her current caseload, she could concentrate on *Commonwealth of Virginia v. J.D. Carson.*

She wished she had the final transcript to go over tonight. Instead, she'd be filling in her notes from today and continuing with materials from the file box Roy delivered, including the piecemeal daily transcripts.

One thing for sure, whether the certified version Scott would provide or the dailies from her files, this transcript would not be a fun read.

She blotted her face dry and hung the towel.

At the jury trial she'd prosecuted after *v. J.D. Carson*, she'd watched the burglary defendants, with their would-be tough-guy slouches, and waited for the verdict.

No question came into her mind.

No whisper about innocence.

Nothing except satisfaction at the "Guilty."

That weekend, she'd read the Carson trial transcript for the first and only time.

What had made the difference were her mistakes. That's why the jury decided she hadn't wiped away reasonable doubt, the reason they set Carson free.

One of her bigger mistakes was Teddie Barrett.

Hit and run accident. Though how they can call it an accident when somebody's so evil he doesn't stop to help, especially a soul as harmless as Teddie Barrett.

She thought of Teddie's face as he'd giggled at her calling him Mr. Barrett. And she thought of his mother.

Maggie sat on the window seat, staring out. Other than the reflection of the bedside lamp, it showed only dark, yet the dark seemed to move with the wind in the trees on the opposite bank.

She had tried to get the trial's lunch break timed immediately after Teddie's statement that he'd recognized Pan's and Carson's voices, letting it sink in with the jury.

But she'd gone through his testimony too fast. That let Dallas get started. During the break, jurors chewed over Teddie saying he'd been *told* his memory came from the day of the murder.

Chewed it over and swallowed it.

After lunch it went from bad to worse.

That damned video. She fought it. But Judge Blankenship allowed it. It had been recorded only two days before Pan's murder as part of a commercial series on waterfalls of the South. A company spokesman testified nothing on it was altered.

Still, she should have fought harder. She should have kept it out. Somehow.

✧   ✧   ✧   ✧

9:56 p.m.

CHARLOTTE SCRATCHED "CRAB puffs" from her menu for the memorial gathering that would have to suffice until authorities released the body.

Allarene insisted on too much garlic in her crab puffs. Last thing needed, with the hugging and cheek-kissing, was everyone's breath reeking.

The mini spinach tarts would do. Laurel hated them, but then, she wouldn't be there.

Soon enough she'd be buried deep in the earth of Bedhurst Cemetery. Odd to think of Laurel lying still beside Mama, solitary in the silk-lined coffin Charlotte was almost certain would be her selection.

Odd to think of Laurel lying solitary anywhere.

That was what those people had been getting at—Laurel was a slut. That's what they'd wanted her to say.

She would have. She had no trouble speaking the truth about her sister. But she'd looked ahead and seen where it might lead—like the crab puffs and garlic breath. She'd refused to be drawn into a discussion of Laurel's indiscretions.

Indiscretions? As if she'd ever had *discretion.*

Not since she'd been thirteen years old and Charlotte had seen her with that delivery man in the back of the old garage.

Charlotte, nearly seventeen, hadn't been kissed, and there was her little sister fucking the help.

"Honey? Aren't you coming to bed?"

She did wish her husband wouldn't say honey. It was common. Sweetheart or darling or—her mouth pursed—babe were no better. That was why she did not ask him to drop honey. He would have if she asked, but the danger was he would fall into worse.

"I have a number of things to do still."

"You're running yourself ragged, honey. You don't have to do it all. Tell me and I'll do whatever you need."

Of course, she had to do it. No one else could be relied on to handle things correctly.

"I'm fine, Edward."

"Okay. Uh. I, uh, I thought I'd go to the office tomorrow. Unless, of course, you need me here."

"No, that will be fine."

His office and, by extension, the courtroom defined him. It was what had brought Edward Smith to her notice.

Besides, she had a full slate of appointments tomorrow about arrangements for the memorial and eventual funeral. Edward would be underfoot.

It occurred to her that if he didn't die beforehand, she would need a detailed plan for his retirement.

He patted her hand, the motion slightly awkward, despite three years of marriage, then kissed her on the cheek. From the corner of her eye, she caught sight of his attire, and her gaze followed as he straightened.

Why he insisted on these pale blue cotton pajamas instead of the burgundy silk she'd bought...

"Good night, honey. Don't work too hard."

Not even a robe.

✧ ✧ ✧ ✧

DALLAS SIPPED HIS wine, staring at Ruth's silver candlesticks on the mantelpiece.

Every time Evelyn dusted and left them angled, with the silver bowl slightly in front, he returned them to side by side, in line with the bowl, the way Ruth liked.

That and refusing to marry him were Evelyn's only flaws.

The day Ruth hired Evelyn, she said Evelyn had a lot of good qualities. All he'd cared about was the quality of her fried chicken, and that Ruth was pleased.

They'd been friendly, but it was until a year and more after Ruth passed they'd started their talks.

A case came where he was sure old Sheriff Hague coerced a confession. The defendant denied it.

He'd been in his chair, reading files. Evelyn came in with her coat on, surely to say good night. "Trouble, Mr. M?"

"Yes."

She'd unbuttoned her coat, sat on the couch, and waited.

He'd talked.

Two days later, when her leaving time came, she'd brought in two glasses of Madeira, sat in the same spot, and he'd talked more.

Then she pointed out his defendant was alone since his elderly mother died and the sheriff was feeding him three squares a day, making him the closest thing to a friend the man had.

Eventually, he realized she'd been his best friend for years. Only looking back did he realize that at the moment he'd recognized friendship, he'd already loved her.

Sometimes he wondered what Ruth would say.

She'd treated every soul with kindness and dignity. And she held Evelyn in high regard. But she hadn't been much of one for folks pairing up outside their race, class, or church. She liked things neat that way.

Like candlesticks side by side.

Evelyn liked angles, unsymmetrical yet balanced. Over the years, he'd encouraged her to arrange things how she liked. To look out from his chair at all her touches made him feel as if she were here even when she wasn't.

Except the candlesticks. Those remained Ruth's way.

━━━━━━━━

Commonwealth v. J.D. Carson

Witness Theodore Barrett (prosecution)
Cross-Examination by Mr. Monroe

Q. Teddie, is that what the falls sounded like the day you say you heard those voices arguing?

A. Sure, that's what they sound like every day.

Mr. Monroe: No further questions.

Ms. Frye: Redirect, Your Honor?

THE COURT: Go ahead, Ms. Frye.

Ms. Frye: Did you hear voices at Bedhurst Falls about 6 p.m. August 12th?

A. Like I told you—

Q: You need to answer yes or no, Mr.—Teddie.

A. But—

Q: Did you hear voices at Bedhurst Falls, yes or no?

A. Sure. Like I said, I—

Q. Are you convinced that the day you heard them was August 12th, the day Mrs. Wade was killed there, yes or no?

A. Yes. And—

Q. Are you convinced those voices belonged to Mrs. Wade and the defendant.

A. Pan and J.D., yeah.

━━━━━━━━━━━━━━━

✧ ✧ ✧ ✧

9:58 p.m.

THAT DAMNED VIDEO.

The narrator's voice had shouted to be heard over the rush of the falls. People in the background appeared to yell, yet no sound came through.

All was drowned by the rush and roar of the falls.

Teddie had been unperturbed, clearly not recognizing Monroe had wiped out his credibility, along with his testimony.

That was the only night of the Carson trial she hadn't gone directly from the courtroom to the office to prep for the next day.

She'd ditched Ed, almost incoherent with apologizing for not seeing the flaw in Teddie's testimony. "I'm more local. I should have known," he'd said over and over.

She'd driven to the crime scene, and seen how she'd screwed up.

From where Pan Wade was murdered, you couldn't hear the falls. On the map, they were close. But as she'd followed the path, she'd realized it dropped sharply to where the falls sat in a sort of natural amphitheater, concentrating their sound, while blocking out sounds from beyond.

Standing there, Teddie couldn't have heard dynamite explode on the service road, much less voices arguing.

Either Teddie hadn't been where he'd said he was, or he hadn't heard those voices. He had no reason to make up the story. So, most likely, he had heard them, and he'd confused which path he'd been on.

It made no difference to the trial, because his testimony had been shredded into confetti.

And she'd let it happen. She should have prepared better. She should not have allowed herself to be lulled by Teddie's earnestness.

She'd vowed to never again be caught like that.

The phone rang.

Not her phone, but a clunky, black old-fashioned twin for the living room phone. This one hunched on the small nightstand on the far side of the bed.

"Frye," she answered.

Nothing.

"Frye," she repeated, less patiently.

Still nothing.

"Hello." No static, no clicking, no feeling of dead air.

She disconnected with her thumb, her thoughts returning to their earlier track.

She'd let Dallas lead her around too much today.

She was the prosecutor. Setting out the case, calling the moves.

Let them react to her.

Instead of looking at the victims for a connection, what if the connection—if there was one—was the murderer. Who had reason to kill both Pan and Laurel? A lover, spurned or otherwise, of course. Who el—

The phone on the bedside table rang again.

She pulled her briefcase to her with one hand while picking up the heavy receiver with the other. Said hello.

As it registered that once more no one was responding, she flipped open her briefcase.

She sucked in a breath and didn't let it go.

The plastic envelope, the one always kept in the pocket of the lid, instead sat atop the files in the bottom of the briefcase. Not the way she'd left it.

Through the clear covering, a photo that had never been in that envelope. An autopsy photo of Pan Wade's dead face.

CHAPTER TWENTY-TWO

WITHOUT KNOCKING AT the back door, without catching her breath, Maggie burst through the kitchen and into a scene of domestic tranquility in the old-fashioned living room—Dallas, Evelyn, and Carson sat before a small fire, Mozart playing softly in the background.

Carson came out of his seat from one end of the couch, book in hand. He dropped it behind him. "What's wrong?"

She demanded of the other two people in the room. "How long has he been here?"

"What?" Dallas blinked slowly from an easy chair angled toward the fire.

"Since you left after supper," Evelyn said from the other end of the couch, her hands suspended, one extended with needle and thread apparently just drawn through a shirt button pinned in place with her opposite thumb.

"What's wrong?" Carson repeated.

"Someone's been in the guesthouse. In my things."

"I'll call 9-1-1," Evelyn said.

"Already did."

Carson scowled. "What things?"

"My briefcase for starters."

"Somethin' taken?" Dallas asked.

"Not that I can tell. But—Where are you going?"

Carson didn't slow. "To see."

She hurried to keep up, not knowing if Dallas or Evelyn followed. At the path, Carson broke into a jog, and any doubt she'd harbored about whether he'd let her follow him up the hillside at the crime scene yesterday was put to rest—he could leave her behind whenever he wanted.

"Hey!" she shouted. "What if I don't want you in there?"

"You already believe I messed with your things. What's a second time?" he asked over his shoulder.

She caught up at the guesthouse's back door, only because he'd stopped.

"Did you leave the door open?" He voice was barely a breath.

"No. Wh—?"

The door was wide open.

"Stay here."

She didn't. She followed him in. She stayed behind him, but watched every move.

Not difficult because he didn't make many.

He eased into the kitchen so slowly her muscles screamed in protest as she mimicked his motions. Finally inside, she reached to push the door closed, but his gesture stopped her.

For what seemed a good ten minutes they simply stood. Then he moved toward the living room. The slow motion journey ended in another interlude of stillness.

He relaxed.

She couldn't identify a motion or expression that told her, but she was sure.

Then she heard an approaching car.

"Sheriff." He didn't move, but his voice was normal.

She stepped toward the front door. He shifted his weight, blocking her. "Out the way we came in. Less we disturb the better."

Stung more by her failure to remember that basic rule than by his reminding her, she pivoted quickly. Too quickly. Her balance wavered. Carson grasped her elbow, the grip not as tight but its solidity as effective as when he'd kept her from falling down the hillside.

Her back still to him, she steadied herself and walked out of his hold and through the kitchen.

Dallas, breathing heavily, was at the base of the back steps. He looked his question past her, at Carson.

"Nobody's there." Carson moved ahead, leading the way to the front of the guesthouse. From his slowness and movements of his head, she gathered he was searching for marks on the path.

Double-checking if he'd left any?

No. Carson wouldn't have left anything behind unless he'd meant to.

Still, it could be for show.

Near the front door, he stepped off the path, crossing spotty grass to the hard surface where a deputy was getting out of his car, parked behind Maggie's Honda.

"Got a call you had a break-in, Dallas." The deputy looked at Carson.

She stepped past Carson. "I called. The break-in was here. The guesthouse where I'm staying. And my—"

She broke off because another car had arrived. This one emblazoned Sheriff.

Gardner emerged slowly. "I heard the call. What's the status, Abner?"

"Just got here myself. Evelyn called in a break-in. Ms. Frye was starting to tell me."

The sheriff nodded at her. She started over and told her story, only saying items in her briefcase were rearranged.

"...When I got to the main house, Carson was there with Dallas and Evelyn. He said he'd been there since before supper, but—"

"Evelyn said it," Carson interjected.

She met his gaze. "Evelyn said he'd been there since before supper." Not looking away, she added, "But I was out of the guesthouse before the briefing. Carson had left my car this afternoon, approximately four blocks from here."

"Anyone could have gotten in while you and J.D. and I were together," Monroe said. "A number of people have keys."

"Half the town," murmured the sheriff.

"Half the county." His deputy looked down when the sheriff gave him a level gaze.

Carson addressed the sheriff. "No one's inside. We entered through the kitchen, went to the edge of the rug in the living room.

Straight line in, straight line out."

Gardner looked over his shoulder from a contemplation of the building. "We?"

"I told her to stay outside. She didn't. Followed me in. Loud enough to scare off anybody who might have stuck around." Maggie made a sound. "Not likely anybody there by then. They had an easy target when she came to the house—noisy, no weapon, alone. Back door was open when I got to it. She says she closed it."

The sheriff shifted his bleary gaze to her.

"I pulled it closed," she said. "I didn't wait to see if it latched. May I have a word with you in private?"

He jerked his head toward his car. Aware of the others all watching them, she took the passenger seat.

"I have some photos. From cases. They were removed from the pocket in the lid of my briefcase and put in the main part so I would see it as soon as I opened the briefcase. Also, the order of the photos was changed," she told him.

After a couple breaths, he asked, "Anything taken? Anything else moved?"

"Not that I'm aware of and I believe I would be. Another thing. He won't have left fingerprints."

"He?"

She shrugged. "Whoever. This was not some idiot breaking in for drug money. They got what they came for as soon as I opened my briefcase."

"You're saying you don't want your belongings fingerprinted?"

"I don't think there's a chance in hell you'd find anything and with all that's going on… But I'll leave that to your professional judgment."

After a moment, he gave a quick nod and they climbed out.

"Maggie," Gardner ordered, "go back to the house with Dallas. J.D., you go with Abner while he looks around out here. I'm going inside."

"But I could lo—"

He cut off her protest. "Now."

Dallas took her arm, a gentlemanly gesture that allowed him to steer her. "Come. We're not wanted."

CHAPTER TWENTY-THREE

DALLAS WATCHED MAGGIE pace from the fireplace to the door and back.

Let him.

Her mind was running four times faster than her feet. She'd barely acknowledged Evelyn's departure as soon as they returned to the house.

Would Carson have had time this afternoon to get to the guesthouse between leaving her car and being at the office? Maybe not, but he'd had enough time while she'd been talking to Theresa Addington after the briefing.

What could he have hoped to gain? What could anyone have hoped to gain?

A message to keep Pan's murder uppermost in her mind?

That might point to Rick Wade. Or Pan's parents.

Theresa or Kevin Addington breaking into the guesthouse and intruding on her privacy might seem far-fetched, but she'd learned a long time ago, apparent niceness was no guarantee.

That long-ago understanding, patient voice. *Are you sure? Are you absolutely sure?*

Dallas cleared his throat. "I knew J.D. hadn't done it."

The abrupt reference to the trial didn't throw her.

"You're going to tell me you'd known Carson all his life and he couldn't hurt a fly?"

"I *have* known him all his life and I've known him to kill flies beyond measure. But I knew he hadn't done the crime you were prosecutin' him for."

She snorted. "Defense attorneys always know their clients are innocent."

"I can't speak for other defense attorneys, but in my case, you are quite wrong. It's the knowin' that was different with J.D. Not knowin' is muddy water, and muddy water quenches a defense attorney's deepest thirst for reasonable doubt. Now clear, cold facts—that's what a prosecutor wants. Sureness. To see clear to the bottom. Defense attorneys are a different breed. We have the capacity for not knowin' and being satisfied with it."

What if he's innocent?

That instant.

That frozen instant, looking at Carson.

The words as if they'd come from someplace outside her.

Dallas was going on, unaware she'd dipped below the surface of his muddy water. "That's why it was different with J.D. I knew he hadn't done that crime."

"How could you know?"

Satisfaction folded his face into a smile. "It comes from the bones, through the sinews, and into the flesh."

"I don't have the bones and sinews for knowing if someone's innocent?"

"Not your bones and sinew, young lady. J.D.'s. It came from that boy's bones, through his sinews, and into his flesh."

Bones. Sinews. Flesh.

She snapped her head up, found what she expected—Dallas watching her, taking in every nuance of whatever she failed to hide.

She braced for probing. Instead he waxed philosophical.

"They say the eyes are the window to the soul, but eyes can be taught to lie. The body isn't as adept. That's the basis for polygraphs, as I'm sure you know. Physiological changes come with a lie. So, who's to say there's not a physiological change when a soul's tellin' the truth—soul-deep truth—and another body can't feel it?"

"That's all fine and sentimental and ethereal. But you know and I know there was plenty of evidence to convict him. I believe he murdered Pan Wade."

"You think he might have, but you don't believe down to your toes. That's what bothers you. That's—"

Gardner stepped into the room from the kitchen.

"I don't see anything out of place, Maggie. Are you sure—?"

"I am sure. There are items I keep—"

Carson and the deputy appeared behind Gardner, two more taking advantage of Dallas' lax security to arrive unannounced.

"Didn't see anything," Abner reported. "But it's hard to tell for sure at night. Something might be visible come daylight."

"Thank you for comin', Sheriff," Dallas said. "With all you have on your mind to take time out to deal with this little domestic matter—"

"If that's what I thought, I wouldn't have come. A break-in while Maggie's looking at these murders and staying here isn't a coincidence I like. But there's nothing more to be done tonight."

"Yes, there is," Carson said. "Call a locksmith. Get new locks tonight. Or get her out of there."

She squared off to him. "I won't be scared out."

"And I won't be blamed for anything happening to you."

Gardner held up a stop-sign hand. "Already called. He'll be out in an hour."

"You'll stay here until he arrives, Maggie," Dallas said.

Carson crossed to the corner of the couch where he'd been earlier, picked up his book and sat.

"I don't need you to—"

He interrupted. "I need you—to witness I was under your watchful eye from the time the sheriff left until the new locks were on."

Wednesday, 12:37 a.m.

DALLAS ROSE, YAWNED. Everyone gone at last. Needed sleep to be half useful tomorrow.

He detoured to the mantel. And yet, with the cool silver under his fingertips, he didn't move the candlesticks.

He stared at them, seeing Maggie's fretful fingers shifting them to an unsymmetrical angle.

Maggie Frye, who he would have predicted with absolute confidence would line them up into perfect order. Even more than Ruth.

Could he have missed an aspect of Maggie?

THROUGH BINOCULARS, J.D. Carson watched Rick Wade enter the showroom from the back lot. Where had he been?

He sure wasn't just returning from the guesthouse after all this time.

Wade poured himself a mug of coffee, then went to his office, closing the door. He rolled up his shirt sleeves, sat at the desk, and opened a program on his computer.

J.D. adjusted focus, trying to read what was on screen. No good from this angle. He saw the format, not the characters.

Wade appeared settled in.

J.D. shifted the view to a salesperson doing paperwork. This late? Had to be trying to impress the boss.

When he'd tracked Wade here this afternoon there'd been a handful of people around.

He put away the binoculars.

CHAPTER TWENTY-FOUR

4:04 a.m.

MAGGIE WAS AWAKE when the phone on the bedside table rang.

It still made her jump.

Both those facts—she was awake and she jumped—made her snap "Hello?"

Nobody was there. Just air.

She gave a second "hello?" More air.

She hung up.

Tried to get some sleep.

Commonwealth v. J.D. Carson

Witness Melanie Forbes (prosecution)
Direct Examination by ACA Frye

Q. Thank you for that concise explanation of the cause of death, Doctor Forbes. To recap in layman's terms, would you say it was fair to say that Pan Wade was shot at close quarters with her own gun?

A. No more than eighteen inches.

Q. Thank you. In your autopsy for the state medical examiner's office, did you find other wounds, such as might be expected if someone tried to defend herself?

A. None.

Q. Mrs. Wade made no effort to defend herself when someone raised and aimed a gun at her from eighteen inches away, as if she trusted the person who—?

Mr. Monroe: Objection. Asked and answered.

THE COURT: Sustained. Proceed, Ms. Frye.

Q. Will you tell us, please, what—if any—items you found in your examination of Pan Addington Wade?

A. In addition to the usual clothing ,items, which we sent to the forensics lab for examination, we found a piece of paper with handwriting on it.

Q. Where did you find this paper?

A. In her mouth.

THE COURT: Silence. There will be no outbursts in this courtroom. Proceed, Ms. Frye.

✧ ✧ ✧ ✧

6:41 a.m.

MAGGIE LET HERSELF into the office with the key Dallas gave her last night—right after the locksmith gave one new key to the guest-house to her and the only other one to Dallas.

The upside of sleeping poorly was she'd been awake to leave the guesthouse before anyone sidetracked her.

Even that early, though, she'd had to sidestep behind a rhododendron when she saw Evelyn entering the back door, and heard the murmur of her morning greetings with Dallas through an open window.

She'd passed under that window in time to hear Dallas describe her as "flinty-eyed Maggie Frye."

She allowed herself satisfaction as she walked to the office of Monroe & Associate. Nice to know she'd been right about his Southern chivalry crap.

If she'd encountered anyone, she'd say she arrived at the office this early to avoid the temptation of an Evelyn breakfast.

Not switching on lamps, she used daylight seeping in through the front window to deposit her briefcase, then returned to the hall, waiting while her eyes adjusted before she went to the closed door on the left.

She hesitated with her hand on the knob. But not long.

She stepped in to Carson's office.

The small room had a single window, which at first glance appeared to have been bricked over. Second glance recognized it had a view across a narrow gangway to the brick wall of the building next door. A shallow puddle of sunlight touched the floor below the window, barely strong enough to cast a shadow.

Small, lacking natural light, and ascetically neat. It could have been a cell—in a prison or a monastery.

She scanned the ordered bookshelves, labeled file drawers, desktop clear of everything except a computer.

Not that she expected to see anything incriminating.

Carson was far too smart to leave anything where it could be easily found, and in a semi-public place, no less. Besides, he was almost certainly too controlled to keep anything at all.

No trophies, no spill-all journals, not for J.D. Carson.

The room told her he was neat, orderly, precise.

While there'd been a strong undercurrent of emotion in the murders—the face-down posing of the bodies, for instance—the scene and victims were meticulously devoid of clues. Someone who knew what he—or she, Maggie added scrupulously—was doing and disciplined enough to do it.

So, what was this niggle of surprise she felt, looking over Carson's office?

Contemplation of that abruptly gave way to alarm and adrenaline.

A sound behind her spun her around.

CHAPTER TWENTY-FIVE

"**IF IT'S NOT** just like Laurel Blankenship Tagner to make her exit from this earth a spectacle that's thrown everything into an uproar," Evelyn said from the sink, her back to him.

Dallas knew she'd taken in the evidence of his sleepless night with one look.

He grunted. "Including boxing J.D. even tighter into never leaving this county."

"Can't blame Laurel for all of that."

"I should've gotten him out of here," Dallas said.

"It'd've taken dynamite."

"At least we wouldn't have flinty-eyed Maggie Frye searchin' for a way to charge him with murder again. You saw her last night—she looks at him like she'd like to take a bite out of his jugular."

"Or something," Evelyn murmured.

"What?"

"I said—" She faced him. "—or something. There're times she looks like she'd like to bite something on J.D., not his jugular."

"You think…?"

"I think." She tied her apron. "Not that she'd act on it the way things are. Not in a million years. Same as him."

"Same as—What are you saying?"

"It's not one-way. You know that, don't you?"

"*Good Lord!*" He leaned against the counter, reviewing tones, looks, silences. "She tried to convict him of murder." He wasn't arguing. He was commenting on the outlandishness of humanity.

"He does work in mysterious ways." She took the pitcher of orange juice from the refrigerator.

"Evelyn, you always do make me feel better." He chewed over what she'd said. "You know, if Maggie became convinced J.D.'s innocent that might be enough to make him see leaving here isn't running away. If you're right—and you most always are—that could make it easier…"

"Or harder. That one—" She tipped her head in the direction of the guesthouse. "—won't fall over with a puff of wind. Besides, how could you hope to make her sure he's innocent?"

ED SMITH SMILED at the girl who took his money through the drive-through window. It was harder to smile when she handed him the white bag with the telltale smells.

Guilt.

He preferred Cheforie's burgers and fries, but it was easier to stop for coffee and a sausage sandwich on his way to the office without Charlotte knowing.

She didn't approve of Cheforie's.

He wasn't clear if her disapproval stemmed from nutritional or social issues. The outcome was the same. No Cheforie's within reach of Charlotte's knowledge.

He circled the cup of coffee, finding the opening in the lid by accustomed feel as he drove one-handed. The first hot, potent sip, brought an "Ahh."

Whatever benefits tea—herbal, Charlotte insisted—might claim, it couldn't match this.

Once, he'd been late leaving for his hour-plus drive to work, and caught sight of the judge in the drive-through. They never spoke of it, and Ed made sure never again to hit Cheforie's at that hour.

Out of town, on the familiar twisting road, he peeled back the coated paper and bit through layers of biscuit and sausage patty.

God, he'd missed this.

It was a small enough thing to sacrifice while he stayed home with his wife grieving for her murdered sister.

He took another bite.

His particular branch of the Smiths had never dealt with a tragedy like the death of Yvonne Blankenship when the girls were young. Though he wondered—not for the first time—if anyone truly could have been the marvel of womanhood and motherhood the family made her out to be.

And now the murder of Laurel.

He finished the biscuit sandwich and wedged a napkin between his left hand and the steering wheel to better wipe his greasy right fingers. He started on the second sandwich, finishing well before traffic increased at the edge of Lynchburg.

The gantlet of condolences from his superiors, colleagues, and support staff took him by surprise. Each person he encountered expressed shock and sorrow, and each encounter slowed him, allowing more and more people to add their sympathies.

He thanked them, concentrated on the shock and horror, promised to ask for help if there was anything they could do.

Finally, in his office, with the door closed with solicitous gentleness by the assistant, he allowed himself the thought that perhaps what would help the most was what had already happened—the removal of Laurel Blankenship Tagner.

Society was unlikely to agree.

That was the problem that threatened to sweep away the life he knew.

He found the button by feel and pressed it.

He would ordinarily handle the mundane task himself. But she offered.

"Would you find out who represents Eugene Tagner, and if he drew up a will for Laurel?"

In his stomach, the coffee and sausage biscuit churned acid, making him feel exactly the way Charlotte warned about.

CHAPTER TWENTY-SIX

"I'M SORRY. I'M sorry. I didn't mean to startle you."

Scott's face shifted. Had it struck him he was apologizing, yet she was the one who was where she shouldn't be?

"No problem." She walked past him to the coffee machine.

From the corner of her eye she saw him look into J.D.'s office, then at her. "Do you need something? Something I could help with or...?"

"No. Thanks. I heard a sound." She lifted a shoulder. Thankfully she hadn't started going through drawers. "Didn't see anything. Probably a mouse."

He laughed. "I don't think even a mouse would dare go in J.D.'s office uninvited. Now, Dallas' office could host a whole convention of mice."

"Great. Thanks for that image," she muttered. She squinted at the unfamiliar coffee machine. If it weren't dark in this hallway she'd be able to figure out the damned thing.

"Mama used to say the crumbs on Cousin Dallas' shirtfront could feed an entire family."

She pressed a button. Nothing happened.

"Here, let me get that for you."

She stepped back.

"Mama had a way with words. She could talk anyone into anything."

Except her husband into staying, Maggie thought, considering what Dallas had said.

"Certainly could talk me into anything." Scott's cheeks and throat tinted mottled red, his eyes misting. "Such a shock when she passed. Cous—Dallas helped me so much. Drew my interest to the courtroom. Such a fascinating theater. One where I'm privileged to play my small part on the stage of justice."

Maggie imagined how Nancy would respond to that description.

"But the pain lingers. It does linger. That's why I know how it must be for you now."

What was he talking about? Her mother was remarkably healthy and blessedly three thousand miles away—not that Maggie would tell him that. She didn't want to encourage discussion of her family.

And there's the fact you're all from complicated families … Google's a wonderful thing.

At this point she didn't even want coffee. But since he blocked any graceful exit, she would stay until the coffee machine finished.

"It's got to be hard, keeping your mind on this investigation."

"Not hard at all," she said grimly.

"Oh, I'm sure you'd never shirk your duty, but when the heart's involved, it's difficult to keep your head from following."

Her heart had nothing to do with it.

"Maybe you and Roy will get back together after this is over."

Roy? Oh.

"Scott, do you have the transcript from *v. Carson*?" It was an abrupt change of subject, but if he thought she was sensitive about Roy, maybe he'd accept that and she could get on to something useful. "If it's going to take much longer—because of your other duties—I can—"

"Oh, I'll have it ready real soon. I'd've had it by now but I didn't expect to take this many calls for Dallas and Jack Dan."

"Jack Dan?"

His brows rose. "Carson. Didn't you know?"

"His legal name is J.D." She'd checked and double-checked he hadn't been charged under an improper name, leaving a loophole for him to climb through.

"Well, all I can tell you is everybody in the county knows J.D. stands for Jack Daniels. Rick Wade found out when we were kids and told everybody, like he told everybody the birth certificate says 'unknown' under 'Father.' "

"Rick said Nola Carson named her baby J.D. because all she remembered about the man passing through who most likely fathered him was he drank Jack Daniels."

Whatever she thought of the adult J.D., Maggie had a sudden image of the child, hearing that and more.

God, what people did to kids.

Tomlinson might have sensed her reaction, because he hurried into speech. "Everybody called him Jack Dan growing up." Something passed across his eyes before he added, "Except Pan."

Maybe he was a bit of a gossip, but that was sorrow in his face.

Scott cleared his throat, "It wasn't until he came back on leave that some folks shifted to J.D. Following Pan's lead, most like. And, once he was charged with murder and the papers had J.D., people got used to it. But growing up it was Jack Dan."

He seemed lost in a memory, then added, "His mama called him J.D."

"You remember Nola Carson?"

"Sure. She wasn't mean like most of the Carsons. An uncle and a brother of hers died in prison. Her cousin Marie's still in for knifing some guy. Nola's father was killed in a bar fight, and another brother smashed up driving drunk. Nola wasn't like that. Oh, she drank. Drank hard, and it kept costing her jobs. Used to hear men joking they'd never know which bar they'd walk into next and see Nola working there. Same way she was about men, moving from one to another."

"Social services never took him away." She'd checked. She'd needed to be prepared for a sympathy play by the defense.

"Never heard Nola hurt him. But I suppose if anyone raised him it was the Wood Witch."

"The who?"

He chuckled. "Sorry, that's what we called her as kids. She was Bedhurst's bogeyman. When I heard the Hansel and Gretel story, I knew it was about the Wood Witch, and she'd eat kids for sure. Since J.D. spent a lot of time with her, nobody messed with him. Nobody knew where she came from or when. Thought she was a squatter. Could have knocked folks over with a feather when it came out Anya owned the land."

"Anya Nouga, the woman Carson inherited the cabin from?" Carson had testified the inheritance was why he'd requested leave to return to Bedhurst.

Scott nodded. "Shack more like. Plants all over. Had a club she shook at us that rattled like a snake. She was forever cooking stuff in huge pots outside. Potions, maybe poisons."

She remembered the tiny cabin—one room and cramped loft— she'd visited as part of the frenzied trial preparation. It had been rundown, yet tidy. Yes, there'd been fire pits in the yard, but all in all, Maggie could see why a boy preferred it to the shell of a trailer that had once been home to Nola Carson.

"You'd go out there, by Anya Nouga's cabin?"

"Sure. We all did. Even Charlotte." He grinned. "Daring the devil, you know. Irresistible to kids. Would creep through the woods to spy on her stirring those pots and talking gibberish over them, for the thrill, trying not to get caught by her or Jack Dan—J.D."

"What happened if you were caught?"

"Kid stuff. Run off, shouted at. Here's your coffee." He handed her a cup, finally stepping back and opening the way.

"Thanks." The coffee was good. Sipping as she went, she returned to Dallas' office, retrieved her bag, took a final swig before leaving the cup, then headed for the door.

"Where are you going?" Scott asked from the dimness of the hallway. "Dallas should be here any minute."

"Tell him I'll be back soon."

"But—"

She was out the door before she heard more. She nearly collided with a figure on the sidewalk before it sidestepped to avoid the contact.

"Sorry. I didn't mean to—Oh. Carson."

"Good morning." His tone was even. "No more alarms during the night?"

"No."

She stepped past. He pivoted and fell into step with her. She stopped. "What are you doing?"

"Going with you."

"You have no idea where I'm going."

"True."

"I won't be long. Tell Dallas I'll be right back."

"Scott will tell him."

She frowned, then resumed walking.

Might be better to know where he was. Plus, it would delay his hearing from Scott that she'd been in his office.

Two blocks past the square, she turned left, went a block and a half to a faded blue frame house, with bright daffodils unfurling in front.

A dent showed beside the scar near his mouth as Carson murmured, "Good work, Maggie Frye."

She didn't respond, studying the house.

"Round back," he said.

She walked down the driveway and saw a small sign on the converted garage: Doranna's Do's.

In answer to her knock, a voice invited her to "Come on in, hon."

She was aware of a reaction from Carson, but he smothered it too quickly for her to catch. It left a small dent by the scar near his mouth.

"Never thought to live to see the day you're early, but it's—Oh." A short, wiry woman with unnatural dark red curls froze between the two chairs, with a brush in each hand.

"Doranna Ruskin? I'm Maggie Frye, Assistant Commonwealth's Atto—"

"Oh, I remember you, hon. Just never thought to see you in my shop, not if I lived forever. Hey, J.D."

"I have questions that might help in investigating the murders of two young women in this county."

"Well, I never thought you'd come for a shampoo and cut. But I can't tell you a thing more about poor Pan getting murdered than I did in that courtroom. And nothing about Laurel."

"I understand both murdered women were your custom—"

"My word." She clapped one hand—still holding a brush—in the vicinity of where her heart would be beating under the brightly flowered smock. "I never thought of it that way. Could give a woman a turn, except near everyone in the county's been a customer now and again."

"Can you—?"

"Sit. Here, take this chair, hon, and I'll..." She moved to a side chair in front of a wicker chest with magazines neatly fanned on top.

"No, thank you. If you could—"

"Well, I'm sitting. I'll be on my feet the rest of the live-long day. Thank you, hon," she added to J.D., who'd slid the chair forward.

"Ms. Ruskin—"

"Doranna."

Maggie gritted her teeth. Was she ever going to finish a sentence?

"Now you go right ahead and ask me your questions," Doranna invited kindly. "Though I can't begin to imagine—but never mind, you go right ahead."

"Do you remember either woman talking about her personal life?"

"Of course. Everybody does. But nothing that'd say who murdered those girls. If there had been, I'd've been to the sheriff first thing. Especially with that nonsense about J.D.—" She didn't finish, clearly remembering Maggie's role in the *nonsense*.

"Was there anyone either woman expressed concern about—Let's take this one at a time. Pan?" Doranna shook her head. "Laurel?" Another shake.

"Threats?" Two more shakes.

"Anything unusual in the weeks leading up to their murders?"

"Laurel hasn't been here for years, but even back before Pan was murdered, there was nothing. As for Pan, like I said at the trial, she was happy with J.D. home on leave—said how nice it was to have such a loyal friend."

She smiled at him. Maggie wondered if there'd been a shade of emphasis on *friend*.

"How about Laurel, who were her special friends?"

The woman's eyes gleamed. "You're meaning lovers? I'd say talk to

Barry at Shenny's. Supposedly he hears all the dirt and claims he doesn't spread it. I did hear tell some things from a girl who works in a fancy salon Laurel's patronizing in Lynchburg. Nothing to swear to, you understand?" Maggie nodded. "Seems Laurel was pretty free and easy right along that she hadn't stuck to the forsaking all others portion of her wedding vows. Word was she was going on and on a while back about somebody *on another plane*—whatever that means. But when she was in last time, and her girl asked about somebody *on another plane*, she waved it off, saying it was over—or would be soon—and she'd had her fill. It's gossip, pure and simple, but seems to me that's what you're asking for."

"Thank you. What about Pan Wade?"

Doranna leaned forward, demanding eye contact. "Pan Addington never broke a promise in her life. And it's sure as all she didn't break a single one of her wedding vows—didn't so much as wrinkle them. Anybody who hints otherwise is a worthless, self-centered child in man's clothes."

Clearly not Rick Wade's fan.

"What about before Pan married? Anyone show special interest in her?"

"Near everybody her age."

"Names would be helpful."

She flapped her hands. "Pull out the yearbooks. Okay—okay. Let's see. My Trent for one. Was couple years behind her, but he had it bad. Rick, of course, though he never treated her the way he should. My nephew, Ralph, bless his soul—died in a car accident not a year out of high school. That Hank Berkin who went to college on a football scholarship with Rick, but was real smart, and became a professor. J.D. here, of course, and Scott. And then the Everly boy in your class, J.D.—or was he the one turned out to be gay?"

"Ben," he supplied. "He was crazy about Pan and he is gay."

"Like I said, three-quarters of this town was nuts for Pan—all the guys and half the girls. Be easier to say who wasn't."

"Who wasn't?" she asked immediately.

"Like I said—half the girls."

"Specific names would—"

She laughed. "Any girl who wanted any one of those boys. Okay, okay." She narrowed her eyes, abruptly serious. "Only one comes to mind was Laurel. Now that girl looked to be seriously put out by attention that went to Pan. That won't help you much, since she got murdered herself."

"Were they ever friends?"

"No. Not enemies or snarling, but distant-like. Pan more friendly than Laurel, but that was her way. Both their ways, come to that."

Maggie used a tactic she sometimes employed, abruptly changing the direction of her questions. Even well-intentioned witnesses stuck in a mental track, and this could shake things loose.

"Did Pan and Laurel have appointments with you around the same time?"

"So they'd overlap, you mean?" Doranna tapped the back of the brush on her thigh. "Might have happened a time or two, but nothing regular. I sure don't recall talk between the two of them to be thinking of it now."

"Can you think of any similarities between Pan and Laurel? Anything that would link them?"

"Pan and Laurel similar? Not hardly. No, no link at all."

"I will need the name of the woman you mentioned in Lynchburg."

Doranna pursed her mouth. "She'll be telling everyone she's the star witness. SherriAnn Pendergast." She added an address and phone number.

Maggie thanked her and started out. She had the doorknob in hand when she realized J.D. hadn't followed.

"Doranna, will you think some more?" he asked. "Small town, a lot of people in common, there must be links."

The woman peered up at him. "Well, sure. But no more links than any other two souls. You know how it is, J.D.—went to school together, their mommas were distant cousins or some such. Anyway, they went to all the same weddings and funerals and all."

"That's a link," Carson said. "Pretty strong link. Folks in the same circles see a lot of each other in the county."

She tipped her head, considering. "S'pose so. As I said, they were kin of some kind. Not that kin necessarily makes for friends. If that were so, Laurel and Charlotte wouldn't have been at daggers-drawn most their lives. But I do s'pose you're right. Even though Laurel was younger than Pan and you-all, there was mixing at parties and such, wasn't there?"

He nodded. "There was."

"But like I said, not much more than most any two souls in this county."

CHAPTER TWENTY-SEVEN

"**NOT A LOT** there," he commented as they walked back.

"Cases are made from putting together a whole lot of not a lot."

He grunted. "Theresa Addington suggested Doranna?"

"Yes."

When Maggie called Pan's mother from the high school yesterday, she'd asked her to think about any connections Pan and Laurel might have had. At first she said none beyond a distant family tie and living in the same county.

Maggie floated specifics—"Friends in common? A restaurant both went to all the time? A favorite store? A service provider. An auto mechanic, or—"

"Hair. Of course. They both went to Doranna to have their hair done. At least Laurel was going there when Pan—" As with many family members of murder victims, she hesitated at the next word. "—died. I heard she started going to Lynchburg after she married Eugene."

Interesting Dallas and Carson hadn't mentioned it.

"Why'd you press Doranna about a link?" Maggie demanded of Carson. "I'd expect you to want everyone to believe the murders are unrelated."

"Why would I want that?"

"If Laurel's murder isn't related to Pan's, it puts more distance between it and your trial."

"I was found not guilty." His left eyebrow arched. "Remember?"

"Not guilty is not innocent."

Something glittered deep in his eyes. "I never claimed to be innocent." He let a beat pass, then, "Except when it comes to murder."

"Murder's what we're talking about. And I know you're neither innocent nor not guilty."

"Know." He rolled it over on his tongue. "Based on?"

"Evidence."

"A jury didn't agree with you."

"That particular jury."

"You think there was something peculiar about that jury?" This was a different glint in his eyes. Humor? Malice? He seemed to be dangling the possibility there *had* been something peculiar about the jury.

Dangling it in front of her like candy to lure a child away from the main path, into the woods.

"That particular hometown jury," she clarified without actually answering, "bought the hard-scrabble upbringing story Dallas pitched."

"They told you?" Offhand interest was the best she could describe his tone.

"They told Ed Smith."

"What did they tell you?"

"Nothing." She left the post-trial interviews to Ed.

"Might have been interesting."

"Why would you care? You got off."

"Curiosity."

"Well, I'm not curious. Not about that. They went with the illogical view that someone who'd bettered himself according to some incalculable scale, couldn't murder. The sentimental view that someone they knew who was reasonably attractive couldn't murder. Some juries look for a slavering maniac, preferably from another county, caught on tape committing the deed. Anything less they consider open to reasonable doubt because—What?"

"I didn't know you thought so highly of me."

She reviewed what she'd said. *Reasonably attractive.*

"I could have sworn you did consider me a slavering maniac. Since you don't see me as a slavering maniac and you base your beliefs—excuse me, your knowledge—on evidence, we'll get along fine."

He lengthened his stride, making her aware he'd been letting her set the pace. Once ahead of her, he grasped the doorknob to Monroe & Associate, but didn't turn it.

"Before you send your assistant on more chases, Doranna's son, Trent Ruskin, has been in the Air Force since we graduated high school. He's married, with two kids. Loves his wife. I know, I know that means nothing, not by way of evidence, but there's this, too. He was stationed in Japan when Pan was killed, and he's in Germany now. Wasn't on leave either time. His cousin, Ralph, did die in a car accident. Ben Everly is gay and he's been in the Seattle area since college. Hank Berkin's teaching at Michigan State and the only time since high school he's been here was when he testified as a character witness at my trial. You might remember him. The rest of us you know"

She said nothing.

He swung the door open. "After you…"

"Maggie!" Dallas called. "Is that you?"

"Yes." She walked into his office. "Good morning."

"Good morning." His smile was broad, his eyes sharp as they cut from her toward the doorway. "Missed you at breakfast."

"I wanted to get work done before we start." Dallas opened his mouth, but she kept talking. "We'll head to Rambler Farm first, to question Charlotte Blankenship again. She must know more than she said yesterday. But first, let me tell you what Doranna Ruskin had to say."

Dallas lowered his eyes, the creased lids hiding his expression, as he listened.

At the end, he said. "We will require your chauffeuring skills once more. My vehicle remains incapacitated."

"Fine."

✧   ✧   ✧   ✧

IT WASN'T THAT simple.

Dallas received a phone call. His grimace and exaggerated shrug indicated it wouldn't be short.

Carson left and she heard his office door close.

She hadn't touched anything. He wouldn't know she'd been in there unless Scott told him. Still, while she retreated to the hallway to email Nancy, she kept an eye on his door.

It remained closed. She called the sheriff, filling Gardner in on what Doranna Ruskin had said.

"If Laurel was seeing someone in secret…" She let it hang.

Carson? He could have learned a lesson from courting Pan publicly. He could have persuaded Laurel Tagner to be discreet.

"We'll follow up with that hair place in Lynchburg, see if we can get a line on anything."

As the sheriff spoke, Carson's door opened. Its light showed Scott, at his desk, facing her, clearly listening.

Whatever they'd heard didn't matter, since Carson had been there to hear the original, and Scott was privy to the investigation.

But she concluded her call without suggesting that whoever went to Lynchburg take along photos of Carson.

Scott hopped up. "Maggie, are you okay? Dallas was telling me about the scare you had last night. How awful."

"Someone rearranged some of my things, that's all."

"But someone getting in—If you'd been there—"

"I wasn't and it won't be an issue going forward."

He nodded. "New keys. Dallas said. Way, way past time. If you ever need help, day or night…"

She couldn't get away without putting his number in her phone.

She went outside for "fresh air," but actually to make her next two calls out of earshot of all denizens of Monroe & Associates.

The first thing Nancy said was, "Henry Zales was the divorce attorney Pan Wade consulted even before Carson got back in town, right?"

Of course, he was. Maggie had to be losing her mind. First to forget details of Wade's alibi and now this.

Nancy reported Chester Bondelle and Henry Zales, the lawyers Maggie had asked her to check, showed no red flags of any kind.

"Speaking of red flags," she continued, "Vic's snorting like a bull with one flapping in front of him. Making noises about you being on a boondoggle."

She'd known he'd be restive with her out of pocket, but not this fast. "I just got here."

"Better call," Nancy said.

She did that next.

The first bad sign was Sheila put her right through.

"Answer your goddamn phone."

"The signal up here's like Swiss cheese. About a tenth of the calls get through and a quarter of the messages."

He humphed. "I want you in tomorrow."

"No. The sheriff requested my help. You agreed. We've barely scratched the surface—"

"You don't work for Gardner. You work for me—"

"And the people of Fairlington County."

He ignored that. As usual. "—I'm not waiting around forever while you work out the burr in your butt about this case."

He hung up.

All in all, that went better than she'd expected.

CHAPTER TWENTY-EIGHT

BACK INSIDE, SHE heard Dallas saying good-bye to his caller, and entered his office. "Ready?"

"Near enough."

When Dallas paused at the corner of the desk, leaning one hand on it, picking up a pen with the other and cocking his head at her, she wondered if it was a ruse to take a few extra breaths.

"You know, Maggie," said Dallas. "You're different from when you were here before."

"Things change in more than four years."

He waved his hand. "A few wrinkles, a gray hair or two, deepen a woman's allure for a man of sense."

"Thanks a lot," she said dryly.

"Dallas, that's absolutely—" Scott started in protest.

It was drowned by a sound it took a second for her to name.

J.D. Carson's laughter.

She caught her jolt before it became a full-blown cessation of motion. Except Carson noticed.

Scott's protest continued, now audible. "… a lovely woman—beautiful—and deserving of the best treatment, even if that boyfriend of hers—"

She pulled out her keys and—letting a hint of impatience seep in—said, "I left the car at the guesthouse. I'll be right back."

"No need, no need. Scott, run get Maggie's vehicle, will you?"

"Sure." Scott snagged the keys from her and trotted into the hallway's dimness.

"Wait. I—"

"There's a backdoor," Carson said, as if that had been the basis of her objection.

"I don't need valet service. And—"

Dallas interrupted as if the subject hadn't changed. "That's not the difference I detect. It's an attitude."

He tapped a finger against his chin, gazing out the window. Then focused on her.

She'd discovered long ago that the way to handle this game was to not play. That worked in a squad room full of testosterone trying out the new ACA and would work now.

"I can't quite…" Dallas murmured.

"It's because she's not trying a case."

"Explain yourself, J.D.," Dallas demanded.

She set her purse's strap on her shoulder.

Carson said, "This is different from trying a case. You have to be open to everything, taking it all in, anything can be important. For a trial, it's narrowed. You take in only that trial. And Maggie—" He stepped back, clearing the doorway as she reached it. "—filters everything else out, focusing completely on the trial."

"I believe you're correct, J.D. I do believe that is the difference I detect in our Maggie. This suits you, my dear." Dallas checked the narrow window beside the door, then straightened. "J.D., open the door please, let our Maggie out into the sunshine. She'll want to be involved in this."

"Involved in—?"

Carson had the door open with one hand and the other under her elbow. She could have escaped his hand, stood her ground, but the open door revealed Charlotte Blankenship Smith about to walk past.

"Charlotte, my dear," Dallas said from behind Maggie, crowding her forward. "Good morning, good morning."

Maggie quickly stepped down to the sidewalk. Dallas was out behind her faster than she would have believed. Carson came last.

Had Dallas seen Charlotte coming? Had his huffing and puffing been a ruse to time their exit?

Maybe.

Charlotte slowed, said a monotone "Morning" in the direction of the street, then took her next step.

Dallas blocked her path. "How propitious you were walking by as we came out."

Maggie updated *maybe* to *probably*.

"I'm certain," he continued, "you're most anxious to hear how our inquiries are proceeding."

"Sheriff Gardner keeps the judge apprised of the investigation."

That didn't stop Dallas. "We've been talking to any number of people who knew Laurel, getting a picture of her, a well-rounded picture. We've come to hear … well, she was a healthy young woman and beautiful."

Charlotte stared at him without expression.

"We'd like to hear your take on it, Charlotte. Give you an opportunity to tell us the truth of the matter."

"What makes you think you haven't heard it?"

Dallas didn't blink at the blandly hostile words. "It would be most helpful to the effort to find Laurel's killer if we knew who her most recent, ah, interests were. Who better to know than a sister?"

"I did not spend time keeping up with such transitory matters."

Dallas pulled in air in apparent preparation for another try, but Maggie figured his head had met the brick wall more than enough.

She asked, "Did you know Laurel and Pan went to the same hair stylist at the time of Pan's murder?"

Charlotte's gaze came to Maggie. "Of course. Doranna."

"They must have crossed paths there and at family and other events."

"Nothing to bother about."

Maggie's head started to ache from contact with that brick wall. "As the sister and friend of these two women, you are in a unique position—knowing them well and observing them interacting with others. Your insights might help us know if there is a connection, which in turn might help solve these murders."

Charlotte stared off absently. Just when Maggie became certain she wouldn't reply, her voice started slowly.

"What people didn't know is she had a blind spot. She thought the way people responded to her on the surface was how they truly felt."

"Who?"

"I don't know any particulars. Now," she added, already moving, "I have a great many duties to perform before the memorial."

Charlotte walked away with no more expression than when they'd started.

"That was…" Maggie stopped.

"Yes, indeed," Dallas said cheerfully, as her car with Scott behind the wheel came around the corner. "What was that old song about sisters?"

Maggie knew immediately. From *White Christmas*. Vivian's favorite movie. "There were never such devoted sisters? Somehow that doesn't fit the Blankenship sisters."

"Ah, but there's another line in the song, about no sister better get between me and my man."

She waited for him to explain. He didn't.

"You think that's what she was saying? She and Laurel wanted the same man?" Ed? Really? Or someone from when they were younger. Someone Charlotte might have had a crush on and Laurel stole away. Rick Wade? Or—She glanced at Carson. "I thought what she said about a blind spot meant Laurel didn't recognize the dark side of someone she knew. That she only saw the surface. What about that?"

"Maybe." Rather than elaborating, Dallas waved Carson to the front seat and hefted himself into the backseat.

She thanked Scott and got behind the wheel.

"No opinions, Carson?" If either of them expected her to protest the change in seating arrangements she wasn't going to. It would be easier to catch Carson's few reactions with him in the front seat.

"You and Dallas covered it. Besides, you ever seen three dogs with one bone, Maggie?"

She didn't answer. She looked over her shoulder for traffic. None.

"Two of 'em square off," Carson continued, "while the third sits back and awaits developments. At worst, third one has one dog left to fight. At best, he slips in and grabs the bone while the other two are distracted."

"Just what bone is this you think you'll grab?" She eased away from the curb.

"The truth."

"Right. The truth. And how do you think you'll grab that?" Her sarcasm wasn't subtle. "If her sister doesn't know about Laurel's life leading up to the murder, then I don't see how you hope to—"

"Ho!" Dallas hooted from the backseat. "Your words reveal you as not a sibling, my dear. There are many and many a sibling who would tell a stranger on the street his most intimate secrets before confiding in a fellow from the same nest. With Rambler Farm now unnecessary, I think Shenny's next, don't you, J.D.?"

"Yeah. Turn left here," he said to Maggie.

"The sheriff will have covered Laurel's movements in the days leading up to her murder. Standard operating procedure." But she turned.

"Then we shall go for premium operating procedure, including what Doranna said about Barry."

"A right at the stop sign," Carson directed. "One thing I side with Maggie on—just because Charlotte didn't tell us about Laurel's life, doesn't mean she doesn't know."

CHAPTER TWENTY-NINE

SHENNY'S RESEMBLED A shoebox, with a flat roof and narrow windows set into siding above chest-high brick.

Cut off from the highway by a belt of trees, a graveled area fronted the building. Maggie parked beside a maroon pickup, forming the closest thing to a row among the scattered vehicles.

"One thing before we go in," Dallas said from the back. "I heard some about Laurel's business with Henry Zales."

Maggie twisted around to him. "The divorce lawyer Laurel saw in Lynchburg? That was the call you took? Why didn't you tell us in the office or during the drive?"

"I was enjoying spring."

What he was enjoying was springing it on her.

"My source says those two peas weren't so happy in the pod. Eugene'd learned a bit from his first three wives—at least from divorcin' them. Before the fourth wedding, he got himself a real strong lawyer from up your way, Maggie, and had Laurel sign an agreement. Sort of two-barreled affair—a regular pre-nup in case of divorce, but also an agreement on what her allowance would be during the marriage. Could have been a union contract, with cost-of-living increases and raises for seniority and all. Laurel was lookin' to Henry Zales to renegotiate."

"Her attorney volunteered that?"

He gave an easy wave of his hand. "Not saying I talked to Henry Zales. Not saying it at all, though we do go way back. And even if I did talk to him it'd be a matter of confirming, rather than volunteering, because I had an inkling." Dallas' gaze flickered to the back of

Carson's head.

Maggie filed that away, but kept to the main thread. "What argument was Laurel using?"

"According to my source, her only argument was she wanted more. She was mad as a wet hen when Henry Zales told her the agreement didn't leave him a glimmer of daylight. Stirred up the whole office with her exit scene. This was *before* she left Eugene.

"And then, last week, she waltzed in to his office and ordered him to start working on a new document that would give her exactly what she'd wanted. When the matter of Eugene and his lawyer was brought up, she laughed and said his lawyer had no say in it and Eugene would sign all right. She'd made sure of that."

"She'd *made* sure of it—it was already settled?"

He nodded. "That's what she told Henry. I have the name and number for Eugene's lawyer, if we get Eugene to agree he can talk to us."

Maggie looked out the back window past Dallas. "From what you've said, Eugene was nuts about her at the start. If he had enough control over his emotions to be practical then would he reverse himself now when—from what we've heard—the bloom was off the rose and her power over him had waned."

Dallas' eyes lit. "The bloom off the rose, yes, and Laurel's sexual power over him waning. But there are other kinds of power."

"Like?"

"They are as varied as the human race, my dear."

"Can we narrow it down some?" Maggie heard, but didn't respond to Carson's grunt of amusement. "What—?"

But Dallas was maneuvering himself out of the car. She could follow or be left behind.

Carson held open Shenny's glass outer door. A second set of doors opened to a constricted area with benches to either side. Beyond were three arches—to the left opened to a restaurant, straight ahead pointed to restrooms and telephones, to the right could pass for a cave. In the center was a lectern, with a dark-haired smiling woman behind it.

"Why, Dallas Monroe, it's about time you came by. We haven't seen you in a month of Sundays." The woman's smile slid over Maggie, then broadened for Carson. "And J.D.! Well, if this isn't a fine day!"

Carson smiled. "Good to see you, Janice."

"You two young people go on in, and I'll catch up after I say a real hello to Janice here." Dallas gestured to the cave on the right. Carson put his hand under Maggie's elbow. Moving forward was the best way to avoid it.

Carson pointed to a small table beneath a curtained window and across from the bar. Three men sat at the bar's far end, with two other patrons widely separated along the length. A man with gray hair in an uneven ponytail was bartending.

Carson pulled out the chair with its back to the bar, presumably for her.

She took the chair closest to her, angling it. "To interview the bartender, we should be at the bar."

He left the chair she'd refused and took the one opposite her. "Dallas is clearing the decks with Janice. She owns the place. Besides, talking at the bar wouldn't get us a thing from Barry. If customers know he gave up their secrets, he won't hear more. He'll come to us."

"We're supposed to sit here and wait?"

His left eyebrow quirked up. "You could have a drink. Relax. What do you do to relax, Maggie?"

"Read."

"Anything besides case materials and legal opinions?"

She ignored that, because the answer was no. Remembering her conversation with Jamie, she said, "Garden a little."

"You find that relaxing, do you?" He didn't believe her.

"No."

He was going to laugh again.

She moved the dish with pink and blue packets of fake sweetener to the precise center of the table, prepared.

No sound came from him.

She looked up. He watched her, laughter lightening his eyes without mobilizing his mouth.

Abruptly, she said, "What you said—about what it's like when someone's trying a case."

"When *you're* trying a case," he corrected immediately.

"That was based on your experience?"

"You mean my handful of times representing a client in a court-room? No. Most haven't lasted long enough to need to filter out anything except a couple flies buzzing around. I recognized it four and a half years ago in you. I've seen it in combat."

"Oh, come on!" she scoffed. "You're likening my concentration during trial to a soldier in combat? What, I'm afraid to die? I'm prepared to kill an enemy?"

He rubbed his chin. "Could be—afraid to die, prepared to kill an enemy, in legal terms. To make sure no one storms your position, to defend your certainty."

"If I'm not certain, I don't go to trial."

His mouth stretched in a quick, sardonic grin. "No claiming you were just following orders for you." He added a nod, as if he expected no different. But his gaze went far away. "When a soldier's in combat, there's a sort of bubble … a zone…" Slowly, he brought his gaze back to hers. "That's what I saw in you. When you tried me. And at other trials."

Something went up her spine. "What other trials?"

"A few of yours in Fairlington."

"You haven't—I've never seen you."

One side of his mouth lifted. "I wasn't part of those trials. I was filtered out."

Was it possible? Maybe. After one of her earliest cases, Jamie and Ally said they'd been in the courtroom and she'd had no idea.

"Why would you go to my trials?"

"To be a decent defense lawyer, I need to know how the best prosecutors operate to counter their moves. You're a damned good prosecutor."

She'd done the mirror image—watching top-notch defense attorneys, no matter how hard it had been.

It was reasonable. Yet his answer didn't satisfy her.

"You were fascinating to watch," he added. "Determined to make everyone see it your way."

"As I said, I don't prosecute unless I know they're guilty."

"Know." He hooked one elbow over the back of his chair. "Such certainty." She braced for a probe. Instead, he said, "Whatever Dallas says to the contrary, that on-a-mission concentration suits you."

"Gee, thanks." Her monotone had more impact than sarcasm.

She shifted to see Dallas still talking to Janice. The bartender moved from a solitary customer to the trio. Carson continued to watch her.

"This is a waste of time." She pushed her chair back.

"Dallas is coming."

"Here you are," Dallas said, as if he'd been searching for them. He took the chair facing the bar. "Any moment now, any moment."

Before she could ask what that meant, the gray-haired bartender showed up. "Can I get you folks something?"

"Have a seat, Barry," offered Dallas.

The bartender gripped the back of the empty chair. "That's okay, I've got work."

"Janice is covering for you, and she said to take all the time you need."

Barry's hands tightened enough to show white at the knuckles, then he pulled the chair back and sat.

"You might not remember me, I'm Dallas Herbert Monroe. I knew your momma, Barry. Fine woman she was. This is Ms. Maggie Frye, and I think you know J.D."

Barry dipped his head toward her and mumbled, "Carson." He looked at Dallas. "What's this about?"

"We'd like to talk to you about Laurel Tagner."

"You and everybody in the county." He sounded more pleased than disapproving.

"This is an official enquiry."

That was pushing it, but Maggie didn't object.

"Official?" His voice flattened. "I already talked to the sheriff. Told him when she was last in, who she was with, all that."

"Good, then you've cleared the surface and we can get below it. I understand Laurel's been coming here regular for quite a while."

"Not real regular, not recent."

"What's recent? Last week?"

"More'n that."

"How much more?"

Barry darted a look over his shoulder. Janice, now behind the bar, looked back. Barry's shoulders jerked and he faced them with a new attitude. "Not as much since she moved back to Rambler Farm."

"But before?"

"Sure. Ever since she was, uh, legal age."

"What about her sister?" Maggie asked.

"Charlotte? In here? No way."

"When Laurel came in after she moved back to Rambler Farm," Maggie pursued, "who did she come in with?"

"Nobody. Always walked in alone."

"Who'd she leave with?"

"Always walked out alone."

She'd kept Carson's face in view as she'd asked and Barry answered those questions. Still, it surprised her when Carson interposed, "In between walking in and walking out?"

Barry smirked, then tried to cover it. "Little bit of everything with three legs. She was a pretty girl, who didn't hide it. Most everyone appreciated that. She had 'em all wrapped 'round her little finger."

"Ever cross your mind one of them might have killed her?" Dallas asked.

"Nah. They were the same guys sniffing around her since she was a kid. If they were going to kill her for being a tease, they'd have done it years ago. Besides…"

"Besides?" Dallas insisted smoothly.

Barry's eyes darted to her, then Carson. He sighed. "She said some stuff that made me think there might be somebody else. Not one of the regular clowns."

"What did she say?" Maggie asked.

"Small stuff, you know? One time she said something like people you thought would never be worth knowing could come in real useful.

That sort of thing."

"She never mentioned a name?" Carson asked.

He could be asking to be sure Laurel hadn't mentioned him, though that was a gamble.

"Nah. Said she'd promised. Said it wasn't like any other relationship she'd ever had. I thought she enjoyed making it a mystery."

"Was it like her to keep a secret like that?" Dallas asked.

"Nah. She liked talking, especially about whichever guy was wrapped tightest around her finger at the moment."

"You believe this mystery person was a man?" Maggie slipped in.

It *could* have been Carson. He might have intrigued Laurel, someone dangerous, someone outside her social group. He could have sworn her to secrecy to avoid gossip or because it would end his cordial relationship with the judge.

"Laurel didn't give much thought to women," the bartender said.

"Maybe that's what was different this time," Dallas said.

Barry shrugged.

"Who were some of these guys she had wrapped around her finger?" Carson asked.

"Christ, I could be here all night. Easier to say who wasn't."

"Even after she married Eugene?"

"Sure."

"Married men?" Was Dallas directing this away from Carson?

"Yup. She liked married men—and those about to be."

Maggie asked, "Did she mention Carson?"

The grooves across Barry's forehead shot up. "You kidding, lady?"

"No."

Barry switched to Carson, whose expression hadn't changed from concentrated interest, then back to her. "Not that I ever heard."

"What about Teddie Barrett?"

"Teddie?" His voice rose with surprise, possibly something more. "What about him?"

"Did you see Teddie in here?"

"A few times," he said cautiously.

"Drinking?"

"That's what folks do here."

"With anyone in particular?"

Muscles shifted in his face. Was that supposed to be amusement? Or was it slyness pretending to be amusement? "You're not thinking he was one of Laurel's entourage, are you?"

"You're saying Teddie Barrett didn't drink with Laurel?" Maggie pursued.

"Yeah, I'm saying."

"Who did he drink with?"

"Anybody who'd buy him a drink."

"Did that include Carson?"

Barry's brows rose. He turned to Carson. "She's really not part of your fan club is she?"

Neither was Barry, apparently.

Carson's expression never changed. "What's the answer, Barry?"

"Not that I recall."

WHILE DALLAS WANDERED toward the trees to call Scott at the office, Carson returned her stare over the top of the car. Nothing about his look invited questions. That never stopped her.

"Do you maintain you never gave Teddie alcohol?"

"Yes."

"And you have no idea how he happened to be drunk that night you happened to take him home, the night before he happened to die—or be killed?"

"That's correct. I have no idea." He added, "It's not your fault."

"There's an entire universe of things that aren't my fault."

He gave her a steady look. "These murders."

These murders. But another—?

With a vinegar sharp twist of her lips, she said, "You're telling me not to blame myself for not convicting you?"

"I'm telling you not to blame yourself for prosecuting me."

"And of course, the secondary meaning you're trying to convey is that I let the real murderer go?" That didn't carry the bite it needed. Because one or the other statement was true.

"Not you alone. Us. All of us. Dallas and me and most of Bedhurst County, all of us who knew I hadn't murdered Pan, but didn't find out who did."

He was good. He was very, very good.

"This is a waste of—"

"I've noticed something that's changed since you prosecuted me."

She didn't respond.

"You get involved in investigating your cases now."

"A good prosecutor needs to know—"

"You didn't do it before."

"I was learning. And—"

"You're obsessive about it. Won't go to trial without delving into the investigation yourself."

"I am not—"

"Obsessive. That's your rep. But what I've got to wonder is why someone as obsessive as you are never came back and checked this case again."

"I never doubted your guilt."

Slowly he pivoted as he opened the car door, then came back in as close as possible with the car between them and looked over its top at her. "Most lawyers are better liars."

"I have never doubted your guilt," she repeated.

In the background, Dallas ended his call.

Carson's eyelids dropped lower. "Yes, you did. And we both know when."

She snorted, dropped into the car seat, jammed the key in, and adjusted her seatbelt.

He got in, faced her. She had to still to hear his low voice. "If you stop cross-examining me, I might tell you more."

"Cross-examining is what I do."

"Doesn't always work, though, does it?"

Before it deteriorated into a staring contest, Dallas opened the back door and got in.

"Let's make another stop while we're out here on the highway," he said.

"Where? Did you learn something from the call?"

"One thing at a time, Maggie, dear. We're not far from the place of business of Eugene Tagner's second wife."

"Why would we want to talk to Eugene Tagner's second wife?"

"Because Eugene's been seein' Renee," Dallas said.

Maggie faced Carson's profile. "You said that when we talked to Tagner—he'd been seeing Renee. How'd you know?"

"Heard some things."

"As have I. But what's most interesting is what I haven't heard." Monroe's eyelids drooped sleepily. "Neither Louelle nor Janice shared with me exactly what Eugene and Renee have been doing when they're together."

CHAPTER THIRTY

"NOW, BEYOND THAT stand of rhododendron, you make two quick rights, and be prepared to climb," Dallas concluded the directions that had brought them east of town.

They stopped in a parking area softened by lush plantings that directed Maggie's eyes to a log building set farther uphill, flanked by trees swelling with buds amid a scattering of evergreens.

It was a skillful blend of old and new. The log construction, a massive stone chimney, wide front porch overhung by a shake roof gave the impression of a cabin that had been there for centuries. Skylights in the roof, the pristine condition, and a discreet sign promising "Luxury Mountain Homes" assured modern amenities would be attended to.

One step inside the double doors, and Maggie caught her breath.

The back of the building was mostly glass and two stories high, with a view of a gorge, opening to a meadow with roll upon roll of rounded mountain tops beyond. A loft lined the room, with offices on either side of a central sitting area.

"May I help you?" a fresh-faced girl asked from a reception desk.

"We're here to see Renee," Dallas said, leaving it open to interpretation whether they had an appointment.

"She's in a meeting. If I could let her know you're here...?"

"That would be fine. Tell her Dallas Herbert Monroe is here for a little word, along with two colleagues."

The girl led them to the seating area in front of the stone fireplace. Carson snagged the chair with the best view of the room. Maggie settled for second-best, the chair at the other end of the coffee table.

Dallas sank into the deep couch, leafing through a magazine.

Maggie's phone picked up a signal to her surprise. Each time she looked up from checking email and messages, Carson was surveying the surroundings.

He stood as a woman somewhere between thirty and sixty approached. She gave an impression of softness—rounded figure, loose hair to her shoulders, easy slacks and tunic—except her eyes. They were shrewd and intelligent.

She smiled at Carson, gave Maggie a cordial nod, then rested a hand on Dallas' shoulder.

"It's been forever since you came to visit me. I don't believe you've ever been here to our new office."

"It's my loss, Renee. Missing seeing this magnificent facility and even more missing seeing you."

"My, you are a flatterer. Is that why you've come today? To end the missing of me?" It carried a hint of an edge.

"Of course," he said promptly. "And, perhaps, to call on your expertise in a matter or two."

"Now if I thought you were ready to make use of my expertise, to sell Monroe House, and move to one of our modern, convenient homes, I'd be beside myself. But if I can help you in any way, you know I am most willing. I tell you what, let's sit on the porch a bit. It's sunny for now, and I can indulge my vice."

Renee Tagner led the way without waiting for a response.

At the end of the porch, she gestured them to a pair of settees at right angles, extracting a cigarette and lighter from a pocket.

With a vague phrase about the investigation, Dallas introduced Maggie, then gave her a nod, inviting her to start the questions.

She waited until Renee Tagner exhaled smoke and looked at her.

"Tell me about Eugene."

"Hah. How long've you got? I've known him since he was twenty-seven and I was twenty. Started off as his secretary and receptionist when he was breaking into insurance. Man can't organize a paper bag. I ran the office. Got my real estate license when we got offered a deal on some land. Developed and sold that parcel off, and that was the start of this."

Her gesture took in the building and grounds.

"Impressive. Business must be good?"

"Could always be better." Her eyes narrowed. "You're not here to talk about my business. You want to know if Eugene would have killed Laurel. I'll tell you—no. And it's not because I've got the notion somebody I've known so long and so well isn't capable of murder. Bull. Most everybody's capable of it, if pushed."

Renee tapped cigarette ash over the railing.

"And for some a touch'd be as good as a push. Sure would be interesting to know how Barry up at Shenny's comes to have a fancy new truck from Wade Motors each of the past four years. Doranna, bless her heart, proves a woman can be as big a fool as a man, but she doesn't have that sort of money to give him."

Interesting. On many levels, including Doranna and Barry. As well as Renee mentioning Barry. Could she know they'd just talked to him?

In this county? Hell, yes.

"But that's not what you came to talk to me about, either, now is it? Let me tell you about Eugene. He married his first wife because he was young and stupid and thought that was the only way to get sex from her. He married me because he wasn't quite so young or so stupid, and he knew I was good for him. Plus—" Lines of humor fanned at the corners of her eyes. "—it sure as hell was the only way he'd get sex from me."

The lines at the corners of her eyes shifted, joined by lines around her mouth. Faint remnants of pain, long mastered. "He divorced me and married Cissy because he was still stupid enough to think it was the only way to get sex from her. Why the fool didn't set the tart up as a mistress is beyond me. I would've had to work like a demon to make it reasonable that I didn't know, but it wouldn't have lasted long, and the long-term payoff would've made the short-term inconvenience worth it. Sorry if I've shocked you, Ms. Frye."

"Not at all."

The lines of humor returned. "I figure love and all's like business—you gotta look at your ROI—return on investment. Once you put it in those terms you avoid mistakes from silly things like hurt feelings, pride, and such."

Eminently sensible, Maggie almost said aloud.

"But Eugene was a fool, and once he asked for the divorce, my hands were tied."

"You did get control of the business," Dallas murmured.

"Of course. He would've run it into the ground in a year, eighteen months. And I would've had to start all over. My God, he was talking about tearing this place down and building a *personal architectural statement.* No concept at all of what city folks come to the mountains for. So, I set it up that he and the tart had enough money to live in his architectural statement, where it wouldn't hurt my bottom line while offending the fewest eyes possible."

She grimaced. "Got to admit I never thought they'd get that far. Eugene'd been nursing pretensions about modern architecture as long as I knew him. But he and the tart never would've gotten around to building that boil if she hadn't found a picture in a magazine."

"How did you get the business, Renee?" Carson asked. "I've wondered."

She grinned at him, and Maggie realized the older woman had a deep reservoir of charm she hadn't bothered to tap in this interview. Yet.

"I got myself a nice, young lawyer—a lot like you, J.D., not as handsome, but otherwise a whole lot like you—and I molded him. Give the boy credit, not only was he smart enough to let me, but he learned real fast. He's got himself a real nice practice now." She chuckled. "In fact, he's done real well out of Eugene. Laurel, naturally, went another direction. Henry Zales isn't a bad choice. But he's a sight too conventional for my taste. Not to say he wouldn't have gotten Laurel more'n she deserved. Course I set it up to keep their hands off the business. Her and Cissy and even Eugene. But they did have their hands deep in his pockets."

More ash went over the railing. "So, back to what I was saying. Eugene was gettin' tired of the tart, when along comes Miss Laurel Blankenship, displaying her wares. No more subtle than the tart, but

Eugene had learned a thing or two. Tried to get her into bed without marriage, but Laurel held out. 'Bout the only time she did from what I hear," she added without heat. "The girl knew what she wanted and how to get it. In that way, she reminded me of myself. Maybe not as smart—"

"And without the ethics," Carson said.

"Why, thank you, J.D." Renee smiled at him from under her lashes. "How sweet."

"I do hate to rush you, Renee," Dallas said. "Maybe it's my poor old brain, but how's this building up to your certainty that Eugene didn't kill Laurel?"

Maybe his poor old brain, her ass, Maggie thought. He wanted to divert attention from Carson's indictment of Laurel as being devoid of ethics.

If they'd been having an affair and he'd been disillusioned...

"Because it doesn't fit Eugene's pattern. Sorry, Dallas. Sorry, J.D., but Ms. Frye here and I know men follow a pattern in affairs of the heart. More'n likely it starts with their mamas like those old Greek plays say. But whatever it is, unless they're smart enough to heed a strong woman, they keep repeatin' it. That's Eugene. What does he do when he decides he wants a woman? He marries her. If he's already married, he divorces the previous one. Killing? That's not Eugene's pattern."

"But Eugene wasn't going to divorce Laurel. They'd reconciled," Maggie said. "And this time he didn't have another woman he wanted to marry."

With bland certainty, Renee said, "Yes, he did. He does."

"Who?"

"Me."

A long beat of silence was broken by Dallas' amused and impressed hoot. "Renee, you are a one. Yes, you are."

Maggie frowned at him. Had he known all along?

She leaned toward Renee. "You're saying Eugene *was* going to divorce Laurel?"

"Yep."

"But Eugene told us they were reconciling."

Renee sighed. "Yes, he did. Told you and the sheriff. Poor baby. I'd instructed him early on to let everyone believe that. When Laurel got murdered, he froze up and did exactly what I'd told him, and wouldn't you know I was in Atlanta, and he was so worried about ya'll tracing calls, he didn't even call me. My assistant told me about the murder, and I cut my trip short, but it wasn't 'til I got back Tuesday night I heard what all had been happenin' and what Eugene told you."

"You maintain they weren't reconciling?" Maggie said.

"Oh, no, they were reconciling. Temporarily. It was what you might call a strategic move. See, early on, and under the influence of the tax accountant cousin of one of his poker buddies—no longer Eugene's accountant, I can guarantee you—my poor baby had Laurel sign some papers, thinking he was smart to not have his name on them. They were reconciling long enough to get that squared away, and then there'd be a permanent break."

"You approved of that?"

"Honey, like I said, it's all a matter of long-term payoff versus short-term inconvenience." A slight tuck appeared between her brows. "Course, I wasn't counting on Laurel getting murdered. Now, I'll be taking Eugene to that new sheriff and explaining it all. Dallas, I do hope you'll vouch for me and how Eugene is, since Sheriff Gardner doesn't hardly know us more'n to say hello."

"I would be happy to give you a character reference, and to describe Eugene as the fool he is, if Sheriff Gardner's willing to hear it," he said.

"Can't ask better. Thank you kindly, Dallas."

Maggie interrupted the Virginia courtesy fest. "But you, Renee, you're not part of Eugene's pattern as you described it."

"Recall what I said about how heeding a strong woman could break the pattern. Eugene finally got his brain around knowin' I'm the exception to his pattern. Because there's more than sex. He can talk to me. He can trust me. And he can relax. That's why he keeps coming back to me, one way or another."

CHAPTER THIRTY-ONE

THEY LEFT RENEE still smoking on the porch.

"Well, that was right interesting." Dallas' chuckle came along with a creak as he settled himself. "Renee and Eugene back together. What do you know."

"If she was telling the truth," Maggie said.

"She's too smart to lie about it." Carson raised a hand in acknowledgment of Renee's wave from the porch as Maggie steered toward the entrance to the highway.

"She could have killed Laurel to be sure she was out of the way. Atlanta's not that far. We—The sheriff should check her alibi closely. Maybe Eugene was wavering. Maybe the papers he had Laurel sign were a bigger deal than Renee let on."

Carson objected, "She's also too smart to need to kill Laurel to get her out of the way—for love or money."

"Eugene could have done the killing, and she's trying to clean up after him." She stared straight ahead, not pulling onto the highway.

It wasn't significant she was tossing out scenarios that featured someone other than Carson as murderer. She was doing what Bel said—checking all angles.

"Possible. But I don't think so."

"Wouldn't put the business at risk," Dallas agreed. "This does shine a light on what power Laurel wielded to force changes in the agreement. Another call on Eugene is in order."

Maggie snorted. "He'll have his orders long before we could get there. Don't you think she was overselling how ineffectual he is, trying to make out like he couldn't possibly have killed Laurel? Though it was interesting what she said about Barry's new trucks."

"From Wade," Carson said. "He needs to provide some answers."

"On less than a rumor?" she scoffed. "She fed us that tidbit at least partly to steer us away from Eugene. Maybe we could go back to Shenny's, but—"

"But," Dallas picked up, "same issue as with Rick Wade. We need more information before we tackle Barry again."

"Leverage," she agreed.

"Exactly. Let's head to the office. See what we can find out, pick up some lunch. Oh, yes, and Scott said he might have materials for us."

"The transcript?" Maggie turned toward town. "Does this mean you're finally looking at what the sheriff actually wants from us?"

Apparently unaffected by her sarcasm, Dallas murmured, "Could be, could be."

✧   ✧   ✧   ✧

DALLAS SETTLED BEHIND his desk with satisfaction.

J.D. had gone to his office. Maggie sat at the table and pulled out her gadget.

Scott came in. "The phone is leaving me no time to do any real work at all, Dallas."

"The transcript?" Maggie didn't look up.

"That's what I'm saying. I'll never finish at this rate. If you'd get me an assistant. Evelyn could come in and answer—"

"Evelyn DuPree is not your assistant." He stopped himself. Dina had not done right by the boy, spoiling, then ignoring him. But when it came to thinking Evelyn … No. "Set the recording to answer, check every hour, and call back as needed. Now, what's this material from the sheriff you mentioned on the phone?"

"I heard from a contact that a number of reports were available. I knew Maggie would want to see—"

Maggie stopped tapping on her gadget. "What reports?"

"—fool Abner thought he wouldn't give them to me, but I set him straight. I—"

"Why don't you bring us those reports, and tell J.D. to join us. Thank you, Scott. Good job."

The boy came back with an armload of papers, which he took to Maggie. Dallas didn't blame him—she was decidedly more attractive than Scott's old cousin.

Maggie frowned. "Aren't these available digitally?"

"Dallas still prefers paper," Scott said. "There's preliminary forensics and initial interviews. But the one you'll find most interesting, Maggie—" Scott placed a stapled set of papers in front of her, the rest stacked to the side. "—has interviews with staff at Rambler Farm."

Maggie gave Scott a sharp look, but didn't voice her apparent objection to his reading the material.

J.D. came in, took two sections from the bottom of the stack, handed one to Dallas and sat on the sofa with the other.

Dallas began reading the report on the sheriff's interview with Eugene. Nothing there beyond what he'd told them.

Maggie, having finished reading, tossed that set of stapled pages onto his desk. He started reading. When he finished, he held the papers out. J.D. came from the sofa and collected them. And around they went.

Not that Dallas couldn't have done the fetching and toting himself. A spell of days running here to there wouldn't do him in, for all that Evelyn kept at him. No, it was the worrisome that dragged on a man of his years.

The worrisome. One of Dina's pet phrases. He probably hadn't used it since she'd passed on. Strange how things like that went through a family.

He contemplated Maggie for a minute. Now, her family was interesting. Real interesting.

As soon as the last report left her hands, she started typing away at her little gadget.

Dallas handed the last report to J.D., and considered what he'd read.

The full-time cook-housekeeper said little. But a place like Rambler Farm required a lot of upkeep. Landscapers, carpet cleaners, window washers, furniture experts, appliance repairmen. Folks who counted Rambler Farm as one client among many, and thus talked freely.

None had provided a full picture, but, together, their observations painted one.

In varying tones of pleasure (youngster on the landscaping crew), approval (appliance repairman), discomfort (carpet cleaner), and everything in between (six more accounts) it was revealed Laurel appeared in unexpected areas of the house in her underwear. She showed no discomfort at encountering strangers in this attire. She was hot (youngster on the landscaping crew), flirty (appliance repairman), shameless (carpet cleaner) in these encounters.

What they all agreed on was she put on a special show when it came to her brother-in-law, including rubbing against him "every which way there is" (youngster on the landscaping crew) until he "had a woody you could hang a flag on" (appliance repairman), and was "sweating and red-faced" (carpet cleaner.)

Since they were at the house at different times, it was not an isolated incident.

They were divided about Ed's reaction, but all cast him in a passive role. The judge was never on hand, but two reported Charlotte arriving on the scene.

The appliance repairman had been the appreciative recipient of Laurel's flirting while she wore a nightie that showed more than it concealed. Until her brother-in-law walked into the breakfast room and she'd immediately gone to Ed Smith. With the laundry room door open, the repairman watched. She kept advancing, Ed kept retreating with worried glances in the direction of the front door.

Ed grabbed his briefcase, and had almost reached the entryway when Charlotte appeared.

The repairman said Charlotte took in the situation, including Ed's physical state. Having had other encounters with Charlotte, the repairman mostly closed the door. He couldn't see what happened next, but he heard.

Charlotte sounded calm when she said Ed would be late if he didn't leave for the office. Ed hightailed it out.

Charlotte then told Laurel to go to her room and put on clothes.

Laurel laughed, saying she had on just the right amount of clothes.

Less calmly, Charlotte hissed something about not airing dirty laundry in front of the help.

Laurel laughed again and said she'd take off her dirty laundry right then and there.

He'd heard Charlotte heading down the hallway, her angry voice growing more distant, and Laurel laughing and laughing, apparently pursuing her sister.

The youngster from the landscaping crew said Charlotte stopped cold at the doorway to the sunroom where Laurel appeared to be trying to give Ed a lap dance, while he remained stiff—in more ways than one—in his chair. Then she strode in, slapped Laurel hard enough to send her to the floor, called her *whore*, and walked out. Ed scrambled out of his seat and followed. There'd been raised voices, a distant door closed, and the youngster heard no more from them.

Laurel got off the floor, her face red and her eyes "looking crazy." Then she'd spotted him beyond the window, where he was cleaning out a flower bed.

It took a bit for the deputy to get the boy to say what happened next, but since he'd bragged about it and they had statements from several of his friends on what he'd told them, he finally came out with it: Laurel unhooked her bra, let it drop. Then she beckoned him inside, and they had sex on a chaise.

He was fourteen.

"No phone records," Maggie said as J.D. flipped over the last page of the last report.

"Sheriff might be holding those close to his chest."

She grunted. "Maybe. One thing's clear. We have to go back to Rambler Farm."

"You think this time will be the charm with Charlotte?"

Sometimes that tone of J.D.'s riled Maggie. This time she rolled right past it.

"Not Charlotte. The cook."

CHAPTER THIRTY-TWO

"**Did you see** her answer to whether she knew any connection between Laurel's death and Pan Wade's? *I don't see how there could be.* There's something there," Maggie said.

"It's an expression," J.D. objected.

"That's the response of someone who doesn't want to give the real answer, but isn't willing to outright lie."

"You're accusing her of obstructu—"

"Maybe. Or maybe she doesn't know what she knows. Either way, I'm going to talk to her."

Dallas spoke for the first time. "We'll all go." Wouldn't do to have Maggie running around by herself. "But not now. The meetin' at the high school's about on top of us. Then we go back to Shenny's."

"Shenny's? But this—"

"Renee's hint about the trucks gives us a bit to pry Barry open more. But we need to be there before business picks up for the evenin'. We'll go there from the meetin', then to Monroe House for supper."

"To keep Evelyn from getting after you for missing the careful supper she fixes," J.D. added with a deadpan glint.

Dallas chuckled. "Yes, there is that, keeping in good with Miz Evelyn."

"Forget supper," Maggie snapped. "After Shenny's, Rambler Farm to talk to this cook—"

"We can't go banging on people's doors at suppertime. It's not polite." He saw she was about to say she'd go banging on people's doors at any time. He pulled air from his gut to lend power to his voice. "It makes folks 'round here unsettled. Show up at their door and they feel obliged to invite you in to share their supper. Say yes, and now you're their guest, and asking questions rubs wrong all-round. Say no and you're saying you think you're too good to sit at their table—or they're too bad, because you're suspectin' them of things." He raised his hands, palms up. "See? Better all-round to leave people be at suppertime. As for talkin' to Allarene at Rambler Farm, absolutely not."

She cocked an eyebrow at him, but let him finish. He did believe the girl was improving.

"It will require care to keep from flushin' Allarene full out of reach. At the farm, with her employers right there? No, no. we'd be done-for at the get-go. I'll see she knows we'd like a word—in private. But first, like I said, the meeting, back to Shenny's, then Evelyn's nice supper at Monroe House. Though I could be talked into ice cream and pie at the café after, because it's certain Evelyn won't serve them."

He sobered.

"But Maggie, you're clear right about one thing. We will need to talk to Charlotte again. And keep talking at her until we hear the truth."

Because these reports showed a change from how it had always been between Charlotte and Laurel.

Charlotte had fought back.

Definitely worrisome.

✧ ✧ ✧ ✧

4:52 p.m.

THE SHERIFF CONCLUDED the update with a vague recap of the crime scene scientists' progress, basically amounting to none, but said they were still sifting through the collected soil.

"Hail Mary pass," Wade grumbled from the far side of the group.

Gardner ignored him.

"For those who haven't heard, there's a memorial gathering tomorrow afternoon at Rambler Farm. Open to all."

Before the briefing, Dallas had said they'd like a word with the sheriff. After, he was stopped twice, but eventually reached them.

"Wanted to tell you what we've learned of Laurel's legal machinations, as well as a whiff of the unsavory that's wafted our way," Dallas started. More succinctly than she would have expected, he recapped Laurel's efforts with the Lynchburg lawyer and the hint Renee had fed them about Barry.

Gardner noted the names. "There's nothing I recall from the files. We can run a basic background check. But it'll have to get in line for anything deeper. I don't have the manpower."

"What about Eugene?" Maggie asked.

"His financials are solid. His alibi—" The sheriff waggled his hand.

"His story about reconciling with Laurel might not be any better." She nodded to Dallas, who told what he'd seen and Eugene's reaction.

"I'll talk to Henry, in light of his client's murder—"

"No. If I need you to talk to him, we'll arrange something down the road. Do not approach him. Right now it's enough to know it's not solid."

"Suspect you'll want to talk to Wade, too, but with all you've got to do, we could have a word with Barry," Dallas said, watching the sheriff closely.

No doubt, he saw what she saw. Gardner wanted to do the questioning himself and was practical enough to know he couldn't. He didn't have half the time to do half of what he needed to do.

The sheriff narrowed his eyes. "A word. Nothing official. Report to me. And don't make it so I can't come back to him. Now, what about connections with Pan Wade's murder?"

"Nothing solid."

"But?" Gardner prompted.

"But here's a thread runs through both," Dallas said. "Money."

"Sex," Maggie said at the same time.

The sheriff's grimace might have been intended as a grin. "Two threads. Neither exactly earth-shattering. How many murders don't involve one or the other, if not both?"

Not many, Maggie conceded as they walked out.

She glanced at Carson's unyielding and unrevealing face.

What about a third thread frequently woven in?

Revenge.

CHAPTER THIRTY-THREE

As Carson pulled the outside door of Shenny's open for her again, Maggie turned to him and Dallas. "I'm asking the questions this time."

She lengthened her stride to preserve the head start they'd given her, and went straight to the pony-tailed bartender.

"We have a few more questions." She kept it quiet, but couldn't do anything about two stool-sitters watching them.

Barry heaved a sigh, gave the bar a wipe, and jerked his head toward the far end, protesting when they got there, "I don't have time and I told you everything I know about Laurel's murder—which is nothing."

Monroe and Carson joined them. She didn't look away from Barry.

"It's interesting how often a murder investigation surfaces other crimes." She let that hang.

Barry's face wasn't bad, but he shifted his weight.

"How's business since Laurel's body was found?"

He seemed confused, but said, "Great. Everybody wants to come to her hangout—that's what the paper called Shenny's. Tips are good. Everybody's real generous when they think it might give them the inside scoop."

"But you keep the inside scoop to yourself, don't you? Especially when it's rewarding. Say that nice shiny new Wade Auto truck you get every year."

Dallas had taken a call from the sheriff as they'd arrived and relayed that Gardner said his deputy confirmed Barry had driven a new truck with a Wade Motors sticker each of the past four years.

"I'm in a position to do him good—talking up his cars here. He's grateful. That's all."

"Or maybe he's grateful because you've done him good another way. Have to be something ongoing to keep getting trucks. Some service you're doing him. Or—here's a thought—something you're not doing?"

Barry puffed up with indignation. "I don't know what you're driving at, but—"

"We're driving at what you might know that would make Rick Wade grateful enough to want to see you in a brand new truck each year since—now, how long has it been?" She locked eyes with the bartender. "Four, nearly five years."

Barry dropped his head, indignation deflating.

"Interesting timing. You said you'd told us all you knew about Laurel's murder, what about Pan's?"

His head jerked up. "What? *Whoa*. You're talking crazy, lady. It has nothing to do with—uh, anything."

"Two young women murdered, found in the same place—they might have a lot to do with one another."

"Not with me," he insisted.

"Tell me about her."

His mouth sagged. "Pan? What about her?"

"She frequented this place. What did you talk to her about? Who'd she come in with?"

He'd started shaking his head before she finished the first sentence. "I knew her to say hello, but she was strictly on Janice's side."

"The restaurant," Dallas murmured.

"Yeah," Barry said eagerly. "She came in often enough, but to the restaurant. I don't know that I ever saw her on this side. I told you honest what I knew about Laurel, and I'm telling you honest I know nothing about Pan Wade. Nothing."

He started to step back.

She didn't have enough to push him on the trucks or—by extension—a connection to Wade. Only enough to make him edgy, though that could do more softening up than a week of questions.

But among the things Bel and Landis had taught her was to make it clear you decide when the interview's over, not the interviewee.

"Are you saying that to your knowledge Laurel had no connection to any of the people affected by the murder of Pan Wade?" The question was meant to close off any you-didn't-ask-that excuses.

His eyes flickered. "Didn't say that, now did I?"

Maggie concentrated on keeping her face still. "What connection or connections did she have?"

"Well, it wasn't like she was involved in the murder." Barry glanced at Dallas and Carson, either for confirmation or hoping they'd rescue him.

They said nothing.

"What connection or connections did she have?"

"It was what you said before—about people affected by Pan's murder. One of those things, you know. Not like it was the first time for either of them, or nothing. Only not with each other 'til then. Odds were they'd get around to each other by and by. Only reason to remember was it was right when Pan got killed. That's a connection, I guess."

Maggie pieced together those fragments. "You're saying Rick Wade was having an affair with Laurel Tagner four and a half years ago?"

Barry smirked. "Yeah, I'm saying. Those two went at it like—"

"That's enough." Carson's voice was low and cold.

For the first time, Maggie shifted focus from Barry.

Wouldn't Carson be more surprised if he were hearing for the first time that Pan's husband had been having an affair with Laurel when Pan was murdered?

On the other hand, his training involved controlling and masking emotions. Plus, she'd seen a good number of criminals put on convincing acts.

"All right, I get it. Just the facts," Barry said. "She was Laurel Blankenship when it started, about this time of year, making it five years back, but otherwise, yeah."

"How do you know?" Maggie asked.

"She told me. And one night after closing—about a month before

Pan got killed—I was heading out, and saw Rick's pickup with the dealer tags. Headlights hit them and I saw them doing it. No mistaking." Barry chuckled. "Bet the poor slob who bought that Wade pickup didn't know how it was christened."

"Was the affair still going on when Laurel was killed?"

"No way. Stick with somebody that long, either of them?" He rubbed at the bar with a rag. "Come to think of it, I never saw them together after Pan got killed. Laurel got together with Eugene not long after."

"Who else knew?" Dallas asked.

"Don't know. Wasn't much talk at the time, now I think about it. Not one Laurel bragged about. There were two kinds with her. The ones she kept close, like money tucked in her bra—only a few of those—and the ones she flashed around to impress folks."

"But she told you," Carson said.

"Yeah," Barry said, with no hint of defensiveness. "She liked telling me things. I don't run my mouth. She liked talking—liked it a lot—and who else was she going to tell things to? Tagner after she bagged him? The judge? That sour sister of hers? Besides, she was entertaining. In her way."

"Sounds like you were fond of her."

"I guess you could say—Hey, wait a minute. Are you saying—? You got to be shittin' me." He laughed. He looked at Dallas and Carson, as if sure they would get the joke. "Doranna would kill me if I screwed around on her. And God help me, she'd know. Listen, I gotta get to work. It's not like I can tell you anything that'll help find who murdered those two girls. Honest."

DALLAS TOOK MAGGIE'S arm and demonstrated a surprisingly strong grip when she would have gone toward the restaurant.

"We should question Janice about connections between the victims," Maggie protested.

"What she had to say about Pan is in the file. As for Laurel, she knew her as little as Barry knew Pan. There are those who come here for a pleasant meal, and those who don't. The two sides of Shenny's are divided by a nearly impenetrable wall."

Outside, she said, "Barry knows an awful lot about someone supposedly a customer. Not a bad motive for Doranna."

Dallas shook his head at her subtext. "He's right about Doranna. She'd kill him, not the other woman."

Maggie snorted. "We need corroboration about this supposed mystery lover in Laurel's life. It only comes from Doranna and Barry."

"It matches with the calls," Dallas said. "Need to see if Sheriff Gardner's caught up with that beautician in Lynchburg."

"Hope he doesn't call her a beautician." Maggie started the car. "He won't get a thing out of her."

Carson spoke for the first time. "Wade will be at the dealership. First right, then take a left at the stop sign at the bottom of the hill."

"You think he was Laurel's new love interest? Or repeat love interest. But—Oh. You want to talk to him about having an affair with Laurel five years ago? Barry's information needs to be corroborated before we'd talk to Wade."

"With you or without you I'm talking to the sonuvabitch."

No clenched jaw, no narrowed eyes, no ticking muscle in his cheek, yet J.D. Carson's face displayed the same attitude she'd heard in his voice. Implacable.

If she'd gotten him to show that face at the trial the jurors would have known he was capable of murder.

Discomfort pulsed through her.

Which was stupid. She should be accustomed to reminders of her failure to get him convicted.

"Generally, I would agree with you, Maggie," Dallas said, as if discussing a hypothetical legal nuance. "However, in this case, what we lose by not having more information from additional sources, might be offset by talking to Wade before he likely hears what Barry has told us. Besides, the husband is the most likely suspect."

She started backing the car out. "He had an alibi." She hadn't looked up the details of that alibi yet. Maybe tonight.

"Ah," Monroe drew out the pleased syllable, "you did consider him as a suspect back then."

"I wasn't considering suspects. That was all done before I got handed the case. I read the file. If Wade had been a strong suspect, Carson wouldn't have been on trial."

"It's refreshing to find such trust in one of your temperament, Maggie. Naiveté, I might even say. Of course, you haven't spent much time in a community like this."

"You're saying Wade's family name protected him? Are you going to spout conspiracy theories next?"

"Family is the greatest conspiracy of all. Especially in Bedhurst County."

"If you'd believed that, you would have used it at trial to bolster reasonable doubt. Besides, as I said, Wade had an alibi."

She glanced in the rearview mirror, braked to a stop, then twisted around to Dallas.

His gaze never wavered from the back of Carson's head as he said, "Unlike a prosecutor, a defense attorney must balance sometimes conflicting elements of his obligation to his client."

She got it. She just didn't buy it.

"You expect me to believe Carson instructed you not to go after Wade?" She leaned back against the driver's door, looking at the man in the passenger seat. He offered only his profile. Implacable had lost no ground. "There's sure no love lost between you and Wade. If you and Dallas seriously want to sell me that, you better start talking."

"Alibi," Carson said.

"Yeah, Wade had an alibi. Still, Monroe could have thrown enough dust over any alibi to make the jury wond—Shit."

Because Rick Wade had been the most likely choice for the defense to bring up as an alternative murderer, she'd studied all the material on him, having Ed and Nancy re-interview him, and preparing to interview him herself if necessary.

It hadn't been necessary, because the defense hadn't brought up Wade. That unused prep work had sifted to the bottom of her mental file on *v. Carson*.

Until now.

"Wade's alibi was Laurel."

CHAPTER THIRTY-FOUR

"**WELL, WELL, WELL.**" Dallas murmured. "We arrive at last."

"Wade said he and Laurel were working on a charity event, and according to the sheriff's report, Laurel confirmed it," she said.

She hadn't known then how unlikely it was that Laurel Blankenship bothered to work on a charity event, but she did now.

"You knew he was having an affair with Laurel," she accused Carson.

His silence sat dense with unvoiced thoughts.

She faced Dallas. "Why the hell didn't you use it at trial?"

From the back of Carson's head, his gaze dropped to his hands, bringing his wrists together.

His hands had been tied.

Bull.

"You let your client dictate that you would not use that information? C'mon. Reasonable doubt for tossing some mud, and you wouldn't use it?"

"Tossing mud?" Carson repeated, low and cool. "No. Smearing Pan."

"But you're willing to have it come out now? Why?"

"You think after that—" His head jerked back toward Shenny's. "—it won't come out? If Barry has been blackmailing Wade and his leverage is gone because the authorities know, that affair will be too juicy a piece of gossip to keep to himself."

"In addition," Dallas said, "if Charlotte did, in fact, know her sister's amorous partners, that's another means for the information to emerge."

"If she knew and hasn't said—"

A horn blared. Maggie jumped, looked over her shoulder at a rusted white pickup. She gave an apologetic wave for blocking the exit.

As she faced forward, Carson's profile brought back a moment in the trial.

The one moment during her cross-examination he had not met her gaze fully.

The one moment when he had looked toward his attorney.

The moment when she had asked if he and Pan had talked about her marriage.

Q. Did you also talk about her marriage to Richard Wade at that time?
A. Pan did.
Q. Pan did? You were silent on the subject?
A. Yes.

A waitress from Shenny's had already testified she'd observed Pan weeping and had heard her refer to *my husband*. Maggie had thought Carson was being cute, acknowledging the bare minimum of what was already in the record.

Had he, instead, been reminding his attorney of the limits of what he would testify to?

"There was one thing in the original file that was interesting. Pan went to Rambler Farm the week before she died and had a long conversation with Charlotte. Perhaps another try at Charlotte is in order."

CHAPTER THIRTY-FIVE

"FOUR AND A half years ago, you told the sheriff Pan Wade came here the week before she was killed. Why did she come here?" Maggie asked.

Charlotte shook her head.

The two of them were in a glassed-in room Maggie suspected was the sunroom described in the statement by the youngster from the landscaping crew.

When she and Dallas and Carson had arrived, they were admitted by Allarene. The Rambler Farm household was finishing dessert. The judge welcomed them all into the dining room. But Charlotte insisted she and Maggie withdraw, while "the gentlemen enjoy their cigars and brandy."

Good Lord, what century was this woman from?

Not that Maggie objected. Talking to Charlotte solo suited her fine.

She'd started by asking about Wade's alibi for Pan's murder.

"I have no idea if he was with Laurel," Charlotte said coolly. "They were not at the meeting for the charity auction. I was."

More questions didn't garner more details, so she'd moved on to Charlotte seeing Pan shortly before her murder.

"What are you denying? That you said that? That Pan came here the week before she died, because we have other statements—"

"I did not say it to the sheriff. That would have been tolerable. Instead, he sent an underling to get my statement."

Definitely not this century.

"What did Pan talk about?"

"I've said all this before."

Maggie could try to hammer at Charlotte, or she could finesse. "We find having people repeat information frequently brings up more detail. Especially with people who have a lot on their minds—many responsibilities. Someone with many other things to deal with can't remember everything the first time. Repetition brings more out with people like you."

Charlotte bought it. "She said she came by to visit. But it wasn't long before it became clear she was troubled. About her marriage to Rick. She cried."

"She confided in you because you'd known each other so long?"

"Yes."

"Any other reason?"

Charlotte gazed at Maggie's face, but she had no sense of the other woman probing past the surface.

When Charlotte didn't answer, Maggie suggested, "Perhaps she confided in you because of your connection—an indirect connection—with the immediate cause of her marital problems? If there'd been gossip—and you're far too socially astute to think there wasn't— when the gossip reached Pan, she might naturally come to you and—"

"I hope you are not saying I was the one who told Pan—or anyone else—her husband was screwing Laurel all over this county."

Maggie had actually been angling toward the idea of Pan coming to Charlotte as a source of information. But this was too damned interesting a thread not to follow.

"It would make sense. Your sister, your friend. Who better to let the wronged wife—" This past century stuff was contagious. "—know the situation?"

"Who better? Laurel."

"What?"

"Laurel," Charlotte repeated distinctly, as if Maggie's hearing were the bar to her understanding.

"Laurel told Pan about the affair?"

Charlotte's mouth stretched. "Affair is far too genteel. But, yes, Laurel told Pan."

"Why?"

"To get Pan out of the way, of course."

Was the woman saying her sister killed Pan Wade?

Charlotte continued, "Laurel went after Wade. But she wanted marriage. To get that, she prepared to remove the obstacle that he already had a wife. She wanted that marriage to break up. Since word wasn't getting around fast enough—or Pan wasn't catching on fast enough—Laurel told her. She advised Pan to give Wade his freedom *so we can find happiness together.*" The woman added evenly, "Pan said Laurel also showed her pictures—photographs of Laurel and Rick in the act."

Maggie closed her mouth, tried again. "Laurel must have been happy when it looked like Pan would leave with Carson."

"At first. But then Rick became the issue. He said he was done with her and wanted Pan back."

Giving Laurel a motive to kill Pan.

But then who would have killed her?

Unless Rick found out she'd killed Pan, and wanted revenge.

The same motive applied to Carson.

Revenge would explain the similarities in the crime scenes—and the dissimilarities.

"She must have been furious—Laurel, I mean," Maggie said. "How did she intend to get him to change his mind?"

Charlotte gave her a scornful look. "I told you we were not prone to sisterly confidences. She didn't tell me what she had in mind. But it was clear by the trial she'd tired of waiting for Rick. She'd set her sights on Eugene Tagner."

CHAPTER THIRTY-SIX

"**THAT COUNTS** *AGAINST* Laurel as a suspect for Pan's murder. She'd already moved on. There's no motive to kill the competition when she's no longer competition," Maggie said—not for the first time since they'd left Rambler Farm.

J.D. didn't disagree, but he had a different priority.

"Wade's the one we should be talking to," he said—also not for the first time.

At Rambler Farm, he and Dallas had finally shaken loose of the judge's hospitality, but barely reached the hallway outside the dining room when Maggie came from the back of the house, jerking her head toward the front door in silent order.

Dallas demurred, but didn't physically resist when she took his arm and ushered him out.

As she drove to Monroe House, she'd recounted her conversation with Charlotte.

There'd been a brief break when they arrived, while Evelyn issued orders to all of them that got their delayed dinner on the table in short order.

All of them included Scott.

He'd stopped by to drop off copies of the transcripts for Maggie and Dallas. Evelyn insisted he join them for dinner.

In light of Dallas' comment to Maggie about people feeling obliged to ask you to stay for dinner if you came by at a certain time, J.D. suspected Scott timed his arrival to get a dose of Evelyn's cooking.

No matter what motives were at work, the five of them sat down for the meal—and for Dallas' grilling of Maggie, aiming to pull out every last detail of her talk with Charlotte.

Neither Evelyn nor Scott said anything, but J.D. doubted they missed a syllable. He sure didn't.

At the end, he repeated, "Wade next."

"Not yet." Maggie didn't look his way.

"Wade's done everything but paint a sign on his back. What more do you want?"

"Evidence."

"You want an eyewitness, too?" The sarcasm was sharper than he'd intended, and he saw her absorb the slice, then reassure herself he couldn't possibly know…

He did know.

Her family history. The trial. What followed.

The facts, those he knew. Where or how those facts made her vulnerable, he didn't know. Not completely. Not yet.

"Hard evidence is always better than an eyewitness," she said.

Having been an eyewitness all those years ago, she would know.

Yet she made no effort to soften that judgment on herself. Whatever else, he admired that in her.

"Not with a jury," Dallas said.

"Juries are built to be led," she shot back.

"Who better to lead them than a good eyewitness?"

"That's an oxymoron—a good eyewitness. All witnesses are bad, tainted by their biases, by their hopes, by their beliefs, by their—" The break was more a breath than a hesitation. "—weaknesses."

"That's where a good lawyer comes in," Dallas said. "To make the most of a witness. Shore up the weaknesses if it's your witness and spotlight the weaknesses if it's not."

"And the hell with the truth?" Before Dallas could respond, Maggie slashed air with her hand. "This is all terrific fodder for discussion, but we have work to do. And that's to get information to the sheriff—"

"I'll call when we finish here."

"—and pursue what we discover with an eye to whether the two cases connect."

"Wade," he said. "He's got means, opportunity, motive. For both."

"Motive? Why would he kill Pan when she was going back to him?"

He noticed her slight emphasis on *he* and its implication that Rick's motive wasn't clear, while J.D.'s was.

"She changed her mind again," Scott said. "She could have. Told Rick it was over. Rick hates losing at anything and especially..." He looked up, then away.

"Especially to me," J.D. filled in.

The trailer rat, the whore's bastard, the witch's pet.

Maggie's frown deepened. "You said on the stand that she *wasn't* leaving him, that she'd decided to give it another try."

As her gaze came toward him, he dropped his to that tapping fork.

"We'd agreed she would go back to Wade and give it another try. I encouraged her. If I hadn't, she might still be alive. I have to live with that."

"Only with that? I notice you don't proclaim your innocence, Carson."

"Not since the trial, no. Waste of breath. Wouldn't convince those who believe I'm guilty and it's not necessary for those who believe I'm not. Besides there's already enough proclaiming going on."

"Meaning Wade?"

"Meaning accusing someone else could be one hell of a diversion."

Her brows arched. "Given that some thought, have you?"

"Have you noticed I didn't accuse anyone until evidence pointed to Wade?"

She slapped the fork on the tablecloth. "Supposition. It's all supposition. And without saying Wade killed Pan, there's no motive for him to kill Laurel. Unless you're saying Laurel killed Pan."

"The guilt of having an affair with her," Dallas said, "and how he betrayed Pan."

"Why now? The affair ended four-and-a-half years ago."

"Guilt built up over time until he couldn't handle it," Dallas said.

She grimaced.

"Laurel threatened to topple his alibi," J.D. said. "If Laurel thought

she wouldn't get more money out of Eugene, she might have tried
Wade. He'd realize his alibi wasn't safe."

"Blackmail," Dallas murmured. "Could be, could be."

"*Could*. But Laurel *was* going to get more money out of Eugene.
She was holding those papers he needed signed as hostage." Maggie
tapped the tip of her unused dessert fork on the tablecloth. "Besides,
you missed an obvious possible reason for why now."

"J.D., will you pass me that fine potato casserole of Evelyn's?"

"Dallas," Evelyn protested.

"Just another bite."

As J.D. passed the dish to Dallas at the head of the table, Maggie
continued as if she hadn't heard the potato casserole exchange—and
maybe she hadn't. "Because Carson's back in Bedhurst full-time.
Anyone hoping to deflect suspicion onto a likely suspect would think
of that."

He didn't turn his head toward her, but he didn't try to stop his
eyes.

Yes, it was there in her face—she knew it represented the first time
she'd offered anything that might indicate his innocence in this
murder.

It didn't last, of course. He wasn't fool enough to expect it would.
But it was a step, a necessary step.

CHAPTER THIRTY-SEVEN

FOR A SUSPENDED moment of stillness and silence, he held her gaze, right there where he wanted it.

She jerked up from her chair. "Thank you for dinner, Evelyn. I'm going to the guesthouse now to start on the transc—"

"But Maggie," Dallas interrupted, "I thought you wanted to talk to the Blankenships' cook."

ALLARENE ROBINSON'S HOUSE was among the small brick boxes before the highway slowed to Main Street. The gravel drive bled into scrubby grass. But the brick-based porch was lined with pots of flowers and young vegetables so healthy they promised to spill over their mismatched pots as soon as full spring arrived.

A slender, middle-aged black woman answered their knock.

"Allarene," Dallas said. "We hope to have a word with you if we may. This is Maggie Frye from Fairlington, and you know J.D."

She looked toward Maggie's car, and beyond it to the road. She kept looking, even as she opened the door and silently invited them in.

"It's just us," Dallas said. "This is an informal discussion."

She gestured them to seats in the tiny living room. Dallas took one of a matching pair of chairs, Allarene the other, which left Maggie and Carson the loveseat.

The woman said, "I need that job, Mr. Dallas."

"I know you do. Takin' care of your boy and all." Dallas' drawl deepened and widened. "We can't swear not to use what you tell us if it helps find who killed Laurel. But if it doesn't, none of us will ever share a word. Isn't that right, Maggie? J.D.?"

"That's right," Carson said.

Maggie's silence brought the older woman's attention to her. "I will do my utmost to preserve the confidentiality of your information. However, if it contributes to a case against a murderer, you could be called to testify."

From the corner of her eye, Maggie caught Dallas' frown. She kept her gaze on Allarene Robinson. At last, she lowered her head, a single, slow nod.

"What do you want to know?"

"The sheriff has reports from a number of folks who did work 'round Rambler Farm. Those are official. We're not askin' for official from you, Allarene. But what you can tell us is the other side, the human side. Nobody else can give us that. These reports, they're sayin' Laurel was—" Dallas cleared his throat. Maggie figured it was to make way for a convoluted euphemism. She was wrong. "—sexually teasin' her brother-in-law."

"She tormented that man."

"And Charlotte?"

"Oh, yes. That's what she was after—tormenting Charlotte. Laurel's done that all her life one way or another. Showing her power. I don't know she truly meant evil by it. More like a cat keeping its nails sharp by taking regular swipes, not heeding that the scratches went to the bone."

Maggie felt as if her vision of Laurel had been a waft of smoke until those few words condensed her into solid form.

"Did you feel sorry for Charlotte?" Maggie asked.

Allarene said without emphasis, "No."

Dallas nodded. "Tell us about the mood in the household."

"A pot on bubble, ready to boil over every minute. Judge the only one didn't know it, feel it. He was happy having Laurel there." Her tone added a slightly sharper undercurrent. "And having Charlotte run things."

"Like before Laurel got married?"

"Worse. Laurel'd been careful like around Judge before. Coming back, she wasn't. And Charlotte was more stiff-necked, thinking she ruled the Farm, like her mama used to."

"Well, Charlotte does run things, doesn't she?" Dallas asked mildly.

Allarene gave a dismissive snort, barely audible. "That one'll never be her mama. She was a lady, through and through. Judge is a fine man. Those two girls…" She glanced toward the loveseat, as if remembering her additional audience.

Dallas said, "We've heard Laurel might've been receivin' phone calls."

"Not many on the house line."

"What about on her phone?"

"Oh, that was forever going off. She didn't let another soul touch it, much less answer, even though she left it here, there, everywhere. Drove Charlotte mad, especially when Laurel accused her of trying to listen. Why, she even cut up Judge when he picked it up when it was ringing and ringing in the sunroom. He kept trying to find it to stop the noise. Finally tracked it to under a cushion. Laurel comes flying in, snatches it from him and snaps about leaving her things alone. But that was early on before she changed about it."

"Changed?"

"To start, she was having a high time with the calls. Giggling, talking low, lots of sugar, like it was some secret game. Got less like that after a while. Toward the last, she went sour. Most often snapping it off when it started to ring. When she did answer, not wasting a speck of sugar."

"You said at the end—how long before she died would you say?"

Tipping her head, she stared at her scrubbed-clean hearth. "Near a week, for sure."

"Do you know who was callin'?"

She shook her head emphatically. "Didn't know, didn't want to know."

"Thinkin' back to when Pan Wade was killed, can you recall anything that might connect her death and Laurel's?" The woman slowly shook her head. "Some similarity you might have noticed? Or something you heard? Or—What is it, Allarene? Something you heard?"

"Not—It's only, it hadn't struck me till this instant that Miss Pan visited the Farm the week before she died. Spent time with Charlotte."

"What did they talk about?"

"I was workin'. Not eavesdropping," she said quietly.

"I most sincerely apologize for makin' it sound like anything else would be the case, Allarene. If you could tell us anything you remember of that visit, we'd be most grateful."

"But it couldn't have no bearing on Miss Pan getting killed. Or Laurel."

"Anything we can piece together of the days and weeks before each death might help. Even something routine like visitin' an old friend."

Allarene put a hand to her forehead, obscuring Maggie's view of her face.

"Wasn't routine for her to visit the Farm. Used to happen more when they were girls, going to school together and all. But not later. That time poor Miss Pan came in looking like a rainy day trying to fool everyone it was sunny. She and Charlotte sat outside. They were talking about old times when I brought out the iced tea, about being youngsters at school with you—" She nodded toward Carson. "—and all. Later, I remember seeing Miss Pan curled up like on the swing. I heard her voice—not words—and there were tears in it. Made me sad, such a nice young lady. And also knowing … it wasn't a good day to come calling on Charlotte. We had a big do—you recall that dinner with the Attorney General?"

"I do," he said. "And I recall you did yourself, the judge, and Bedhurst County proud with that dinner, Allarene."

She bowed her head in regal acknowledgement. "Learned my cooking from my mama, but learned how to do for important folks from Miss Yvonne. She had a grace. Brought it together easy-like. Charlotte gets worked up. Tighter and tighter. Reconsidering when there's no more time for it. Making lists, all sorts of do-remembers and double-check-what's-been-dones and keeps on even when folks are there and she should be enjoying the guests—leastwise making sure they're enjoying themselves."

She fell silent, and no one stirred, letting her memory reach back.

"After a while, I heard Charlotte's voice getting louder and stiffer, and I got a here-we-go thought, because that's how she is before a big do—even Laurel'd steer clear of her then. Then she shouted. Something about Miss Pan getting everything without doing anything. Miss Pan must've left soon, though I can't say for sure because I was in the kitchen, polishing silver, and she didn't come say good-bye and give a word of thanks the way she always did. Last time I saw that sweet girl."

CHAPTER THIRTY-EIGHT

9:06 p.m.

"**Week before she** died was when Laurel changed about those calls—right when she went to Zales' office and told him to draw up those papers. Interesting," Maggie said with them all back in the car. "Wish we could talk to Henry Zales."

"He wouldn't tell you a thing anyway," Dallas said with apparent satisfaction from the backseat. "Besides why be sour when she was getting what she wanted?"

Maggie backed out of the driveway. "The calls could explain that. Her *other plane* lover had given her what she needed—enough to force Eugene to give in—and she wanted Mr. Other Plane Lover gone. He didn't want to go."

She felt Carson's gaze on her. Was he reminded of what he'd heard between her and Roy? At least the part about wanting him gone and him not wanting to go.

"Might not have been a lover, the way people talked. And she might have gotten information from another source," he said.

"Possibly," she conceded.

Dallas clicked his seatbelt closed. "One thing's closer to buttoned up. Eugene was telling the truth about the calls."

"Not necessarily. He could have been the one making them."

"I admire you not limiting your thinking, Maggie. But some avenues have to be closed off, at least temporarily, or you'll never get far enough down the others to know if they lead somewhere."

"There's no—"

"What Dallas is saying," Carson interrupted, "is it's less likely Eugene was lying about the calls, because Laurel was giggling and happy about them when she was trying to punish him, and her sour attitude coincided with Eugene coming to heel."

Maggie kept her attention on the road. "Good point. Unless he was threatening her as well as grudgingly renegotiating."

Carson made a sound.

"Okay," she said, "so Eugene doesn't seem like the threatening type."

"I was thinking Laurel wasn't the type to be threatened."

"Never underestimate the nastiness of a fearful man backed into a corner," Dallas said. "Eugene's not in the clear. Need more checking on him."

"Before that, we need to dig more at Rambler Farm. The follow-up on what Allarene said, including—" She looked at Carson. "Earlier, when the judge said something about Pan being Charlotte's friend, not Laurel's, you didn't agree."

"I didn't say that."

"No, but you looked it. You don't think Pan was Charlotte's friend."

"Pan was her friend."

His even tone gave away little, but she got it. "Pan was Charlotte's friend, but Charlotte wasn't Pan's friend. If you think that, all the more reason to get back to Rambler Farm now and—"

Dallas interrupted. "No, even if we hadn't already been there today. We go and start askin' Charlotte questions, she'll know Allarene told us things. Least four cars passed slow enough to note your car. Word'll be back to Rambler Farm anytime if it isn't already. So, we go other places, ask other folks, and when we do get back around to Charlotte, there'll be no straight line she can follow to Allarene."

"You wouldn't know a straight line if it hit you between the eyes," she muttered. "Okay, then Eugene."

"Entirely too late. We keep early hours here in the country."

SCOTT CAME OUT of Monroe House as she braked to drop off her passengers.

"Still here?" murmured Dallas.

"I was getting ready to leave when—I kept him here. Took some doing, but I was sure you'd want to talk to him. Especially when he's in such a state."

"Who?"

"Rick Wade."

J.D. started toward the door, but Dallas laid a hand on his arm, slowing him, at the same time he asked Scott, "What kind of state?"

Maggie shut off the car and got out.

"He's all wound up. Insists on talking with Maggie tonight. I tried to tell him—"

"What did Evelyn say?" Dallas asked.

"She invited him right in and sat him in front of the fire."

Who'd kept him there? Maggie wondered wryly.

"Well, then, let's go see what he has to say."

✧ ✧ ✧ ✧

EVELYN SURVEYED DALLAS, quickly but comprehensively, then rose and excused herself.

Wade sat in the chair Dallas usually occupied, his head down, his hands rubbing up and down his thighs.

"Rick," Dallas said pleasantly, taking the other chair.

"I understand you want to talk with me." Maggie sat on the end of the couch across from Wade. Scott took the other end of the couch and Carson pulled up a side chair.

Wade's head came up. "No. I won't talk to you with *him* here."

J.D. stood.

Maggie pointed to him. "Sit." He did.

She said to Wade, "You're both staying here and you're talking." Playing them off each other might be the best way to get to the truth.

Wade glared at her. "You're like all the rest. I told you. I warned you."

She was aware of Carson looking at her. She kept her attention on Wade. "Never mind that."

"Never mind it? It's what started everything. Pan fell for his crap. The jury fell for it. *Everybody* fell for it. And Laurel—"

"Now, Rick, you can't be sayin'—"

Maggie sliced through Dallas' objection. "Do you have evidence? Was Carson involved with Laurel?"

"Laurel?" Wade sounded confused. "Not that I heard. But he fools people. So many people. Pan."

"Yes, let's talk about Pan," Maggie said. "When Pan was killed, Laurel was your alibi, Laurel and being at the charity meeting, right?"

"Yeah."

"We know you weren't at the meeting. Where were you?"

His gaze bounced around. Abruptly he dropped forward, his face in his hands, his elbows between his legs.

"Oh, God, Oh, God. I did … Oh, God. … Pan…"

Maggie felt something thrum through her. Was he saying…?

Carson hadn't budged. The only change she saw was the lines in his face tighten as he watched Rick rock forward and back, forward and back.

"Tell us what happened, Rick," Dallas said in his most soothing voice.

Wade lifted his head a few inches, but otherwise remained almost doubled over. "I did that to Pan—God, to Pan. I must have been crazy. To fall for that little tramp Laurel. To break Pan's heart over a bitch like that. I *was* crazy."

Dallas huffed out a breath, and Maggie's shoulders eased. He was confessing to the affair. Not murder.

"So, you're confirming what we've heard from others—you were carrying on with Laurel, back five years ago or so?" Dallas asked.

"Yeah. I was a fool, but… Yeah."

Maggie asked again, "Where were you when Pan was murdered?"

"With Laurel. At Piedmont Manor. We thought… We went to the

meeting, well before the meeting, saying hello to people, making them remember us being there, then we slipped out. That's how we—We did that regular."

"Is keeping that quiet why you give Barry a new truck every year?"

"God, you, too? Gardner's been going on and on about that. It's marketing. He can do us some good, talking up the dealership at Shenny's."

Interesting he'd used the same phrase as Barry.

"Did Pan know about you and Laurel?"

"Not at the start. She found out ... later."

Maggie thought Carson moved. But, no. No movement, no expression, no reaction.

Or was an absolute lack of reaction a reaction?

"How did she find out?" she asked Wade.

"I don't know. She wouldn't talk to me. Said she needed time to think. If I could've gotten her to talk to me, to make her understand—"

"Understand?" Carson's voice was low and cold. "Understand you betrayed her, adding on humiliation by doing it in Shenny's parking lot, where more people than Barry were certain to see, certain to talk, until everybody knew except her. You couldn't have found a better way to hurt her. You—"

"Like hell! It was *you*—you came between a man and his wife. You were pulling apart our marriage."

"You'd already done that yourself, you asshole. You never knew what you had, you never gave her the love she deserved. You did it, Wade. All you."

If he'd killed Wade it would make more sense.

The thought shot through Maggie's mind, but this was not the time to consider it.

Wade shouted, "Everything was fine until you came back."

"You're lost in your own fairytale, as always, where you're Prince Charming. Pan was done—"

"She loved *me*."

"She had. Until you squandered it, you sonuvabitch. Fucking Laurel in Shenny's parking lot. You never thought about anybody but yourself. What do you think that did to her? Knowing you were running around on her. And she knew Laurel wasn't the first."

"Because you told her—"

"I wasn't here."

Wade froze. Maggie suspected it was Carson's abrupt return to rigidly calm control.

In the same tone, Carson continued, "But other people were here to tell her. It was eating her up inside."

"But she was still with me," Wade said. It was a rally of sorts. "Until you came and tried to get her to run off with you."

Carson's posture didn't change, yet Maggie had a sense of infinite weariness coming over him. "She wasn't leaving with me, she was going to give you—give the marriage another chance."

"Like you were some fucking marriage counselor?" Wade said with an ugly twist to his face. "Like hell! She told me. That last day. She told me she was going away with you."

"That was earlier. We talked it over again and—"

"After that. After you left her in the clearing. She called me and said it was over between us and she was going away with you as soon as she made you see it her way. Like she had to beg trailer trash—"

Carson's face went hard, yet there was a sense of movement beneath the surface.

But Maggie had no more attention to spare for him.

She leaned across, cutting the space to Wade, shutting off his words. "Pan called you from the clearing? After Carson left? Is that what you're saying?"

"Yeah."

CHAPTER THIRTY-NINE

DALLAS MADE A sort of crowing sound.

Wade looked from her to Dallas and back. "So what?"

"You never told anyone." It came out as accusation. That was completely restrained compared to what she wanted to do, which began with lopping his head off with a dull object.

"Yeah, I did. I told Sheriff Hague right off. He asked when I last saw her and I told him the day before, then I said I'd talked to her on the phone."

Maggie felt the muscles in her jaw going rigid. "You never told my second chair and assistant when they interviewed you, you never said anything on the stand."

"Nobody asked. If it was important, they'd have asked."

How could they ask when they didn't know about it, since it never made it into the pathetic official file?

Forcing her jaw muscles apart enough to let out the next words, she said, "I'm asking now. We're asking now. Tell us exactly what she said."

"Exactly? I don't know—"

"Tell us," she snapped. "When did she call you?"

"She said Carson had just left, she was going home to her parents' but she wanted me to know she'd made her decision and it was final. She was getting a divorce and she was going off with Carson. I tried to talk to her, but she wouldn't listen and then she said someone was coming."

"Who?"

"She didn't say."

"Was she scared? Worried?"

"No. She was crying, but said she wouldn't change her mind. Didn't sound scared. Said it was someone she needed to talk to. Don't you see?" He looked only at her. "It was *him*. He came back and he killed her. I figured the sheriff and you prosecutors knew the best way to handle it and since nobody brought it up, I was sure—"

"You're lying. You didn't want everyone to know she was leaving you."

"I knew he was guilty. I knew it. He *is* guilty. He killed her." He jerked his head around to Carson. "You killed Pan."

Carson returned the glare, his cold implacability in full force. "You're an idiot."

Maggie watched those three words defeat the certainty Rick Wade had held close for nearly five years. Then slowly, slowly, Wade shrank back into the chair, tears sliding down both sides of his nose.

"He killed her," he whimpered, "He killed her."

Evelyn appeared with her handbag over her arm. She hooked a hand under Wade's arm. "Come along, Rick, come along. I'm taking you home now."

"My... my..." But he was already rising.

"You'll get your truck in the morning," she said firmly.

Evelyn surveyed the rest of them one by one, ending with Dallas. "Plenty enough work for one day. Time for everyone to get some rest."

With that pronouncement, she escorted Rick Wade out.

The sound of the back door closing brought movement into the room as they shifted their frozen stances. Except Carson. He remained absolutely still.

Dallas heaved a breath. "I could have gotten a *second* acquittal on that alone."

She grunted. There probably wouldn't have been a trial if that had been in the file she received. Too much reasonable doubt. Wade was right, Carson could have returned and killed Pan. But with the limited forensic evidence...

"It doesn't prove anything," she argued. "Wade said she said someone was coming. No knowing who."

She could have pointed out someone who'd left coming back was more likely than a total stranger arriving on the scene. She didn't.

Dallas responded with a reproving, "Maggie, Maggie, Maggie. Well, I'll call Sheriff Gardner and let him know. First about the timin' of Laurel's mood changes. Maybe that'll accelerate havin' a conversation with Henry Zales. Suspect he'll be less interested in what we just heard, because it doesn't help on Laurel's murder. Sure would be fascinatin' to know if old Hague hid it or forgot it."

"Or if Rick's telling the truth. Who's to say he's not lying," Scott said.

"We won't figure that out tonight." She rolled her shoulders, stood, then stretched. "Now I'm really going back to the guesthouse to read that transcript." She added another nod of thanks to Scott.

Carson spoke for the first time, sounding his usual unemotional self. "You'd be more comfortable here with Dallas."

"Of course," Dallas said immediately. "Stay here. The nights are still chilly and it's comfortable here by the fire."

"No. Thank you. I prefer to work alone. I'll go over the file again. And the transcript—"

"Don't hesitate to call me if you have any problems or questions," Scott said. "Or—"

"I'm sure I won't."

"—if you need background files or anything, let me know."

"There is one thing. If you can get us the phone records the sheriff's department has so far. They weren't with the reports."

"Sure, sure. Damn Abner. He must have held them back. Or forgot to copy them. Anything else, call me, contact me. Any time. I've listed them all here on my card. If there's anything you have a question on, my original notes are stored at the guesthouse and I can—"

"Thanks. I'm sure I'll have everything I need." She secured a transcript.

J.D. suggested smoothly, "Scott, why don't you walk Maggie to the guesthouse? I'm sure she'd appreciate company for that dark walk."

And, said his subtext, she'd be a lot less jumpy than if he accompanied her.

"No need. My car's here. I'll drive down."

SHE READ THE official transcript fast this first time. She would read it many times before she was done, some slower, some not. Hopefully, she wouldn't be as tired for those next times.

Still, there'd been no way she'd sleep without getting this first read in.

Something tugged at her.

She saw her mistakes, of course. Was that it?

Frustration with the investigation? Oh, yes. Make that plural—investigations. This one and the one four and a half years ago.

Dallas was right. Rick Wade's revelations tonight didn't help Gardner any with investigating Laurel's murder.

At least not directly.

You've missed an obvious possible reason for why now ... Because Carson's back in Bedhurst full-time. Anyone hoping to deflect suspicion onto a likely suspect would think of that.

She hadn't said that *was* the situation. Not for a moment. But she'd be a fool not to look at the defense's point of view—to look at Carson's explanations.

Who better to lead them than a good eyewitness?

Why had Carson said that? Eyewitnesses barely figured in his trial, not after Monroe disposed of Teddie Barrett's testimony.

He couldn't possibly know...

Hard evidence is always better than an eyewitness.

She'd learned that a lifetime ago. At a cost beyond measuring.

She sucked in a breath and picked up the transcript.

Read. Just read.

―――――――――――――――

Commonwealth v. J.D. Carson

Witness Oliver Zalenkia (prosecution)
Direct Examination by ACA Frye

Q. Among the items you examined in your capacity at the state forensic lab as you have described for us was there one that was unusual?

A. Yes. The note that the medical examiner's office found in her mouth.

Q. Is this the note, previously entered as an exhibit?

A. Yes.

Q. It appears stained and smeared in areas. Were you able to ascertain what is written on it?

A. Yes, we were.

Q. Will you explain to the jury how you did that?

A. We examined and photographed it extensively in its original state first. We were able to make out the left-hand side of the five lines of writing in that state. That's three lines together, then a single line, then another single line.

Q. This is a photograph that was taken with the note in its original state?

A. Yes. You can see that the first three lines appear to be from an address. The first single line begins in the format of a phone number. The second single line begins with the word 'One and two-bedrooms with…'

Q. Those elements are quite legible. But the right-hand side is not because of that stain. Did you have any success reading that side?

A. Yes, by applying ALS—Alternate Light Source—as you see on this next photo. Fortunately, the writer used durable ink, which we determined was used by the defendant's Army unit. If we put the photos of the two sides together, we see the complete address, phone number, and line of description.

Q. Do you know what this information refers to?

A. We called the number and checked the address. It is off-base housing for a nearby army installation.

Q. Were you aware this is where the defendant—?

Mr. Monroe: Your Honor, the defense stipulates that this note about off-base housing was written by Captain Carson, in durable ink, as favored by his unit, and was given to Pan for her information.

CHAPTER FORTY

THE PHONE RANG.

Okay. This was definitely not a coincidence.

Three out of three nights she'd been here, a call in the middle of the night on the guesthouse phone.

Noting the time and resolving to find out more about the calls Laurel might have been receiving—and to check if Pan had experienced anything similar—Maggie concentrated as she picked up the receiver.

She said nothing.

Breathing. Audible, but not loud. With a faint, faint sibilance.

She closed her eyes, trying to sharpen her ears.

It didn't match J.D. Carson. Not the sound, not the rhythm.

She shook her head.

For God's sake, thinking she could recognize someone's breathing? Make an ID by breathing? It was nuts.

"Carson?" she demanded.

An intake held the breathing, then it released in a soft hiss.

Click.

She replayed that reaction in her head. Surprise? Displeasure?

Could it have been Roy?

True she had dented his considerable ego, but would he resort to such childish tactics? Absolutely. He'd certainly know how to avoid leaving a trail in the phone records.

Or could the reaction have been something altogether different? Pleasure…?

Shit.

She could no more interpret that sound than she could ID breathing. She was grasping at straws.

What if he's innocent?

The voice spoke in her head as it had at the trial.

Except it wasn't the voice she'd first heard while she'd awaited the verdict in *Commonwealth of Virginia v. J.D. Carson*. That voice she would never forget, always hate.

This was the unknown voice from the second time she'd heard the question.

Where had that come from? Why now and—?

"No."

She said it aloud, breaking the thoughts.

It was a memory. Stirred by rereading the transcript.

Sleep. She needed sleep.

✧ ✧ ✧ ✧

MAGGIE JOLTED AWAKE to blood-thudding, ears-humming, muscle-tensing physical preparedness. Her brain tried to catch up.

The phone rang a second time, and she recognized the cause of her reaction.

That pissed her off—at herself, at the caller.

"What?" she snapped into the receiver, refusing to grant a polite "Hello."

"Well, shit, don't take me head off," groused Vic Upton, as she realized it was her phone she was answering, not the guesthouse phone.

"Oh, for God's sake." She slumped against the pillows. That put her in position to see the alarm clock. "Six o'clock? You can't be serious."

"I'm already up and on the way to the gym. If you got on a regular schedule, you'd be up being productive, too. That's what I called about."

"My circadian rhythms?"

"Being productive. You're not. Not while you're there."

"You agreed to Sheriff Gardner's request for me to help."

"Not indefinitely. You're too good to go off on a tangent like this, Frye."

Nancy would be screaming—or at least mouthing—*manipulator* at this point. And she'd be right.

But Vic might be, too. Was this brief sabbatical derailing her hard-built career? Probably not. Though she might be putting a kink in the rails. But she'd survive. She was sure she would.

"I'm staying through the weekend, Vic. There are a number of lines of inquiry we've started."

"We?"

She pushed the pillow more firmly behind her back. Fog turned the windows into blank walls. "That's the investigatory we, similar to the royal we. Judge Blankenship's well-connected in the state. It doesn't hurt to have a representative of the office here."

He humphed, but she'd scored. "At your desk, first thing Monday morning."

He hung up.

✧　✧　✧　✧

8:18 a.m.

THE ADDINGTONS WOULD not only not hear her apologies for imposing on them so early, they insisted on feeding her breakfast.

It wasn't quite Evelyn's standards, but it sure beat her usual small carton of old yogurt, if she remembered at all.

And they were pleasant company.

Seeing and listening to them here, interacting, it was almost like she could imagine the Pan Wade of the static wedding photo brought to life as a blend of these two people, with a dash of her special individuality, walking and talking … and living.

That made it harder to contemplate shifting the focus to the circumstances that had ended Pan's life.

As if sensing her reluctance, Theresa said, "Well, now, what did you want to ask us about?"

The talk with the Addingtons mostly gave her more background, several strikeouts, and one possible nugget.

The background included that the animosity between Carson and Wade went back to childhood. It also confirmed that they remained certain Carson hadn't harmed their daughter.

Their recollections of Pan interacting with Laurel remained sparse and vague.

They had no memories of Pan talking about a new person in her life, someone who might have been a mystery arrival at the clearing. Their daughter would have told them if there had been someone important. She always did.

The nugget was that, yes, Pan might have been receiving odd phone calls before she was murdered. How bad was it that she considered *might have been* a nugget?

That came after she'd heard herself telling them about the calls she'd received.

First, Kevin said, "She didn't talk to me about any. Theresa?"

"I think there were calls," she said slowly. "But it was mostly an impression. They didn't scare her. More like an annoyance. And a puzzle."

How many calls or when or anything else about them was not in their memories.

"But if we think of something, we'll call. In the meantime, you be careful."

CHAPTER FORTY-ONE

MAGGIE'S PHONE RANG as she got back in the car.

The irrational thought that the caller somehow knew she'd been talking to the Addingtons about him ... or her? ... came before she could stop it.

She grabbed the phone.

Caller ID was one she knew, not to mention this was her cell, not the guesthouse phone. Still, she let out that breath and drew in a new one before answering. "Hey, Bel."

"What's wrong, Maggie?"

"Nothing."

"You sound tense."

"Frustrated."

"Hah. We told you about starting from scratch."

"Yeah. Did you call to gloat?"

"Nah. A lucky bonus. Heard a couple things you might be interested in."

"A pebble?"

"Maybe. I got thinking about that search you asked me to do for similar murders in the region, and coming up with nothing. I checked your guy's military record and—"

Her heartbeat tripped, picked up. Something she'd missed? Something—

"—decided to search where he'd been posted. At least the ones I could find out about. Half the time nobody but a couple generals seemed to know where he was. But I checked where I could."

"And?"

Belichek huffed out a breath. Irritation at being rushed or reaction to what he'd found, she couldn't tell. She didn't care.

"Nothing."

"Nothing?" Her voice sounded thin to her.

Belichek didn't comment. "One maybe, but it was two years before he got there. So, yeah, I'd call it nothing."

"Okay. It was a good thought. Thanks. I—"

"Hold on, Mags. I'm not done. I figured as long as I was doing the tracking, I should do it right. I asked about attacks short of murder—assaults, rapes. Still nothing. Not where he'd been posted. But then I went back to folks around the region.

"I know the sheriff up there was checking murders around the state, but I thought it was worth a few calls to see if he'd checked other crimes. Most murderers don't bat a thousand to start. With the limited physical evidence, it's tough, but I used the calls and the description of the victim."

"Bel—"

"Bingo."

She pushed the microphone away from her mouth, in case her breathing sounded as harsh as it felt.

"A case two years ago. In the western part of the state."

"Roanoke."

"No. Lynchburg."

"Lynchburg?"

"Yep. Caught a break, too, because my buddy remembered the guy assigned to the case talking about it, and put me through to him. Seems a woman came in, real nervous, asking to talk to someone. She said how she'd thought this guy was great at the start, but then she got an uneasy feeling. When she tried to pull back, it got worse. She talked a lot about phone calls and how they escalated. And—get this—she said the guy tried to strangle her. She showed him the marks. But then, she not only wouldn't press charges, she wouldn't tell him the name of the suspect. He said she got real jumpy, and scooted out of there. He's getting me a copy of the incident report. What he did remember is when he checked back, she'd moved right after she talked to him. Moved fast, no forwarding information, but a neighbor said she came to this area. I'm tracking her, but just my luck, her name's Johnson. Darcie Johnson. She's a teacher. When I find her, I'll interview her."

Maggie's lips twitched at the *when I find her*—no doubt in Belichek's mind that he'd accomplish what he set out to do—but her mind was still wholly occupied with Lynchburg. Not Roanoke.

"That's good work, Bel. Real good work." She reached around, tapped in a site one-handed and pulled up a map of Virginia. Lynchburg was a heck of a lot closer to Bedhurst County than Roanoke was. But why...?

"There's more." His voice yanked her attention from the map, even as her fingertip lingered on Route 460 connecting Lynchburg and Roanoke. "Not sure if it's even a grain of sand, much less a pebble, and it could have nothing to do with any of this."

Hedging was not like Belichek.

She waited.

"Three of the guys I talked to in Virginia gave me grief about triple-teaming them."

"Triple?"

"The sheriff's official inquiry about murders, my unofficial inquiry about short of murder. And, in between, an unofficial inquiry about murder cases from somebody saying he was doing a favor for an ACA."

Carson?

Why would he do that? He could have Dallas call. Unless there was some reason Carson didn't want Dallas knowing he was looking for a connection to other murders?

Rick Wade?

Investigating on his own? But why?

Eugene Tagner?

Could she imagine Eugene bestirring himself to make such calls? And why?

Charlotte? Oh. *Or Ed Smith on behalf of Charlotte?*

But, like Dallas, he wouldn't need the excuse of saying he was doing a favor for an ACA.

"Maggie," Bel's voice stopped the whirl of speculation in her mind. "It was Roy."

SHE FOUND ROY at the Piedmont Manor.

Dallas and J.D. had been right. She couldn't have stayed here. She would have been calling the sheriff all night long to report the misdemeanors scattered over the parking lot, and the felonies surely lurking behind the ratty façade.

Roy, with his knack for compartmentalizing, had no trouble shutting a door labeled, "Not My Jurisdiction."

That, she realized, was how he'd been genuinely surprised she didn't agree his fling with Officer Hundley didn't—for him—have anything to do with her.

Roy opened the door, impatient, wiping shaving cream from his jaw. Then he saw her. A moment's hesitation before he extended one arm above his head and leaned on the door frame.

"Decide you were letting a good thing go?"

"If you ever use my office, my name, or me in any way whatsoever without direct, written authorization, I will pursue disciplinary charges against you as fast and completely as possible. Do you understand?"

"I'm trying to help. This podunk town doesn't—"

"Do you understand?"

"Yeah, I understand. I understand you have a stick up your—"

She turned and left.

CHAPTER FORTY-TWO

THE INSTANT MAGGIE walked into Dallas' office, J.D. Carson stood from the sofa and demanded, "Why the hell haven't you told us you're getting phone calls?"

It was as if the confrontation she'd left behind at the motel morphed into a new storm coming at her full force, recharging the anger and adrenaline already churning her stomach.

"What phone calls?" Dallas asked from his desk.

Carson answered without looking away from her. "Hang ups, breathing, late at night, like Laurel got. Like the Wades say Pan got— now that they've been reminded by Maggie's questions this morning. And like Maggie's been getting and hasn't told us about."

Breathing in through her nose, out through her mouth, she boxed her reaction. "How could you know about my getting calls unless you're making them?"

"Use your brain, Maggie. I know because Pan's parents called me to add something they forgot to tell you. They assumed I knew all about it, since we're supposedly working together."

Another reaction surged in. It did little for the agitator in her stomach, but her head cleared.

"Is that what you're pissed about? That I left you out of the loop because—"

"I'm not pissed you left me out of the loop. I'm pissed—"

"—I haven't told anyone."

"Oh, that's a hell of a lot better. In fact, that's fucking great. Are you trying to—?"

Dallas cleared his throat, a sound that carried to the back of any courtroom.

A beat passed, then two. J.D. took half a step back. "I told you," he said in his normal voice. "I don't want any more dead women in my county."

"There's no reason to think I'm in danger."

"The hell there isn't. You look like them. You're getting the calls. And you're going after whoever the killer is."

"So's the sheriff. And Dallas. And you."

A glint like sunlight on metal came off his eyes.

She wouldn't take back including him. Not because she didn't suspect him, but because he knew she did. No reason to repeat it simply because she'd misspoken.

"If I may intrude," Dallas said, "what was it the Addingtons had to add to their conversation with Maggie?"

"They remembered Pan had asked her cousin who works at the phone company to check into the calls. I talked to the cousin—"

"You didn't think I was in such horrible danger that you failed to follow that up."

"Pan was killed before her cousin could act," he said with heavy emphasis.

"Unfortunate," Dallas murmured. "But this does give us an interesting line of inquiry to pursue—discretely, of course—at the memorial service this afternoon."

"I told Gardner about you getting calls," Carson said.

"That was—"

Dallas interrupted. "Smart. The brief he gave us is to make connections and that's a promising one."

Since he was right, silence seemed her best course.

THE SHERIFF GROWLED at her about not telling him about the calls, dismissing her "Three. Three calls is hardly a pattern." But he limited it to one short growl because the briefing, in addition to its usual vague, was also early and short today, with the memorial overlapping their usual meeting time.

Although no matter when they met it probably would have been short because there was not much to share.

Nothing seen on security footage from around town.

Nothing unusual in Laurel's financial records.

Nothing from the hairstylist in Lynchburg, except confirmation of Laurel's exultation when Eugene agreed to her demands and a possible dip in her mood at her last appointment, when she said someone was trying to rain on her parade but wouldn't succeed. Who, how, and all the other basic questions were unanswered by the hairstylist.

While Carson returned to the office—in what might have been a demonstration of tact or, more likely, for reasons of his own. She and Dallas remained after the rundown to update Gardner on last night's discussion with Rick Wade, who was not at the briefing. According to Gardner, no one had heard from him.

"Does that bring us any closer to linking these two murders?" the sheriff asked.

"No," she said.

"Although the possibility of another person arriving at the clearing—someone Pan needed to talk to—does offer an interesting echo to Laurel's *other plane* companion," Dallas said.

"*Echo.*" Gardner looked as if he'd roll his eyes if he'd had the energy.

Dallas was in an odd mood in the walk back to the office. He hummed snatches of some old song and kept glancing at her, then away.

It made her edgy. Not enough to ask him what he was thinking— he'd tell her, and she didn't want to know—but enough to have a solid base of irritation when Scott greeted her with the news that she had a call he'd put through to Dallas' office and why didn't Dallas come have a cup of coffee while she talked in private.

She should have asked Scott who it was. Presumably the caller's identity prompted him to take those measures. It was stupid to feel asking him would somehow reveal weakness.

So, she was stupid.

If it was Roy, it was a couple dozen straws past a broken back. Was Vic on another rampage? Or—*Quit speculating and find out.* "Hello?"

"Maggie? It's me."

Jamie.

"Why are you calling this num—Is something wrong? Ally? Your folks?"

"No, no. Everybody's fine. I didn't mean to scare you."

"Then why—" She stopped. Swallowed.

"I've called and called your number, but you never answer or return my messages. I know you don't support—I know we don't see eye to eye, but we're still cousins. We still have memories—good memories when we were all together. Memories only you and Ally and I have now. They're important. And a connection that won't ever go away. Please, Maggie. Please, talk to me."

"I'm really busy, Jamie. I have work I have to do."

"I know. I know the work you do is very important. But this is important, too. And I'm going to say it, no matter how much you don't want to hear it. You have to forgive—"

"*Forgive?* No, I don't. I don't share your sweetness and light view that murderers and rapists and all the rest should be forgiven. They should get justice. That's what I'm here for. You forgive, but without people like me, you'd get to forgive them again when they commit the next crime. That might be what happened here. There was forgiving all over the place—" Along with a shoddy investigation. "—and now another young woman's dead."

She was aware of the silence lengthening to awkwardness. But dammit, she was tired of Jamie trying to push her where she didn't want to go, wouldn't go. Maybe couldn't go.

"I'm sorry, Maggie. Truly, I'm sorry you're carrying the burden of that. Of all the people in the world… But I was going to say you have to forgive yourself, Maggie. Finally and completely. Most of all you have to forgive yourself for not being able to run the world the way it should run. It's *not* all on your shoulders. Not for a murderer killing again up there and not for Aunt Vivian. She's the last person who'd want you to—"

"I gotta go. Bye, Jamie."

She replaced the receiver in its stand. It rattled from her hand shaking. She put her hand behind her back.

She took two breaths, then walked out to tell Dallas he had his office back.

He was nowhere in sight. Neither was Carson. His closed office door might account for both.

Scott hurried up with a cup of coffee he pressed into her hand—hands—she used both to hide any remaining tremor.

Concentrating on that, she was ambushed by his gush of words.

"Oh, my God, Jamison Chancellor is your cousin? Jamison Chancellor of the Sunshine Foundation?" Curiosity glittered in his eyes the way it always did when people heard she was related to Saint Jamison ... and they realized Jamie's story, broadcast far and wide. was Maggie's, too. "Of course she is, what am I saying. I admire her so much. And the work she does with the Sunshine Foundation. Amazing work she—the foundation does."

"Yeah."

"Building such good from a personal tragedy—a *family* tragedy."

She stiffened.

"I mean the Sunshine Foundation is amazing. I wish I'd had that sort of imagination when Mama died. You know, to do something really special in her memory." His voice vibrated with emotion. "A commemoration of what she meant to me. I don't want to pry, but—"

"Thank you," she got in, overlapping the *but* that always followed *I don't want to pry*. Because that's what everyone wanted. To pry open her head, her heart—her past. To drag it all out where they could see it and talk about it and demand answers about it. Some indulged in prurient curiosity. They were easy to shut down. Some—the well-intentioned ones like Scott—wanted to offer sympathy or thought they could help. They couldn't and they were harder to shut down.

"Roy said you'd had it tough," he added. Roy gossiping with this man? That made the shutting down easier. "I'm sorry I hadn't made the connection. I want to express my sympathy—"

"Thank you. But this investigation comes before personal matters."

She softened the shut-down by touching his arm.

As Nancy said, she had to work with people even after she'd slammed the door on them.

"Tell them," she tipped her head toward the closed door, "I'll see you all at Rambler Farm."

"I'd be happy to drive you—"

"No thank you. I'm going alone."

3:28 p.m.

CHARLOTTE LOOKED AROUND one last time.

Perfect.

No one could say otherwise.

Her eyes filled.

"Oh, my dear, I know you'll miss that lovely, lovely sister of yours." Janice patted the back of Charlotte's hand where it rested on the damask upholstery imported from the same English company that supplied fabrics for royal palaces. Janice always came early. "Like a breath of spring she was. Always just so, and that smile. Such an ease about her. Oh, I know you'll do your best to go on, but it won't be the same, especially for Sundays at Rambler Farm."

Charlotte thanked Janice for her words—and she wasn't lying. She did thank the woman for her words. Not the sympathy, but the reminder that things would not be the same. They would be better.

She straightened her jacket and went to join the judge by the door as more guests arrived.

From now on, there would be no Laurel, there would be only Charlotte at Rambler Farm.

CHAPTER FORTY-THREE

LAUREL BLANKENSHIP TAGNER was memorialized on a day that displayed every mood of spring. The early fog had burned off. The mourners started outside on the sloped lawn behind Rambler Farm's main house, steaming gently in a preview of sun-scorched summer. Shortly after, they were herded inside, as a front pushed wild clouds, and cold rain lashed down.

Maggie hadn't packed for a memorial service during her quick stop at her townhouse Monday on her way to Bedhurst. She made do with the slacks and shoes she'd worn from the office, a white blouse, black jacket, and black and white scarf.

The drive alone to Rambler Farm gave her a chance to sort her thoughts.

Roy was on the verge of becoming a real problem. When she got back, she needed to have a come-to-Jesus talk with him. If that didn't work, she'd go over his head in the department. Not a fun prospect, but she would not let this grow like a nasty mushroom when bright light could stop it in its tracks … Or expose it as truly serious.

Carson getting bent out of shape about the calls and raising alarms with the sheriff pushed her buttons, but not that big a deal in the scheme of things.

As for button pushing… Jamie.

Yeah. That was a major button pushed.

Especially with Jamie—*Jamie*—acting like *she* was the mother hen. That had always been Maggie's role. *Born to be the oldest, a responsibility junkie.*

Refusing to identify the remembered voice that had said those words, Maggie still disputed the *junkie* part. Besides, responsibility wasn't a bad thing. She'd always felt protective of the youngest of their triumvirate of cousins. That's why she'd picked up on...

No. Wasn't going there.

Get her head back to where it belonged. Here. Now. Watching and listening. Picking up nuances of the interrelations of the people they'd been talking to. Looking for contradictions.

She gave up her keys to a teenage boy providing valet service at Rambler Farm's stately entrance, proceeded slowly through the house, not recognizing anyone except a glimpse of Allarene Robinson handing a tray to a waiter, and Teddie Barrett's mother, small and uncertain, perched on the edge of a chair in a side hall.

Maggie smiled and said hello to her, but continued on, carried by an inexorable tide—no doubt responding to some gravitational requirement ordained by Charlotte—through the sunroom and onto the back lawn.

By a buffet table, she spotted a clot of law enforcement, including Sheriff Gardner. None looked comfortable, but that didn't stop them from indulging in the offerings.

Carson, Dallas, and Doranna talked not far away. Barry stood separately, staring at the ground. He might as well have a sign on him saying, "I'm in the doghouse."

The Addingtons were at the core of a group of people exchanging hugs and shoulder-pats. Rick Wade broke away from it and headed for the house. Even from a distance she guessed he hadn't combed his hair or shaved since they'd talked yesterday, though he had changed to a suit.

He detoured around what amounted to a seated receiving line.

Eugene occupied a chair. The judge, sitting slightly in front of him, appeared to grace a throne. That's how highbacked and elaborate the carved chair was. Ed Smith stood, a page on the alert to fulfill the king's wishes.

Or the queen's, because Maggie saw Charlotte say something to Ed that immediately started him toward the buffet table. Then Charlotte was off in another direction.

Renee Tagner held court of another kind, wearing a dress that looked black until she moved and it glowed the darkest red, and surrounded by what had to be the cream of Bedhurst County's business class.

"Quite the gathering."

Maggie found Scott at her elbow, offering her a glass of white wine.

"This is what's on offer here," he said. "For the bourbon and whiskey, you need to be invited to the judge's den."

"Thanks, this is good." And it was.

As if expanding her thought about Renee's group, Scott added, "Drawing dignitaries and leaders from all the surrounding counties, as well as Bedhurst—that's Henry Zales there saying a word to Eugene." He was a slender man of barely medium height with straight, pale hair cut to show every bit of elf ears. He wore a bow tie, offset by a seriously square jaw. "None of them strangers to Rambler Farm and its Sunday gatherings. Though it's the first time coming through the front door for a number of people here."

Maggie thought of Mrs. Barrett looking awed and uncomfortable and wished she'd stopped longer.

She felt an itch between her shoulder blades. The kind that required a backscratcher, another pair of hands, or flexible arms and no compunction about contorting in public.

Was it the desire to grab Henry Zales, hold him upside down, and shake until whatever he knew about Laurel's machinations came out?

This wasn't the place. Not to mention Gardner would have a fit. Plus, the little fact that Dallas was right that he was far more likely to get information out of his crony than she was.

Maddening.

"You appear to be in the appropriate mind-frame," Scott said with a smile.

She yanked her thoughts from the tunnel they'd been following. "Mind-frame?"

"For a funeral—excuse me, memorial. Do you like funerals? Some people do, you know." He lowered his voice, as a group passed them, clearly led by a red-head in a silk suit that would have been stunning if it hadn't been two sizes too small for her otherwise decent figure. "Take Robin over there. She specializes in funerals. Had to. Her sister, Mary Kay, specializes in weddings."

Maggie felt a twitch pulling her lips, but said only, "This is a lovely setting for either."

"Oh, yes, Rambler Farm has seen any number of both. Always well done, too."

"The Sunday gatherings—Laurel would have been expected to be here every week?"

"Expected, yes. She didn't always attend."

"But she'd told people she would last Sunday, apparently to announce she was returning to Eugene, that they'd worked out their differences."

"Mmm."

It was an interesting sound, agreeing with her while adding a large measure of doubt.

"Which Laurel told some people and Eugene confirms meant he'd agreed to increase the allowance," she pursued.

"Mmm?" Doubt topped agreement. He smiled. A cat who had swallowed the canary, but now was dying to share it.

"We have multiple sources that Laurel was saying—"

"Oh, I don't doubt she was saying that. And now Eugene's saying it, too. But saying and doing aren't necessarily the same."

He had all her attention. "You have evidence he didn't intend to increase her allowance?"

"Evidence of intention is whimsical at best," he was relishing this. "What I know is what he *didn't* do. I've worked with people who do work for the firm Tagner uses and no matter what Laurel thought—or told other people—Eugene hadn't changed her allowance. In fact, he'd called to make sure the pre-nup's provisions were ironclad."

"Did you tell Dallas?"

"Not yet. Just found out."

"His lawyers told you?" They sure as hell shouldn't have.

"There's a whole network of information and connections beyond you lawyers. Speaking of which, you'll have to excuse me while I make the rounds." He smiled, then drifted to a group of people she didn't recognize.

If Eugene Tagner lied about changing Laurel's allowance, that was valuable information. Maybe the pre-nup's provisions weren't as ironclad as he'd hoped.

He could have lured Laurel to that isolated spot with the promise of discussing an increase, killed her, and staged the scene to resemble Pan Wade's murder to throw off suspicion.

But why on earth would Eugene Tagner have murdered Pan? True, compared to the crisscrosses of relationships in this county the nation's power grid resembled a straight line, but there'd been no evidence of a connection four and a half years ago.

So that would likely mean two murderers.

She realized she was searching the crowd for Dallas and Carson.

Well, that didn't mean anything special, except her subconscious was ahead of her conscious. If she shared this tidbit with them it didn't mean anything more than engendering good will. What could it hurt? Scott would tell them anyway.

Carson was farther down the slope, his head bent to hear something Renee—now without entourage—was saying. Dallas was closer, talking to Henry Zales.

Before she moved toward either of them, a wind came up and the sun disappeared like a flipped switch. She looked up to a massive black cloud. Enough sunlight glimmered along the bottom to show slanted lashings of rain trailing it like airborne firefighters dropping a load of water.

"Inside, inside!" The call came from every direction at once.

Allarene appeared, overseeing the temporary help gathering the contents of the buffet table. Charlotte led the charge into the house, directing the flow through the sunroom and deeper inside.

Ed brought in the next wave and the judge gathered the stragglers, all with the air of a practiced sequence. Among all those Sunday gatherings, this must be a familiar scenario.

Not caring about the large, vehement drops splashing onto her head and shoulders, Maggie timed her dawdling to be among the last shepherded in by Judge Blankenship. She was unsurprised to find Dallas and Carson beside her, though Zales and Renee had rushed in earlier.

"Inside, inside," he urged them, even as all four of them stepped into a screened porch attached to the sunroom.

Dallas slowed, huffing audibly, and taking the judge's arm. For support or to delay him?

The judge obligingly stopped.

"Glad to have this chance for a word, Kemble," Dallas said between breaths.

"Are you all right, Dallas?"

"Will be in a second. J.D.?"

Carson picked up immediately, saying to the judge, "We have reason to believe Laurel was receiving crank calls while she was here at Rambler Farm. Did she discuss them with you? Seem upset or—"

"No, no. Laurel would have told me if she'd received upsetting calls. She relied on me." He showed no sign of remembering their reference to calls. "Not that she wasn't independent, she was. Can see her as a tot, standing there with her tiny fists on her hips, pointing to Dina and saying *why is she always crying and clinging?* Sorry, Dallas, but Laurel had Dina dead to rights. She did cry, and good Lord, the woman could cling. I thought Bill Tomlinson might break from it. Surprised he had the backbone to leave."

"Every family has its eccentrics."

"That branch of your family grabbed more than its share. Dina's brother Bruce was eleven apples short of a dozen. And there's the legend that Dina's grandmother poisoned her husband. Nobody'd eat her cooking after."

"Now, Judge, that would never pass for evidence in your courtroom. I recall a speech of yours chastising the fine citizens of this county for—I believe your phrase was—*abject failure in applying logic or humanity* when they got up all those charges again Anya Nouga when what it came down to was she chose to live in the woods by herself."

"All right, all right, Dallas. You got the woman off years ago. You can quit trying the case." To J.D. he said, "Can't say I ever approved of her, but she did right by you."

"Yes, sir, she did."

"Strange woman. Sitting on the bench, you see all kinds, but can't say as I've seen the like of Anya Nouga before or since. Now, Nola wasn't such a rare kind. Wish she were. There'd be a lot less unhappiness in this county, and a lot less work for me. Not that she meant anyone harm. Harmed herself—and you—most. Those last years, seemed Nola was before me more days than not. And even then, she meant well, poor soul."

"It wasn't her intentions at fault, it was her actions."

He clapped a large hand on J.D.'s shoulder as he addressed Maggie. "You hear that? Know what this one told me before he headed off for the Army?"

She didn't respond. He didn't need a response. He was clearly a man accustomed to dominating the conversation, if not everything around him. Maggie suspected all around him were deferring to him even more than usual, hoping whatever course he chose led away from the grief drawing his face into sagging folds.

"He told me one of his early memories—"

"Judge—"

He shook his head, not looking at Carson but with his hand still on his shoulder. "I'm going to tell Ms. Frye this. J.D. here said one of his earliest memories was listening to a judge hold his mother accountable for her transgressions. In his young life he hadn't seen that. When she made excuses there in court, this judge cut her off, saying actions speak louder than words.

"I'm proud to say I was that judge, young lady. And I'm even prouder to say this young man has lived by that standard—the words I spoke in court to his mother. Actions speak louder than words. His actions show him as a fine young man. Becoming a top-notch lawyer, too."

Maggie had recognized on their first trip to Rambler Farm that Judge Blankenship didn't suspect Carson of murdering Laurel. But this encomium caught her off balance.

"I didn't realize you were close."

"Don't get that lawyer twist to your mouth, young lady. There was no partiality from the bench. In fact, I'd say the fact you didn't know I'd had an interest in young J.D. is proof I didn't favor him one whit at trial. You'd have spotted it fast enough."

Maggie smiled to indicate the judge won his point.

It was an effort. Because she *should* have been thinking about the effect this relationship might have had on the trial. Instead, she'd been thinking about the strange upbringing of J.D. Carson. And how he'd found such differing champions. Pan Wade, Anya Nouga, Dallas Monroe, Judge Blankenship.

And she'd been realizing the sharp edge of her suspicion had dulled.

Was it a result of extended exposure to people who believed in his innocence? Or was it something even more insidious?

He was a sexually appealing male. God knew she wasn't immune to the species—Roy proved that.

Yeah, there it was. She was physically attracted to J.D. Carson.

Which proved absolutely nothing.

It made sense that the murderer of Pan and Laurel had appealed to them somehow. They certainly wouldn't have met a troll out in the woods. Sexual appeal was a weapon some criminals wielded.

Besides, what solid evidence pointed away from him now that hadn't been there when she'd arrived? None.

Charlotte bustled in with Henry Zales in tow. "Judge, you shouldn't be out here in the damp. The rain is coming in the screens. You and Henry will be comfortable in the library."

"Henry," Dallas said. "I hope to have a word—"

Charlotte cut across. "Perhaps later. I'm taking Henry and the judge to the library now."

"These folks have some questions, Charlotte," the judge said. "About Laurel."

"Again?" she muttered.

Apparently not hearing, the judge continued, "We must help them every way we can to bring to justice the person who… who…"

Zales took the judge's arm. "Come along, Kemble, I want to test your memory on a case our fathers told us about when we were first practicing."

Charlotte would have followed, but Maggie took her arm, stepped in front of her, and said, "We're glad your father's encouraged you to cooperate." She quickly tacked on, "We want to get to the bottom of the phone calls your sister was receiving."

"You asked about that already."

"We didn't know for certain they existed. Now we do. So, I'm asking again."

"I don't remember anything more about phone calls than I've told you."

"Did anything seem to be frightening Laurel, bothering her?"

"Frightening her?" Charlotte repeated as if the thought were foreign. "No. As for bothering, all that bothered her was Eugene not acquiescing as fast as she wanted."

"We know Laurel was asking for an increase in her allow—"

"Asking? Oh, no. She was demanding, using anything to get her way."

"What was she using?" Carson asked.

"She was threatening to tell anyone who would listen about Eugene's sexual inadequacies if he didn't increase her allowance."

CHAPTER FORTY-FOUR

"WAS THAT TRUE?" Dallas' head tipped in seemingly innocent curiosity.

"I have no way of knowing," Charlotte said precisely. "I know only what Laurel said. Now, I have to see to the judge, if you don't mind."

Maggie released the other woman's arm and she went.

Dallas immediately took her elbow, guiding her inside. "Time to mingle, mingle, mingle, and hear what we can hear."

THIS WAS HER opportunity to observe the interactions and connections Dallas and Carson knew in their bones.

Maggie tucked herself in against the half-wall at the base of the stairs, with the main room open before her and the sunroom past it, the door to the library over her shoulder, the entry to the kitchen area down a short hallway to her left. From this spot she watched a few early departers slip out.

At first, the individuals had moved as one through the rituals, held in a unified orbit by the gravity of the occasion. Now that they had partaken of food and drink—especially drink, conveyed by a half-dozen young men in white shirts and dark slacks—the bonds loosened.

A husky voice said, "Fucking social event of the spring." It was the red-head in the silk suit whom Scott called Robin.

"Always is at Rambler Farm," murmured the tousled-haired woman a half step behind her. Her slight smile could have been shy or malicious. Or both. "Whatever else you can say about her, Charlotte does know how to throw a party. Oh, excuse me, a memorial."

Both chuckled.

"J.D. doesn't look too broken up about Laurel," Robin said. "Guess he won't miss the favors she kept trying to bestow on him."

The other woman tittered. "Him and a lot of other guys."

"The widower won't be mourning long, either. Renee won't let Eugene screw up—or around—again. Did you hear about the will?"

"No," breathed the other. "What about it?"

They moved out of earshot, showing no sign of noticing Maggie.

Dallas, talking with Janice, caught sight of the women as they entered the living room, and made a commendable pirouette to put him on the far side of a floor lamp, out of their path. Clearly there were limits to his mingling.

Sheriff Gardner crossed their path with the air of one doing his duty. Maggie thought he exchanged at least a few words with everyone in attendance. In between, his sharp brown eyes scanned the rooms as she was doing.

When Maggie turned, she saw Judge Blankenship, in a leather wing chair, a half dozen other silver-haired men around him, in the library. Over the mantel was a large portrait of a smiling young woman flanked by two young girls, one rounded and solemn, the other blonde and pleased with herself.

Eugene occupied a large chair by the fireplace in the main room. In a steady stream, people approached him, said a few words, then left. No one sat near him, or continued conversation. The only person she saw approach him more than once was Ed Smith, when Tagner otherwise would have been alone.

Otherwise, Ed carried out tasks from his wife. Charlotte was in constant motion. Never in a hurry, but always attending to something, directing Ed and the help, connecting various groups, ushering new people into the library and easing out those she apparently thought had been there long enough.

Renee, Doranna, Barry, Scott, Kevin Addington, and a couple other people seemed at ease by a grand piano that didn't take much of a bite out of the large room. Rick Wade was in earnest conversation with a man Maggie hadn't seen before.

Looking around, she spotted Theresa Addington in the hallway, seated beside Mrs. Barrett.

J.D. Carson had taken a position near French doors to the porch, closed now with the rain. The position provided him a good view, yet was set back enough that those circulating through the room could overlook him, if they chose. Most at least exchanged hellos, and a number made the detour for further conversation. All who did treated J.D. Carson with something she could only call respect.

A lot of folks here think he never should have been tried—not all, but a lot. Sheriff Gardner had said.

The woman in the suit and her companion headed across an open patch of oriental rug directly toward Carson. At that moment Maggie recognized a potential drawback to Carson's position. There was no escaping anyone seeking him out.

The woman in the suit put her hand on his arm, and sent a rapacious smile up into his face.

The J.D. Carson of the trial returned. Cool, impregnable. He didn't withdraw from the touch. He didn't need to. Even from this distance it was clear the woman's touch hadn't truly reached him.

"Ms. Frye?"

Rick Wade. She hadn't seen him approach.

His eyes were bloodshot, putty colored blotches showed on his skin, as if he were under fluorescent lights. He'd deteriorated since last night.

"Do you have a minute?" He looked from side to side, assessing if anyone was around to overhear them. He had her attention.

"Certainly."

"The phone calls … Is there anything else you can tell me about them?"

Did he mean calls she'd received? Had the Addingtons told him? More likely, they mentioned Pan receiving calls. Or he could have heard through the law enforcement grapevine.

She kept her response wide open. "Like what?"

"Like when they started for Pan and for Laurel."

"Sorry, I don't have details to share." She truly was sorry she didn't have more details, not sorry about not sharing. "Were you aware of them receiving calls?"

"Not Pan. I wouldn't have known with Laurel, but I thought… That or—" He shot her a look, decided against what he'd started to say. "The calls could be a tie between Pan and Laurel. That's been bothering me. They were different. Couldn't be more different. Pan was kind and loyal and generous."

And Laurel wasn't. His unspoken words were clear.

"The calls are interesting," she agreed. "But as an auxiliary deputy aren't you assisting the sheriff in specifically investigating Laurel's death?"

"Yeah, yeah. We're run off our feet. I'm just saying it needs looking into. A link. I'm not letting anything get by this time." He stepped in closer, hatred snarling his voice. "That bastard is not going to keep walking around free. Or alive."

His certainty had returned since last night.

"That's the legal system's job to decide, Wade," she said sharply.

He stepped back, seeming to collect his composure. "That's right, it is."

He walked away, toward the back of the house. As she watched him, she was struck that both he and Carson had gotten bent out of shape about calls today.

Though there'd been something else Wade had started to say then didn't.

Charlotte emerged from the library. Shelving questions raised by Wade, Maggie immediately stepped in front of her.

"Charlotte, you've done a wonderful job with this. I can tell you're a phenomenal hostess to make everyone welcomed during such a difficult time."

She was laying it on thick, but she hoped that might soften the other woman's reserve.

"Thank you." Charlotte smiled mechanically, then took a step away.

The wretched woman intended to pull her disappearing act again. In desperation, Maggie snatched a pastry off her buffet plate and held it up. "These are absolutely wonderful. What are they?"

"Cranberry and brie puffs. I'm glad you're enjoying yourself."

An odd comment at a memorial, but that was for later consideration. Right now Maggie wanted to keep her here and keep her talking.

"This is such a great opportunity for me to see Bedhurst society. It's fascinating to watch the interactions." She purposely let her gaze shift to J.D.

In silence they watched a gray-haired man and a middle-aged woman drift over to him, as if a current carried them. The suited woman and her satellite walked away.

"Oh, yes," Charlotte said slowly, "J.D.'s quite popular with a certain element in Bedhurst. Surprising, some of them. Pan included. Suppose they're caught by the sex, like animals in a trap."

Maggie had seen the trap. She wouldn't step into it.

Charlotte continued, "Although with Pan, it was more complicated than sex. Started so young between them, it had to be. That might have made it worse. The fool." Maggie almost missed those two low words. "As for my sister, it was ridiculous for her to lust after him."

"Did he know?"

"I don't know how he could have helped it. Laurel was not subtle, certainly not in her efforts to seduce."

"Did she succeed?" It was important because of what it might mean for the investigation.

"I have no idea. As much as possible, I saw to it that her dealings did not touch Rambler Farm."

Except for Charlotte's husband.

"You don't like him—Carson?"

Charlotte gave a ladylike hitch of her shoulders. "Like has nothing to do with it. Breeding is what counts in the end. Breeding and background."

Clearly Charlotte counted those as two strikes against J.D. Carson.

"We're all supposed to do the right thing. Only some people get applauded for it, like J.D., while others don't. And then there are those who don't need to do anything at all and still get applauded." Charlotte faced her for the first time, studying her. "You're like them, you know."

"Who?"

"Pan and Laurel. Just like them. It all came easy. Never had to work—"

Maggie could have laughed. Never had to work?

"—Never had to work to be loved, either." She frowned, but it was not at Maggie. Her focus had shifted. "Excuse me."

She was gone, taking the arm of one of the servers and speaking sharply, then winding among the clusters of guests. The server picked up a glass from the windowsill, glared at Charlotte's unheeding back, then moved on.

Never had to work to be loved, either.

That sounded like what Allarene had heard Charlotte saying to Pan.

Jealousy there, but how deep, how strong?

She shimmied her shoulders.

If this darn itch halfway between her left shoulder blade and her spine would stop tormenting her, she could think through all the ramifications. The need to scratch nearly blotted out everything. The newel post behind her was too low and she couldn't reach herself without arm-twisting gymnastics and if she went to the restroom, she risked losing this vantage point.

"Poor Maggie, all by yourself?" J.D. Carson's hint of rough rumble came from behind her.

She'd lost track of him.

"Alone by choice." she said, not turning. "And you?"

"I'm not alone. I'm with you. Picking up interesting impressions?"

He put his hand on her back. She jolted, but he renewed the contact. And then he scratched. The exact spot. She would not let herself shiver.

"Nothing earth-shattering? You?" Her voice was even. Good.

"As you say, nothing earth-shattering. A bit here and there."

"Like what?"

Rather than answer, Carson stepped back. Maggie realized the flow of departures had picked up, clogging the hallway.

"There you are, J.D." Dallas came up to them with the judge and Scott with him. "Wondered if you'd mind driving Eugene home."

They all stepped closer to the side hallway to leave room for those heading out the door.

"Don't know how Charlotte came to overlook it when she dismissed the limo," the judge said.

"I'll take him, Judge. No problem."

Dallas said, "Maggie, my dear, if you wouldn't mind my riding with you—?"

"I can take you, Dallas," Scott said.

"No, no. Maggie will oblige, I'm sure. But if you could take Mrs. Barrett home, Scott, that would good."

Discontent flashed across Scott's face.

"No, no, no, no need," the woman fluttered.

"Nonsense," Dallas said. "You're not walking all that way in the rain."

Eugene, flanked by Ed and Charlotte, approached slowly, as if he'd become an old man in the past few hours.

"I'll bring my truck around, Eugene." J.D. offered. "It's still raining some."

Before he followed through, Rick Wade strode into to the group and announced loudly, "It's going to dry up tomorrow and it'll be perfect golfing weather day after."

He looked around the now-still group as if issuing a challenge. Maggie saw only blank expressions.

"I'm playing golf at the Laurelcrest Run Club in Lynchburg. You're a member there, aren't you, Eugene?"

"Been a member for a decade," the other man said with pride, his feeble demeanor sloughing away. "Most exclusive club in western Virginia."

Wade nodded, shifting his gaze from face to face. Over his shoulder, Maggie saw Renee in easy listening range. "That's right. Very selective in its membership. And I'm lucky to have made the acquaintance of a member who's invited me out to discuss certain matters while we play a round. Likes to get away from the office when he can, he said, but he'll bring one of his investigators along. Telecommunications specialist. Business and pleasure."

What the heck was this about? Was this connected to what he'd started to say to her?

Maybe Carson's suspicions were infecting her, because she suddenly wondered if Wade could be trying to cover his tracks somehow. But how? What could he hope to accomplish by this?

Silence greeted Wade's speech, until Scott produced, "You could use a break, what with working so hard on the investigation."

"Yes, I have been working hard on the investigation." The words sounded stilted. "Been going over Laurel's phone records real, real close."

Great, Wade got the phone records, but they didn't?

Wade glared at Carson, still beside her.

She turned. A flash of realization crossed Carson's eyes, but disappeared even faster than it had come. And what he might be realizing, she had no clue.

"And I've come to a conclusion." Wade paused. If it was for a response, he didn't get one. "Jealousy. That's at the core of both these murders."

Carson met his former classmate's eyes, impassive.

"Spiteful, vicious jealousy," Wade said.

Maggie's chest felt as if she were holding her breath, yet she knew she was breathing. Someone had to say something, do something.

Scott gave a rattling ghost of a chuckle. "I won't let jealousy get the best of me. I'll be generous and say I hope the weather holds for a perfect day for golf, Rick."

"Yes, indeed. A good game of golf come spring is a godsend." Dallas backed Scott's effort to break the tension. "Go get your truck, J.D. And the rest of us will be taking our leave, Judge. Charlotte, as always, the hospitality of Rambler Farm was above equal..."

In a stream of thanks, condolences, and farewells, they flowed out the front door of Rambler Farm.

━━━━━━━━━━━━━━━

Commonwealth v. J.D. Carson

Witness Oliver Zalenkia (prosecution)
Direct Examination by ACA Margaret Frye

Q. Dr. Zalenkia, you examined the clothes that testimony has shown Mr. Carson wore on the evening that Pandora Wade was murdered, is that true?

A. Yes, it is.

Q. Did those items include the blue cotton shirt entered as an exhibit?

A. Yes.

Q. What did you discover on that shirt?

A. There were traces of cosmetics on the right shoulder.

Q. Were those cosmetics identifiable?

A. Yes. The brand—

Mr. Monroe: Your Honor, the defense stipulates that the cosmetics found on Captain Carson's shirt were those of Pan Addington Wade. We will even stipulate that they came to be there when she rested her cheek on her friend's shoulder—

Ms. Frye: Your Honor—

THE COURT: Enough. Mr. Monroe, you are not to testify unless and until you are in the witness chair. Ms. Frye, since the defense stipulates that the cosmetics found on Captain Carson's shirt were the victim's, do you have further questions for this witness.

Ms. Frye. Yes, Your Honor.

THE COURT: Proceed.

Q. Dr. Zalenkia, what else did you find on the defendant's shirt?

A. We found hair, subsequently identified as Mrs. Wade's, wound around the button of the right cuff.

Mr. Monroe: Your Honor, the defense also stipulates that the hair found on Captain Carson's shirt was that of Pan Addington Wade.

Ms. Frye: The prosecution accepts the defense's stipulation, Your Honor, only if it also accepts the hair was wound around the defendant's shirt button and that the hair had been pulled from the head of Mrs. Wade, the victim.

Mr. Monroe: The defense will stipulate to the hair being around the shirt button. There is no evidence it was pulled, Judge.

THE COURT: The Court strikes the testimony relating to the hair being pulled. The jury shall disregard that. Proceed, Ms. Frye.

Q. Dr. Zalenkia, were there roots attached to the hair?

A. Yes.

Q. Are roots present when hair is pulled out?

A. Yes.

Q. To spare Mr. Monroe further objections, I will ask you, Dr. Zalenkia, if the roots can indicate the amount of force required to pull the hair out?

A. It depends on the phase of growth the hair is in. The hair found belonging to Pandora Wade was in the catagen phase, when the hair can come out more easily. We know that the hair came out, but we do not know if more force than necessary was applied when it came out.

Q. Thank you, Dr. Zalenkia. Were there any other items your lab examined.

A. Yes.

CHAPTER FORTY-FIVE

ON THE PORCH, a hand took her arm.

Ed Smith. He tugged her toward the far end. "A word, Maggie."

"Of course. How are all of you doing?"

"The shock's wearing off."

"That's good, isn't it?"

"It's hard. You think it will get easier ... This morning, the judge was much himself. And then—" He snapped his fingers. "It was all back."

"He was truly close to Laurel?"

"He adored her."

Not the same, not the same at all.

"And Charlotte?"

"The heart and soul of Rambler Farm. And above all, the brains. The place wouldn't operate a day without her."

"That was clear today. It was particularly impressive considering the burden of grief and shock she must be operating under."

"Working is how Charlotte copes. But I do worry about her. She worked hard getting ready for this memorial. Wouldn't let anyone help. Nobody wants to find this killer more than Laurel's family. If there's anything I could—"

"I have heard Charlotte and Laurel clashed."

"Clashed? That's a strong word. Sisters, you know. Sibling rivalry and personality differences rolled together."

"I understand their personalities were very different." She paused, letting his discomfort deepen. "Ed, was Charlotte jealous of Laurel?"

"Jealous?" His voice rose. Surprise? Discomfort? Nerves? Guilt?

"No. Not at all. They wanted such different things in life. Anyone who says otherwise doesn't know Charlotte the way I know her."

Maggie had her doubts, but this wasn't the place to press him. "Ed, there is something I'm hoping you can help with."

"Anything I can do, you know that."

"I've been reading the transcript. There's something… Damned if I can pin down what it is, though."

He shook his head. "I read it right after the trial. Several times. I don't remember anything strange, and I was reading it carefully because I was, uh…" The man actually blushed.

"Looking for what I did wrong. How I lost the case. I know. I did that, too."

"You didn't lose the case, Maggie. You handled that trial wonderfully."

"I *did* lose the case. That's a fact. But it wasn't only that. Maybe this thing with the transcript is all in my head, but I'd appreciate another set of eyes—eyes of someone who wasn't at the defense table."

"I'll take another look at it if you like."

"Thanks. I'll send you a copy Scott made for us. There's something else, if you don't mind my asking, do you know anything about Laurel's will?"

He stiffened slightly. "I'm checking on that. One thing I can spare the judge and Charlotte. But I don't have information for you right yet." Was that true? "I wish I could spare her more. But you can, Maggie."

"Me?"

"There are so many questions from the authorities for the official investigation… Yet you and Dallas seem to be asking even more questions. I don't want you to ask Charlotte anymore questions."

She considered him. "Ed, you know I can't agree to that. As long as these murders aren't solved, there are going to be questions. Some of them by me. The best thing would be for everyone to cooperate to get them solved as quickly as possible."

"Of course, that would be best. Absolutely."

She wasn't sure she believed that, either.

He walked with her to the bottom of the steps, where Dallas was waiting, then remained there as she got into her car.

Escorting her as a courtesy or to be sure she left?

"TAKE THE LEFT fork up ahead," Dallas told her.

"Why?"

"We're going to talk to Eugene again."

"When was that decided and why didn't you say something when we were leaving?"

"It was decided when an interesting tidbit came along this afternoon that he'd tried to cozy up to Pan after she first left Rick, but she was having none of it. *Shot him down good* was the phrase used. Didn't say anything because I didn't want to give Eugene a preview, didn't want him to get worked up."

"Eugene doesn't know we're coming?" That part she approved.

"No. J.D. will have him feeling all calm and relaxed when we arrive."

"You cooked this up with Carson?"

"Oh, no. He has no inkling, either."

Dallas sat back with a satisfied smile. But that word *inkling* set off a bell in Maggie's head.

"When you told us about Laurel seeing Zales, you said you had an inkling. That's what made you talk to him. That inkling, where'd it come from? Carson?"

"J.D.? How would he—? No."

A piece fell into place. "Scott."

"That would not be discreet of him."

No, it wouldn't be. He shouldn't gossip about who he saw or what he heard while in the lawyer's office, no more than he should have told her what he had this afternoon.

Dallas was going on. "To understand Scott, you must understand about his mama, my cousin, Dina."

Before Maggie could say she didn't want to understand Scott—or his mother—Dallas plunged in.

"Dina never got used to the idea the family money was gone. She married a nice enough fella, but Tomlinson left when Scott wasn't even in school yet. Dina treated that boy more like a pet than a son. Tried to talk to her, but she wasn't one for listening.

"Scott was starting high school when Tony came along. Scott and Dina fought something terrible. Well, he fought. She went on doing what she wanted. Married Tony that spring. Things were rocky until Scott left for college. By then, she'd run Tony into debt. I helped a bit with Scott's schooling, tuition and such. He talked about law, but his grades ... When he raised becoming a court reporter, I thought it might remind him of what he'd wanted and didn't have, but he started strong.

"But damned if he didn't go into a tailspin when Dina died. You'd think there'd never been the fightin'. You'd think it had always been the two of them, close as after his daddy left. Didn't work for months, and what with more jurisdictions using recordings and such, it's been harder."

She remembered Scott's disappointment at not working for the sheriff. And Dallas' response.

"You throw jobs his way," she said to Dallas. "That's nepotism."

He smiled with genuine amusement. "Not in Bedhurst County. Here it's called helping family. But your experience might have been different."

"You didn't say Scott didn't provide the information that gave you an inkling."

"No, I didn't. But what about your family, Maggie?" Uh-huh. This explained the buildup. He'd been trying to work it around to her. "I understand your cousin is in charge of the Sunshine Foundation in Washington. How do you—"

"Here we are."

Carson held his truck's passenger door open while Tagner used it to steady himself as he slowly climbed out.

Dallas murmured, "Perfectly timed, my dear."

CHAPTER FORTY-SIX

SHE FELT JUSTIFIED ignoring Dallas' comment, since she'd been getting out of the car. Nobody could prove she'd heard it.

Standing at his truck, Carson's brows rose in question. She shrugged slightly.

Dallas, moving at a surprisingly good rate, was already to Tagner. "Eugene, let me take your arm. Yes, yes, right this way. Up the stairs and—Louelle, it's a pleasure to see you. We'll set a while in the card room. No need for refreshments. We were treated to all one could hope to drink or eat at Rambler Farm. Quite the event."

Carson closed his truck door and gestured for her to precede him as they trailed Dallas and his captive inside, past a puzzled Louelle, and to the opposite side of the house from the previous visit.

This room was significantly smaller and more comfortable, with a poker table and chairs on one side, sofa and upholstered chairs on the other. Dallas deposited Eugene in a chair.

Behind them, Louelle made a protesting sound, but Carson closed the door, and the housekeeper didn't try to open it.

Eugene roused himself. "Wh—What's this about?"

"A few questions, a few questions, that's all."

"I already answered—"

"That's the thing with an investigation. Every conversation you learn a little more, and then you need to come back around to those involved and ask again."

"Involved? I'm not involved."

Maggie cut in. "For example, when we hear that you not only

weren't changing your agreement with Laurel, but you'd checked to be sure it was still in its original form, just before her death."

That drew raised eyebrows from both Dallas and Carson.

Eugene didn't notice their surprise. "No! No, that's not right. Not right. I didn't. I never—Renee said don't and I didn't." He breathed audibly.

"We'll check and we'll find out," she said.

"Then you'll find out I didn't. Didn't. You can't be saying things like that. If Renee…" Apparently realizing he'd been about to say something unwise, he shut his mouth.

Dallas picked up. "As for being involved, of course you are. You're the bereaved widower of Laurel, well-deserving of all the condolences extended to you at Rambler Farm these past hours."

"Well, yes, but not … you know, with the investigation of Laurel's, uh, death."

"Laurel's death? Oh, *that's* what you thought we wanted to ask about?" Dallas asked.

Eugene sent J.D. a look over his shoulder. Why? Did he know Laurel had gone after Carson, at least according to Charlotte?

"Uh, yeah."

"Not at all, not at all. It's what happened between you and Pan we wish to discuss."

Maggie would swear Carson didn't move or make a sound, yet it was like he exerted a force that whipped Eugene's head around toward him, even as their reluctant host squeaked, "Pan? Nothing happened between Pan and me. Nothing between Pan and me."

"I didn't—Eugene, please look at me when I talk to you." Dallas waited while Eugene slowly faced him. "I didn't say anything happened, now did I? Though not for your lack of tryin'."

"I—I—"

Dallas talked over him. "Several weeks before J.D., here, came back to town. Out at Shenny's. You'd been in the bar for some period of time. Pan was in the restaurant with two friends. You, shall we say, joined their table uninvited and made statements that also were uninvited."

"How'd you hear that? Not that I admit—"

"Eugene, Eugene, the exchange took place in front of witnesses. Do you truly believe you can deny it to everyone?"

"It's not everyone I'm worried about."

Since he continued to glance at Carson, it didn't require a guess to know who he was worried about.

"J.D., assure the man you will not pummel him over the incident in question."

Carson considered Eugene through eyes narrowed to slits. "If I ever hear you talking about Pan—"

"Never, never with anything but the utmost respect. Utmost respect."

"—or subjecting another woman to unwanted advances."

"Any other woman?"

"Any other woman." He held Eugene's gaze. After receiving an acquiescent nod, Carson concluded, "I will pummel you. I will not over this incident."

Eugene swallowed at the ominous ring of those final words.

"Excellent," Dallas said briskly, "now tell us your account of what happened."

"Nothing. Really, nothing serious. It was like you said, I saw her there in the restaurant when I went to the back to—Well, you know. When I came out I thought I'd go by and say hello. Attractive woman, real attractive. Wasn't a good time, though. She was busy, that's all. Busy."

"You propositioned her for sex," Dallas said in his sharpest cross-examination tone.

Eugene started to turn toward Carson, then appeared to think better of it. "Looking for some fun. Thought she might be, too."

"She was a married woman at the time," Dallas said.

"Suppose so, though she'd left Rick. Oh, you're thinking that meant she was a no-go." He shook his head. "Not my experience. Not my experience. I was married, too, and women came on to me most all the time."

"Not respectable women," Dallas said. Hard to tell if he was truly shocked or putting on a show.

"Oh, yeah, respectable, too." Eugene argued. "Like the Blankenship girls."

Girls. Plural.

Maggie broke the momentary silence to be absolutely sure. "Charlotte, too?"

"Yeah. Pretty sad, really. Not my type. And mostly she talked about what a force we'd be in county politics, maybe the state. Could've taken a lesson from her sister and sat on my lap, unbuttoned her blouse, and popped her tits in my face. God, that girl did have great tits." Tears came into his eyes. "Such a waste, such a waste."

"How'd it make you feel when Pan shot you down?" Carson asked abruptly.

He frowned. "Kinda surprised she was that sharp, because she'd always been nice to me, but not real tore up, either, you know? Well, maybe you don't. Until I had money it was how most females were to me. With the businesses and all, it changed, mostly, but not entirely. I'm still kind of used to it. Used to it."

"You called her a bitch and said she'd regret it," Dallas said.

Carson made a low sound.

"It was the drink talking. The drink. I wouldn't have ever hurt Pan. I *didn't* hurt her. I—"

The door opened abruptly.

Eugene's second ex-wife walked in, with a smug Louelle momentarily visible before the door closed.

Eugene twisted around. "Renee!" You'd think he'd been rescued from being beaten with hoses.

"Why, this *is* a surprise to find you all here with my Eugene." Her sarcasm was too thick to drip.

"My, oh, my," Dallas said with a reproving shake of his head, "you are most fortunate not to have encountered any law enforcement on your way here, Renee. Even allowin' for Louelle telephonin' you with alacrity, you must have severely broken the speed limit."

Unruffled she said, "I was on my way to see Eugene when Louelle called. How are you, darlin'?" From behind his chair, she put a hand on his shoulder and kissed the top of his head. He relaxed, facing forward. "As nice as it is to see y'all—again and so soon—it's been a long day and Eugene—"

Maggie cut across Renee. "Eugene, we'd like to talk to your divorce lawyer, clear up some issues. It could help you a lot."

Eugene looked up at Renee.

She said, "No. Now, if you'll excuse—"

"I have another question." Maggie stepped in close, blocking Eugene's view of Renee, "What does Laurel's will say?"

"Everything comes to me, of course. We had our wills drawn up same time as our other agreement. Mine has bequests—to Louelle, some charities—but Laurel's didn't. She left whatever she had to me. Everything to me."

"None to her family?" Dallas asked.

Renee interrupted, "Nothing odd in a wife leaving everything to her husband."

"Do the Blankenships know?"

Renee clicked her tongue. "They have no kick. Laurel hadn't inherited her half of Rambler Farm yet. Now that would've been something."

CARSON WAS ALREADY at the back door of Monroe House when Maggie pulled in with Dallas once again her passenger.

"Join us for supper," Dallas invited. "Evelyn's made soup and fresh rolls."

"I'm not hungry, but we should talk. Then I'm going to continue with the transcript."

"Yes, yes, come in to talk. If you don't want it now, we'll send soup back with you to the guesthouse when you go."

"Really, I'm not—" Her words stopped at Carson's hand touching the small of her back, nudging her forward.

"If you want to talk about anything else, stop arguing with him about soup." Now inside, she saw Evelyn busy with a large pot on a burner, getting bowls and plates out. "He'll never quit. Faster to take it and throw it out later if you don't want it."

"Throw it out? Evelyn's soup? I never heard of such a thing. Just you wait."

It did smell good, but she had no appetite after the spread at Rambler Farm.

Quickly, they were seated around the table in the kitchen, the other three eating soup and rolls that smelled heavenly.

"Other than Eugene propositioning Pan, what did you pick up at Rambler Farm?" she asked Dallas and Carson.

"You first, since we're eatin'. In addition to that question about the will—where did that come from?"

She told them. "Figured there might be something there."

"Good figurin'," Dallas said. "Wonder if Charlotte knows everything goes to Eugene."

"Except Laurel's share of Rambler Farm. Now Charlotte will inherit it all," Maggie said slowly.

Dallas dismissed it with "Long way off," but Maggie wasn't so sure. Charlotte might take the long view.

"What of Eugene checking on the pre-nup?" J.D. asked her.

"I hate to steal his thunder..." She recounted what Scott said.

Carson's only contribution was that he'd talked with Teddie Barrett's mother. "She said she thought maybe she knew which man it was gave Teddie liquor. But then she named nearly every male in attendance, including the judge and Sheriff Gardner, who was still in Richmond at the time." He lifted one shoulder. "I was mostly saying hello."

They shifted to chewing over what Eugene had said.

Eventually Dallas spread his hands. "It stands like this: He wanted to get back to Renee. But there was Laurel, in the way. Renee wouldn't hold back on letting him know he'd been stupid to have Laurel sign those papers. There's the money, and the worry about getting the papers dealt with, and the prospect of havin' Laurel back in the house, then needin' to get her out again, and the whole divorce process. Not to mention his, ahem, amorous skills or lack thereof... Sure made things smoother for him with Laurel gone."

"Unless he's charged with murder," Maggie pointed out.

"Doesn't look likely, now does it?"

Into the silence, Carson suddenly said, "Remember what Renee said about the design of Eugene's house?"

She waited for a response from the others. When none came, she said, "Yeah. So?"

"Eugene doesn't have original ideas."

Dallas rumbled agreement.

She asked, "What's your point, Carson?"

A tic showed at the side of his mouth. Annoyance? Or a suppressed smile? "Thinking how a man who makes his *personal architectural statement* by copying a picture in a magazine might deal with a wife causing him trouble."

"You're saying Eugene copied the murder of Pan because he wasn't original enough to figure one out on his own?"

"He's not original, doesn't mean he's stupid. Somebody got away with killing Pan to date."

"And by inference, you're saying Wade kills his wife and Eugene copycats to kill his when she becomes an annoyance?"

"Could be," Dallas said.

Carson frowned. "Would be interesting to know exactly what Pan told Wade. Or if he knew by some other means that she'd been back to see Zales."

"All his talk about going to Lynchburg and playing golf," Maggie said. "Why didn't he just go to talk to Zales? Unless Gardner said he couldn't, either. Maybe Zales won't talk, holding attorney-client privilege even after death, but depending on who's executor for Laurel's estate—"

"What is it, Maggie?"

She'd sat bolt straight, facing Dallas. "Inkling. That's what kept poking at me after all your dodging about whether Scott told you about Laurel consulting Zales. You said Carson didn't. But in the car, when you first told us, you looked at him."

"I have no idea what you're talking about. J.D., if you'd pass me the rolls and butter?"

"When you said that about an inkling. In the car at Shenny's. You looked at the back of his head," she insisted.

Carson, holding the basket of rolls, shifted his gaze toward Dallas.

"Really, my boy, it was ... nothing." Perhaps he heard how unconvincing he sounded, because he sighed deeply, then raised and dropped his hands in surrender. "It was about Pan."

"What about Pan?"

"She'd been to see Zales the day before she died." After a pause, he added, "She'd decided. She was leavin' Rick. For good. I have it on excellent authority and it backs up what Rick said, that she had told Zales to start the divorce process."

"Why keep that from Carson?" Maggie asked. "It gives him less motive."

"No, it doesn't," Carson said, "because I didn't know until now that she was killed because she was coming away with me."

Dallas clicked his tongue. "Investigatin' is one thing, but there's such a thing as being too dispassionate, J.D."

"No there's not." Before Dallas could respond, she added, "Have you told the sheriff all these connections with Zales? It's a strong potential link between the cases."

"My dear, going to Henry Zales connects nearly every woman in Bedhurst County who has contemplated divorce and can get themselves to Lynchburg."

Commonwealth v. J.D. Carson

Witness Oliver Zalenkia (prosecution)
Cross-Examination by Mr. Monroe

Q: Now, Dr. Zalenkia, we wrangled a good while this morning about whether you can tell if a hair was pulled from someone's head by some perfectly innocent means such as being caught in a friend's cuff button and—

Ms. Frye: Objection. Mr. Monroe is once again trying to testify.

THE COURT: Sustained. Ask your question, if you have one.

Q. I do, Your Honor, I do. Now, Dr. Zalenkia, you also examined clothing from the laundry hamper that Pandora Addington Wade was using while living with her parents, the Addingtons, is that correct?

A. Yes.

Q. And on that clothing, did you find any hairs?

A. Yes.

Q. In addition to Pan Addington Wade's own hair, whose else could you identify?

Ms. Frye: Your Honor, I continue to object—

THE COURT: And I continue to overrule. You may answer the question, Dr. Zalenkia.

A. I identified hairs belonging to Theresa Addington, Kevin Addington—

Q. Her parents?

A. Yes. Also Richard Wade, Junior.

Q. Her husband?

A. Yes. Also Sheriff Hague.

Q. My, oh my, the sheriff of Bedhurst County?

A. Yes.

Q. Anyone else's hair that you attached a name to?

A. Yours. At least—

THE COURT: Order. Order in the court.

A. May I clarify, Your Honor?

THE COURT: You may, Dr. Zalenkia.

A. It was only an initial test that indicated it was likely that Mr. Monroe was in the division of subjects who could have donated that hair.

Q. I do thank you for that clarification. I'm quite relieved not to have been arrested myself.

CHAPTER FORTY-SEVEN

BELICHEK WAITED UNTIL he was off-duty to make more calls.

He liked what he'd heard about Sheriff Gardner, not what he'd heard about the murder investigation of Laurel Tagner.

As for the first case, nothing since Carson was found not guilty.

He called Maggie last.

She answered the first ring, but she sounded like her attention was elsewhere.

"How's it going?"

"Fine and dandy. I'm rereading the transcript."

That explained her distraction. "Anything?"

"Not yet. Except a nagging feeling there is something or should be something or could be something. Maybe it's wishful thinking. Because the deeper we go with this, the less concrete everything seems to be."

"Happens that way a lot. Who'd you talk to today?"

"Nearly everybody."

She updated him on the information from the Addingtons about the calls, tried to be casual about the ones to her—he let that go, since he already knew Gardner was checking on them from a friend of a friend with connections to the investigation—then detailed what she'd learned at the memorial, followed by Eugene Tagner.

"…and in addition to Dallas reporting to him, I wrote Gardner an email saying that if Eugene—more accurately Renee—would let us talk to his lawyer, a lot of this uncertainty could be cleared up."

"That might be why they don't want you talking to the lawyer," Bel said dryly. "Guilty doesn't want things cleared up."

"True. It's possible Eugene killed Pan for that rejection, but I don't buy it. So, if he killed Laurel, using Pan's murder as a how-to, that means there could be two murderers."

"Don't get ahead of yourself."

"Hey, you're the one who raised the possibility the first time we talked."

"Possibility, yeah. Conclusion, no. You gotta—"

"I know, I know, build a mountain of evidence a pebble at a time."

"That's right. And only when you have a lot of the pebbles that belong to your particular mountain do you start seeing its shape. You waste a lot of time trying to guess at what the mountain will end up like when you've only got a few pebbles."

"Great. Did you call to give me the Rutherford Belichek Criminology 101 Lecture—again? Because please don't tell me you're going to pull a Vic and say I need to get my butt back to Fairlington when I'm only helping out the new sheriff."

He pulled in a bushel of air.

"Is that all you're doing?" Along with the question, he expelled the air, trying not to let it come in a gust. "Do you have a feeling this reminds you of something?"

"Of course. The murder of Pan Wade."

"No, I mean starting with her murder."

"What are you getting at? Are you saying Pan's murder reminds you of another case?"

He heard the heightened interest in her voice. "Not like you're thinking, Mags. And it wouldn't be reminding *me* of another case. I meant reminding you of another case. Of ... the case."

Silence.

Silence like a vacuum had sucked all the words out of the air, leaving blankness between, around, them, and all along the phone connection.

"Mags..." It was half asking her to forget he'd said anything, half asking her to come through.

"I don't—I won't—"

"I know you don't, and I'm not asking you to talk to me. But listen. And think about it. Sounds like Pan Wade was like—was the same kind of woman. Sweet. Loved by everybody as far as anyone could ever tell. Trusting. Nice. Real tight with her family." He knew that treaded close, and pulled back. "Trying to do her best in life, and by people. Maybe too trusting. Too nice.

"And then think about the kind of murderer who could take advantage of that kind of a woman. Charming. Con man. Going out of his way to be sure he was everybody's favorite. Patient. Patient enough to plan what he wanted. And arrogant, thinking he's smarter than everybo—"

"I gotta go."

"Okay, Mags. Okay. Just think about it. I won't—"

"Bye."

SHE MADE IT to the toilet, but nothing came up.

Not sure her legs would get her back to the table, she sat on the floor, her cheek against the cool smoothness of the toilet lid.

Her hands were shaking, but her mind was working.

Similarities.

I'm saying that in a general way they look like each other—and like you.

There was a strong physical resemblance among the Fryes. If there was a resemblance linking Pan and Laurel and her, then there was a resemblance to another woman. Another victim.

The Bedhurst cases couldn't possibly be related to her aunt's murder. He was dead. No question.

Yet...

Similarities.

Had she recognized that at some level all along? Did that explain the bizarre moment of questioning Carson's guilt?

Carson.

He'd spotted the resemblance. Possibly long before seeing the photos on the board in the high school gym?

Just how much research had he done on her family?

The same kind of woman.

Blood. Savage wounds. Head arched back in ultimate pain—

No. No. She wouldn't. She couldn't. Or her brain would not work. Would stop completely. Forever.

The other, look at the other. Think about that.

Think. That's what she had to do. Think about what else Belichek had said.

Charming. Con man. Going out of his way to be sure he was everybody's favorite.

Was that Carson?

First reaction, she'd say no.

He had some charm, she supposed. That wasn't his appeal.

He was a favorite of some, yes. Certainly not all. With those who didn't favor him she'd seen him make no effort to change their view. More, he seemed indifferent. With an edge, perhaps, but still indifferent.

That rough indifference was entirely unlike—

Was not the hallmark of a classic, smooth con man.

She levered herself upright, washed her hands while leaning against the sink.

But who said all con men were the classic type?

She got back to work.

CHAPTER FORTY-EIGHT

CHARLOTTE SAT IN the dark of the sunroom.

The judge and Ed had gone to bed early, but she was too steeped in the success of the memorial to consider it.

A breeze outside shivered the swing under the broad-arching oak, catching her attention.

Nearly five years ago, Pan had sat next to her on the swing, those long tanned legs tucked under her, her arms wrapped around herself. Tears slipped one at a time down her cheeks.

"How do you do it, Charlotte? How do you hold it together? This house, the judge's social calendar, all the projects and—"

"I work damned hard. I never let up."

Pan had blinked, surprise breaking through her self-absorbed misery. "But … you make it look easy. All the parties, the charities…"

"Never mind."

Pan reached out and touched her shoulder. "No, no. I'm glad you told me. I'm grateful. It's a wakeup call. I suppose I've had this naïve idea of what life would be, how easy it would be. You're right. I haven't worked hard enough. But I will."

Pan, the dreamy little idiot, had been sure Charlotte's words were meant only in her best interest. That's how she saw everything. That's how she thought the world worked—to please her, to make things better for her.

Then Charlotte had blurted out a truth she'd never before spoken aloud.

"It's damned hard, being indispensable. Making it look easy

enough nobody feels uncomfortable or they won't come back, but not so easy they don't appreciate you. It's a tightrope."

Pan had stared at her with the pity of someone who knew the trip across the tightrope would end in disaster. Maybe not this one or the next or the one after, but some trip, some time.

It infuriated Charlotte.

"You can't do what I do." Charlotte had tried to keep the words in. They wouldn't be kept. Her gaze bounced away from Pan's startled face. She stared at the petunias grown leggy and the gladiolas in need of staking. "You've never had to work hard at anything in your life. You, Laurel. Given everything. You think either of you could keep a place like Rambler Farm running? I've had to do everything. You? You've only ever had to be yourself."

Pan had held still while the words jerked out of Charlotte. After, she untucked her legs, planted her feet flat. Charlotte felt oddly chilled.

"You've never liked me. All these years, all the years I thought we were friends, you've never liked me. You haven't known me, either. You're right about a lot of things, Charlotte, but you are wrong about this."

Pan got up, giving the swing a shove that jerked Charlotte in a way she could only believe was deliberate, and walked away.

Charlotte never talked to her again. She saw her at church that Sunday, of course, but it was easy to not cross close enough where talking was required. Charlotte was quite sure nobody noticed.

Soon Pan was dead. And now Laurel was, too.

DAMMIT, THERE WAS something in this transcript trying to tell her something.

If Maggie could put everything else out of her mind and concentrate, surely she'd see it.

A muscle from the back of her neck to her shoulder contracted. She sat upright to ease it, and her back and knees griped at the abrupt change of position after rusting into place. Even her forehead—she rubbed at tightness there—was complaining.

And no wonder. It was after nine. She'd spent hours squinting in concentration over the transcript as if it were a holy rune.

Then her stomach rumbled.

The vote was unanimous—time to get up, move around, get something to eat. She'd come back to it fresher.

After a cup of soup, a warmed-up roll, and a glass of ice water, she noticed the garbage can had reached capacity. She set the filled black plastic bag on the back steps while she fitted a fresh one into the can.

A scratching sound from the shadowy bushes brought her head up. Good heavens, Carson and Evelyn had said to be careful of garbage-digging raccoons, but could they possibly be reacting to the bag already?

She locked the door and grabbed the bag to take it to the main house. No way was she giving J.D. Carson the opportunity for a told-you-so.

A few steps into the rhododendrons and it was tunnel dark. But she knew the path to Monroe House's back door.

Damp leathery touches against her face were rhododendron leaves. She remembered the sensation from the climb to the overlook behind J.D. at the crime scene. What had he been looking for? She'd never asked, he'd never said.

That might have been short-sighted. Truth or lie, an answer could provide—

A sound behind her.

Raccoons following the scent? Wasn't that extreme, even for the pushy behavior Carson and Evelyn described.

And this wasn't the same sound as the scratching in the bushes by the back door. It was more furtive. Yet ... bigger. Something pushing at the leaves about shoulder height at the same time creating a faint footfall.

Footfalls closing in on her.

She went faster. If she ran, could she beat her follower to the back door?

Not if it was Roy.

Roy who wouldn't be above trying to frighten someone in the name of "fun."

She'd reached where one side of the path opened to the oval of lawn, but the deep shadows left it no brighter. She picked up speed.

Behind her, she heard her follower break into a run. Toward her. Coming right at her.

Fury spun her around, and instinct swung the bag of garbage into a high arc. It crashed down on the shape behind her—a person, definitely a person. A man? She thought so, couldn't be sure.

Her follower reached out, a shadowed hand squeezing at her shoulder, trying to grip her. Maggie jerked out of the grasp.

She swung a second time, putting all her strength into it. Hitting head and shoulders as the figure tried to duck. One seam split, spilling a stream of egg shells, tomato stems, coffee grounds, ripe cans that once held orange juice. She let go of the bag, and felt the top give way in another spurt of smelly garbage.

The figure recoiled.

With that momentary advantage, Maggie turned and ran to the main house.

"Dallas!" she shouted. "Call the police!"

Inside the back door—*still* not locked—she slammed it closed behind her, fumbling for the latch. She sprinted through the kitchen and into the hallway, still shouting. Dallas was fumbling his way out of the oversized chair.

"Wha—What is it? Maggie? What's wrong?" He squinted at her from eyes heavy with sleep.

"Someone chased me from the guesthouse. A man. I'm almost sure." She was panting, winded by more than the short run.

"Good God. J.D. will find whoever it was."

"J.D.?" There was no one else in the room.

But Dallas was going on. "We thought we'd work in comfort in here. He's right…" He looked at the couch. On the coffee table sat a neat pile of folders. "He must have stepped out a moment."

At the window, Maggie checked the lighted drive. "His truck's not here. Carson!"

Silence.

Confusion showed in Dallas's eyes. Until he remembered not to show her what he was thinking, and dropped those heavy lids like a curtain.

Chill understanding swept across Maggie, leaving goose bumps.

J.D. Carson's alibi for the murder of Laurel Blankenship Tagner had just evaporated.

Because that Saturday could have unfolded the way this evening had.

When Dallas fell asleep, obviously Carson slipped away without the older man ever knowing. So, when her shouting woke Dallas, he still expected to see his associate sitting across from him.

If she hadn't arrived, Dallas would have slept on in peace. Carson easily could have slipped back in, awakened the older man at some convenient point and presented himself as having been there all along. Dallas wouldn't know otherwise.

As he could have when Laurel was murdered.

As he could have only a few minutes ago when someone followed her. Roy might have motivation to try to rattle her, but who knew the guesthouse and grounds better than Carson?

She picked up the phone on the desk in the corner—her phone was back in the guesthouse—and stabbed in numbers.

"Are you calling the sheriff?"

"No. He has enough to do." She hung up, and dialed another number. No answer at either of Roy's numbers. "What's Carson's phone number?"

She hit the numbers as Dallas recited them. It rang and rang. Until a neutral voice invited her to leave a message. To be sure, she also called the law office, and got the standard message.

She replaced the phone, said to Dallas, "It could have been him."

She saw his recognition that she meant more than chasing her from the guesthouse.

He shook his head, but said only, "Tell me what happened."

When she'd finished, a slight smile lifted his face for a moment. "You're a resourceful woman, Maggie Frye. A resourceful woman.

Moreover, your resourcefulness has put the mark of Cain on the perpetrator. More accurately the stink of refuse on him. If you can find someone who smells, you'll know you have the man."

Damn, if he wasn't right.

But only for a short time.

The person would change, shower as soon as possible to get the stink off.

If it was Roy, he was already heading out of town, and with myriad routes to choose from her odds of catching him were crap.

Carson's options were more limited. If he bore the stink of her counterattack he couldn't risk seeing anyone else, because when word got out about her follower and the garbage spill—and word would get out in Bedhurst—people would connect him with the incident. He had to get home, fast. To wash off evidence.

"Where are you goin'?" Dallas called as she sprinted out.

"I'll be back."

She retraced her route through the house. Outside, instead of the darkened path, she followed the open walk that led to the lane that serviced the guesthouse, then ran down its center to her car, digging out the keys she'd pocketed after locking the guesthouse's back door. She slammed it into reverse and backed up.

CHAPTER FORTY-NINE

10:19 p.m.

IT WASN'T THE shack in the woods she'd seen four and a half years ago.

Not only did the address provide GPS navigation straight to his front door by the new road, but what sat around that front door was completely different.

This was a solid structure with a sharply peaked roof. Not a hut sinking into the forest floor. The wood was weathered gray with no sign of paint. She stepped up three stairs to a porch of the same material, unsoftened by a plant or chair.

She knocked twice on the equally unadorned door. Then called out his name.

No answer and no sound inside. She grasped the wrought iron handle, hesitated, then tried it. The door moved easily, opening wide, and she was in his home.

Lights came on as she entered. She called out again. Nothing.

From the threshold, softly aged wooden planks stretched in front of her, nearly uninterrupted by furniture. The only upholstered piece in the large room was an oversized chair with matching ottoman set at an angle by the stone fireplace. A wooden rocking chair and settee joined it. There was an open stairway to the right, leading to what she guessed was a loft bedroom.

In the back left corner, past a door on the far side of the fireplace, was a compact kitchen with cream-painted cabinets, modern appliances and a small island with two stools on this side. In the back right corner, a desk held a computer setup.

Both of these areas had normal height ceilings, with the loft above. The front of the cabin soared to the peaked roof.

On the front wall were bookshelves. From floor to high ceiling and from one corner to the other, interrupted only by a pair of windows and the door still open behind her.

The wall opposite the fireplace was made up entirely of windows. Actually two sets of windows, she saw as she stepped closer. The interior windows were three sets of sliding glass doors, all open. The room beyond was no more than five feet wide, with a brick floor and a bench along an outside wall, made from more framed windows. It smelled warm and fertile.

Something caught her eye as she stepped into the bricked area, and she saw the ceiling was also made of windows. The moonlight had caught her attention, casting shadows on plants lining the bench.

She backed up. Just plants. That's all. She wouldn't learn anything from them. She went to the seating area in front of the fireplace. There was nothing on the chairside table. The mantel was a single large squared-off log. Atop it was an uncovered tin box with matches and twists of newspaper inside.

He left as little out to reveal himself in his home as he did in his expression.

Except his books.

She started examining the shelves. Law books. Not the volumes of statutes, but books about the law and about those who practiced it.

The next section had military books. On snipers. On military theory. On leadership. Then books on the mountains. Nature. Geology. History. A section of fiction, heavy on Dickens.

"Find what you're looking for?"

She was turning even before her gasp formed.

Wearing only running shorts and shoes, Carson stood inside the side door between the fireplace and kitchen.

Before she marshaled words, he added, "And does anyone know you're here? Hope you called the sheriff before you ventured into the woods."

"You don't lock your door. Out here in the middle of nowhere and you don't lock your door. Why aren't you robbed blind?" It was an approach Vic had taught her: If direct has thrown you for a loop, make your first cross-examination question quick and sharp. To hide that inside you're scrambling.

"You didn't try to get out."

"What?"

"You can come in, but you can't get out. Does no one any good to break in if they can't get out with loot. Besides, word got out fast."

"Word of what?"

He picked a wooden chair up by the back like a lion tamer and pushed it toward the door, touching the handle lightly. A net dropped from the ceiling with lightning speed, but he'd jumped back even faster, leaving the chair captured.

"You booby-trapped your house?"

"Only for unwelcomed—" One eyebrow rose. "—or uninvited guests. Some tried to steal building materials from out here early on. Wasn't comfortable for them. No one's bothered me much since."

Sweat showed on his chest, arms, legs, turned the bottom of his hair shiny dark. She smelled the heat on him. Or felt it.

"You've been running?"

His eyes glinted, but he said simply, "Yeah."

"At night?"

"Yeah."

"This late?"

"Yeah."

"In the woods in the *dark?*"

"Yeah."

Each yeah was more unrevealing than the previous one.

"How the hell do you see where you're going?"

"You don't. You feel it."

"You must have excellent night vision."

He opened a set of doors off the kitchen and grabbed a towel he wrapped around his neck. "Coming out here to ask about my night vision is a waste of your time. You have all the information in my old Army files. Including the fact that night runs were part of training. And since you don't waste time, why did you come?"

"Someone attacked me."

A sharp, assessing look. Drawing a reaction from him that broke through that cool exterior felt like some kind of victory.

"Attack's too strong," she continued. "Tried to spook me, probably. Followed me on the path from the guesthouse to the main house, tried to grab me."

"And you came here."

She had no reason to feel ashamed. She'd acted on logic and reason. "Yes."

"How long ago?"

She checked her watch. "Twenty-two minutes."

"A man?"

"I think so. I couldn't see him—" She shrugged at the pronoun. "It was an impression of size, of ... movement."

She hesitated on that last word. J.D. Carson has a distinct way of moving. Would she have recognized that, even as a shadow? Unless he'd masked it on purpose.

"What did you expect to get from coming here when you couldn't make an ID?"

"I couldn't see the person, but I should be able to smell him. I hit him with the garbage bag and it broke all over him."

He stared at her, his face not quite still. A space by his scar indented.

He was trying not to grin.

That didn't mean he was innocent. He could be wanting to grin because he'd outmaneuvered her.

"Damn. A new self-defense maneuver. Call it the Maggie Frye Defense." He uncrossed his arms, spread them wide. "Go ahead and sniff."

She ignored the offer.

"And now that you've spent all this time eliminating me, it's too late to check anyone else." He let his arms drop.

"You're not eliminated. You could have stripped off your smelly outer clothes and put on running clothes. Sweat could mask whatever smell was left."

"And still get here in time? I'd have to drive here, stow my guilty clothes and run enough to get this sweaty. That doesn't leave much time for thinking out this brilliant plan in the first place."

"I never said you were stupid."

"No, you never did. One thing you haven't accused me of." He went into the kitchen, opened the fridge.

Feeling dismissed, she started to leave. He was right that it was too late to check anyone else. Not only Roy, but Eugene, Rick, even Charlotte or—if it came to that, she supposed—Ed Smith.

"Maggie." He still had his back to her. He seemed to stare out the window into the shadowy woods around them. "If you walk into my home uninvited a second time, you better be prepared."

"Prepared for wh …?" By the third word, she lost the steam of indignant ignorance.

She knew. And no matter how strongly she wanted *not* to know, it was insufficient to stem the knowing.

He looked over his shoulder at her.

Damn it.

Damn him.

Damn her.

Damn.

She gave him back a stare she hoped was saying she'd roast in hell first.

But she knew all too well that not all hopes are granted.

As she drove away, the black sky opened to a deluge, which somehow seemed appropriate.

CHAPTER FIFTY

Friday, 9:22 a.m.

"I'VE GOT THE phone records."

J.D. held up the sheets from the doorway of Dallas' office. Dallas was behind his desk. Maggie sat at the table. The clear space before her had grown another few inches. Another ring of folders had been neatly stacked and—he glanced toward the bookshelves—more books returned to where they belonged. Give the woman a few more weeks, and continued nervous energy, and she'd have Dallas' office presentable.

"How'd—?"

"Sheriff." He dropped a copy on the table, gave Dallas another, then sat on the sofa with the final one. "He had no objection. The technicalese at the start confirms the records for Pan's phone are long gone. Better luck with calls to and from Laurel. Guesthouse are here, too."

Dallas grunted after flipping through the pages. He'd spotted the problem, too.

J.D. pointed out Eugene's home number, as well as two numbers at Rambler Farm. He also ticked off the number to Shenny's, several clothes stores, the hair stylist, a state liquor ABC in Lynchburg.

"What about these incoming numbers?" Maggie immediately asked when he paused. She was making notes on her copy.

"The 555-9624 that shows up only during the day, so not on the records for the guesthouse, is a phone in the courthouse. In an alcove behind Courtroom One, between the courtroom and judge's chambers."

"It's no help," Dallas grumbled. "Everybody having trouble with reception uses it and that's most everybody. There's people wanderin' in and out of there all day. I've seen bailiffs and judges and lawyers and defendants and witnesses and staff on that phone. I've used it myself."

"Next best thing to a public phone," Carson agreed. "Nobody would blink at anybody using that phone. As Dallas said, no help. Then there are four numbers that show a few times each, including for the guesthouse."

"Whose?" she asked.

"Burner phones."

"All of them?"

"All of them. One person using four burner phones? Or Laurel knew four people who used burner phones—"

"No evidence of her using drugs," Dallas said.

"Autopsy's not final."

"I happen to be aware that the preliminary findings show no drug use."

Maggie muttered *happen to be aware*, then said more loudly, "And drugs wouldn't explain the burner numbers showing up for the late-night calls to the guesthouse. I was not ordering home delivery, I promise."

"We'll need evidence of that." J.D. dodged her glare. "Some of these calls are from Rambler Farm to Laurel's number and they're damned late."

Dallas reached over to his phone and punched in numbers, putting it on speakerphone. Charlotte answered. "Charlotte, this is Dallas Herbert Monroe calling. How are you today, my dear?"

"Quite well. How are you?"

Maggie shifted, her obvious impatience squeaking the chair.

"Very well, thank you. Lovely reception yesterday. I told Evelyn about those cranberry and brie puffs, and she might be calling your Allarene for the recipe."

"I'd be pleased to share that with her, especially if she shares the recipe for her pecan pie."

"Oh, now, Charlotte, you know that's a family secret. She'd be run right out of the DuPree clan if she told anyone."

Charlotte said blandly, "I keep hoping."

Dallas responded with an obligatory chuckle.

"Now, Charlotte, I was hopin' you could answer a little question for us. Hate to bother the judge with something like this. It's something to follow up on Laurel's activities the days before the tragedy."

"I was never privy to Laurel's activities, as I've told you." Disapproval snaked through Charlotte's voice. "More than once."

"Just do the best you can, my dear, that's all we ask," Dallas said, pouring it on. "What we'd like to know is why folks at Rambler Farm would have cause to be callin' Laurel on her cell phone at one, two, even three in the morning."

There was silence. Maggie's head came up from the papers she'd been studying. Light filtering through the blinds glinted red off her hair. She sat straighter, looking toward Dallas, leaving him only her profile.

Charlotte's voice her back from other thoughts. "No one was calling Laurel," she said. "Except Laurel. She was forever losing her cell phone, and that's how she'd find it. She'd go to the closest phone to call her own number, listen for the ring. All hours of the day and night."

"Thank you, Charlotte. That's what we needed to know. You've been most helpful, my dear." After another exchange of pleasantries, Dallas clicked off the speakerphone. "It could account for calls from Rambler Farm numbers to Laurel."

Maggie rubbed her eyes. "Or it could have been Ed calling her. Some of those calls lasted a minute or more. And there's what those workmen said about Laurel coming on to Ed."

Dallas heaved a sigh. "Well, this doesn't get us any farther down the road, does it, then. We got Eugene callin' her, and folks at Rambler Farm, which could be Laurel herself, but could also be Charlotte or Ed or even the judge. As for the courthouse, it could be most anybody in town."

"Including Wade," J.D. said, aware of an arrival in the hall. Scott passed the open doorway to greet the newcomer.

"Or you," Maggie shot back. "You have business there as a lawyer."

"Yes, I do. And—"

"Maggie!" Scott's shout came from the hallway.

━━━━━━━━━━━━━

Commonwealth v. J.D. Carson

Witness Oliver Zalenkia (prosecution)
Cross-Examination by Mr. Monroe

Q. Could you determine who put the paper in Pan Wade's mouth?

A. We could not.

Q. Could you ascertain if the paper was put in Pandora Addington Wade's mouth before or after death?

A. We could not.

Q. Thank you. No more questions.

━━━━━━━━━━━━━

Theresa Addington (prosecution)
Redirect Examination by Ms. Frye

Q. Mrs. Addington, you heard the testimony that a piece of paper was found in your daughter's mouth by the medical examiner?

A. Yes.

Q. Was your daughter in the habit of eating or chewing on paper.

A. No. Never. Not even as a child.

━━━━━━━━━━━━━

✧ ✧ ✧ ✧

ROY STOOD IN the office doorway with Scott behind him.

"I told him you were in a meeting," Scott said.

"We are. Go away, Roy."

"Screw your meeting," Roy said. "We need to talk. Now."

She faced him. Her voice was cool enough to chip. "No, we don't. You need to listen. This is over. Over."

"I've said I'm sorry until I'm blue in the face."

"It's way past being about sorry. The fact that you haven't figured that out yet is part of the basic problem."

"Jesus, you are such a bitch."

Maggie's eyes cut to J.D. then away.

A fraction of a second, yet a niggling discomfort sifted through him. He hadn't moved. He had, however, shifted to a higher level of alertness.

Roy was too angry to notice. But she had.

He didn't like that.

"I can take care of myself," she said looking at Roy, but telling him.

"Of course, the great independent Maggie Frye can always take care of herself. Herself and the rest of the world." Roy's sarcasm was as subtle as a battle axe. "What's hard about it, after all? People fall into one category or the other—innocent or guilty. And the all-knowing Maggie decides which box they go into. Clear-cut and tidy, like your cases. That's how you treat people. Assess the crime. Weigh the evidence. Prosecute to the full extent of the law. Nothing less than perfect will do."

He slapped his hand on the back of the file-loaded chair by the door. No one else moved.

"Well, here's a bulletin, Maggie. You're not so damned perfect. Not even the great Maggie Frye is perfect."

"Roy, it's time for you to leave."

Underneath her calm was an edge of impatience, almost disdain that J.D. saw acting on Roy's control like acid on a rope.

"That eats at you, doesn't it, knowing you're not perfect? Ever since you broke down on the stand and let a murderer go free."

Maggie flinched. An involuntary motion quickly controlled.

"You'd think you'd be more understanding of other people's failings. Especially with you—of all people—going to this murderer's place alone last night. *That* won't do your career any good. What the fuck were you thinking?"

Scott snapped a look at J.D., but Maggie never even blinked. "You've been following me? It's none of your business where I go. Got that, Roy? None."

"Unless a fuck is why you went out there."

"You've been drinking. I can smell it from here. Don't drive like that."

"I'm not drunk. Not yet. But I will be. Because it'll take gallons of booze to get the bitter taste of Maggie Frye out of my mouth."

CHAPTER FIFTY-ONE

NONE OF THEM had moved when Scott returned to the room, the sound of the bolt indicating he'd locked the door after Roy.

"Maggie, don't let that guy bother you." Scott would have put his hand on her shoulder, but she shifted away. "You're wonderful, caring, generous. He's a jerk. He doesn't see—"

"I'm sorry for the interruption," she said precisely. "What else can we glean from these phone records?"

Dallas stood. "You and J.D. keep checkin' them. Scott and I need to get to the courthouse—other work, you know. But you two keep on talkin'. About the phone numbers and what they might mean."

❖ ❖ ❖ ❖

10:31 a.m.

"THE IMPORTANT THING is they catch the killer. It will give you and the judge closure—well, not closure, but at least knowing Laurel's murderer has been found."

Ed had been talking for some time. He'd said he stayed home from work today to be available to help her. But she didn't need help.

Except for him to stop talking at her.

As he drew in a breath, Charlotte cut in. "They'll never find out. There are too many choices. She was making it with every presentable man in the county. Marriage didn't stop that, and getting separated only made it worse. They might as well start with the county phone book for suspects."

"Charlotte," Ed said in a strained, hushed voice. And there was no reason after all. Nobody was here. "Don't say that. Don't tarnish your sister—"

"Tarnish? My God, how do you tarnish a whore?"

A power she had never known infused her bones.

He winced. "I know you and Laurel never saw eye-to-eye, but there was good in her. And all that life—"

She cut across his words, harsh and grating. "You were dreaming about fucking her again."

"Charlotte—" She saw him belatedly absorb the last word. "What? What?"

He was panicked, desperate.

"Don't be a fool, Ed. You think I didn't know you'd fucked her? Or should I say she fucked you? And she did, didn't she?" She chuckled a little. "Fucked you, then fucked you again by tossing you aside the way she did everyone. I suppose you were dreaming of her every time we fucked."

"*No.* Charlotte—"

She saw he was appalled even more by her matter-of-fact calm than by her words. And he was thoroughly horrified by her words. Interesting to watch. For a while.

"It doesn't matter. I knew what I was getting when I took you. But I did take you. And you will rise to a level I deserve. Laurel's dead. Fucking her will no longer be an issue or—"

"I didn't—after we were married—never, Charlotte. I swear to you—never."

She considered him. "Well, it doesn't matter now. But that Frye woman…"

"Maggie?" He looked confused.

"Yes, *Maggie,*" she mimicked. She tapped her pen against her chin. "Yes, Maggie. Can't have you fucking her. Have to do something about that."

✧ ✧ ✧ ✧

"...SO I HUSTLED Scott and myself out of there to see if nature would take its course, and came here to acknowledge you are a marvel, woman, to have seen that. Evelyn, marry me."

Dallas held up a hand to halt her reply.

"No, you said your piece before. It's my turn. I won't run for Commonwealth's Attorney again. Don't know I'll keep practicin' at all. This situation..." He cleared his throat. "But I've still got some life left in me, and long as there is, I want to spend it with you. You ... make me happy. I didn't think that would ever happen to me again."

She propped her hands on her hips, but he saw a smile pulling at her mouth. "Well, we can't have it any other way than Dallas Herbert Monroe happy, now can we? There's probably a law saying that."

"Damn right."

She swatted his shoulder as she stepped into his arms. "Watch your language."

He kissed her. "Does this mean you'll marry me."

"No."

"Evelyn—"

"Don't you lawyer-voice me, Dallas Herbert."

"Evelyn—"

Her gaze came up, warning him not to pursue the subject.

"Do you think the furniture in the parlor should be reupholstered?" He had the pleasure of knowing he'd surprised her. Not an easy achievement.

"Some should be reupholstered," she started slowly. "Some should be thrown out."

"Thrown out! That's..." He subsided under her arching eyebrow. "Will you take care of it?"

"No."

He supposed turnabout was fair play when it came to surprise.

He reviewed what he'd said. Ah. His infelicitous phrasing had pushed the task into what she considered employer-employee relations.

"Would you care to redecorate the house to suit your taste, Evelyn?"

"Our taste. Yes. I will see to that."

CHAPTER FIFTY-TWO

MAGGIE TAPPED HER fingers on the table, the sound breaking a good half hour of silence as they'd studied the phone records, making notes, pretending Roy Isaacson had never burst in and said the things he'd said.

J.D. looked at her.

Immediately, she said, "Interesting Laurel was killed Saturday night."

He considered that. "Because her habits meant she was likely not to be missed right away."

"Possibly. Or possibly because it would prevent her from attending another Sunday gathering at Rambler Farm."

He frowned. "Why?"

"Did Charlotte ever have a crush on you?"

"Where did that come from?"

"Just answer the question."

"Yes, ma'am, Ms. Prosecutor. The answer is: Not that I was aware of. Only emotion Charlotte ever showed toward me was disapproval."

"Oh."

"You're disappointed."

"Not disappointed. Just ... I keep thinking about Rick Wade saying jealousy is at the bottom of all this."

"Maybe you should talk to Wade then."

His tone made her look up. But he had his reactions under control again.

"These murders have some of the hallmarks of jealousy," she persisted. "Both victims could have accrued a monumental lump of jealousy: the popular, pretty girl and the sexy bombshell."

"You're thinking Charlotte might have been pining for me all these years. Murdered Pan to clear the way, then waited four and a half years—marrying someone else in the meantime—to murder her own sister on the off chance my fancy went that way? Shouldn't she have gotten rid of Ed?"

"Maybe she didn't consider him an impediment," she said tartly, clearly irked at his sarcasm. "And it wasn't just an off chance your fancy might turn to Laurel, now was it?"

Figured she'd hear about that. "You've plugged into the Bedhurst gossip surprisingly well for an outsider."

"Why were you keeping it a secret that Laurel came on to you?"

He laughed, catching her arrested look. "Some secret in this county. Especially since she did it twice at Shenny's."

"What did she do?" Was her voice too controlled?

"She draped herself over the bar in front of me." His hand had been resting palm up on the bar at the moment she stretched across it, fitting her breast into his palm. She'd slid her free hand over his thigh and into his crotch, cupping and squeezing. "I said no thank you." He'd picked her up, held her away from him, set her on another stool and left.

Maggie said nothing, but he saw her mind going.

"It didn't mean anything. She came on to about every male in the county at one time or another. Jealous?" He kept it light.

She studied him with her serious, intelligent eyes a moment before saying, "Not at all. I am wondering how Eugene felt about all this."

In other words, had Eugene rid himself of his unfaithful wife and duplicated Pan's murder in order to throw suspicion on J.D.?

If that was the scenario she had in mind, she was still thinking he murdered Pan.

Maggie pushed back her chair and began pacing.

After a few minutes, he said, "What are you thinking?"

"Charlotte hated her sister."

"As kids? Yeah."

She pivoted to face him. "You knew? Why didn't you say something?"

"I'm not in any position to say people don't change from what they were as kids."

"What was Charlotte like as a kid?"

"Unhappy."

"So who wasn't? Tell me something new."

"Pan wasn't." He'd thought about that. He'd thought it was what pushed her to befriend him. "She had this huge reservoir of happy most folks didn't. But the last couple years of her life, with her marriage draining away her happy like a dam left open, the waterline dropped low enough to reveal the rocky fears and tangled doubts."

That had rattled her. He'd tried to tell her it was the same for everybody. But she didn't have experience to fall back on. Maybe if she'd had more troubles in her life she'd have handled Wade differently.

More the way Laurel had brought Eugene to heel.

"Laurel wasn't unhappy, either," he added.

"Maybe that was their blind spot," Maggie murmured.

"Blind spot?"

"I was remembering what Charlotte said about Laurel's blind spot being that she thought how people responded to her on the surface was how they truly felt. Maybe lack of unhappiness made her vulnerable in a way. Her and Pan."

After a pause, he said, "Teddie, too.

He knew Maggie was studying him. Watching his face as he'd thought his thoughts about Pan. That didn't bother him. She wouldn't read anything.

What bothered him was his reaction. Tightening zinged toward fullness. There'd be no missing it.

Color rose up her throat—the color of heat. It smoked her eyes.

She pivoted. Back to pacing.

"So, Charlotte was unhappy," she said. "Tell me about that."

"I'm no psychologist."

He was irked. At himself. At her.

Complications. Definite complications. And he couldn't afford any.

"You're observant enough. And don't tell me it's only of woods and animals. I've read your military evaluations—you were good at handling people. You have to be observant to do that."

"Charlotte and I didn't exactly hang out together."

"That's no excuse. You didn't hang out with anyone." She threw that over her shoulder. "You were a loner. But you watched everyone. Come on, Carson. You wanted to be on this investigation, well this is a way you can help."

She came back toward him, scowling with every step. He saw she thought she was going to stop in front of him, but she changed her mind two strides away. Instead, she started her outbound path again.

"What about the rest of them, the ones Doranna mentioned, how'd they get along with Charlotte? Any trouble there?"

"Nothing unusual I ever saw or heard."

"Scott? Do they have a history?"

"Not much of one. Same school. Same group of kids. That's all. Why ask about him?"

"You're all about the same age. Grew up together. What about Rick?"

He considered that, shook his head. "Same as the rest as far as I know."

"Anybody else? Eugene's older, but he said she came on to him, too, after the trial. See any of that?"

"I wasn't exactly the center of Bedhurst's social doings, you know. Working on the cabin, reading law, getting my head on straight. Each a full-time occupation."

"C'mon, Carson.

"Charlotte was a loner. An outsider. Except at Rambler Farm."

"Like you?"

"The opposite—" He stopped. "Maybe some like me. But the judge's daughter, and she held that like a banner in front of her. She got the grades, worked on every committee, volunteered for everything. Never relaxed."

"Laurel?"

"Party girl. Dated early and often. Skated close to the line—with flunking, with the law."

"And the judge adored her while he barely sees his older daughter?"

He thought of the man who had sat in judgment of his mother's transgressions. Transgressions not so different from what Laurel Blankenship Tagner had committed.

"Yeah. Laurel was his blind spot."

"Sounds to me like Charlotte might have motive for wanting her sister out of the way."

"Based on what they were like as kids? Doesn't mean it's the same now."

"It is. That's what I'm saying. The hate didn't stop. Charlotte still hates her sister—even with Laurel dead, she hates."

THE SOUND OF a key in the street door turned them both that direction. Scott entered.

"Oh, there you are," he said, as if they'd been the ones to arrive. Maggie thought there was an undercurrent of tension beneath his surface. "Dallas wants you to go over to the sheriff's office."

"Has something happened?"

He shook his head—not disputing her guess, but a refusal to tell them what it was. "You'll have to talk to Dallas."

Without discussion, she and Carson walked to the courthouse, then downstairs to the sheriff's office.

Phones were ringing as much as when Maggie had arrived Monday afternoon, with the same woman appearing to have never left her spot. A deputy was on one phone, taking notes.

Dallas stood by the window. They went to him.

"Where's the sheriff?" Maggie asked.

Dallas looked weary. "He's not here. Rick Wade's been murdered."

Maggie felt her breath burn in her lungs.

If he'd killed Wade it would make more sense.

She thought that Wednesday night. And now Wade was dead.

CHAPTER FIFTY-THREE

ABNER, THE DEPUTY, either didn't have much information or wasn't sharing it.

But in answer to a direct question from Maggie, he did say, "East of Buena Vista. Looks like he was on his way to Lynchburg." The deputy paused.

"Five-oh-one?" J.D. prompted. When the deputy didn't respond he added, "Sixty?"

"Neither. He was found on Robinson Gap Road. You know it? Six-oh-seven. Crosses the Parkway."

"Why in hell…? That makes no sense, even for—" He bit it off, not stopping anyone from filling in *Rick Wade*.

The deputy shook his head. "No sense at all. But that's where he was. That's where the sheriff is now."

"Okay." Maggie fished out her keys.

The deputy shifted his feet. "I don't know if Sheriff Gardner would like that, you going out there."

"He can tell me so when he sees me. Us." They moved toward the door. "Dallas?"

He shook his head. "But you two young people go ahead, fill me in later."

"You okay, Dallas?"

J.D.'s question made her focus on the older man. His skin had none of its usual ruddy glow.

"I will be come morning. Just need some rest."

As she turned toward the outer door, J.D. plucked her keys out of her hand and dropped them in her open bag. "Hey—"

"My truck. I'm driving."

"I can—"

"You can. You're not going to. Not that road."

"Robinson Gap Road? What's the big deal about that?"

"No big deal. Most useful when VMI—that's Virginia Military Institute—uses it for a twenty-mile march for cadets. Other than that, you'll see."

✧   ✧   ✧   ✧

THE DRIVE TO the town of Buena Vista was uneventful enough that Maggie found herself noticing blooming patches of blue, purple, and white she guessed were wildflowers. Would Jamie or Ally know their names?

She was almost dozing when Nancy called.

When Maggie told her where she was going, why, and with whom, her assistant grunted, then launched into reports on Chester Bondelle of Roanoke—no blots on his record—and Henry Zales. She summed up Zales with, "About as good as you'll get for a divorce attorney. The files doing any good?"

Maggie expelled a short sigh. "Something about the transcript keeps bugging me."

"Which one?"

"Which—? Oh, the official one. I only went through the dailies while I was waiting for the official transcript."

"The dailies are all I've got because the prick was too cheap to get the official, but I can see if anything jumps out at me."

"Thanks, Nancy. I'd appreciate that."

"No problem. You better appreciate yourself back here soon before Vic pops for real."

"I'll be in Monday morning."

J.D. didn't comment when she ended the call. Soon they reached Buena Vista.

"That would be the usual route to Lynchburg." J.D. tipped his head toward the road heading south, while he took one headed east, straight into the mountains.

It started as an ordinary road, with houses spaced out beside it. The houses disappeared. The road narrowed. Trees closed in on either side. The surface crumbled. The slopes going up on one side and down on the other steepened. The curves began.

Gradually at first, but then they came closer together, with a relative straightaway leading to a left hook, a sequence of twists, before what felt like a U-turn. Then smaller curves to the right that seemed destined to take them in a circle. Before they could complete it, official cars clogged the narrow way.

The outpost was an auxiliary deputy from Bedhurst, who greeted J.D. by name and didn't object to them walking past him and between official cars. After about fifty feet, the ground on the right side—the inside curve of the road—dropped sharply away.

If Wade went over the edge, evidence collection would be a bitch.

They came around a large SUV and saw Wade's truck hadn't gone over and neither had he.

Another twenty-five feet away from them, his truck was wedged into the incline on the opposite side of the narrow road, but with the hood facing down, as if he'd driven up the slope, then turned, and started down it. The passenger door was open. His torso was held upright behind the wheel by the airbag, but his head lolled to the side, revealing the blood.

Gardner left a group and came toward them, his face even more haggard. "You made good time. Too good. If you don't want more tickets, Maggie—"

"Carson drove. Ticket him. Any idea yet on when?"

"Some time after ten and before midnight last night."

"That tight?"

"A gas station called in when news got out. Pulled their video. He was pumping gas at nine-forty-five. Give him time to drive to here, that makes it after ten, easy. He was found at eleven-thirty. That's when the call came in, actually, making it tighter on that side, too."

Maggie's brain completed each of the computations, but somewhere deeper than her brain was already shouting, *J.D. Carson could not have done this.*

Could.

Not.

Have.

He had an alibi.

An alibi she could rely on, because it was her.

CHAPTER FIFTY-FOUR

SHE'D BEEN AT J.D.'s cabin at ten-nineteen. He'd arrived no more than fifteen minutes later. He could not have driven from this spot to his cabin, much less get sweaty from a run in the forty-nine minutes after Wade was seen alive on the gas station's tape.

She'd left at ten-fifty. That left only forty minutes before Wade was found. Also not enough time.

J.D. asked the sheriff the question she should have asked. "Who called it in?"

"Car load of kids. On this road, that time, that weather, they could've been up to no good, but they did the right thing, so there's that."

Was it possible for J.D. to be innocent of this murder, yet guilty of one or both of the others?

No.

Everything inside her said they were connected. Had to be. Rick Wade had gotten too close, had figured out too much, the murderer disposed of him.

She kicked her brain back into gear. "The way his truck is positioned, are you thinking it got there before or after he got shot?"

"Not pinned down yet, but before is more likely. Looks like a handgun. Can't see anyone making that shot on this road in the dark from outside the truck."

Carson nodded agreement.

"A passenger who shot while Rick was driving would have risked the truck going down instead of up." Gardner shook his head. "No.

More likely something blocked the road and made Wade swerve. Truck comes to rest. He's stunned. Shooter walks up out of the dark, opens the passenger door, shoots, drives away. But not before using an evergreen branch to rub out any footprints or tire tracks left by the rain."

"Did the carload of kids see any other vehicles?"

"Haven't said so yet. Locals and state are questioning them again now. Also checking their phones, social media in case there's anything there." He shook his head. "Not likely the way this is going. A garroting, a shooting if Pan Wade's connected, and now run off the road. No repeats."

"Teddie," J.D. said grimly.

Maggie quickly explained Teddie Barrett's role as a witness and what she knew of his death. "This was set up with an accident to start, like Teddie. A gun, but no need to be a good shot. Like with Pan," she said.

The sheriff didn't seem impressed.

"You keep following up on Pan's murderer, but for us this takes priority, while it's fresh. We're pulling Barry in for questioning, what with those free trucks. Why Wade was going to Lynchburg's our top priority. Any ideas there?"

Maggie filled him in on what Wade had said at the memorial. Gardner had already heard the gist, and her details didn't answer any of his questions.

They were firmly dismissed.

✧   ✧   ✧   ✧

2:28 p.m.

THEY STOPPED AT a barbeque place in Buena Vista for a late lunch. She was going to object, but her stomach growled. Overruled.

The food and service were good and unfancy, including rolls of paper towel on the tables to cope with barbeque sauce.

Their conversation was sparse since what was on both their minds was best not talked about in public. Especially not when the public was eating.

Back in his truck, where a heat and heaviness seemed to close around her, they still didn't talk. Not until the welcome sign announced they'd entered Bedhurst County.

He said, "Want to go to the office? Get dropped at the guesthouse? Or…"

She looked over, but he was focused on the road, which she'd considered narrow and twisty until she saw Robinson Gap Road.

"You think Dallas is at the office?"

"No."

"No," she agreed. "He needs to rest. And if he knew I was at the guesthouse he'd want to hash things over all evening."

"Yes," he agreed. "We should fill him in, though. By phone."

She nodded. "Not the office, not the guesthouse. So? You said *or…*"

"Or we go to the cabin."

If you walk into my home uninvited a second time, you better be prepared.

But she wasn't uninvited this time.

She also recognized the neutrality he'd used—the cabin, not *my cabin,* which could be construed as a close relative to *my bed.*

That made a difference. A huge difference.

"The cabin."

SHE PUT THE call on speaker and reported.

"What does this tell us?" Dallas asked at the end.

"Could have been somebody at the memorial. That's when Wade talked about going to Lynchburg," Maggie said.

"No help, since everyone was there."

"True, but what if it was something he said at the memorial? Nobody was trying to kill him before that—that anybody knows about. Then hours after he talks about going to Lynchburg, he's dead."

"I'll call Henry. There has to be more to that."

"Good luck. Investigators have got to have him in for questioning. I'll call Bel—Belichek, a detective I know—and see what more he can find out."

She filled them in on Bel tracking Darcie Johnson, another woman who'd consulted Henry Zales.

Carson asked, "What about the phone calls? Rick was studying them."

"How do you know?"

He looked at the road. "Exactly how you think I know. I was watching him. As much as I could. Saw him studying something on his computer, but couldn't see exactly what. Didn't realize they were phone records until—"

"The memorial, when he mentioned them. That's why you reacted."

He frowned, but answered readily enough. "Yeah. That's when I realized what he'd had up on the screen. Phone records fit the format of the list he was checking. Confirmed it when I got that copy this morning."

"We need to see Wade's phone records," Maggie said.

"Surely Sheriff Gardner—"

She cut off Dallas. "With all he has to do, we'd be doing him a favor going over them first."

He chuckled, revealing he'd been pulling her leg. "Welcome to the dark side, Maggie."

J.D. said abruptly, "There's something else Rick's murder tells us. Shooting wasn't the murderer's first choice."

"Sure. Because it was dark and—"

He interrupted her. "He—or she—could have set it up to shoot Wade in the daylight. Or at that gas station, with the target well-lit. That would present fewer variables than with an ambush, even on that road. And Teddie. That was a maybe-it'll-work try. This is the work of someone who wanted the target close and not moving."

"It didn't take good shooting to kill Pan Wade," she said.

"No, it didn't," he said in a thoughtful voice. "Rick Wade was a darned good shot."

"But we don't know for sure Teddie was murdered."

J.D. glinted a look at her. "You were more certain before."

In other words, when she'd suspected him of killing Teddie. "Being skeptical is what I do, and we can't know for sure."

"Certainly lookin' more likely," Dallas said. "And I see what J.D.'s saying. There could be a pattern. Pan's shot with her own gun, but that's on impulse. When the murderer has more time, he—or she—uses other means. Runnin' Teddie off the road—yes, yes, Maggie with the caveat *if he was murdered*—garrotin' Laurel, tryin' to run Wade off the road, then followin' up with a shootin'. I think you have something there, J.D."

"They might not be connected." But Maggie didn't believe that.

These deaths *were* connected.

J.D. Carson hadn't killed Rick Wade, so he hadn't killed any of them.

He wasn't a murderer.

She'd prosecuted the wrong man. The verdict had been right.

And her attraction to this man…

"They're connected," Dallas said. "I'll raise what you said with the sheriff, J.D. Those are good points."

"Not tonight," J.D. said.

Another voice came through the phone—Evelyn, also saying, "Not tonight."

With a lift of the lines at the corners of his eyes, J.D. said they'd sign off now and meet at the office in the morning.

J.D. HAD NOT liked Rick Wade since they were kids at recess. It was an instant antipathy and an enduring one. Then Wade made Pan unhappy. He wouldn't have thought he'd waste a moment's sorrow on the guy.

But damned if there wasn't sorrow in what he was feeling.

Maybe it was because Pan had loved Rick at one time. Maybe it was the loss of someone he'd known his whole life, even if he hadn't liked him.

He'd never expected to feel this. Not for Wade.

He glanced toward Maggie.

There were a lot of things he'd never expected to feel.

Not part of the plan.

Not part of the plan at all.

CHAPTER FIFTY-FIVE

HE OPENED THE cabin door, stepped back to let her go in first.

She flashed back to walking in to the guesthouse for the first time. How she'd made sure not to let him get behind her, to corner her.

But he'd been with her when Rick Wade was killed.

That opened everything to be viewed from a different angle.

"Have a seat." He gestured briefly to the stools at the island. "I'll make coffee."

She watched his efficient movements, said nothing until he handed her a coffee mug fit for his large hand, but requiring both of hers. "Thanks."

She sipped as he settled on the other stool.

"This is *good*. You should make the coffee at the office."

"Only if you want to put Scott's nose out of joint."

She smiled. Tipped her head toward the rest of the cabin. "You've done amazing things here."

"Wanted to do them sooner, let Anya enjoy them. She wouldn't hear of it. She liked things the way she liked them."

"And then she left you her property," she said musingly. "Anya, the woman in the woods…"

His mouth twitched. "At least you called her the woman, not the Wood Witch."

"Was she? With her potions and poisons?"

His eyes narrowed. "You shouldn't listen to gossip. Especially not Bedhurst gossip."

"Give me something else to listen to, then."

She wasn't sure that would work, even when his lips parted. But, sure enough, words came.

"Anya grew herbs, medicinal plants. Collected others from the woods. Guess you could say she made potions. No poisons."

"And she taught you?"

"Yeah. That was one of the things you got wrong at the trial. It wasn't the Army taught me about being in the woods and surviving on my own. It was Anya. Only reason they put me into the unit was I already knew about surviving, and they figured they could improve my shooting."

"Which they did."

"Which they did," he agreed.

"What you said to Dallas on the phone about Teddie's death—" *If you ever stop cross-examining me, I might tell you more.* "—that was interesting. Running him off the road was a second effort. The night before, when you took him home and he was drunk... If someone got him drunk on purpose, it would make it easier, look even more like an accident..."

She clamped down on the urge to follow up.

Okay, Carson, I'm not cross-examining you. I'm not asking you a question at all. You've got the chance to tell it the way you want.

As if he recognized the challenge to make good on his earlier words, he said, "I came out of the restaurant side and saw Teddie weaving on his bike across the parking lot toward the highway. None of his *friends* who thought it was quite the sport to get him drunk considered how he'd get home. Drunk. On a bike with no lights. In the dark."

He stared into his mug as he tipped and rotated it. "Might have been somebody's idea of fun. Kids—and people old enough to know better—used to tease him. Teddie was a gentle person. He never hurt anyone."

"He testified against you."

One side of his mouth lifted. "He didn't know it." Then any semblance of amusement went. "Someone fed him a load of crap."

"And then, the theory goes," she picked up, "killed him to keep him from accidentally disclosing how he'd been manipulated." She felt the mug's surface imperfections against her palms. "I know he didn't hear you and Pan. Not just from the recording. I went there. It couldn't have been the way Teddie said."

"No, it couldn't have. Even if Teddie had been right at the edge of the clearing he'd barely have heard, because we never raised our voices. Though we did have a disagreement."

Now she looked up. She was going to ask this. Not every question was cross-examination. "Did Rick Wade have cause to be jealous of you?"

"Not in the way he was." *Sorrow.* No one element of expression, posture, voice formed it, yet she felt the edges of his sorrow. He'd loved Pan. He'd wanted to be her lover. "Pan came back to Bedhurst after she finished college. She wanted to teach kids, but there weren't any jobs. She told me Rick had come back, too. It wasn't long before they were married. She seemed happy at first. Then she wasn't happy. I got an email from her. Said her marriage was breaking up, and she needed to see me. Would I come home when I could? Anya had left me this place, that gave me a reason to be in Bedhurst."

Less than two weeks later, Pan was dead and he was charged with murder.

She could cross-examine him, as she had in court, and, yes, since. Would she learn more from yes or no questions?

"What happened that day, J.D.?"

He put his mug down, but kept his gaze on it. "She said she was ready to file for divorce. She wanted to come back with me. Start a new life. Together."

In that one final word, Maggie heard hope then, grief now.

"I said she needed to give her marriage another chance, not leave any doubts, regrets. I couldn't have stood it, looking at her and seeing regrets about being with me. If she gave it a real chance with Wade, and still felt that way... She tried to change my mind. We'd talked about it at Shenny's and I wrote out the address of the apartments near the base I'd gotten the day before and gave it to her, to show I meant it about if things didn't work with Wade. Then she drove me back to

Anya's cabin. She wanted to make love. She wanted at least that much. I said no. She was crying when I left." His hands dropped between his knees. "That was the reason…"

"The reason what?"

He straightened, his expressions defiant, determined. *I'm telling you this and you're not going to stop me, no matter how you react.*

"I had this sense someone… I didn't see anyone. Christ, I barely looked. I was too busy making sure Pan did what would be best for me, making sure I wouldn't have any uncertainties or doubts. I told myself it was military instincts on overdrive. And with her crying… If I didn't leave I was going to give in—Give in," he repeatedly harshly. "Besides, what the hell could there be to fear in Bedhurst?"

He waited. She suspected it was for her to make a comment. She had none … and too many to pick one.

"Next day, her mom called, worried because Pan hadn't come home the night before. Wanted to know if she was with me."

Commonwealth v. J.D. Carson

Witness J.D. Carson (defendant)
Cross-Examination by ACA Frye

Q. After you heard that Mrs. Wade was missing, your testimony was that you went straight to the back entrance to the park?

A. Yes.

Q. You went there because, according to your testimony, that seemed the most logical place to start?

A. Yes.

Q. The most logical place for you to find a dead body?

Mr. Monroe: Objection to characterization.

THE COURT: Sustained.

Q. Yes, Your Honor. You testified you went there and found Ms. Wade, deceased, right?

A. Yes.

Q. You said you did not approach her body?

A. That is correct. I did not approach her body.

Q. Was that a shock for you to find the body of this woman you'd known since childhood?

A. Yes, it was.

Q. Yet you testified that you had the presence of mind not to disturb the crime scene, is that correct?

A. Yes.

Q. Because you could see that she was dead from a distance—twenty-two feet the crime scene measured it at—is that correct?

A. Yes. I've seen death before, Ms. Frye.

Q. Yes, you have. You certainly have.

———————

CHAPTER FIFTY-SIX

"**TELL ME ABOUT** that spot, the other clearing, up the ridge from the crime scene."

"You saw it. Smaller clearing, rougher track with a great vantage for watching somebody below without being seen yourself."

"Pan was killed in summer, the leaves were all out. Would've been a lot harder to see below *if* someone wanted to spy."

He nodded. "Also meant better cover for anyone up there. Plus, the plants were five years smaller."

She shifted, facing him. "Tell me about 'Nothing. This Time.' "

He returned her look for ten, then twenty seconds. "There were footprints up there after Pan was murdered."

"*What*? What makes you think that?"

"Not think. Know. I saw them."

"Why didn't you tell—"

"I did. The sheriff. The deputy. Dallas."

"There is not a word in the official file—"

He grunted disdain for the file.

"—and nothing at trial or—"

"Sheriff never checked and they were rained out by the time Dallas could get someone up there. It would have sounded like a desperate story with nothing to back it up." His mouth twitched. "You would have made sure of that."

She sure would have tried.

"What kind of footprints?"

He grimaced. "They were already pretty sloppy when I saw them the day after Pan was found. Wet—soaked ground and a rainstorm—had distorted the size and shape. Hard to tell if they were from a man or woman. Couldn't have come from a real big guy or a kid, that's about all I could tell for size. Probably not hiking boots. Maybe running shoes. The one thing real clear was there were a number of them—a dozen, maybe more—right where somebody would stand for the best view down to where Pan parked her car whenever she dropped me off."

"All made at the same time?"

He shook his head slowly. "I don't think so. Some were in a lot worse shape than others. The ones in the best shape were fairly deep, like the person stood in the same spot a spell and sank deeper into the muck."

"There were no tracks at the overlook this time," Maggie reminded him.

"No. There weren't. This time was different. With Pan, it was a murder of opportunity. The killer watched her, approached her when she was alone. Hadn't brought a weapon, used her gun. Maybe didn't intend to do it at all. Until something set him—or her—off. But the murderer planned to kill Laurel.

"The murderer had to arrange to meet her there. There's no other way Laurel would end up in that clearing. She wouldn't go there on her own. And this time he brought the means."

She was silent half a minute. "How many people know that spot?"

"Anybody who ran these woods as a kid, which is pretty much every soul who grew up in the county."

"I get the feeling you have a love-hate relationship with this county. Why did you stay here after you were acquitted?"

"Everyone here knew who I was, knew I'd been tried for murder, knew I'd been acquitted, and knew some people thought I'd gotten away with murder. Outside Bedhurst, the trial is something for people to find out."

"You've made this another kind of prison."

"The food's a lot better. And so's the view." He stood. "Speaking of food, how about some."

✧ ✧ ✧ ✧

HE HEATED SOUP and made grilled cheese sandwiches in a cast iron skillet that were the best she'd ever had.

When he started cleaning up, she picked up a towel to dry the wood-handled spoons and the heavy skillet while he put the rest in the dishwasher.

As she went to hang the damp towel on the oven handle, their paths crossed.

He stopped.

Directly in front of her but not touching.

...you better be prepared...

Was she?

Waiting, waiting, waiting. Leaving her time to back away, despite his words.

Words echoed now not as a threat, but a prediction.

She hadn't let herself want him yesterday. Now she could.

She wanted him.

Slowly, he raised his hand, brushed her hair back from her forehead with the back of his fingers, watching the movement.

He slid first one hand, then the other along the line of her jaw, under her ear, and around. Touching her, but not holding her, not compelling.

He didn't need to.

Slowly, he bent his head to her. She tipped hers back.

She felt his breath on her lips but still he didn't touch them.

"I've wanted to do this since..."

His lips brushed hers.

Then again. Again. Again.

She stretched up, extending the contact. Kissing him.

She felt it all through her, deep inside her, but also odd spots. As if the back of her knees melted, her palms tingled, her shoulders ached.

Against her lips, she felt the ridge of the scar near the corner of his mouth. A point of friction, the slightest rasp sensitized her lips even more.

She pulled her mouth away. His lips slid over her jaw, down her throat. Lower. A button gave way, another. His mouth grazed the sensitive skin above her bra.

"Say it, J.D.," she whispered.

He stilled, then raised his head.

Not meeting his gaze, she touched her tongue to that scar, tracing it from the corner of his mouth, diagonally across his chin, and disappearing under his jaw. "Say it?"

"No."

"I didn't—I don't mean a declaration of love. I don't need tha—"

"I know what you want me to say."

"Then why won't you? You said it before."

"That's why."

"But…"

His face was impassive. Or was it? The tick of the muscle under the scar at his jaw. And his body. His body wasn't impassive. Not at all.

"But what, Maggie?" he asked, soft and sharp.

But I need to hear it.

Or did she?

An alibi she could rely on, because it was her.

That was proof. That was certainty.

She reached up with one hand, circled to the back of his head and pressed, bringing his mouth back to hers. Under her fingertips she felt the muscles of his neck tighten to resist. She added her other hand. His resistance strengthened.

She came up on her toes, leaning against him, her mouth two inches short of his. Feeling the sharp bursts of air from him. Once. Twice.

Then his mouth came down on hers.

CHAPTER FIFTY-SEVEN

.

THE SECOND TIME they made it up the stairs to his bed. Barely.

Now she observed that odd sensation of weightlessness, like she had no body to move even if she could have commanded her muscles.

J.D. turned his head toward her, but didn't move otherwise. Perhaps he was in the same state.

"What are you smiling about?" she asked.

"Thinking about your expression when Doranna called you *hon*."

She made a noncommittal hum in response. Her mind, feeling as weightless as the rest of her, flitted away. "Judge Blankenship said you were in his courtroom a lot as a kid, watching when your mom…"

He filled in her pause, "Was called up before him. Yeah."

"Is that why you went into law?"

"Mmm. It gave me an early interest. Made me realize words could be actions, too, especially in a courtroom. Being on trial myself got me a little interested, too," he said dryly.

"You really went to my trials? When?"

"Mostly while I was preparing to take the bar. Studied your cases and studied you." He pushed her hair back. "Closes seem to be your strength."

"I work hard on them. In fact, I build the case around them. A lot of people think the opening's most important, but to me it's setting the stage."

"You build around the close?"

"Sure. I figure out where I want the case to end up—what I need to tell the jury in the close—then I build the case, piece by piece to lead to that close."

"No wonder this has been hard for you."

She fought the automatic stiffening against anything like sympathy. "What do you mean?"

"It's open-ended. No sure answers. Putting pieces together with no idea of where it's leading. It's not the way you work."

"You sound like Belichek and Landis. The detectives I told you about." She rolled her head toward him. "Why didn't you go into law enforcement? Lots of ex-military do."

"Thought about it. But I could catch the killer without being a cop. I couldn't prosecute him without being a lawyer."

"Prosecute?" Her laugh was dry. "You're a defense attorney." The only one she'd ever slept with. "Dallas is a—Okay, he's part-time prosecutor now, but he's been a defense attorney most of his career and you couldn't have known he'd run for office when you…" She came onto her side, raising her head to see him better. "Are you saying you were behind Dallas running for CA? To keep pressure on about Pan's murder?"

"What makes you think Dallas would have listened to me even if I'd tried to get him to run?"

"Because you're persuasive." His hand stroked up over her hip, then slowly, slowly down. "You're very… ahhh… persuasive."

He certainly persuaded her to do exactly what he wanted—what she wanted, too—as they came together again.

Saturday, 8:49 a.m.

AFTER SHE OPENED the guesthouse door with her new key, J.D. followed her to the bedroom.

"Looks like a nice bed. Cozy," he said.

She laughed. "No. We have to get to the office. And you're not coming in the bathroom while I get ready."

"What's to get ready? You already showered." They'd done that together at his place, with a number of detours from getting clean. By the end, they were clean ... and prunes.

"Just stay out here. I won't be long."

He wandered to the window seat, looking out at the pollen-flecked, sloped roof of the porch, across to spring green on the opposite rise.

Water turned on and off a couple times. He heard her opening and closing things. Women's mysteries.

"J.D.?"

"Yeah?" He came back closer to the bathroom door, not quite shut, and sat on the bed.

"The first time we talked to Barry. He said something about Laurel being in a relationship and you frowned. Why?"

He took a moment, thinking, remembering. Absently, his hand stroked over the briefcase sitting on the bed. The latch was broken. From the night of the break-in?

"It was what he said she said about it. It reminded me of something Pan said, though it wasn't the same at all once I thought about it. Pan said she'd learned a lesson about being too sure she had someone pegged. Laurel said someone she'd overlooked turned out to be useful. Besides, I figured Pan meant Wade."

"What if she didn't? Could Pan's comment connect to Laurel's *other plane* relationship? Could it—Leave that alone. Don't touch it."

His hand stilled on the closed briefcase. "This is what was disturbed during the break-in Tuesday night."

"Give it to me." She crossed the room, her hair pulled back by a band, a wet washcloth in one hand.

He shifted, blocking her from the briefcase. Holding her gaze, he slowly lifted the lid.

"Don't—" She bit it off, her face rigid.

He knew that reaction. Knew it intimately.

Whatever happened, don't let anyone know how you felt about it. Yeah, he knew it.

He glanced into the well of the briefcase. Reports, notes, files, pads. Any one of them could—Then he saw it. Lines in the soft material of the lid pocket announcing something stayed in that spot long enough to leave the mark. He kept his gaze on her as he slid his hand in, felt the plastic protecting something else.

He drew it out. Looked down.

And took a blow to the chest.

Pan.

Looking straight at him from a wedding photo.

He fought to regulate his breathing. Heard Maggie trying to do the same.

"Why do you keep this?" As he asked it, he recognized the thickness meant this photo wasn't alone. He reached in, freed one photo after another from the plastic protection. Eight women of different ages, races, backgrounds. Some professional portraits, some snapshots. The images and clothing getting older until he came to the last one.

He saw Maggie in the woman.

He saw the resemblance with Pan and Laurel, too.

Slowly, he looked up. "What do these mean, Maggie?"

"Give them to me," she said coldly.

He didn't. "What are you doing, Maggie?"

"Doing?" Her voice vibrated but didn't break. "I'm trying to get justice for them."

He shook his head. "These are from cases, right? The trials are over, the defendants were acquitted. It's done. But you... You hold onto it. You keep their pictures with you. What are you doing to yourself, Maggie? What do you want of yourself?"

She made a harsh sound. "I want them to be alive. I want them not to be dead. I want not to have failed them. I want them not to be dead because of me."

He dropped the photos into the briefcase, taking hold of her wrists.

"Maggie, you know that's not true. Listen to me. Think. You didn't convict the murderer—the person charged with the murder—in these cases. Right?"

He shook her wrists. The motion made her head bob, and he accepted that as confirmation.

"But their deaths have nothing to do with you. They were dead before you ever entered the picture."

"Not all of them."

CHAPTER FIFTY-EIGHT

"**I WAS A** witness in a case. A long time ago." She felt distant, almost dreamy. "I was a witness against my aunt's murderer."

"You couldn't have been. There was no trial."

"How could you know——? Oh. What Roy said."

"No. Dallas. Before the trial, he said he needed to know who the opposition was. Kept grumbling there wasn't enough from studying your cases. Dug back more. The week before the trial, he told me about your aunt's murder, how the murderer was killed in a shootout with police. There was no trial."

"Not for murder."

He looked at her a long moment. She felt it, didn't return in.

He put it together. "The trial you were a witness in was before he murdered your aunt."

"Yes." Stinging tears pooled in her eyes. "He and Aunt Vivian were dating. She was head over heels. And he included us, me and my two younger cousins. You see we'd always spent summers with Aunt Vivian. She'd inherited our grandparents' house and it was the hub for everybody. My parents traveled all the time, Ally's broke up… That house, her, us. That was home.

"Then Glenn showed up and swept Aunt Vivian off her feet. But I could see… There was something *weird* about how he was with Jamie. But nobody believed me. Not even Aunt Vivian. I heard her telling a friend and the friend saying I was making up things against him so he'd go away and I'd have Aunt Vivian's attention again. And she agreed.

"I stopped saying anything then, but I made sure he wasn't alone with Jamie. He knew what I was doing, and sometimes, the way he looked at me... Then he said he was going on a business trip, making a big deal of saying good-bye, hugging and kissing Aunt Vivian while he kept looking at Jamie. But he was gone—gone—and it felt great. I relaxed. The next day, we rode our bikes to an ice cream shop, I was racing Ally. Jamie fell behind. The shop door was around the corner from the way we'd come. Ally and I were laughing, shouting she was a slowpoke. We started to go into the shop without her, but something... I walked back around the corner of the building to check for her.

"Jamie was on the ground, tangled up with her bike and this man in a hoodie was trying to lift her and put her in a van. She was trying to scream. I could see that, but no sound came out.

"I yelled to Ally to get help and I ran toward them. He was trying to lift bike and all by then, but she was kicking and I was yelling and then she started screaming.

"If she hadn't gotten her foot caught in her bike... It delayed him. People started to come out of the building, responding to Ally. He dropped Jamie. Got in the van. Took off. Lots of people got a description, parts of the license plate. They tracked him down after a week. But none of the adults had a clear view of his face. They could say it was the same van, not the same man. Jamie couldn't do it. She'd break down crying. Ally never saw him. It was up to me. I told everybody it was Glenn, but when it came to the trial..." She sucked in a breath. "I failed. I totally failed. And he walked. Twenty-three days later, he broke into the house when Vivian was alone and beat her to death. He came after me, but he found her."

She panted, the rush of words ripping at her throat.

"You don't know that."

"I know it. I knew him. A neighbor called police. That was the shootout. He died. Too late for Vivian. Too late. It had been too late from the moment I fell apart on cross-examination."

"And you've been blaming yourself ever since. You were a kid and you weren't certain, nobody can blame you—not even you, Maggie."

She slowly raised her head. "I *was* certain. Absolutely certain. He was the man and I knew it."

He held her gaze, and she let him. Let him see. Perhaps let him understand.

"The defense attorney," he said.

"Yes, the defense attorney. He chewed me up and spit me out. A masterful construction of reasonable doubt. A masterful destruction of a fifteen-year-old girl."

"So you became a prosecutor to make sure nothing like that happened again—at least in the cases you handled."

She shook her head. A single, tight jerk.

"I became a prosecutor to keep from killing the bastards myself."

HER PHONE RANG.

Not looking at J.D. or caller ID, Maggie grabbed for it, grateful.

"Couldn't get you last night," Bel said by way of greeting. "I found her."

"Found—? Oh. Right. The woman who reported a similar incident in Lynchburg, then disappeared."

"That's her. She didn't want to talk last night on the phone. I'm outside her place now."

"She's willing to talk to you in person?"

"Don't know yet. Have to wait until she comes back."

"She didn't know you were coming," she guessed.

"No sense giving her a chance to say no. I'll wait. See if my honest face persuades her to talk. One thing I did get out of her last night, she'd consulted a divorce lawyer in Lynchburg—"

"Henry Zales," they finished together.

J.D. looked up at the name.

"Same as your two victims, right?" Belichek asked.

"Yes. That's good work, Bel. How long will you stay there?"

"Long as it takes."

"I appreciate it, but—"

"No buts. Be careful, Mags."

"You, too."

"Me? In this area the worst danger is a soccer ball denting my car."

With his chuckle, they ended the call.

"Maggie—"

"No. I'm going to finish getting ready. We'll go to the office. We'll tell Dallas. We'll figure this out."

The words that had gushed out of her could not be taken back, but no more would follow.

They would not discuss her past. They would not discuss the photos she kept with her day in and day out.

✧ ✧ ✧ ✧

AT THE SIGHT of Sheriff Gardner on the sofa in Dallas' office, Maggie stopped short.

J.D. took hold of both her arms to keep from plowing into her. Still, his front pressed against her, the touch and friction popping off explosions in nerve endings that remembered and wanted more.

"Ah, Maggie, J.D., the sheriff here came by to hear more about what we saw in Laurel's phone records. I've filled him in. He's leaving us Rick's records, and he's updated me on what they know about Rick's death."

Maggie moved out of J.D.'s hold, took her usual chair, turning it to face the sheriff, avoiding the speculative glint in Dallas' eyes. J.D. sat beside the sheriff.

Gardner grunted. "What we know about Rick's death… which is pretty much nothing. Once again, no forensic leads. Nothing helpful from the witnesses. We got his phone records right away, but nothing there, either."

"Anything useful from Barry?"

"Useful? No. He has an alibi—working at Shenny's. Seen by a load of people, some of them passably sober. He's covered for the whole time, not just the narrower window."

"Narrower window? What do you mean?"

Gardner snorted. "That was a screw-up. Time on the gas station's video was wrong. Time didn't change automatically with Daylight Savings a couple weeks back like it should've. The manager had his kid change it, only the kid got the time change backward. He made it later, instead of earlier.

"When we thought Rick was pumping gas there at nine-forty-five, it was actually seven-forty-five. We filled in the first half hour—Rick got something at a drive-through, but still, it more than doubles the window when he could have been killed. Autopsy might narrow that some, based on digestion, but still. Why the hell Abner didn't notice the difference in the light—But he didn't. And we wasted time…"

Gardner's words went on, but Maggie didn't hear.

Seven-forty-five.

Doubles the window.

J.D. could have gone there, killed Rick, and still be back at his place in time.

Could he have also been the person she smacked with the garbage? Maybe not, but what did that matter?

He didn't have an alibi for Rick Wade's murder.

He could have done that murder.

And the others.

Every word he'd said, every gesture, every look. Every kiss. Every slide of his body against her. In her.

Shifting, spinning.

You're a fool. You'll get sucked in by him just like all the rest.

That's what Rick Wade had said to her and now he was dead.

CHAPTER FIFTY-NINE

"EXCUSE ME."

Maggie made it to the hallway, but felt J.D.'s presence behind her.

"I have to—"

"No." He took her arm, led her to his office.

She might have been able to pull away, she didn't try. She didn't feel anything, didn't think anything. She was a blank. A sinking, dark blank.

"Maggie, you went absolute white. Are you sick?"

He closed the door.

That stirred something in her.

He stopped dead, seeing her face. Slowly, his head drew back, his hands dropped to his sides. A soldier's stance.

"I see."

Did he? That fast? How could he if he wasn't guilty?

"In the absence of certain proof, you go to certain disbelief. I should have expected ... I built too much on the fact that you wondered four and a half years ago if I was innocent."

She jumped into familiar territory. "Once I reviewed the evidence, I was sure—"

"You wondered."

"I don't know what you could possibly base—"

"The hell you don't, Maggie."

His voice was low. He didn't touch her. Didn't try to. Yet she felt as if she were shrinking from him.

"You looked at me there in that courtroom, and you didn't know.

Screw your evidence and your witnesses and your testimony—you, here—" His finger held steady a centimeter from her breast, "—didn't know."

"No." He drew it out, discovering something in the saying of it. "It's a hell of a lot worse than that. You *did* know. You *knew* I didn't do it. Goddamn it."

He pivoted away.

"I—How could I possibly *know*? The evidence said—"

He slashed the air with one hand. "Be quiet, Maggie. Just goddamn, be quiet." They held like that, the harshness of their breathing the only sound.

A minute. More.

She turned on her heel, strode out. Keeping her back straight, her pace steady. Grabbing her keys, ignoring Dallas' questions. Walking back to the guesthouse. Getting into the car.

✧ ✧ ✧ ✧

INTUITION. THAT'S ALL it had been four and a half years ago. A wobbly, woolly flash of unsupported what-if thinking for a handful of moments.

She *hadn't* known.

Not in any sane, reasoned sense.

She'd looked at a man with evidence pointing toward his guilt, and she'd had an intuition.

What was she supposed to have done with that?

She'd already read the case notes. She knew the investigation was crap, but the conclusion was logical. From the start, she'd heard the closing argument in her head, writing itself. Layering the connections between defendant and murderer, drawing in all the threads. The poor boy from the bad family, who had longed for the town's golden girl all his life. Came back to Bedhurst as a proud and successful man. Found the girl now an unhappy woman, prepared to give him what he'd always wanted—her love. And then, when it seemed she was within his grasp, she pulled back, set to return to the man who had belittled that poor boy all his life.

But he wasn't a poor boy any longer. He was a deadly force in himself. And in that moment, the deadly force was unleashed.

The heat of his emotion was there in the note crammed into her mouth—his note. She had crumpled his dream, as he did the note.

All this on one side.

An irrational flash at the last instant on the other.

There had never been a moment during the days of the trial she hadn't believed in what she was doing. Absolutely.

Not the way defense lawyers believed they had to give their client the best defense, guilty or not. But in the way she had always believed in her cases—giving the best prosecution because the defendant was guilty.

And then that moment before the verdict....

But she hadn't *known*.

She still didn't know. Couldn't know.

She'd made love with him. A man who might be a murderer. A murderer of young women, who looked like her ... and Vivian.

Might be...

Might be.

She stopped along the highway, well out of sight of any house.

She opened the car door, leaned out and vomited.

✧   ✧   ✧   ✧

3:36 p.m.

HER PHONE RANG.

Gave up.

Started ringing again.

Not J.D. Not Dallas.

Caller ID said Rambler Farm.

She answered.

"Maggie? It's Ed. Ed Smith."

"Ed. Hi."

"Are you okay? You sound—"

"Just a little under the weather. I'll be fine. What do you need?"

"Can we meet? Talk?"

"I can be at Rambler Farm in—"

"No. Not here. Where are you?"

She looked around. Grimaced. "I appear to be at the entrance to Bedhurst Cemetery."

"I'll be there in fifteen minutes. There's a bench at the top of a rise on the east side. I'll meet you there."

CHAPTER SIXTY

AFTER HELLOS, HE talked about rereading the transcript. Mostly about how smart she'd been in the trial.

Right.

"Nothing seemed … off to you?"

That moment before the verdict. Thinking something was off, mocking herself…

"No. Nothing. And I was looking after what you said. Sorry to disappoint you."

"Not at all. Thanks for going over it again."

He sat staring straight ahead.

She broke into the silence. "What is it, Ed?"

"Oh. I … nothing."

"Ed, if you know anything about the murders that—"

"No! No, I swear. I don't."

"Or anything about Laurel—" She took a wider swipe. "—Or background about her character or the interactions of people that might explain what's happening now."

His head dropped forward. His shoulders shuddered.

"What is it, Ed?"

"It doesn't have anything to do with her death. It's … God, I feel…"

Light glinted off a trail of moisture beside his nose. She waited, a luxury she seldom had at trial.

"She was so sure, so sexy. I couldn't believe it when she came on to me. And I wasn't imagining it," he added in a stronger voice. "She came on to me."

Maggie's brain teemed with possibilities. "When was this, Ed?"

"We weren't married. I didn't cheat on Charlotte." His words crowded together.

She eased into it. "It was before you started dating Charlotte?"

He shook his head.

"Before you were engaged?"

Another head-shake, this one smaller, his head dropped lower.

"How long before the wedding, Ed?"

"Three weeks. It only lasted nine days."

Maggie sat back, leaving him to his misery. Laurel had gone after her brother-in-law-to-be three weeks before her sister's wedding. And kept it going until days before the wedding.

Ed was sweet, but not exactly gotta-have-him-or-I'll-die material. So why? Power? That fit with what they'd come to know of Laurel. Control? Over him? Or—?

"Did Charlotte know?

Ed's head snapped up. "No! Absolutely not. No idea."

He was too emphatic.

"She knows now, though." And from what she'd seen of Charlotte, the woman would not be surprised.

Maggie had a sudden longing to see and talk to Ally and Jamie. Maybe it was the certainty that whatever strains there were between and among them, they would never do that to her, each other, or anyone else on the planet. The toxic sisterly relationship between Charlotte and Laurel had her longing for her cousins, which at least had the benefit of involving ethical human beings with shared old memories. Good memories. Despite what followed.

"I don't know why you'd think she—"

"Ed."

He stopped.

"How did she react?"

"She's hurt. Of course. Unhappy. But she knows I take our vows very seriously. And we're happy together. We have a good marriage. She'll put it behind us, as I've put it behind me."

"When did she find out." No need to ask if he'd told her. Damn clear he hadn't.

"I told her ... a day ago." *Lie, lie, lie.* "She's had too much to deal with already with her sister's murder, and supporting the judge, and now this. I'll never forgive myself for adding to her burden."

"She must be jealous. Any woman would be, under the circumstances, but even more jealous considering Laurel's...ways."

"No."

"The kind of jealousy and worry about a relationship that could push a woman to viole—"

"No!"

"Violence," Maggie repeated the whole word, "even against her own sister."

Ed straightened some. Though his shoulders still rounded forward he achieved a kind of dignity. "I better leave now, Maggie. I've told you, my wife didn't know anything about this until after Laurel's death. It's my guilt, my shame. And I won't burden her further by talking about it ever again." He looked at her, half stern, half pleading. "And you won't either."

"Not unless it figures in the investigation," she said.

They both knew she would tell the sheriff. How confidential it stayed beyond that was anyone's guess.

He stood. "I need to go home to my wife."

SHE THOUGHT SHE'D been okay driving back to the office. But when she got out of the car, her legs were rubber.

Outside the black door under the "Dallas Herbert Monroe & Associate" sign, she hesitated, took three slow deep breaths, then walked in, going straight to Dallas' office, but unable to not see J.D.'s open door.

"Anything from Henry Zales?" she asked Dallas.

"Haven't been able to get through to him. He's bein' grilled six ways from Sunday by as many jurisdictions as can get in line, with

Sheriff Gardner at the front."

"How about a copy of Rick's phone records?" She dropped her things on the table.

"Maggie."

"If they're not, I'll—"

"Your copy's there, but now, while it's the two of us here, there's something more—"

"Leave me alone, Dallas."

"Trust your gut."

He couldn't have chosen a worse metaphor considering how her gut felt. "I trust my gut to tell me when I'm hungry or sick, not to ascertain legal matters."

"This isn't a legal matter. It's deeper than that. You believe in him. You know you do. Look into your heart, girl. Look into your soul. You do know."

"Knowing is built from evidence, and I *don't* know. I thought there was proof. But—You don't *know*, either. He could have left you sleeping by the fire, killed Laurel, and you'd never have known."

"It's more than timetables, Maggie. And you better wake up and realize that. You can't go through this life waitin' for every last piece of evidence to line up. You got to rely on yourself. You got to look beyond what you see to what's really there. You got to feel what's right. And what's wrong."

Rely on herself? No. "I'm not—I need evidence. I need proof."

"You got it backward. Totally backward. You want proof that J.D.'s not a murderer. But here you stand, like a divinin' rod of truth. Don't you see it, girl? Don't you understand? It's you. You are his proof of innocence. You're the only key that will finally let him out of this county."

CHAPTER SIXTY-ONE

SHE OUTLASTED DALLAS by refusing to respond and by keeping her head down, studying phone records.

Evelyn came by around six and announced Dallas was done for the day. He started to protest. She said he was coming home, having dinner, and resting or she was calling the doctor. Immediately.

She gave Maggie a couple shots, too, about working herself to death doing no one any good.

Maggie outlasted her, too.

They left, Maggie remained.

Her eyes, though, might have the last word.

Studying the logs of Rick Wade's calls over the past ten days, then comparing them to Laurel's and the guesthouse's, had her longing for a little light reading among legal precedents.

She rubbed her eyes. This was entirely too up close with phone records.

Rick Wade had called every number listed to and from Laurel's phones in the days leading up to her murder.

At most, his calls to those numbers lasted a minute or two, many of them considerably less. Except his call to the main number of Zales' firm. Presumably it took some conversation to set up a golf game.

But *why*?

She sighed. If there was anything to learn from Henry Zales, Gardner, the state guys working with him, and his counterparts in Rockbridge County, where Wade had died, were hard at it. No hope anyone else would get a crack at him any time soon.

But there was something else intriguing. Shortly after hanging up with the firm, Wade had called a number in Northern Virginia.

Could it be the woman Bel had tracked down?

As Maggie Googled the number, she was anticipating calling Bel, being told it was the woman's number, closing one damned loop in a made up entirely of open loops and—

The number was an elementary school. Certainly closed over the weekend. She called it anyway. No answer.

With her finger still on the screen from ending her outgoing call, one came in.

She hit answer immediately, saw it was Jamie, and recognized she didn't regret answering it.

"Hi, Jamie."

There was a pause on the other end. Her cousin might have been as surprised as she was.

"Maggie. How is your case coming?"

"It's not a case yet, and likely won't be mine if it ever is one. I seem to be sort of investigating."

"Oh? Is it going well?"

"It's going shittily."

A single syllable of amusement came from Jamie. "Sorry. I didn't mean—"

"It's okay. It's not your fault the whole situation sucks."

"Maggie, are you—?"

"Don't say it, Jamie. Don't say it. I'm so sick of people asking me if I'm okay."

"I'm sorry. I won't. I get that. I'll just—Will you be in town Monday? Lunchtime?"

"I better be or I won't still have a job."

"Oh. Well, will you come to lunch? Ally and I can come to the courthouse area so you don't have to go far."

"Chad's aunt's still in town?"

"Yeah, and Ally's agreed to come. I really need to talk to you both."

"Are you—?" She couldn't ask what she wouldn't answer. "I'll be there. Set the time with Nancy. I—"

The bell chimed, announcing the office's front door had opened.

"—gotta go now. Somebody's here. See you then."

Charlotte Blankenship Smith stood in the doorway of the office.

"Was that my husband on the phone?"

Maggie looked at the screen as if it might answer that odd demand. "Ed? No. Are you trying to get in touch with him?"

"No. I am here to tell you to *not* touch him."

Maggie pulled in a long breath, hoping her calm would be contagious. Though Charlotte did not sound angry or agitated. Just delusional.

"Charlotte, Ed and I are colleagues. Friendly colleagues."

"I know you talked to him this afternoon."

Did she? How? Listening in on phone calls? Following him? How deep did this paranoia go?

"Yes, we did talk. About your sister's murder and the progress of the investigation. He's very concerned about the toll Laurel's death has taken on you."

Uninvited, Charlotte pulled out a chair. She put one hand down first and lowered herself to the seat with the weary care of the elderly.

"Laurel's *death* has taken a toll? No, no, not her death. Her life. Do you know what she told me about why she fucked Edward before our wedding? To be sure he wasn't worth taking away from me for good."

Maggie had interviewed her share of witnesses with mental illness or addiction or the always popular daily double of both. But the combination of Charlotte's pedantic tone and the hostile words chilled her.

"She thought I'd seen something in him she'd missed. Isn't that laughable? What I'd seen was a man who might interest the judge. And she never had to worry about that. Just being was all she had to do. The judge always saw *her*—looked for her, wanted her there. But I—" Her voice shook for the first time. "I had to be his slave, marry a man he could talk to, and even then he hardly noticed me. And her—her— she didn't have to do anything. So all she'd missed in Edward was what she'd never needed."

"Then why were you worried she might try to take him away?"

Charlotte raised her eyes without moving her head. They said, *You stupid woman*, clear as day. "Because she could. That was reason enough for Laurel. As it is for other women. Like you."

CHAPTER SIXTY-TWO

"ME? CHARLOTTE, YOU are completely wrong if you think—"

The front door bell sounded again. Almost immediately, Scott walked in and stopped, looking from one to the other of them.

Behind him came Eugene and Renee.

All three of them appeared surprised to see anyone still in the office.

Into the frozen moment, Charlotte rose, picked up her purse, and started out.

Maggie stood. "Charlotte, you are wrong about—about what you said. If you want to talk more—"

The bell chimed again and Charlotte was gone.

"Sorry if we interrupted." Scott appeared confused.

"It's fine."

"We stopped in to pick up work I did for Renee that I left here. Are you still working? You haven't had any dinner?"

"Not hungry."

"Oh, honey, you got to have something. We were just considering supper, too," Renee said. "Eugene, you go get us all something from Cheforie's and when you come on back, Scott and I'll be done with our business."

Maggie thought she saw protest brewing in Eugene. If so, it passed before any expression of it emerged. He took orders and left.

Renee followed Scott to the back, Maggie returned to Dallas' office and the phone records.

Eugene delivered and they ate at the cleared end of the table with desultory conversation, carried mostly by Renee and Scott. Eugene kept shooting Maggie looks as if he expected her to strike.

He did not encourage lingering when the food was finished. At least he, Renee, and Scott said good-night when they left.

As she put her things together more than an hour later, Maggie's mind returned to Charlotte's strange visit.

She certainly had a chip on her shoulder about her sister. Possibly with cause.

But did that chip apply to more than Laurel?

We're all supposed to do the right thing. Only some people get applauded for it, like J.D., while others don't. And then there are those who don't need to do anything at all and still get applauded.

Driving away, Maggie saw a vehicle close behind her. Uh-oh. Had she pulled out in front of them without looking? If so, she'd been away from Fairlington too long. She'd also been away too long if a little tailgating bothered her.

You're like them, you know … Pan and Laurel. Just like them. It all came easy. Never had to work. Never had to work to be loved, either.

Presumably the flip side was Charlotte *had* had to work—filling her mother's shoes as mistress of Rambler Farm, taking care of the judge, upholding the family name. Charlotte the reliable. Charlotte the indispensable. Charlotte the unappreciated.

Oh, yes, she saw herself that way.

And what about love? Her father's? Her husband's? She felt she'd had to work for that while Laurel waltzed through life taking for granted she deserved to have whatever she wanted?

Thinking about Charlotte was giving her a headache.

No, Maggie realized, the piercing glare of the headlights still behind her were causing the headache. She flipped the lever on the rearview mirror to dim the lights.

Too bad it wasn't as easy to switch the angle on her thoughts.

Charlotte clearly resented Laurel. Couldn't totally fault her for it, either. Unless it had led to murder.

Charlotte had lumped Pan in with Laurel. Yet there'd been no direct competition between the two women. At least that Maggie knew of. Certainly not for the affections of the judge or Ed, who hadn't come along until after Pan's murder. Or for the affections of J.D., because Charlotte's lack of interest there rang true.

Maggie left Main Street, automatically noting the lights followed. Probably a truck, since the lights were higher than her sedan.

What about Rick Wade?

Could Charlotte have harbored resentment against Pan from their school days when the girl everyone loved won the town's destined-for-success golden boy? Even after the gold tarnished and his limited success came ready-made from his family's business?

Possibly.

On the other hand, Charlotte had included Maggie in her mix of people who had never had to work, including for love. Which nudged Charlotte significantly closer to off-the-charts whacko.

✧ ✧ ✧ ✧

DALLAS WATCHED EVELYN put away the clean dinner dishes.

"I'm old, Evelyn."

Her rhythm never broke. "Getting there."

"I should have died when Ruth did."

"You've got too much imagination for that."

"What does imagination have to do with it?"

"Comes in handy for all sorts of things, but folks surely need imagination to see living a life—a good life—after someone they love's gone."

"You had such imagination?"

"Had to," she said flatly. "Had it then. Have it now."

"Imagination," he repeated. "Imagination to keep on living."

Voices tumbled through his head. Voices of the departed, and of those still here. When he spoke, the words came before he'd formed and polished the thought. "Maybe imagination to keep on killing, too."

"Maybe." She sorted utensils into the drawer.

The tumbling sped up. Whirling, kaleidoscopic flashes of blinding colors mixed with glimpses beneath that surface to dank, depthless shadows. Too fast. Too sickeningly fast.

Clammy sweat oozed on his forehead, under his arms.

9:16 p.m.

MAGGIE MADE THE final turn into the dirt lane that dead-ended beside the guesthouse, and frowned again into the rearview mirror The lights had followed.

She flipped the lever on the rearview mirror to normal and the glare jumped out.

Could it be someone coming to see her? If so, they didn't know how quickly the end of this lane was approaching.

She slowed. The vehicle behind her didn't, narrowing the gap until she imagined she felt the other engine's heat on her back. She eased her foot off the brake, tapped twice, flashing the lights to the other driver.

In that instant the vehicle's high beams burst on, blazing through her car and out through the windshield, creating a spotlight on the fence.

If you count on that fence holding you, you're going to find yourself smashed up.

Maggie hit the brakes hard. If the idiot hit her, she'd deal with a damaged bumper.

The vehicle behind her—yes, a pickup—banged her bumper. Her car pulsed forward. She jammed the brakes as hard as she could.

This was no accident, no lost driver.

In the narrow lane, there was nowhere to go, no room to escape.

"DALLAS?" EVELYN'S VOICE sounded distant.

You got to look beyond what you see to what's really there. You got to feel what's right. And what's wrong.

His own words. But why? Why had they joined the whirl?

Was his heart giving out? Or had he seen—

"*Dallas!*"

Fear.

Evelyn was afraid.

It pulled him back. He grabbed his head in both hands, forcing the kaleidoscope to stillness.

"What? What's wrong?" His own voice sounded odd.

She peered out the window toward the guesthouse. "Sounded like a car crash from back at the end of the lane. But it was wrong. No brakes or—There. Hear it?"

He did. He lumbered up, heading for the door.

"Call the sheriff!" he ordered.

She already had the phone in her hand.

"Don't you do anything stupid, Dallas Herbert," she ordered as she hit numbers.

The sick feeling came back. The feeling the kaleidoscope was getting worse.

CHAPTER SIXTY-THREE

THE TRUCK CONNECTED hard with the Honda's bumper. Maggie heard the engine revving behind her, the tires of the truck biting into the dirt. Without letting up on the brake pedal, she yanked on the emergency brake. The smell of heat and rubber rose.

She reached for the door handle, felt the Honda's tires jerk forward, skidding on the dirt.

Before she could get the door open, the fence rose up.

...*Smashed up*...

Sixty feet. Sixty feet of trees and rocks to the creek below.

Trees...

Damned if she was going nose down to her doom.

She popped her foot off the brake and yanked the steering wheel as hard as she could to the left, hoping the passenger side would take the brunt. The truck behind gave another shove, and the right front of the Honda broke through like the fence was straw, the rear end swinging around under the force of her yanking. The car skidded over the edge of the earth. It felt as if the rear caught on something, but she felt the front angling down, a sensation like being at the top of a slide, in the moment before the plunge.

A plunge into blackness.

CHAPTER SIXTY-FOUR

"MAGGIE! MAGGIE!"

The dim form slumped over the wheel of her Honda didn't stir at Dallas' call.

The sky still showed faint daylight, but little reached under the canopy around the guesthouse and none down the drop-off to the creek.

J.D. took it all in. Gave his first order. "Aim the light at the driver's door, so I can see."

"You can't go down there, J.D. Evelyn has called 9-1-1. Wait until help comes. Until we can see—"

"Fuck that."

He heard the lack of control in his voice. Made himself draw in a breath, let it out. Draw in another, let it out.

He sprinted to the side of the guesthouse, unwound the hose until there was one loop left around the holder to add strength. It was too thick and unpliable to tie around his waist, but at least it would give him something to climb if necessary.

Her car angled down at forty-five degrees, the rear passenger side caught by the sizable stump of an old tree with the front held only by the trunks of two small trees, neither much more than a sapling. If they let go, the whole thing would go.

He ordered, "Keep the light steady."

Tuning out the older man's exhortations to wait, he started down.

Testing roots and branches, not only for helping him down, but for whether they would hold when he climbed back up with Maggie.

He moved slowly. Pulling down a branch or bush or starting an earth slide could dislodge the slope's hold on her car.

Sweat traced down his back, but his hands were dry and steady.

He checked over his shoulder for a final foothold and let himself look into the car for the first time. Maggie stirred, trying to sit up, pushing her hair out of her eyes.

"Stay still, Maggie," he commanded.

She turned toward him. Blood tracked down her right cheek, but he saw recognition in her eyes—of him and of the situation.

"Don't move until I tell you." He called up, "Dallas. Get the light on the front. Yeah, now down, to the tires."

The upside tire had nothing to stop it. He couldn't see the other front tire, the one on the passenger side, not without climbing down and he wouldn't be able to see anyway, not without better light.

He moved back to the door, wrapped the hose around his shoulder twice, braced his legs then tried the door handle. It was locked.

He met Maggie's gaze through the closed window and for a fraction of time thought she would refuse to open it. Instead, she reached across and unlocked the door.

He held her gaze as he slowly opened it. Halfway, a groaning creak came from somewhere on the far side of the car.

"Can you move?" he asked.

"Yes."

"Undo your seatbelt. Good." He extended his right arm. "Grab my wrist." Their grips overlapped. "Slow and steady."

She pushed partway out. The groan from the far side intensified. Her grip reflexively tightened.

The hell with slow. He pulled her out, wrapped her against his side, her feet scrambling for a hold.

"You said slow a—"

"Save your breath for the climb." He kept her against his side.

Above, he saw Dallas shift the flashlight and J.D. caught a glimpse of the older man's anxious eyes pinned on them.

Then the light steadied, guiding their slow, cautious climb, with Maggie tight to his side.

Up, handhold by careful handhold.

Until, finally, he heaved her, then himself over the edge, to horizontal ground.

Dallas fussed over them, but she looked straight at him.

As soon as her breath came back, she said, "Where did you come from?"

"As I pulled in, Dallas was heading out with a flashlight to see what had made noises he and Evelyn heard."

"You must have seen him—it. The truck that pushed me over."

"Somebody pushed you?" Dallas asked.

"A truck. You must have seen it leaving." That was directed at him. "Unless—"

Her suspicion was back in full force.

J.D. sat on his heels. Looking at her.

"I went over the edge and then there you were, right away. You … You must have seen the truck."

He supposed he should thank her for her hesitation.

"You lost consciousness, Maggie. Who knows how long you were unconscious," Dallas said.

She didn't take her eyes off him.

"You were out when I started down after you," he said.

"But Dallas heard sounds, *then* came to check. The timing…"

The woman was bruised and battered, yet still piecing together bits of information, still checking his alibi. Didn't she realize what trouble that could get her in?

"Oh, my dear, there was certainly some passage of time between first hearin' the sounds and arrivin' where J.D. saw me. I wasn't at all certain I'd heard something, and then there was the matter of puttin' my hands on a flashlight. And I do not move with the speed I once did," Dallas concluded.

The siren-wailing vehicles came to a stop, ending Maggie's putting together of clues.

They treated the cut in her scalp—"Not bad," said the medic.—while the sheriff arrived and took over the scene.

After Gardner confirmed Maggie was okay, he ordered them to

"stay where you are and don't talk until I get back."

He returned when he was satisfied the situation was under control. Then he looked from one to the other of them. "What the hell happened?"

"A vehicle—truck, I'm pretty sure—tried to push my car into the ravine," she said.

"Maggie thinks it might have been me," J.D. said evenly. "You're welcome to examine my truck."

"It wasn't, J.D. He *saved* her," Dallas jumped in. "I came from the house and—"

Gardner raised a stop sign hand. "Hold on, Dallas. Maggie?"

"I... I don't know. He got here so fast. But I—I think I better tell you about a conversation I had."

They sat in Dallas' den, and he watched her bruises begin to bloom and her movements stiffen as she told them about another of Laurel's sexual conquests and her sister's threats.

AFTER THE FIRST time she reported her conversations with Ed and Charlotte, the sheriff gave several orders, then they all went to the sheriff's department, where she repeated it, waited for the formal statement to be printed, read it over, and signed, while J.D. and Dallas were questioned separately.

Now they all crowded into the sheriff's office.

"J.D.'s truck came back clean," Gardner announced. "We're going out to Rambler Farm now."

"I don't know if you have enough, Sheriff," she'd said.

He scrubbed a hand across his face. "No sense waiting. At this rate, I can't take the risk. If she's wild enough to try to do that to you... Besides, word'll be all over by morning."

"There could be other explanations. Someone else—"

"First thing is we'll check for damage to any of vehicles."

"Even if... It doesn't mean she killed the others."

"You're defendin' her?" Dallas asked with a hint of humor.

Gardner said, "Jealous of her sister, that's clear motive, and if Rick was figuring it out, that's motive. Fits with this attack on you, too. You're real fortunate J.D. was right there."

Gardner and his deputy left for Rambler Farm, while she, Dallas, and J.D. returned to Monroe House.

Evelyn and Scott were waiting there.

Scott jumped up. "Maggie! Are you okay? I came as soon as I heard. It's all around Shenny's. The guys from the wrecker that pulled your car out came in and were talking all about it."

"Sheriff Gardner was right," she muttered. Then she groaned. "My *car*. How am I going to get home?"

"My second boy has a couple car rental places," Evelyn said. "I'll have him have a car here for you tomorrow."

"Thank you. That's very kind of you. I don't know how I didn't think about it until now."

"Well, you can just not think about it anymore," Dallas said. "Like you don't have to think anymore about something naggin' you from the transcript."

"The transcript? Was there something wrong with it?" Scott asked.

"If there is, I couldn't ever pin it down," Maggie said dryly. "I kept thinking there was something, but I read it over and over and couldn't find it."

"If you couldn't find it, it must not be there," he said with a smile.

She tried to smile back. She wasn't sure those muscles worked anymore. Especially when she looked at J.D.

CHAPTER SIXTY-FIVE

Sunday, 4:43 a.m.

THE CALL CAME shortly before five a.m.

They were all still in Dallas' den, waiting. None of them willing to leave.

Another judge had sworn out a warrant and Charlotte Blankenship Smith was in custody for charges connected to the attack on Maggie.

Not only was there damage to her vehicle in the right place and what initially appeared to be the right colors of paint transfer, but Charlotte hadn't denied it, despite her husband's and father's shock. In fact, she said nothing.

"Best thing for her to do," Dallas said. "Well, that's that."

Maggie stood. "I'll leave in the morning—uh, later. After I get some sleep," she amended.

"No need, no need," Dallas said.

"No reason for me to stay." She was aware of Dallas' and Evelyn's gazes going to J.D.

He did not look up as he said, "She's got to get back to her real job. Her boss wants her there Monday morning."

True. All true.

Yet it was a dismissal.

She walked alone to the guesthouse in pre-dawn light that seemed brighter than it truly was because it was pushing against the dark.

No need for an escort now.

But once inside, as she went to close and lock the door behind her, she sensed a presence out in the shadows.

J.D.?

Making sure she got in all right?

Maybe Dallas sent him. Or Evelyn.

That was probably it.

MAGGIE WOKE UP stiff and with an ache where the scalp cut had let loose all that blood.

But the afternoon was sunny and warm. She got up and opened the big windows. The lack of screens didn't matter this early in the season, before mosquitoes arrived. The wind moved branches into restless nods and swept into the room.

That helped her fog.

A hot shower helped more.

A text invited her to come to Monroe House for brunch as soon as she was up.

She dressed and packed quickly. A new car was waiting down the lane ... behind the police tape marking off where her Honda met its end.

Evelyn was cooking for a steady stream of law enforcement, passing through for food before leaving town.

Dallas was there, of course. Scott was talking with Deputy Abner—she never had found out if it was his first or last name—the state trooper, and the woman from the front desk.

To her surprise, Eugene and Renee Tagner were there, as well, chatting with Doranna and Barry. She recognized other faces from the memorial service, including the redhead Robin and her sidekick. Maggie steered clear.

No sign of J.D.

"Hasn't been here," Dallas said quietly to her. "Addingtons came by earlier, said to give you their best and hope you'll stay in touch. I believe they were headed to Rambler Farm to console the judge and Ed. Good people, those two."

Sheriff Gardner came in, looking worse than ever, yet with a hopefulness deep in his tired eyes.

He packed away a considerable amount of food. Maggie pecked at hers. They finished at the same time and walked out through the kitchen together.

"Thank you, Mrs. DuPree—Evelyn. Thanks to you, too, Maggie." Gardner extended his hand.

They shook, meaning it.

He left. She didn't envy him the paperwork ahead of him.

Evelyn gave Maggie the keys and papers for the rental car. Scott and Dallas came in, each of the three of them hugged her. She did not get hugs from Eugene, Renee, Barry, or even Doranna.

Then she was walking down the lane to a strange car, to leave a place she'd barely recognized when she'd returned a week ago, feeling … something she couldn't pin down.

J.D.

He stood in the center of the lane, not far from the car parked well back from the police tape around the remnants of the fence, watching her come toward him.

She wouldn't let herself falter, closing to two feet before she stopped.

"I was wrong, J.D. I'm sorry. You should not have been prosecuted."

He looked at her for a long moment, his expression revealing nothing. "You know why I wouldn't declare my innocence to you Friday night?"

She had no answer.

"Because as long as I didn't say it, I didn't have to know you didn't believe me. I should have known how strong your need to see the ending is. The way you build a case, you need to know where you'll be at the end. But that's not how it works with people. Good-bye, Maggie."

He stepped aside.

Her breath stuttered. But she pushed herself forward, reaching the car, unlocking it. With the door open she faced him.

"I'm truly sorry, J.D. I wish you well."

He declined his head in acknowledgement. "Go back to your job, Maggie. You are one hell of a prosecutor."

He was still standing there, watching her car the last time she checked the rearview mirror.

CHAPTER SIXTY-SIX

SHE DROVE. SHE saw the road, the rare other vehicles, the sky, the trees, all with no consciousness of seeing them. Except to notice the designs the lengthening shadows of budding trees made on the road's surface.

Designs…

Patterns.

They look like each other—and you.

Had Charlotte followed a pattern?

Are you testing if I know up-to-date research says many serial killers don't stick to the rigid timelines and MOs popular media portrays? I do.

J.D. said that at the Monday briefing. He was right.

The image of serial killers operating like clockwork was only one behavior. They could react to triggers that had nothing to do with time, sometimes spaced out, sometimes not.

Had Charlotte's trigger been thinking Pan and Laurel would get their happy endings—Pan going off with J.D., Laurel getting the money she wanted from Eugene.

But, wait, how could Charlotte know Pan was going off with J.D.? Only Rick and the divorce lawyer had known that. Everyone else thought Pan was going to stay, to work on the marriage.

Except the mysterious "someone coming." Pan could have told that person.

Charlotte?

Standing up on that ridge, in the woods, watching Pan until her shoes sank deep in the muck?

It was possible. Emotions strong enough to drive someone to murder could overcome other habits.

But which emotions had been strong enough?

Had Pan been killed because the murderer thought she was going back to her husband? Or because the killer knew she wasn't?

And the same thing with Laurel.

Another connection—the uncertainty of their marital futures.

Patterns.

What was it Renee Tagner said about men following a pattern when it came to affairs of the heart?

More'n likely it starts with their mama's like those old Greek plays say... and unless they're smart enough to heed a strong woman, they keep repeatin' it.

Eugene, for sure. Rick Wade, with his affairs.

Ed Smith?

Being controlled by Blankenship women, perhaps. Anything else?

J.D. Carson.

He had let Pan go—telling her to go back to her husband. Just now he'd told her to go back to her job.

But she wasn't part of this pattern. She was outside of it. Except for the calls.

And the break-ins?

No sign there'd been break-ins for Pan or Laurel. But then they'd been living with their families. Harder for anyone to break in undetected.

Complicated families.

Jamie and Ally. ... Aunt Vivian.

Not going there.

Stick to patterns. What Renee had said.

But instead of Renee Tagner's voice in her head, she heard Mrs. Barrett's.

Teddie would talk about the other boys, this one saying that funny thing and that one making this joke, but the names came so fast and it seemed all were the same, if you know what I mean. This one somebody's brother or uncle or cousin.

Why did that gnaw at her? Gnawing—like the something in the transcript? God, if something was telling her to dig deeper into Teddie's death, she hoped she had better luck than she'd had with the transcript.

There was no indication Charlotte had a motive for hurting Teddie. Didn't fit any pattern.

Jealousy could give her a motive to kill Pan, certainly to kill Laurel. And covering her tracks could explain Rick Wade if he got on to something. But then why was he making those phone calls? Happenstance? And what about Teddie?

His mother did some sewing for Charlotte, but what direct dealings did she have with him? Certainly not sitting in Shenny's plying him with drinks, directing his memories. They'd have heard that.

No. To have Charlotte be the murderer, Teddie's death had to be an accident.

Her gut said it wasn't.

She chuckled shakily. Great. Listening to her gut.

Her phone rang. Audio caller ID announced Nancy Quinn.

"I heard about the arrest of the judge's older daughter. Where are you?" her assistant asked.

"On the way back."

"Are you okay?"

"Yeah."

"You don't sound it."

"Nancy—"

"Fine. I'll butt out. Heard Bel got you some intel. Any help? Did it fit in?"

Fit in with the pattern.

Maggie braked, saw a crossroad ahead, braked harder, and flipped on her signal.

"No, it didn't help. Yes, it fit in."

"What does that mean?"

"It means I'm going back, Nancy."

"You mean you're coming back."

"No. I'm turning around and going back to Bedhurst. You're right. What Bel found doesn't point to Charlotte, but it does fit the pattern. That needs to be looked at."

Nancy was silent a moment. "I don't know what that's about, but you sound more like yourself. The most like yourself you've sounded since you went up there. Hell, since before you got involved with Isaacson. What should I tell Vic in the morning?"

"Nothing."

Maggie could imagine Nancy's smile as she said, "My favorite thing to tell Vic Upton."

✧ ✧ ✧ ✧

ONCE HEADED TOWARD Bedhurst, Maggie hit speed dial.

"I'm not going to make lunch tomorrow."

"Oh?" There was something odd in Jamie's voice. Not the usual I'm-too-upbeat-to-show-I'm-disappointed tone that served up double scoops of guilt.

"They've arrested someone in Bedhurst."

"But then why…?"

Was Jamie asking why was she headed back there or why was she telling Jamie about it? Couldn't blame her for either question. Neither answer made much sense based on Maggie's history.

"I don't think she's the one—well, she *is* the one who pushed my car down a ravine, but—"

"Pushed your car—? With you *in* it?"

"Yes, but—"

"My God, Maggie—Are you all right?"

"I'm fine. A little sore, but fine. J.D. got me out in time."

"In time," Jamie echoed faintly. Maggie regretted the phrase. Jamie had already moved on. "J.D.? *J.D. Carson?* The guy you prosecuted up there?"

Now she regretted saying anything. "Yes. It's complicated. But maybe it's one of those omens you like so much, because it turns out I forgot to give the key back when I left. Anyway, the point is, I'm not going to make lunch. There's more to do up here. You and Ally—"

"What more is there to do up there? What do you know, Maggie?"

"Know? Not much. It's not a matter of knowing." She gave a harsh laugh. "You'll love this, Jamie. It doesn't *feel* right.

✧ ✧ ✧ ✧

6:45 p.m.

MAGGIE HADN'T SEEN Bedhurst anywhere close to busy this week, but Sunday evening, sliding into twilight, it was beyond slow.

No visiting cars remained around Monroe House. Nothing stirred.

If Dallas and Evelyn were smart they were tucked up for a long nap or early-to-bed. He'd looked wan at brunch. Relieved, but wan. The man definitely needed rest. She felt the effects of a sleep deficit herself.

She sent Dallas a text that she'd returned, was in the guesthouse, and they needed to talk as soon as he was rested.

In the guesthouse bedroom she unpacked only the files. The rest could wait.

She spread them out on the bed, organizing them one way, then another. Jotting notes on a legal pad.

Then she picked up the transcript and began reading again.

Commonwealth v. J.D. Carson

Closing Statement Excerpts
Assistant Commonwealth's Attorney Margaret Frye

Reason, not emotions.

Mr. Monroe has focused your attention on emotions during this trial. The story of a man from a difficult background who seemed to make good in his adult life. He has focused on emotions because that is all he has.

What you have are facts. Reason and facts that the testimony of all these witnesses have given you.

Even J.D. Carson acknowledges that his relationship with Pan Addington Wade had taken a turn from the friendship they had enjoyed since she befriended him in childhood. Even J.D. Carson acknowledges that they had spent a great deal of time together and that they were seen in public places in intense and intimate conversations. Even J.D. Carson acknowledges that he had given her the address and phone number for an apartment complex near where he was posted at the time. And here is where your reason is put to use—why would he give that to her if he didn't want her to leave her husband and run away with him?

And, finally, even J.D. Carson acknowledges that Pandora Wade had been last seen by him at the spot where she was found dead—also by him. The defense asks you to believe that she drove him there, they had an ordinary conversation, then he left, walking down the path to his cabin in the woods. What? No breadcrumbs to follow later? Because it sounds just like a fairy tale doesn't it?

The defendant also says that he heard no gunshot.

For that to be true, there would have to be a gap between the time he says he left her and the time she was murdered.

Apply your reason here, too. Why would Pandora Wade remain by her car after J.D. Carson left after this friendly, ordinary conversation? Waiting for some stranger to happen along and kill her? Pure coincidence?

And what about the other facts we have given you? Pandora Wade was shot with her own gun. There was no sign of struggle, no signs she was trying to get away or escape. Reason says that rules out the stranger-happening-past theory. Reason says she was killed by someone she knew, someone she trusted. Someone she never believed would hurt her.

And here are more facts for your reason to consider. J.D. Carson found Pandora Wade's body. He would have plenty of opportunity to remove or alter evidence at the crime scene. Ah, but there was no evidence at the crime scene, was there—because someone had time to wipe it away, thinking he had erased every bit of it.

But he didn't. Not every bit of it. Not Pandora Wade's hair wrapped around the cuff button of the shirt you've heard witnesses testify he was wearing that last day of Pandora Wade's life.

And here's another fact for you to consider. J.D. Carson is a trained killer. An expert marksman. A man who could shoot Pandora Wade through the heart in a blink.

The last to see her alive, the first to find her dead body. That, ladies and gentlemen, is the murderer of Pandora Addington Wade. That is J.D. Carson.

———

CHAPTER SIXTY-SEVEN

SHE WOKE TO darkness.

She'd barely gotten past her opening statement before sleep had hit her.

Now, someone was here.

Making no sound. But breathing the same air. She was sure of it.

She also wasn't surprised.

So much for believing in Charlotte's guilt, thought one segment of her mind. The rest of it was on hyper-alert.

A shadow moved.

J.D.

Relief swept across her, sank into her tensed muscles.

Followed immediately by realization that with her defenses down, mind shut off, with no evidence except her gut, she not only sensed his presence, she trusted him.

"J.D.? What—?"

He turned on the small bedside lamp. "I saw movement, but I knew you were asleep. I came in."

"How did you know I was here at all?"

"Followed you. Out of town, then back in. Damn it—why the hell didn't you keep going? Just keep going back to where you belong?"

"Wh—?"

"Go ahead, call the sheriff. I ignored a feeling of someone being around before Pan was murdered. Not again. No matter how much you say you're able to take care of yourself. No matter how much you don't trust me. Here, dial 9-1-1, get Gardner. Get the whole department. I'm not leaving you alone."

"But—"

"I'm not convinced Charlotte's the murderer, and even if she is there's something else going on."

"What I've been trying to say is I agree, Charlotte isn't the murderer." For once, she thought his silence was from surprise rather than control. She sat up, piled pillows behind her. "That's why I came back."

She drew her legs to one side. She looked from the space on the bed created by her movement, to him.

A flicker of the heat she'd seen in his eyes the other night flashed. Then was gone.

He took her sweater off the suitcase where she'd dropped it and handed it to her. "Chilly in here."

Looking down, she saw her blouse had unbuttoned halfway down. Awareness of her nipples, hardened and straining against the silk of her bra, swept heat through her. She buttoned hurriedly and pulled the sweater on. Hoping he would mistake her flush for embarrassment.

She couldn't have him again. Not unless she did a lot more sorting out.

Was that for herself? For him? Did it matter?

"There's a pattern, J.D. I can't see it, but there are glimpses."

"What pattern?"

"That's the problem. I don't know."

Renee's words... *Affairs of the heart.* But with Rick Wade dead, who could that be? Except J.D.

Unless it was Wade who killed Pan and Laurel, attacked the woman Bel had found named Darcie Johnson, then someone else killed him?

Eugene? But would he kill to avenge Laurel?

Ed—

J.D. sat on the edge of the bed, one leg drawn up, his knee touching her calf. "Where'd you go just now."

"I was remembering what Renee said about patterns and affairs of the heart. I can't grab hold of it. And there's something else. Almost from the start, I've had this nagging sense of the transcript trying to tell me something. Trying to tell me something was wrong." She grimaced. "At least not quite right. I know it sounds crazy, but—"

"Trust your gut, Maggie."

"I wish people would stop telling me that."

He persisted. "What's the first thing that comes to your mind? No thinking, say it."

"The opening statement. I keep going back to the opening statement." Before she finished the words, he'd reached into the carton from Nancy, which was on the floor near him, and pulled out the rough transcript, handing it to her.

She took it, but shook her head. "I've been over and over and over it. Nothing."

"Go over it again. Now. Read it aloud."

She hesitated, reluctant to speak her words declaring his guilt.

"Maggie."

She tipped the transcript to catch light from the small lamp and began.

✧ ✧ ✧ ✧

"**...PANDORA WADE WAS** found with the note the defendant, J.D. Carson, wrote representing his plans to run away together stuffed in her mouth. She'd said no and he couldn't take that..."

"Keep going."

"Something... There's something..."

She re-read the words from the transcript.

Pandora Wade was found with the note the defendant, J.D. Carson, wrote representing his plans to run away together stuffed in her mouth. She'd said no and he couldn't take that.

She stared at the paper she held until the words disappeared, she slipped under the surface of the trial, into the depths of it again. Surrounded by it. In it. Completely.

Standing in front of the jury. Seeing each face. Hearing the slight movement of Judge Blankenship to her side.

And she spoke.

Each word sounded in her memory, echoed in her head.

Each word she had spoken.

And the words she had not spoken.

"In her mouth."

Her voice sounded strange to her. Muffled. The liquid volume of the trial buffering it.

She shook it off, pushing up from the memory. Returning to now. Looking at J.D.

"I *didn't say that*. Not in the opening statement. I left the detail of where the note was found out of the opening to have more impact during testimony. Maximum effect. It was the end of the second day." She flipped through pages. "With the medical examiner on the stand."

"I remember that testimony."

She did, too. She also remembered him in that moment.

She'd turned away from the medical examiner, made eye contact with several jurors to be sure they understood the import, then she'd seen his face.

Rigid. Taut. Controlled. ... Yet, under the control, shock.

"You hadn't known." She didn't ask it as a question, because she knew. She'd known then, as hard as she'd tried not to. It was the seed that grew into *What if he's innocent?*

"Not until that testimony."

The paper hadn't been visible when he found Pan's body. Still wasn't visible for sheriff's department personnel to spot—and blab about.

Only the murderer who had shoved the note into Pan's mouth, then posed her face down had known about it.

J.D. said, "Are you sure about this? You've been reading this transcript over and over."

"Sure. I must have read that opening a dozen times since I came up here but I never—Oh, my God. Oh, my God!"

CHAPTER SIXTY-EIGHT

"WHAT? MAGGIE—"

She scrambled off the far side of the bed, pawed through the papers on the table, frustrated by the lack of light.

"Maggie?"

"Wait. Just wait!" She had it.

Too impatient to walk around the bed, she crawled back across it to the pool of light. Her hands shook as she flipped the pages. J.D. tried to read from beside her, but clearly didn't have the right angle.

She read it. Then read it again, slowly. To be sure.

Her hands stopped shaking.

"What I just read from, what had me including the note being in Pan's mouth in my opening, which we agree I *didn't* say—" She sucked in a breath. "—and what you're holding now, J.D., is a copy of the transcript my assistant made from dailies she'd pulled out of storage and sent to me. My boss wouldn't pay for the post-trial version because it wasn't our jurisdiction. I kept the dailies and put them in the file."

She tapped the page of the transcript from the table—the copy she'd been reading and rereading, unable to find the flaw.

"*This* is the copy I was given here in Bedhurst after Laurel's murder. This one reads: *Pandora Wade was found with the note the defendant, J.D. Carson, wrote representing his plans to run away together. She'd said no and he couldn't take that.*

He got it.

Still, he held his hand out for the copy she held. He touched his fingertip beside the passage. Then he put both copies under the brightest light from the lamp and looked from one to the other.

"Could Dallas have told him?" she asked. "Did he work on your case or—"

"No. Dallas kept him out of my case, so he could work as reporter. Plus, Dallas had stopped using him for depositions a while before and wasn't confiding in him. But he has contacts at the sheriff's department. Buddies who—"

"None of them knew. No one knew except me, Dallas, and the professionals at the regional medical examiner's office in Roanoke."

His big hands spread on the pages, he stared straight ahead. "Scott."

"Yes. Only Scott could have put it in the dailies and only he could have left it out of the complete."

"Fuck," he said low. "He removed it because he realized he shouldn't have known that fact during your opening statement."

"Exactly. He must have anticipated I'd say it, and typed what he expected to hear rather than what he actually heard. After hearing testimony that only the medical examiner saw the note, he realized he couldn't have known before the testimony unless he was the one who shoved the note in Pan's mouth … after murdering her. When he put together the complete, he fixed his mistake and took it out."

"*Scott* murdered Pan? Why? *Why*? She never did a thing to him. She was only kind to him, was his friend."

"His friend. Maybe that's it. Maybe—Oh, my God, he said she'd changed her mind about going back to Wade. He covered it, but he said it the night Wade came to Monroe House. How could Scott have known that unless she told him? That day, in the clearing. At the same time she told him she was going away with you. He must have thought… The pattern. The pattern Renee talked about." *Starts with their mamas like those old Greek plays say.* "He follows a pattern."

"Laurel, too?"

"Laurel, Pan, the girl in Lynchburg—all of them. Befriends them when they're vulnerable. Offers support. But when they don't need that anymore. Oh—oh! But with Laurel it was different. She didn't cry on his shoulder. She wanted information. And he gave it to her. The papers Eugene had her sign. What do you want to bet Scott was aware of that, too—the work he does for Renee Tagner. I bet he found out then."

"And you. He was trying to be your shoulder to cry on about Isaacson. What—? Shit." From *shit*, J.D. went into a stream of low, but heartfelt and colorful curses.

"What?"

"The key. On Scott's key ring, he has a shiny new key."

She got it immediately. "A key to here, but—How?"

J.D. stood. "Soap, clay, hot glue and silicone—a minute to make a mold, then make the copy at leisure."

"But he'd have to have the key. Only Dallas and I had one."

"When he brought your car around to the office. While we were talking to Charlotte on the—"

CHAPTER SIXTY-NINE

NOISE ASSAULTED MAGGIE'S senses.

A door crashed open. Shouts. A head-snapping jolt. A crushing weight. A roar like a train. Then weight sliding off her.

Acrid burning.

Shouting, shouting.

"Maggie! Maggie!"

"J.D.?" But it wasn't his voice.

She raised herself up, reason sorting through the fragments.

Someone had burst in—from the storage closet, where something was burning—and fired a shot.

J.D. had pushed her to the bed, covering her with his body, then slid to the floor, carrying the bedspread with him. He wasn't moving. Cold fear shuddered her heart.

Scott stepped into the room, holding a gun with both hands. Still aimed at J.D.

"It's him, it's him! He's the murderer," Scott shouted.

She started to drop to her knees beside J.D. Scott grabbed her arm, dragging her up, holding the gun away with the other.

"No! Carson's the murderer. He shot Pan, strangled Laurel. Now he's after you. Get away from him!"

Maggie backed away from J.D. to get Scott and the gun farther from him.

J.D.'s head spilled red streams onto the bedspread, where it wicked across the threads as if trying to run away. He lay still. She couldn't see his eyes from this angle. Conscious? In shock? Worse? He was breathing. She held on to that.

"That's right." Scott talked fast and high. Behind him fire cackled at the closet's treasure of paper fuel. Heaps of notebooks and paper. He was destroying his original notes from the trial, made while he'd lived here, sitting in that closet the whole time. "This time will be different."

He stepped forward, aiming the gun at J.D. with both hands.

"Scott. Tell me, tell me the truth." She reached for his arm. He flinched and backed up, the gun pointed up. Would playing along gain necessary time or use up time J.D. couldn't afford? "You're the only one who can tell me, Scott. The only one."

His lips twitched. "I'm the only one who knows everything. That's what none of them understood. But you do, Maggie, don't you?"

"Yes, I understand. But first you have to tell me, Scott."

"I listened. To all of them. Mother, others. Listening, always listening when they needed someone. But they wanted…dirty things. Like Mama. But with Pan … oh, Pan was different. No one else knew. I told her it was because of working for her divorce lawyer—confidentiality. I had her all to myself. She asked me things, asked about me. She loved me. It was over with Rick. She hardly even talked about him. We were going to be happy. Really happy.

"Then Carson came and she stopped calling, stopped seeing me. She didn't have time. But she had time for *him*. Every day, every night. Everybody in town talking about it. That's how I heard. Not from her. She had told me everything, every thought and fear and feeling. And now she wasn't telling me anything. I had to call to know if she was home or out. I had to follow her to know where she went.

"The other times at the clearing, they'd talked in the car and I couldn't hear. But that day, when he got out, she followed. Calling out, throwing herself at him. Practically begged him to fuck her. Hanging on him, touching him like a common whore. Needs—God, needs! Need more than companionship. Need a man. Even when I didn't want to, even when it was disgusting. But she needed—she needed everything!"

That last wasn't about Pan, was it? His voice had changed. Risen, out of control. Now he sucked in air, calming himself.

"It was ruined. She ruined everything."

"Laurel, too," she murmured.

Laurel wouldn't have hesitated to use Scott as a convenient and sympathetic audience. And once she thought she had Eugene by the short hairs to dump him.

"That tramp told me she didn't need me, because she'd fixed things just how she wanted. Like she got to decide." His sneer faded into resolve. "This time it'll be different, Maggie. It'll be perfect. Roy's out of your life. Just one more."

J.D.

Was he stirring?

"But Teddie?" she prompted.

"Like Mother—memories all jumbled. They'd start jabbering. Telling what was *secret*. Had to go.

"Got him stinking drunk. Cost a hell of a lot more than I'd counted on. And then Carson scooped him up like some fucking guardian angel, and there wasn't a damned thing I could do.

"I wasn't doing that again. Next day, got out ahead of him, put good skidding gravel in the right spot, brought the car around, and came straight at him. That bike hit the gravel, he jerked the wheel, and plop, over he goes. No more moron. Perfect. Never touched him. No forensics at all.

"Like with Pan. Even when I didn't have time to plan, I thought of everything. Leaving her because it was close to his shack. Wiping out the prints—because that's what he'd do. He should have been convicted! Death row. I dreamed of recording those words. Now I have to finish the job."

"No!" She forced calm into her voice. She had to delay him. Someone would see the smoke. Someone would call it in. Dallas. Evelyn. A neighbor. Someone. Help would come. "No, Scott. Think. We'll call the sheriff. He'll be tried. I'll prosecute. I'll get a guilty verdict this time."

"No. I'll finish him, my notes will burn. I have you to myself."

He raised his arm, aimed at J.D.

She dove.

Her shoulder slammed into his chest, she swung her elbow into whatever it could find. He made a sound, mixed of surprise, rage and yes, pain. She clawed at his arm, his hand. Empty.

Where was the gun?

She pulled back. Looking frantically. She hadn't heard it against the wood floor, but—

And then she saw it at the back of the window seat cushion under the middle window.

Scott saw it, too.

They reached it simultaneously. He had the stronger grip, but she had a better angle.

If he gained control, there would be no talking to him, no delay tactics. It would be over before anyone had a chance to help.

J.D.

Trust your gut, Maggie.

She released the gun, grabbed Scott's arm and pushed with all her weight behind it. Caught off guard and off balance, he offered no resistance. His wrist cracked against the window frame. He screamed and released the gun. He lunged for it, but it was gone, scratches tracing its path as it skidded down the roof, then a glint in the dark when it skied off the edge.

She never heard it land.

Scott lunged. Pain exploded in her jaw. The blow knocked her back off the window seat. She felt herself falling.

Then nothing.

CHAPTER SEVENTY

COUGHING DRAGGED MAGGIE upright.

Smoke. Fire. Pain.

The circle of her senses widened. Grunts and curses. Movement. A moan.

J.D.

She opened her eyes.

Scott had J.D. on the window seat. Grunting against the dead weight, he was trying to position J.D. at the open window so all it would take would be a good shove to tumble him out, down the steeply pitched roof, into the rock-strewn creek bed.

"No!"

Maggie launched herself at Scott. Trying for his eyes.

He yelped, but his elbow connected with her cheekbone. Maggie stumbled, caught herself. But her ankle folded under her. No chance of catching or protecting herself, she went down, the side of her head slammed against the floor.

She wouldn't pass out again. She couldn't.

She reached her knees, holding her breath against the swirling smoke.

Scott had J.D. in the open window. He pushed. Pushed again.

"God dammit!" Scott screamed.

J.D. held the frame with one hand. He was alert enough and strong enough to do that. Thank God.

Scott pried at J.D.'s fingers.

Maggie surged to her feet, lurching, reaching out.

J.D. disappeared from the frame.

No! No!

A dual cry rose. Her horror, Scott's triumph. But no sound from J.D.

She pulled herself onto the window seat, leaning out the second open frame while Scott did the same beside her, trying to see. There was nothing. But she heard. Creaking wood. Grunts. A soft swish, a sharper rip.

Then a thud.

Solid male tumbling to wooden floor, wasn't it?

Or was it the cracking and shattering of something in the house below them from the fire?

But how could he have—She didn't care how, just please, please, let it be.

"You're like them—*all of them*. Leave me for some shit who fucks you. I'll show you like I showed them. You bitch! You godamn bitch!"

Scott lunged to push her out the window after J.D. She feinted one way. He fell for it. She scrambled off the window seat and toward the door.

One step from the windows and the thick, dark smoke stung her eyes. She covered her mouth and nose with one hand, crouched and plunged deeper in. A patch of flames brought some illumination. The bed, she realized. She'd gone too far to the left. She had to get around it to reach the door. She scuttled to the right, her eyes streaming. Coughing wracked her.

And then, out of the hot swirls, a hand grasped her wrist.

She couldn't break the hold. She couldn't breathe.

He swung her around like children playing Crack the Whip. She had no strength left to save herself from crashing into the window seat.

He was on her immediately, shoving her legs out the window. She grabbed for anything. Her fingers scraped across raw wood gouged by J.D. She held on, scrabbling for a foothold on the slanted roof. Scott jammed the heels of his hands against her, driving splinters deeper. She clung.

"You're just like her. Trying to throw me away. No more!"

He loomed above. Standing on the window seat. In the flash before his foot stomped on her fingers, she released one hand, dangling now.

His foot landed on the frame where her other hand had been, barely missing her one-handed. She caught his ankle and yanked. Momentum already carrying him forward, he pitched out the window, landing on the roof beside her. She heard his hands tearing at the shingles, trying to catch hold, anything to fight the gravity pulling him.

Maggie reached up to grasp the frame with both hands, the motion swinging her feet to one side.

Oh, God! Scott had caught her left foot.

His weight pulled her like the rack. Arms, shoulders, torso, left leg, all screamed with the burning stretch.

"You, too, Maggie. You, too."

The harsh whisper came from the dark closing over her. She had no voice to beg for her life.

She felt the yank on her foot, knew he was no longer trying to save himself. He wanted only to kill her. To kill her as he had Pan and Laurel. She would be a victim, like the women in her photographs. No longer there to fight for them.

Like Aunt Vivian.

She saw her face. Heard her.

Maggie.

It would be okay. Aunt Vivian would fold her in her arms, and it would be okay. She wouldn't fight any more. She could let go...

No... No, Maggie. Live. Not for me. Live for yourself. Fight, Maggie. Fight. And live.

A sob sucked air into her lungs. She kicked out with her right foot. Once. Twice. And again.

She caught him the third time. His head, she thought. He screamed. The unbearable drag on her leg disappeared, and he screamed again. The descending crash of branches swallowed the scream. But not its echoes.

Finally, she heard only her own wheezing pants, and the voracious crackle of fire.

She was beyond pain. Beyond struggle. Beyond letting go. She would stay here. Right here. Until... Until.

Smoke billowed out of the windows. She coughed. Turned her face to the side.

The harsh pebbles of the shingles pressed into her cheek. She closed her eyes and concentrated on a pain she could fathom.

"Maggie."

Was that the last thing in her mind before she died? J.D. saying her name? Shouldn't her entire life flash before her eyes? Or was it a mercy to not get her entire life? To have simply his voice?

She looked up, but smoke filled the window above her.

Then she felt a strong hold across the back of her waist. From here, out on the roof.

"J.D.?" He was real. "You're here."

"Yeah." He was doing something. Lying on his stomach next to her, but not sliding.

"You didn't fall off the roof."

"Caught the gutter. Swung into the porch." He was tying a rope. That's what he was doing. Tying a rope around her waist. Connecting it to himself.

"Scott fell off. Down—"

"I know. I tried to get back before—But you're not going to fall. We're getting off together."

"Okay."

"Good." He tugged at the rope. "Draw your legs up to the side, like a frog. Good. Use the side of your feet. Press against the shingles. That's right. Now, let go of the window."

Her fingers wouldn't open.

"Maggie, I've got you." His arm crossed over her back. "You can let go."

Sooty tears slid into her mouth. "I'm trying."

He shifted, reached over her, and pried her fingers open. Fire licked at the vertical window frame.

"Here we go," J.D. said. Calm, unhurried.

They edged their way across the roof like peculiar crabs. No, frogs. He'd said frog.

She focused on his voice. And the inch in front of her.

Voices came from below. Voices shouting about their safety. About the fire. She listened to only one voice. The one closest to her.

They reached the edge, it was easier to breathe here. Slightly. Though with each breath that benefit lessened, as the smoke followed.

J.D. checked the rope.

"The ground's not solid enough where the roof's lower. We have to drop to the ground from up here. I'm going over the edge first, Maggie." He brought his face close to hers. Looked into her eyes. "When I tell you, lower yourself down. Wait for my word, then let go and I'll be there."

He stroked her hair once. Looked as if he might say more. Instead, he left. And she was alone.

"I won't be able to hold here long."

Who was she telling? J.D.? Herself? Vivian? Jamie and Ally? Bel and Landis? Nancy?

A little longer, Maggie, they all said.

A little longer.

She'd do that. She owed it to all of them.

A little longer.

"Maggie." His strong voice came from below. She released the breath she hadn't known she held. He hadn't disappeared into the abyss. He'd reached ground. "Slide over the edge now."

Her muscles shook as she slid one leg then the other over the edge of the eave, each move accompanied by the scrape of the shingles. She didn't have the strength to lower herself slowly, her weight jerked her down.

"Okay, Maggie. Let go."

She couldn't. She hung, her hold weakening, the stretch in her shuddering arms becoming more impossible each second. But she couldn't let go.

"I'll get you."

She closed her eyes. And she saw his face. Seeing the blood. Seeing the pain. Seeing the loner. The survivor. The innocent man.

"Trust me, Maggie. Trust me."

She looked down, between her arms and to the side. Saw a slice of his face.

"Shut up." She gulped in air. "And get me on the damn ground."

He grinned, altering the path of the blood running down his cheek. Stretched his arms higher, narrowing the gap she would fall but unable to close it.

"C'mon, then."

CHAPTER SEVENTY-ONE

Monday, 10:32 a.m.

DALLAS SAT AT the kitchen table when Evelyn came in. She studied him as she put on an apron.

She'd stayed last night—the hell with what her boys or anyone else thought—she wasn't leaving him with all this.

The fire.

J.D. and Maggie.

Scott.

She'd persuaded Dallas to bed as dawn came, but sleep was another matter.

"Morning, Dallas. No stirring from the guest rooms." Maggie and J.D. had followed the doctor's orders to rest, but not until most of the night had gone in questions, answers … and horrors, as officials worked along the creek bed to retrieve Scott's body.

Dallas grunted. "When they get up, tell them I've gone to the sheriff's department. Have a lot of things to go over. They say confession's good for the soul. I'll be confessin' my blindness and my arrogance."

It was worse than she'd thought.

She'd known he would blame himself for not seeing signs of Scott's problems. At some level maybe he had known. Those dizzy spells, the tiredness, all the ways his body tried to make him listen to what his heart couldn't bear.

All because he and that strange son of a strange mother shared a trickle of blood. The old fool.

Her old fool.

"Dallas, I have something to say."

He looked up, not much interested.

"Yes," she said.

"Yes?"

"Yes. I'll marry you."

A spark lit his eyes, but then they narrowed. "Why now?"

"Because before you thought you were rescuing me."

Automatic denial came to his lips. He stopped it. "I'll have to think about that." He added, "So now my name is disgraced, you're rescuing me?"

She made a sound. "As if roaring into court as the underdog wouldn't get your blood pumping like it hasn't in years. Besides, you know as well as I do that if there'd been rescuing—one or the other—we would have suited all this time."

He lowered his eyelids. "Then why now?"

"Don't go closing your eyes like you think it'll stop me seeing into your head. Why now? Because I've got the imagination to live with you, but I'm not sure I have enough to live without you."

✧   ✧   ✧   ✧

CHARLOTTE BLANKENSHIP SMITH'S laughter could be heard throughout the jail.

Sheriff Roger Gardner could still hear it long after he'd informed the prisoner she was no longer suspected in her sister's murder, although she continued to be held on charges associated with the attack on Maggie Frye.

Charlotte had hardly seemed to hear what he'd said about how Scott's confession to Maggie and J.D. of murdering Pan and Laurel affected her. She was already laughing.

Laughing and laughing.

Maggie had heard it, too. Probably why her exit just now had been speedy.

She'd likely be back for an official tie-up, but for now she was headed home.

Home.

The sheriff locked his office door. At the front desk he told Dorrie, "Abner will be back when they finish dismantling at the gym. I'm going home. I'm going to sleep for a week. If you need me tonight or tomorrow—"

"I won't. You sleep well, Sheriff Gardner."

She put on her headset, even though the phone hadn't rung.

He hoped it shut out Charlotte's laughter.

And her occasional shouts. "Scott Tomlinson! Fucking Scott Tomlinson! The one man she didn't screw!"

SHE STOOD AT the prosecution table, her fingertips trailing over the wood.

"Maggie."

She whirled, the way she had a week ago when he'd startled her in this same spot. This time, she relaxed as J.D. stepped out of shadow.

She even gave a half-grimace, half-smile. "Who sent you to see if I'm okay? Dallas or Evelyn?"

"Came on my own. *Are* you okay?" He leaned in. "Your hair doesn't smell like smoke anymore."

"Thanks to Doranna. Even cleared her shop so I wouldn't be bothered by questions. I will be okay. You?"

"Better than you."

"Right. Because you only got shot. In the head." Her sarcasm slid away. "I still think—"

"No hospital. Mostly scalp wound. After your tangle with Charlotte, you know how they bleed. Besides, I told you, I was mostly playing possum to gain the element of surprise."

She took his arm, trying not to wince at the bandage on his head and those *mostly*s, and started toward the door. "You couldn't have surprised him *before* he threw you on the roof?"

"He thought he'd disposed of me. That added more surprise. If you'd just been a little more patient, instead of dealing with him yourself…"

She grimaced wryly. Then she sobered as the doors of Courtroom One closed behind them. "We have all the things Scott said to us— me—but will we ever know for absolute certainty?"

"Guilt can be as much a matter of guesswork as innocence is. But—"

"*Guesswork?* That's—

"Belief then."

"I'm crap at believing."

His laughter startled her. Again. After a moment she smiled.

"I was going to say," he said, "that evidence goes a long way to eliminating the guesswork. Not only do we have what he told us, but Scott being the guy makes sense of a lot. Like using Pan's gun—that was impulse. But for the other killings he didn't use guns—he always was a lousy shot."

She nodded as he held the outer door for her. "Sheriff Gardner said he probably used what he'd picked up from trials and work for the legal system to avoid leaving evidence or a pattern."

"No pattern in how he committed the crimes, maybe but there was in the relationships that led to them."

Amazing how fast information could be accumulated once you knew the answer.

With Monroe, Gardner, some of the other investigators, assisted by Bel and Landis by phone, they'd pieced together that Scott had encountered Pan and Laurel at Zales' office, doing depositions on other cases. Zales, apparently, had no idea.

Bel provided a detailed account from Darcie Johnson, the third woman Scott had met.

Eighteen months ago, Scott was balm during her bad divorce. But as Scott became both possessive and increasingly volatile, the woman withdrew. The more she withdrew, the more demanding he became, until she was spooked, then terrified.

She'd talked to Lynchburg police, changed her mind, and moved to Northern Virginia, covering her tracks… Or so she thought until

Belichek found her.

The investigators could only speculate Pan and Laurel had dismissed any similar internal warnings—if they'd had them—because they'd known Scott all their lives.

Their blind spots. Charlotte of all people had spotted that.

She thought the way people responded to her on the surface was how they truly felt.

And Rick? Would he have gone to that isolated spot for promised evidence against J.D., even if he'd been suspicious of Scott? Almost certainly.

When Maggie didn't respond to Scott's overtures as her comforter, he upped the stakes with calls, following her, looking through her belongings, using the guesthouse key.

After she left Bedhurst, he must have thought it was safe to use the new key, planning to destroy his original trial notes. He was trapped when Maggie returned. Some argued he'd started the fires by accident. She wondered if he'd been that clearheaded.

She stopped on the courthouse's bottom step. "Do you think he killed his mother?"

"From what I heard..." He'd caught some while he'd fought for consciousness. "Yeah, though that's something we won't know for sure."

J.D. took her arm to lead her across the street to her car, as if to steer her clear of nonexistent traffic. There was none.

He continued, "Mrs. Barrett says that when Scott dropped her off after the memorial, he took the road toward Lynchburg instead of heading back to town, and he was on his phone as soon as she was out of his car."

"Gardner told me."

"Probably a burner phone. He had them stashed in his truck, his house—his mother's house—even the office. More phone records."

"At least I won't have to look at them." She shook her head. "I can't believe I fell for it when Scott fed me that misinformation about Eugene making sure the pre-nup was ironclad. There was no downside for him, he could always say his informant got it wrong. In the meantime, he'd diverted us to Eugene while he set up Rick."

At her rental car, she beeped the trunk open, took off a sweater—spring had a firm hold on the mountains—folded it and dropped it inside. The sweater, along with the leggings and shirt she wore were on loan from Theresa Addington.

Her clothes were held for evidence. Everything else she'd had here was lost in the fire that had destroyed much of the guesthouse.

Including her briefcase and the plastic sleeve of photos.

"So, you're leaving." His voice was perfectly level.

She stilled with her hand on the trunk lid, then closed it with a neutral thunk.

J.D. rested his butt against the rear door on the driver's side, his head toward her.

Bones. Sinews. Flesh.

"Need to get back and find out if I still have a job."

He tipped his head in acknowledgement of her point of practicality.

"How's Judge Blankenship?" she asked.

"Devastated."

"And Dallas? How do you think he's really doing?"

Dallas said his informant about activities in Henry Zales' office was a disgruntled associate trying to curry Dallas' support. Maggie had suspected Scott, with Dallas masking his indiscretions. But Scott had reasons far larger than indiscretions for not wanting anyone to connect him with the women going to Zales.

She worried about Dallas, though the doctor said he'd be fine physically with a good stretch of rest and no stress.

"Better. A lot better, I think. Ed Smith called him not long ago."

"Oh?"

"Asked Dallas to help with Charlotte's defense for attacking you."

She shook her head. Defending the woman who'd tried to kill her, yet proclaiming his never-ending friendship. Trouble was, she believed him.

"That must have cheered him up."

"Almost as much as the fact that he and Evelyn talked—same

topic, new response. They're getting married."

"Really? That's great." She saw he was thinking about their own talks, of whether they were in a position to have a new talk on a new topic—the future instead of the past. "Isn't it?"

"Who knows with a hard-headed woman."

She studied the unfamiliar set of keys in her hand. "What about you, J.D.? Are you leaving?"

His silence stretched a minute. "Don't know yet. Too soon. I do know I'm not locked in anymore. Thanks to you."

His hand covered hers and the keys, two of their fingers connected, held, then slid apart.

"J.D., when you were getting me off the roof, I couldn't let myself think about what had happened, or how we'd get to the ground. I concentrated on your voice. On looking at the inch that came next. That's all I let in. That's how I made it. Your voice and looking ahead one inch at a time."

After a pause, he said slowly, "That sounds like a plan. A good plan."

She glanced up, then away, nodding. "Yes. I think so, too."

As she slid into the driver's seat, he went to the outside of the car door. With the window down all the way, he cupped both hands over the doorframe and closed it. He was too close for her to see his face, hidden by the top of the door.

She stared at his hands, even as she fumbled to start the car.

The engine caught immediately.

"Well," she said, forcing out words. "I'll be seeing you."

He bent, caught her face between his palms and kissed her. Hard. Emphatic. Fast.

Too fast.

He released her and stepped back.

This angle allowed her to see his face. His eyes, intent and dark, were locked on hers. His mouth shifted, creating that indentation she knew to look for now.

"Yes," he said, "you will. You will be seeing me, Maggie Frye."

✧   ✧   ✧   ✧

Thank you for reading Maggie and J.D.'s story in PROOF OF INNO-
CENCE. *If you enjoyed it, here is a glimpse into* PRICE OF INNOCENCE,
the next book in The Innocence Trilogy.

THE MIDDLE-OF-THE-NIGHT PHONE call woke J.D. Carson to
immediate alertness. In that instant, without turning on a light, he
grasped where he was, the time, the weather conditions ... and a gun.

No name on the phone's screen. A 703 area code. Not Maggie's
number.

"Hello."

"Carson? J.D. Carson?" Male voice. The calm of authority. But
something besides that... Pain. Worry.

"Yes."

"This is Detective Belichek of the Fairlington police department.
You know Maggie Frye."

Not a question.

Belichek. Maggie's friend.

Calling in the middle of the night.

He was up, pulling out his ready bag. Ignoring a squeezing twist
inside him.

He confirmed the non-question anyway. "Yes."

Almost on top of his single word, the voice said, "She's okay.
Physically."

"What the—?"

"Listen. I don't usually—I know some of what happened up there
in the mountains, in Bedhurst. You and Maggie. And I'm saying you
should get down here to Fairlington. Fast. Her cousin's been found
dead. Looks like murder."

Murder.

Maggie's cousin ... which one?

Detective Belichek of the Fairlington police department spoke
again. "She knows. She's on the way to the scene. It's going to be
rough. Maggie needs ... a friend. Support."

✧   ✧   ✧   ✧

To solve this murder Bel Belichek will risk everything—his friendships, his reputation, his career, his heart ... and his life.

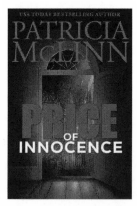

PRICE OF INNOCENCE

And in conclusion ...

PREMISE OF INNOCENCE

Book 3 of The Innocence Trilogy

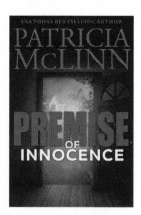

The last woman Detective Tanner Landis is prepared to see is the one he must save.

To get briefed on upcoming books, as well as other titles and developments, join Patricia McLinn's Readers List and receive her twice-monthly free newsletter.

www.patriciamclinn.com/readers-list

Maggie, J.D., Dallas, Evelyn, Bel and Tanner ask if you'll help spread the word about them and The Innocence Trilogy. You have the power to do that in two quick ways:

Recommend the book and the series to your friends and/or the whole wide world on social media. Shouting from rooftops is particularly appreciated.

Review the book. Take a few minutes to write an honest review and it can make a huge difference. As you likely know, it's the single best way for your fellow readers to find books they'll enjoy, too.

To me – as an author and a reader – the goal is always to find a good author-reader match. By sharing your reading experience through recommendations and reviews, you become a vital matchmaker. ☺

If you'd like to investigate Patricia McLinn's mysteries with humor and a hint of romance, try her **Caught Dead in Wyoming** series:

SIGN OFF

Divorce a husband, lose a career … grapple with a murder.

LEFT HANGING

Trampled by bulls—an accident? Elizabeth, Mike and friends must dig into the world of rodeo.

SHOOT FIRST

For Elizabeth, death hits close to home. She and friends must delve into old Wyoming treasures and secrets to save lives.

LAST DITCH

KWMT's Elizabeth and Mike search after a man in a wheelchair goes missing.

LOOK LIVE

Elizabeth and friends take on misleading murder with help—and hindrance—from intriguing out-of-towners.

BACK STORY

Murder never dies, but comes back to threaten Elizabeth, her friends and KWMT team.

COLD OPEN

Elizabeth's looking for a place of her own becomes an open house for murder.

HOT ROLL

One of Elizabeth's team of investigators becomes a target.

REACTION SHOT

Homicide on the range, where clouds darken over Elizabeth.

BODY BRACE

Everything can change ... except murder.

"Colorful characters, intriguing, intelligent mystery, plus the state of Wyoming leaping off every page."

—Emilie Richards, USA Today bestselling author

And the **Secret Sleuth** series:

DEATH ON THE DIVERSION
Final resting place? Deck chair.

DEATH ON TORRID AVENUE
A new love (canine), an ex-cop and a dog park discovery.

DEATH ON BEGUILING WAY
No zen in sight as Sheila untangles a yoga instructor's murder.

DEATH ON COVERT CIRCLE
Sheila and Clara are on the scene as a supermarket CEO meets his expiration date.

DEATH ON SHADY BRIDGE
A cold case heats up.

DEATH ON CARRION LANE
More small-town mystery.

"Move over Agatha Christie, there's a new sleuth in town. Patricia McLinn has created a fabulous new murder mystery series with ... wonderful characters, both human and canine, [and] an interesting backdrop. I highly recommend."

—*5-star review*

If you like Patricia's romantic suspense, you might also try:

Ride the River: Rodeo Knights

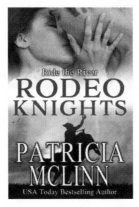

Her rodeo cowboy ex is back … as her prime suspect.

BARDVILLE, WYOMING

A Stranger in the Family

A Stranger to Love

The Rancher Meets His Match

Explore a complete list of all Patricia's books

www.patriciamclinn.com/patricias-books

Or get a printable booklist

www.patriciamclinn.com/patricias-books/printable-booklist

Patricia's eBookstore (buy digital books online directly from Patricia)

www.patriciamclinn.com/patricias-books/ebookstore

About the author

USA Today bestselling author Patricia McLinn spent more than 20 years as an editor at The Washington Post after stints as a sports writer (Rockford, Ill.) and assistant sports editor (Charlotte, N.C.). She received BA and MSJ degrees from Northwestern University.

McLinn is the author of more than 50 published novels, which are cited by readers and reviewers for wit and vivid characterization. Her books include mysteries, romantic suspense, contemporary romance, historical romance and women's fiction. They have topped bestseller lists and won numerous awards.

She has spoken about writing from Melbourne, Australia, to Washington, D.C., including being a guest speaker at the Smithsonian Institution.

Now living in northern Kentucky, McLinn loves to hear from readers through her website and social media.

Visit with Patricia:

Website: patriciamclinn.com

Facebook: facebook.com/PatriciaMcLinn

Twitter: @PatriciaMcLinn

Pinterest: pinterest.com/patriciamclinn

Instagram: instagram.com/patriciamclinnauthor

Made in United States
Orlando, FL
07 April 2022

16560029R00236